THE VIOLENT LAND

JORGE AMADO

TRANSLATED FROM PORTUGUESE

BY SAMUEL PUTNAM

 AVON
PUBLISHERS OF BARD, CAMELOT, DISCUS AND FLARE BOOKS

Originally published in Portuguese in 1943 as *Terras do sem fim* by Livraria Martins Editora, Brazil.

AVON BOOKS
A division of
The Hearst Corporation
1350 Avenue of the Americas
New York, New York 10019

First Avon Books Trade Printing: April 1988
First Avon Books Mass Market Printing: November 1979

AVON TRADEMARK REG. U.S. PAT. OFF. AND IN OTHER COUNTRIES, MARCA REGISTRADA, HECHO EN U.S.A.

Printed in the U.S.A.

OPM 10 9 8 7 6 5 4 3

*Blood Fertilized These Lands**

The cacao lands, a region embracing all of the southern part of
the state of Bahia in Brazil, were fertilized with blood. They were
conquered foot by foot in ferocious struggles of indescribable
violence. They were barbarous lands, where banditry and death,
implacable hatred and the cruelest revenge flourished; there was
a time when they were the symbol of anti-culture and anti-
civilization in Brazil. Men had set out to conquer the forest,
to clear it and transform the landscape and the economy of a
vast area. But those who set out were many, and they went
armed. As though there were not land enough and to spare for
all, they fought one another, disputing each foot of that humid
earth, ideal for the planting of cacao. At the very time that the
seedlings were being planted, crosses were being set up to mark
the spots where the brave had fallen, victims of ambushes or of
encounters between hired gunmen.

All this happened only the other day, at the end of the past
century, at the beginning of the present. When I was five or six
years old, in 1917 and 1918, shootings were the daily fare of

---

*This foreword was written by Senhor Amado especially for this new
edition of *The Violent Land*, which was first published in English in
1945.

v

those cities, of Ilhéus and Itabuna, and of the hamlets recently sprung up in the woods. I saw the birth of the village of Pirangy, which today is the city of Itajuipe; my father was one of its founders around 1920. I witnessed encounters of the cacao "colonels," fights to the death, when bullets whistled through the night in both jungle and cities. My father was wounded when I was a year old. I was with him on the veranda of his plantation house on the land that he had conquered, cleared, and planted to cacao. I saw the end of those struggles; I could say that I was born amidst them, was nourished on them, and that they made me a novelist.

Very little time was required—fifty years at most—for the cacao trees to come to maturity and bear fruit, for the plantations to grow, for the living conditions and economy of an immense area to change, and it is curious to realize how in such a brief period a civilization and a culture grew out of so much spilled blood.

At a given moment in the last pages of this novel, one of the characters says that cacao produces everything, even a bishop. Today I can add that cacao also produced a literature. In the complex of Brazilian letters and within the limits of the literature of Bahia, there is a genre with its own well-defined characteristics, with its own unmistakable brand, born of cacao, bearing a certain flavor of blood in its pages, a certain bitter aftertaste of death. It is the literature of cacao, a product of the cacao civilization, its finest product.

As for me, I was the first of these writers and, perhaps for that reason, slightly barbarous, like those lands at the time of my birth; I led the way. Then came the young masters of today: Adonias Filho, with his densely packed novels on which weighs the solitude of man in the midst of new lands; James Amado, in whom the sea and the forest are mingled with the tragedy of children and workers; Jorge Meduar, with his stories of the zone of Agua Preta, his immigrants, and his *fazendeiros*; Helio Pólvora, the storyteller of Itabuna; Emo Duarte, with his city of Ilhéus. They are the flowers of a literature that grew out of blood, flowers of cacao which come to re-create the reality of yesterday and of today, to give us the exact measure of the extraordinary saga lived by the men who built that civilization.

Many of those men came from the backlands or from the neighboring state of Sergipe; they were avid for wealth, disposed to build a world. And they did so, but not before traversing the roads of hell. Others came much greater distances, from the far-away Orient, from Syria, Lebanon, Arabia, following the trails of the conquistadores, carrying their trunkfuls of baubles and gewgaws, setting up trade. Men came from many other lands and established themselves there. All made their contribution.

In a series of novels I have tried to tell the stories of those cacao lands and of how a culture was implanted there, and of how that culture gained strength and originality. In *The Violent Land* I told the beginning of that great adventure: the thrust into the forest where men struggled with one another as enemies. It was the epoch of the cacao colonels, indomitable, titanic men of unlimited courage, for whom life had no value. It was worth exactly the price of a swig of rum, sufficient pay for the hired gunman who hid behind a guava or breadfruit tree, waiting for his designated victim to come into the sights of his repeating rifle. In other novels I have told of the growth of the cities and of progress, of the twilight of the colonels, of the appearance of the urban bourgeoisie and the rural proletariat, of the new problems, the new world of conflicts much more subtle than the primary conflict between the colonels and the land or among the colonels themselves. No other of my books, however, is as dear to me as *The Violent Land:* in it lie my roots; it is of the blood from which I was created; it contains the gunfire that resounded during my early infancy.

Today the cities have grown; the country is so well cared for that it is like a garden. But I know that cities and plantations alike were built on the blood of men. Generous blood. Never have the cacao trees flourished so rapidly, never have they borne fruit so early as here, in these lands of killing and death.

A motion picture has been made from this book, which has also been adapted for the stage, television, and radio. Editions of it have appeared in twenty-five languages; some twenty editions have appeared in Portuguese. I believe that all this is owing to those colonels of indomitable courage who took up arms and went to face the forest and the phantoms, the other armed men, and the future's challenge.

JORGE AMADO

Translated by Harriet de Onis

Contents

1

The Boat

〰〰〰〰〰〰〰〰〰〰〰〰〰〰〰〰〰〰〰〰〰〰

1

The boat's whistle was a lament, piercing the twilight that lay upon the town. Standing upon the deck, Captain João Magalhães surveyed the jumble of old-fashioned houses, the church spires, the dark roof-tops, the streets paved with enormous cobblestones. His gaze took in the roofs of varying shape, but he had no more than a glimpse of a bit of street where no one passed. Without knowing why, he found those stones, with which the hands of slaves had paved the street, deeply moving in their beauty. Beautiful also were the dark roofs and the church bells which were just beginning to chime, summoning the pious city to benediction. Once more the boat's whistle rent the twilight that shrouded the town of Bahia, and Captain João extended his arms in farewell. It was as if he were taking leave of a loved one, some woman dear to his heart.

Aboard ship men and women were engaged in conversation. Some distance away, at the foot of the gangplank, a dark-skinned gentleman, felt hat in hand, was kissing the lips of a pale-looking young woman. At João's side a fat fellow, leaning back in a deck-chair, was striking up an acquaintance with a Portuguese travelling salesman. The latter glanced at his watch and announced in a voice that all could hear: "Five minutes yet."

João reflected that the salesman's watch must be slow, for the

1

whistle now sounded one last time, and those who were staying behind left the boat, while those who were sailing took their places on deck, crowding about the rail.

A sudden rumble of the engines, and he was certain they were under way; and then it was that he turned to gaze at the city once more, with a strange emotion as his eyes rested on those ancient roof-tops and the bit of street paved with huge blocks of stone. A bell chimed, and João fancied that it was a call for him, inviting him once again to make his way through the city's streets, to look on at its solemn processions, to take his early morning *mingau** in the public square, to drink rum with aromatic herbs, to play a game of cards in a corner of the market-place of a forenoon, to play seven-and-a-half of an afternoon at Violeta's place, where there was always a good gang, to play poker of an evening in the café with those rich fellows who treated him with so much respect. And then along toward daybreak, to come out into the streets once more, his mop of hair down over his eyes, and to giþe at the women as they passed, arms folded over their bosoms on account of the cold, in quest of male companionship and the strains of the guitar in the Lower Town. Afterwards there would be Violeta's sighs as the light streamed in through the window of her room, with the wind swaying the branches of the two cocoa trees in the garden outside. The sighs of love would be wafted on the wind, all the way to the moon, perhaps—who knows?

The sobs of the pale young woman distracted his thoughts. She was saying, with a tone of infallible certainty: "Nevermore, Roberio, nevermore." The man was kissing her, in great excitement; he was deeply grieved, and it was with difficulty that he replied:

"I'll be back in a month, my dear, and bring the children. And you're going to be a good girl. The doctor told me—"

The young woman's voice was full of pain, and João shared her anguish as he heard her say: "I know very well that I'm going to die, Roberio. I'll never see you nor the children again." And dropping her voice, she repeated: "Nor the children." Then she burst into sobs.

The man wanted to say something, but could not; all that he could do was to shake his head, eye the gangplank, and let his gaze wander in João's direction, as if seeking aid and comfort there. The woman's voice was a sob: "I'll never see you again."

* For Brazilian terms see the Glossary at the end of the book.

2

The dark-skinned man continued to gaze at João; he was alone with his grief. João remained undecided for a moment; he did not know how he was going to be of help; he felt like running down the gangplank, but the sailors were already drawing it in and the boat was getting under way. The man barely had time to kiss the young woman's lips once again, a prolonged, ardent kiss, as if he wished to contract the disease that was gnawing at his wife's bosom. Then he leaped aboard. His grief, however, was greater than his pride, and the sobs burst forth; they appeared to fill the departing ship, and even the fat colonel left off conversing with the travelling salesman.

From a distance someone was calling, shouting almost: "Write to me. Write to me." And there was another voice: "Don't forget me. Don't forget."

2

A few handkerchiefs waved, but from one face alone tears were streaming, the young face of a woman whose bosom heaved with sobs. Bahia's new pier was not in existence then and the water came up almost into the street. The weeping girl waved her handkerchief, also, but among those on board who waved in return, the one to whom her heart belonged was no longer to be distinguished. The boat had begun to pick up speed, and those who had come down to see it off were leaving now. An elderly gentleman took the young woman's arm and led her away, murmuring words of consolation and of hope. The ship was lost in the distance.

During the first minutes of the voyage the various groups on board were mingled in confusion, after which the women began retiring to their cabins, while the men stood watching the ship's paddles as they churned the sea, for in those days the boats that ran between Bahia and Ilhéos were of the paddle type, as if instead of going forth to conquer the great open sea where the south wind held sway, they had merely to navigate some fresh-water stream.

The wind blew up more strongly and bore toward the night that lay over Bahia fragments of the conversation of those on deck, words uttered in an emphatic tone of voice: land, money, cacao, death.

3

As the houses dropped from sight, João twirled the ring on his finger, seeking to avoid the gaze of the dark-skinned man who was wiping his eyes and saying, as if in explanation of the entire scene: "She's consumptive, poor girl. The doctor says there's no hope."

João stared at the sea, dark green in color, and it was only then that he remembered why it was that he was fleeing the city. The engineer's ring fitted his finger perfectly. "Might have been made to order," he murmured to himself.

He smiled as he recalled the engineer. An easy mark. He had never seen such an easy mark. The fellow did not understand the first thing about poker, but had let himself be taken, even to his ring. That very night a week before, João had cleaned them all, taking from Colonel Juvencio alone a conto, a thousand milreis. Was he to blame for it? He had been well enough off as he was, stretched out half naked on Violeta's bed, with the young woman singing to him in that frail little voice of hers and running her fingers through his hair, when Tabaris's boy had put in an appearance, saying that he had been all over town looking for the captain.

Rodolfo always contrived to get him a seat in a game. When a table was not full, he would say to the players: "Are you gentlemen acquainted with Captain João Magalhães—a retired captain?" There was invariably one who knew him and who had played with him before.

"He's not a sharper, is he?" the others would ask; and Rodolfo would wax indignant.

"The captain," he would say, "plays a straight game. He plays well, I grant you that. But what I mean by a straight game is the kind of game the captain plays." He would lie with the most cynical face in the world, and then would conclude: "A table without the captain is no table at all."

In return for this rigmarole Rodolfo had his commission; and he knew, further, that the table where João Magalhães sat was one where the drinks would flow and the house's kitty would be no light matter. And so he had sent the boy for João as he prepared the decks.

That was the way it had been that night. João had been taking his ease, Violeta's fingers in his hair and her voice all but lulling him to sleep, when the boy had come. He had thrown on his clothes and a moment later was ensconced in the back room of the casino. From Colonel Juvencio he had taken one conto, and from the engineer all that the latter had in his pocket, even to his university ring, which the chap had tossed on the table when he found that he held four queens in his hand, on João Magalhães's deal. He lost, for the reason that the captain's four was a four of kings. The fourth player alone, a merchant from the Lower Town, was also lucky; he won two hundred-odd milreis.

At the table where João played, the fourth man always won; this was a part of his technique. And inasmuch as the captain (so his intimates asserted) had an exquisite flair for such matters, he would always pick the winner by the colour of his eyes, eyes which most nearly resembled a pair that had stared him out of countenance in Rio as they studied the professional's face with repulsion and contempt.

It was morning when they all rose from the table; and Rodolfo had valued the ring as being worth more than a conto. The engineer had bet three hundred and twenty on his four queens. João laughed to himself, there on the ship's deck. "Only a fool would stay on queens."

He had gone to Violeta's house feeling thoroughly fit and thinking how happy she would be next day when he brought her that blue silk dress that she had seen in a shop window. Who would have thought that the engineer, instead of keeping his mouth shut, would go to the police with a cock-and-bull story? What he had said about João had been a plenty. He had wanted to know in what army the captain had held his commission; and if the police had not called João in for a little talk, was not that possibly due to the fact that they had been unable to find him?

Rodolfo had hidden him away and had made a good job of it; Agrippino Doca had told him marvels of Ilhéos and the cacao country; and now here he was on board this ship, after eight months spent in Bahia, bound for Ilhéos, where the cacao grew, and with it swift-made fortunes, the engineer's ring upon his finger, a deck of cards in one pocket, a hundred professional cards in the other:

CAPT. DR. JOÃO MAGALHÃES
Military Engineer

Little by little the sadness he felt at having to abandon the city he had so loved during those eight months was disappearing, and João began to take an interest in the view: a distant glimpse

5

of trees and of houses growing smaller all the while. The ship's whistle blew and water splashed his straw hat. Removing it from his head, he ran his perfumed handkerchief over the crown and stuck it under his arm.

Then he smoothed down his tousled hair, which was left purposely uncared for and wavy. Darting an eye about the deck, he let his glance roam from the dark-skinned man whose gaze was still fixed upon the quay, no longer visible now, to the fat colonel, who was telling the travelling salesman of feats of daring in the semi-barbarous São Jorge dos Ilhéos country. As he twirled the ring on his finger, João studied the physiognomies of his fellow passengers. Would he be able to find the players for a little game? True, he had a comfortable amount of swag in his purse, but money never did anyone any harm. He whistled softly to himself.

Aboard ship the conversation was becoming general. João Magalhães had the feeling that it would not be long before he was drawn into it, and he was thinking of how to get up his poker party. Taking out a cigarette and striking a light, he strolled up and down the deck. Then once more he became interested in the view, for the boat was now drawing near to land as it crossed the bar of the harbour. From in front of a mournful-looking mud hut a couple of naked urchins with enormous bellies shouted at the passing ship. From another house a young girl with a pretty face, half hidden by the window, was waving an adieu. João reflected that this must be intended either for the ship's stoker or for all on board, but he took it upon himself to respond to it, extending his thin hand in a cordial gesture.

The fat colonel was astonishing the travelling salesman with the account of a row that had occurred in a house of prostitution in Bahia. Some young rowdies were making fools of themselves and had tried to get the better of him over a little mulatto girl. All that he had had to do was to draw his six-shooter.

"Come on, you! I'm from Ilhéos, I am!"

And the rascals had slunk away.

The travelling salesman was astounded by the courage that the colonel had displayed.

"That's what I call a man," he said, "a real he-man!"

Captain João Magalhães strolled slowly up to them.

4

Leaving her stateroom, Margot crossed the ship from one end to the other. Twirling her fluffy parasol and catching up the ample train of her dress, she permitted herself to be admired, by the travelling salesmen, who made lewd remarks as she passed, by the plantation-owners, who stared at her open-eyed, and even by those third-class passengers who were on their way to look for work in the regions of southern Bahia. Begging pardon in a voice that was little above a whisper, she made her way through the various groups, and over each group a silence fell as she drew near, in order that they might be able the better to see and to desire her.

Once she had passed, however, the conversation came back to the one eternal theme: cacao. The salesmen would laugh as they watched Margot and the planters. They well knew that what she was looking for was money, easy money, and that it would cost these rude fellows a pretty penny before they were through with her. But they did not laugh when Juca Badaró emerged from the shadows, took Margot by the arm, and led her over to the rail, where they might have a view of Itaparica as it dropped from sight, and of the distant mass of dwellings that formed the city of Bahia. Night, meanwhile, was falling rapidly as the ship splashed onward through the water.

"Where are you from?" And Juca Badaró let his tiny eyes run over her woman's body, to come to rest on her thighs and bosom. Lifting his hand to her buttocks, he caressed them, feeling the firmness of the flesh.

Margot assumed an offended pose. "But I don't know you. What do you mean by taking such liberties with me?"

Juca Badaró took her chin in his hand and raised her blond head, his eyes looking straight into hers.

"Don't forget," he said, measuring his words, "that you are going to hear much of Juca Badaró. And remember, you are mine from now on. See that you behave yourself, for I'm a man who means what he says."

Then, abruptly dropping her chin, he turned on his heels and made his way to the stern of the ship, where the third-class passengers were crowded about and whence came the melodic strains of harmonica and guitar.

5

The moon had begun its climb in the heavens, an enormous red moon that left a bloody wake on the darkness of the sea. Antonio Victor drew up his long legs and rested his chin on his knees. The song which the back-countryman beside him was singing was lost in the immensity of the ocean, and it filled Antonio's heart with longing. It brought back to memory those moonlit nights in the little town where he had lived, nights when the lamps were not lighted, nights when he and so many other lads, and so many lasses as well, would go to fish from the bridge, bathed in moonlight. Those were nights of story-telling and of laughter, the fishing being little more than a pretext, with a clasp of hands as the moon hid itself behind a cloud.

Ivone was always beside him. She was a girl of fifteen, but already at work in the factory, the spinning-mill. She was the man of the family, supporting her sick mother and her four small brothers, ever since the night when her father had slipped away. No one knew where he had gone; that was the last that was heard of him. Ivone had had to go to work in the factory in order to feed all those mouths, and these nights on the bridge were her only diversion. She would recline her head with its dark hair on Antonio's shoulder and would give him her ripe, full lips to kiss each time a cloud came over the moon.

As for himself, he with his two brothers cultivated a millet plot on the outskirts of the city; but the income was small, and there was said to be much highly paid work in the lands to the south, where there was a fortune to be made in cacao. And so it was that one day, like Ivone's father, like his own older brother, like thousands of others, he had left the little town in his native province of Sergipe and had embarked at Aracajú. He had slept for two nights in a cheap waterfront hotel in Bahia, and then had taken third-class passage in a boat bound for Ilhéos.

He was a tall, lean *caboclo*, with protruding muscles and big calloused hands. He was twenty years old, and his heart was filled with sadness. A sensation he had never known before now took possession of him. Did it come, perhaps, from that big red moon, almost the colour of blood? Or from the back-countryman's mournful melody? The men and women, jostling one another on the deck, were speaking of their hopes, hopes bound up with those southern lands.

"I'm headed for Tabocas," said one man who was no longer

young, with a scraggly beard and kinky hair. "They tell me it's the coming place."

"But they say it's a wild one, too, with all the killing that goes on, God forgive me." It was a little fellow with a hoarse voice who spoke.

"I've heard tell of that, but I don't believe a word of it. You hear all kinds of things."

"That is as God may will." This from an old woman with a shawl about her head.

"I'm going to Ferradas," announced a young lad. "I have a brother there who's doing very well. He's with Colonel Horacio, a man of money. I'm going to stay with him. He has a job for me. And then I'll come back to get Zilda."

"Your sweetheart?" a woman wanted to know.

"My wife. We have a little girl two years old and another on the way. A pretty little kid."

"You'll never come back," said an old man wrapped in a cape. "You'll never come back, for Ferradas is the ass-hole of the world. Do you know what it means to work on Colonel Horacio's plantation? Are you going to be a worker or a cut-throat? The colonel has no use for any man who's not a killer. You'll never come back." And the old fellow spat fiercely.

Antonio Victor heard this conversation, but the music that came from the other group, the lilt of harmonica and guitar, carried him back once more to the Estancia bridge, where the moon is lovely and life is at peace. Ivone had always begged him not to go. The millet plot would be enough for the two of them. Why was he so eager to go seek for money in a place of which they told such ugly tales? It was on those moonlit nights, with the stars filling the sky, so many of them and so dazzlingly beautiful, feet dangling in the water of the river, that he had planned his departure for the Ilhéos country.

Men had written back, men who had gone there, saying that money was easy to get, saying, also, that it was easy to get hold of a piece of land and plant it with a tree called cacao, one that bore a golden-coloured fruit worth more than gold itself. The land was there waiting for those who would come and take it; it belonged to no one as yet. It would be his who should have the courage to plunge into the wilderness, clear the forest, plant cacao, millet, and manihot, and live for a few years on meal and wild game until the cacao began to bear fruit. Then there would be riches, more money than a man could spend, a house in the city, cigars, fine leather boots.

From time to time, on the other hand, there would come word of someone who had died from a bullet or a snake-bite, who had been stabbed in a row in town or shot and killed from ambush. But what was a mere life when so much wealth was to be had? In Antonio Victor's home town, life had been poverty-stricken and had held no hope for the future. The men, almost all of them, would leave, few to return. But those who did come back—for a brief visit, always—came back unreconciled to the life there after all the years of absence. For they came back rich, with rings on their fingers, gold watches, pearls in their neckties. They spent money right and left, threw it away on presents for their relatives, gifts for the churches and their patron saints, and donations for the feast-days at the end of the year. "He's come back rich," was all that you would hear about town. And every man who had come back only to leave again because he could no longer accustom himself to the tranquil life of the place was one more invitation to Antonio Victor. Ivone was the only thing that held him there. Her lips, the warmth of her breasts, the entreaty of her voice, her pleading eyes. But one day he had broken with it all and had gone away, leaving Ivone sobbing on the bridge where they had said good-bye.

"I'll be a rich man in a year," he had promised her, "and then I'll come for you."

The moon of Estancia was over the ship now, but it was no longer the golden moon that had bathed the lovers on the bridge. This was a red moon, and there was an old man who said that no one ever came back from the land of cacao.

Antonio Victor had a feeling he had never experienced before. Could it be fear? Could it be homesickness? He himself did not know what it was. That moon brought back Ivone's lips, pleading with him not to go away; her eyes, filled with tears that night they had said good-bye. There had been no moon that night; there had been no one on the bridge fishing. It had been dark, with the river murmuring down below, as she met him there, her body warm-glowing, her face wet with tears.

"You have made up your mind to go?" There was a long minute of silence, a gloomy silence. "You will never come back."

"I swear I will."

She had shaken her head by way of negation; and then, afterwards, she had lain down on the river bank and had called to him. She had let him possess her without saying a word, without so much as a moan. When it was over, she had lowered her calico dress, its faded flowers stained now with blood, had covered her face with her hand, and had said to him in a broken voice:

"You will never come back. Another would have had me one of these days, and it is better that it be you. That way you will know how much I care for you."

"I swear I'll come back."

"You will never come back."

Despite the pleasure that her body gave him, he was deeply moved at having possessed her in this manner and by the thought that he was leaving a child behind him. He told himself that he was going to make money for her and for the child, and that he would be back within a year. Land was easily had in Ilhéos; he would plant cacao, would harvest the fruit, and then would come back for Ivone and the young one. True, her father had not returned and no one knew where he was. And here was an old man saying that no one ever came back from that country, not even a man with a wife and two children. Why didn't that harmonica stop playing? The music was so sad. And what was the meaning of that moon, that blood-red moon above the sea?

6

The song is a sad one, like an omen of trouble to come. The wind, scurrying over the sea, snatches up the musical notes and scatters them, until it seems they will never die. Sadness comes with the music and lays hold of the third-class passengers, among them the pregnant woman who clings to Filomeno's arm. The strains of the harmonica serve as an accompaniment to the melody the young man is singing in a voice that is loud and strong. Antonio Victor draws his long legs closer still to his body as the picture of peaceful Estancia and of Ivone giving herself without a murmur mingles with the fresh images of a land as yet unconquered, a land of brawls and bullets and sudden death, of money and heaps of banknotes. One man who is travelling alone and who speaks to no one makes his way through the groups and stretches out on the deck. The moon leaves a reddish wake on the sea as the song tears at their hearts:

> *My love, I am leaving you now,*
> *Nevermore to return.*

11

Comes now a vision of other, distant lands and of other peoples, of other seas and other shores, or of a rustic backland country flayed by drought; and many of those on this little boat are leaving a love behind them. Some are going by very reason of that love, to find the wherewithal with which to win the loved one, to look for the gold that purchases happiness. That gold which grows in the land of Ilhéos, on the cacao tree. The song says they will never come back, that in those lands death awaits them from behind every tree. And the moon, the moon is red as the ship heaves and tosses on the ruffled waters.

The old man in the cape is bare-legged, with no shoes on his feet. His eyes are hard as he draws on the butt of a cigarette. Someone asks him for a light, and the old fellow gives a puff to revive the spark.

"Much obliged, Pop."

"Don't mention it."

"Looks like a storm coming up."

"It's the season for the south wind. There are times when it blows so hard no boat can stand up against it."

"Ceará is where they have the storms," the woman puts in. "You'd think it was the end of the world."

"So I've heard," says the old man. "Yes, that's what they tell me."

They had come up to a group that stood conversing about the men who were playing cards.

"Are you from Ilhéos?"

"I've been in Tabocas, going on five years now. I'm from the back-country."

"And what are you doing down there at your age?"

"My son, Joaquim, went down there first. He was doing well for himself, had a little grove. The old lady died, and he sent for me."

He fell silent then. It seemed that he was listening attentively to the music that the wind carried away to the city hidden in the night. The others waited expectantly, but only the murmur of voices from first-class and the song the Negro was singing came to break the silence.

> *Nevermore to return,*
> *In those distant lands to die.*

The song continued as the men shuddered from the cold. A swift and violent wind was blowing up from the south, and the

12

ship was bouncing over the waves. Many of those aboard had never been on a boat before. They had crossed the inhospitable scrub forests of the backlands in a train made up of carload after carload of immigrants. The old man with his hard eyes looked them over.

"You hear that song? 'In those distant lands to die.' That's the truth, that is. Whoever goes to that country never comes back. It's like a spell laid upon you; it's like a trap. I'm telling you, that folks—"

"But there's easy money there, ain't that right?" The young lad faced him with kindling eyes.

"Money—that's what gets 'em. Folks come, make a little money, for, bless the Lord, there *is* money there—but it's money that brings bad luck; it's money with a curse on it. It don't stay in anybody's palm. You plant a little cacao..."

The music now was low and hushed. The card-players had finished their hand. The old man looked the young one straight in the eyes, after darting a glance around at the others who were hanging on his words.

"Did you ever hear tell of an 'ouster'?"

"I've heard it's some kind of monkey-business with a lawyer who takes the land away from other folks."

"An attorney comes along with a colonel; they work an 'ouster' and take away the cacao that folks have planted." Once more he glanced about sharply, then spread out his big rough hands. "You see those hands? They've planted many a cacao tree. Me and Joaquim, we set out grove after grove; we worked like beavers, we did. And what did we get out of it?"

He was putting the question to them all—to the card-players, to the pregnant woman, to the young lad. Then he appeared to be listening to the music once more as he gazed at the distant moon.

"They say when the moon is the colour of blood like that there'll be trouble in the street that night. It was like that the night they murdered Joaquim. They had no reason for killing him; they did it out of pure wickedness."

"But why did they kill him?" the woman insisted.

"Colonel Horacio and Lawyer Ruy worked an ouster; they took the cacao we had planted—claimed the land belonged to the colonel and that Joaquim had no right to it. Colonel Horacio came with his cut-throats and a bunch of certified records. They drove us off the land and even kept the cacao that was drying and about ready for market. Joaquim was a good lad, not afraid

13

of hard work; but he was done for when they took the grove, and he started to drink. And one time when he was drunk he told people he was going to have revenge, that he was going to do away with the colonel. One of the colonel's *cabras* overheard him and told his boss, and they laid for Joaquim in ambush and killed him the next night, on the road to Ferradas."

The old man fell silent and his listeners asked no further questions. The players returned to their game, the dealer threw down a couple of cards, and the others bet. The music was gradually dying away in the night. The wind was blowing harder and harder every minute. The old fellow took up his tale again.

"Joaquim," he said, "was a law-abiding man; he would not have killed anybody. Colonel Horacio knew that very well, and his men did, too. Joaquim just said that because he'd been drinking; he wasn't going to kill anyone. He was a hard-working man; all he wanted was to earn a living. He felt bad because they'd taken the plantation, that's true. But if he hadn't been drinking, he'd never have said what he did. He wasn't a killer. They shot him in the back."

"Were they arrested?"

Again the old man spat, contemptuously.

"The very night they killed him, they were drinking in a wine-shop, bragging about it."

Silence fell on the group. "Seven," said one of the players. But the winner did not even rake in his money, so absorbed was he in watching the old man, who stood there all bent over, seemingly oblivious of the world, alone with his sorrow.

"And you?" said the pregnant woman in a low voice.

"They shipped me off to Bahia, told me I couldn't stay there any longer. But I'm going back now." The old fellow suddenly drew himself erect, his eyes once more took on the hard gleam they had lost as he finished his tale, and it was with a firm voice that he went on speaking:

"I'm going back now, going back for good. No one is going to drive me away. It's fate, woman, that decides what is going to happen to folks. No one is born good or bad; it's fate that twists us all crooked."

"But—" The woman paused.

"Go ahead; say what you like."

"But how are you going to live? You're not the age now to do hard work."

"When people make up their minds to something, woman, things always get straightened out somehow. And I've made up

14

my mind. My son was a good lad; he wouldn't have killed the colonel. And neither would I soil these hands of mine with blood." He put out his hands, calloused with the toil of earth. "But they killed my son."

"So you—" began the woman, fear and trembling in her voice.

The old man turned his back on her and slowly walked away.

"He'd kill all right," was the comment of a lean-looking individual.

The music once more grew in volume in the night as the moon swiftly climbed the heavens. The one who was dealing the cards nodded his head by way of confirming what the lean man had said. The pregnant woman grasped Filomeno's arm.

"I'm afraid—"

The music of the harmonica ceased. The moonlight was like a pool of blood.

7

José da Ribeira dominated the other group. He was speaking of things that had happened in the land of cacao; stories and more stories. Every other moment he would spit, happy at being in a position to do the talking and tell these people what he knew. They listened to him attentively, as to one who had something to teach them.

"I almost changed my mind about coming," said one little woman with a suckling child at her bosom, "when they told me there was a fever going around down there that takes people off in a flash."

José laughed as the others turned to him. His tone was a knowing one as he replied.

"They didn't tell you any lie," he said. "No sirree, lady. I've seen many a man who was stronger than an ox come down with that fever. Three nights of it and he was done for."

"Isn't it something like the smallpox?"

"There's a lot of that, too, but that's not what I'm talking about. There's smallpox, and chicken pox, and all kinds of pox, and then there's the black fever, which is worse than any of them. I never saw a man come out of the black fever alive. But that's not what I mean. This is a new kind of fever. Nobody knows what it is. It don't even have a name. It comes on you unexpectedly and takes you off in the blink of an eye."

"Saints preserve us!" said another woman.

José spat as he went on with his reminiscences.

"There was a doctor came down there, with a diploma and everything. He was a young fellow, didn't even have a beard, and good-looking, too. He said he was going to put an end to the fever in Ferradas, but the fever put an end to him and to his good looks at the same time; for he was the ugliest corpse I ever saw, uglier even than Garangau, the one they stabbed to death at Macacos—they cut him all to pieces, gouged out his eyes, cut off his tongue, and stripped the hide from his chest."

"Why did they do that, poor fellow?" said the woman with the child.

"Poor fellow?" José da Ribeira laughed, an ingrowing laugh; it appeared that he was enormously amused. "Poor fellow? As if there was ever a worse cut-throat in all the south country than Vicente Garangau. Why, in one day he did away with seven men from Juparana. He was as mean a man as God ever put breath into."

The group was impressed, but a man from Ceará spoke up.

"Seven is a liar's count, friend José."

José laughed once more and puffed on his cigarette; he was not offended.

"You're a child," he said. "What do you know about life? You see me here, don't you, with the weight of fifty years on my shoulders? Well, I've covered a lot of ground; I've spent ten years in those woods. Before that I was a soldier in the army and saw plenty of trouble, but nothing in the world to compare with the kind of trouble you see there. Did you ever hear of an ambush?"

"Yes!" exclaimed one of the men; "they say it's where you lie in wait for some one and shoot the poor fellow from behind a tree."

"Well, then, see here. I know a man who made a bet of ten milreis with a friend of his. He bet the man to be killed would come from one direction and his friend bet he would come from the other; and the first one who came along got the bullet that was to decide the bet. Did you ever hear of anything as cursed as that?"

The man from Ceará shuddered. One of the women could not believe her ears.

"And they did that just to win a bet?"

José da Ribeira spat once more as he went on to explain.

"I've been there, I've seen a lot of the world, I was a soldier and I've seen things to make your hair stand on end. But I've never seen anything like what you see there. They're real men, all right, but money is what talks. If you're quick on the trigger, you get along well enough."

"And what do *you* do down there?"

"I was a police sergeant for a while; then I got me a little grove, which is better than being on the force, and I live on it. I've been up to Bahia for a vacation and to buy a few things I needed."

"And you're coming back third-class, Pop?" said the man from Ceará, banteringly.

José smiled again, that ingrowing smile of his.

"The girls," he confessed, "took all my money, son. The wildcat in the forest is what woman is in town. Whenever you see a white one in the capital, it seems to turn your head. They took me, cleaner than a whistle."

No one had any comment to make on this, for at that moment a short man with a whip in his hand and a sombrero on his head had stopped in front of them. José turned and spoke to him respectfully.

"How are you, Mr. Juca?"

"How are you, Dad? How goes the plantation?"

"I've been away, going on a month. I aim to clear more woods this year, the Lord willing."

Juca Badaró nodded his head, eyeing the group as he did so.

"You know these people, Dad?"

"I'm just getting acquainted with them, Mr. Juca. Is there any reason why you ask?"

Instead of replying, Juca made his way into the centre of the group.

"Where are you from?" he said to one of them.

"From Ceará, boss. From Crato."

"What were you, a mule-driver?"

"No, sir, begging your pardon. I had a little farm." And without waiting for the question: "The drought finished me."

"Do you have a family or are you single?"

"I have a wife, and a kid on the way."

"Do you want to work for me?"

"Yes, sir; thank you kindly."

Thus Juca Badaró went about, hiring hands: the man who was dealing the cards, one of the other players, the man from Ceará, the young lad, and Antonio Victor, who was gazing up at the sky with its thousands of stars. Many offered their services and he refused them. He had had a wide experience with men

17

and could readily tell which ones would do for his plantation, for felling the forest, working the land, and looking after the crops.

8

Captain João Magalhães had them bring down Portuguese wine. The travelling salesman accepted some, but the colonel declined; the swaying of the boat upset his stomach.

"That's a devil of a wind. If I took any wine, I'd throw my guts up over the side of the ship."

"Beer, then? A cognac?"

The colonel did not care for anything. João Magalhães was telling tall stories of his life in Rio, as an army captain and a rich business man as well.

"I own many houses—stocks and bonds, too."

He rapidly made up a yarn of an inheritance that he had received from a millionaire aunt who had no children of her own. He spoke of the prominent politicians of the day, his friends—so he said—whom he called by their first names, and with whom he drank and gambled. He had retired from the army and was now travelling around, seeing the country. He had come from Rio Grande do Sul and expected to go as far as Amazonas. He believed in seeing Brazil first before visiting other lands; he was not one of those who, when they had made a little money, went to spend it with the French in Paris. The colonel approved of this; he thought it very patriotic; and then he wanted to know if it was true about the "French houses" in Rio, if they really did "everything," or if that was just a lot of dirty talk. For he had heard there were women there who did things like that. João Magalhães confirmed the fact, and went on to elaborate, giving all the lurid details, being supported by the travelling salesman, who also wished to show that he knew all about such things (he had been in Rio once, and this trip was the most important event in his life). The colonel was delighted.

"But what's this you're telling me, captain? Why, that's downright filthy."

With this, the captain proceeded to lay it on. He did not spend much time on these descriptions, however, but returned to the subject of the fortune that he possessed and the good connections that he had. Was there nothing he could do for the colonel in Rio? Was there, perhaps, some important politician with shom he could put in a word? If so, the colonel had but to let him know. That was what he was there for, to be of service to his friends. He only wished they had known each other before; they would have got along splendidly together, and he would have been only too happy to do anything he could. The colonel, as it happened, stood in need of nothing in Rio, but he was much obliged all the same.

At this moment Maneca Dantas passed. He was a heavy-set man, inclined to corpulence; his shirt was covered with perspiration and his hands were clammy. The colonel called him over and made the introductions.

"This is Colonel Maneca Dantas, a big landowner from down our way. He's got more money than he knows what to do with."

João Magalhães rose; his manner was extremely courteous.

"Captain João Magalhães, military engineer, at your service." Taking out one of his visiting-cards, he presented it to Colonel Maneca. Then he offered him a chair, pretending not to have heard the salesman's remark to Colonel Ferreirinha:

"A distinguished chap."

"Well educated, you can see that."

Colonel Maneca accepted some wine. He was not subject to seasickness.

"I'm as comfortable here as I would be in my bed at Auricidia. Auricidia is the name of my little plantation, captain. If you would care to spend a few days down there—that is, if you can put up with dried beef—"

Ferreirinha laughed derisively.

"Dried beef! Why, captain, at Auricidia every luncheon is a banquet and every dinner a baptismal feast. Dona Auricidia has some Negro women in her kitchen who can cook angelically," and Colonel Ferreirinha ran his tongue over his lips like a gourmet, as if he could see before him the dishes he was describing. "They make a blood pudding that will give a Christian visions of paradise."

Maneca Dantas smiled, vastly pleased with these eulogies of his cuisine.

"That's about all you get out of life, captain," he explained. "You live down there in the wilderness, felling the timber so that you can plant cacao, slaving like any back-country clodhopper, dodging snake-bites and bullets fired from behind a tree—and if you don't eat well, what are you going to do? We don't have any big-town luxuries—no theatres, women, cafés, nothing of that sort. It's work day and night, cutting timber and planting cacao."

Ferreirinha bore him out: "It's hard work, all right."

"But there's a lot of money to be made," put in the travelling salesman, wiping the wine from his lips.

Once again Maneca Dantas smiled.

"That's the truth," he said, "there *is* money to be made. It's good land, captain, worth the labour that it takes. The yield is good, you raise a lot of cacao, and you get a good price for it. There's no complaint on that score. You always have enough to be able to offer a bite to your friends."

"I'm going to be in that neighbourhood on the 16th," the salesman said, "on my way to Sequeiro Grande; I'm spending the night there."

"At your service," said Maneca. "And you, captain—will you come along?"

João Magalhães said it was quite possible that he would. He was thinking of staying in the region for some little time. As a matter of fact, he wanted to see if it was worth his while to invest a little money in cacao land. He had heard of this country down in Rio and of the money that was to be made there, and he was tempted to invest a portion of his capital in cacao plantations. True, he likewise had no reason to complain; the greater part of his wealth was in Rio de Janeiro real estate and it gave him a good return; but he had a little left over in the bank, some dozens of contos, and he also had large holdings in government bonds. If it was worth while—

"Indeed it is worth your while, captain." Maneca Dantas's tone was serious. "It is certainly worth while. Cacao is a new crop, but the land there is the best in the world for that purpose. Many experts have been down to look it over, and they are all agreed on that. There is no better land for cacao-raising. And the yield is all that anybody could ask; I wouldn't trade it for coffee, nor even for sugar-cane. The only thing is, the folks down our way are a rough and ready lot, but a gentleman of your courage shouldn't mind that. I am telling you, captain, in twenty years' time Ilhéos will be a great city, a capital; and all the little towns of today—they will be big cities, too. Cacao is gold, captain."

Thus they went on talking, of the voyage and one thing and another. João Magalhães spoke of other places he had visited, of his journeys by rail and on great ocean liners. His prestige was growing moment by moment, and the circle of admirers was also increasing as story after story was told and the wine flowed freely. All the while, the captain was subtly endeavouring to steer the conversation to the subject of cards, and they ended by getting up a poker game. Colonel Totonho, proprietor of

Riacho Sêco, sat in, but the travelling salesman did not—the ante was too high for him, the game too fast. And so João and the three colonels made up the table, the others looking on.

"I don't know much about this game," Maneca Dantas remarked as he took off his overcoat. Ferreirinha burst into another guffaw.

"Don't you believe that, captain. Maneca is a master hand at poker. I've never seen his match."

Maneca now stuck his revolver in the pocket of his overcoat, so that it would not be in plain sight there in his belt; and João Magalhães pondered the question as to whether it might not be a good thing for him to lose at first and not display his abilities all at once. The bar-boy brought a deck.

"Joker wild?" Maneca inquired.

"As you like," replied João Magalhães.

"Joker wild is not poker," said Totonho, speaking for the first time. "Don't keep the joker, please."

"Very well, my friend," and Maneca tossed it in the discard.

Ferreirinha was banker, and each one bought five hundred milreis' worth of chips. João was studying Totonho attentively. The latter had a vacant eye and wore three rings on one of his hands. He was silent and sombre-looking. It would be well to give him the cards. The captain had made up his mind not to cheat, but to play fairly, even foolishly if possible, to lose a little something. That way he would have these fellows for another game which would pay a good deal better.

He held a pair of kings, and made his bet; Maneca Dantas raised him sixteen; Ferreirinha passed, Totonho stayed, and João "saw" the raise. Ferreirinha dealt the cards; Maneca drew two, Totonho one.

"It's up to you gentlemen," said João.

Totonho threw down his cards; Maneca bet, but no one "saw" him, and he took the pot. He was bluffing and could not refrain from showing his hand.

"A three-wheeler," he said. He held a king, a queen, and a jack and had drawn for a straight. João Magalhães laughed and slapped him on the back.

"Very good, colonel; that was very good."

Totonho was eyeing him grimly, but said nothing. The captain proceeded to lose all he had to the other players. There was no doubt of it, he would make a fortune in the land of cacao.

9

Tired of watching the game, the travelling salesman went up on deck, where Margot stood leaning over the rail, drenched in moonlight and lost in thought. The sea was dark green, and the last of the city's lights had long since disappeared. The boat was tossing, and nearly all the passengers had retired to their cabins or were lying stretched out on deck-chairs, wrapped in heavy blankets. In third-class the harmonica again was playing a languid air. The moon was in the centre of the heavens now, and a cold gust of wind blew in from the south, lifting Margot's blond locks. She grasped the rail as her hair floated on the breeze. When he saw that she was alone, the salesman whistled softly to himself and approached her gradually. He had no definite plan of action, no more than a vague hope in his heart.

"Good evening."

Margot turned, putting up a hand to her hair.

"Good evening."

"Turning cool, isn't it?"

"Yes, it is."

Once more she gazed at the sea, where the stars were reflected. Drawing a kerchief over her head to restrain her hair, she moved over to make room for the salesman at the rail. There was a prolonged silence. Margot appeared not to be aware of his presence, being lost in contemplation of the mystery of sea and sky. It was he who finally spoke.

"You are going to Ilhéos?"

"Yes, I am."

"Going to stay down there?"

"I don't know. If I make out all right—"

"You were in Lisia's place, weren't you?"

"Uh-huh," and she nodded her head.

"I saw you there, last Saturday. You were with Lawyer—"

"I know." She turned back to gaze at the sea, as if she did not care to continue the conversation.

"Ilhéos is the land of money, big money. A kid as pretty as you ought to get herself a grove. There can't fail to be a colonel among the customers."

She took her eyes away from the sea and looked hard at her companion. It was as if she were doubtful whether she ought to speak or not. Then she gazed back into the water without saying a word.

"Juca Badaró," the salesman continued, "was talking to you a little while ago. Better be careful."

"Who is he?"

"He's one of the rich men of the country—a brave one, too. The workers on his plantation are a hell-raising lot, they say. They are bullies and braggarts; they run over other people's land and kill folks right and left. He's the master of Sequeiro Grande."

Margot was interested, and he went on.

"They say the whole family is brave, men and women alike, that even the women are killers. Want some advice? Don't get mixed up with him."

Margot stuck out her lip disdainfully.

"And who told you that I was interested in him? He's just an old rooster who runs after every young pullet that he sees. I want nothing to do with him. I'm not out for money."

The travelling salesman gave an incredulous smile and shrugged his shoulders, as much as to say that her opinion mattered little to him.

"There was one young girl," he said, "who was friendly with him, and Juca's wife had her done in."

"But what ever put it in your head that it's any concern of mine? He can have as many women as he pleases; he's not going to have this one." And she struck her hand to her bosom. Once again she seemed on the verge of speaking, and then apparently made up her mind.

"You saw me dancing with Virgilio, didn't you? Well, he's in Ilhéos, and I'm going to him."

"That's right—I'd forgotten. He *is* down there, sure enough. Practising law—lad with a future, eh? They tell me Colonel Horacio sent for him to come down and take over the leadership of the party." The salesman nodded his head as if convinced. "If that's how it is, I've nothing more to say. My only advice is: watch out for Juca Badaró."

He walked away. It was not worth while talking to her, for a girl in love is worse than a virgin. But what would Juca Badaró have to say to it?

Margot undid the kerchief and let the wind lift her hair.

10

A shadowy figure glided up the stair and, before setting foot in first-class, glanced around furtively to see if anyone was about.

The man smoothed down his hair, adjusted the scarf that was tied about his throat. His hands were still swollen from the treatment he had received at the police station. The big ring with the false stone was no longer on his finger. The sergeant had said there was nothing to do but to crack the fellow's hands, so that they would not go into another person's pockets. Fernando climbed the last step and made for the side of the boat opposite where Margot was standing. Catching sight of a member of the crew, he went up to the rail, as if he were a first-class passenger taking the night air; after which he stole slowly over to the deck-chair where a man was snoring. His deft hands slipped under the blanket, under the overcoat, touched the cold steel of a revolver, and drew out from his victim's pocket a fat bill-fold. The man did not stir.

The thief returned to third-class. Tossing the bill-fold into the sea, he stuck the money into his own pocket. Then he tiptoed along among the sleeping passengers looking for someone. In one corner, stretched out as if he were lying on the ground, the old man who was going back to avenge his son's death was snoring away sonorously. Taking out a few of the banknotes, Fernando, with all the dexterity of which his hands were capable, crammed them into the old man's pocket. Holding his breath as he did so, he hid the remaining ones in the lining of his overcoat and then went over to the far-distant corner where Antonio Victor lay dreaming of Estancia and of Ivone's warm body beside him.

11

It was cold in the late hours of night, and the deck-passengers huddled under their blankets. Margot caught the sound of voices at a distance.

"If cacao brings fourteen milreis this year, I'm going to take the family to Rio."

"I'd like to build a house in Ilhéos."

The speakers were drawing nearer, talking as they came.

"That was a nasty business, having Zequinha shot in the back."

"But there will be a trial this time, I'll guarantee you that."

"Let's hope so."

They came to a stop in front of Margot and stood looking her over without the least ceremony. The short man smiled beneath an enormous moustache, which he stroked every other minute.

"You'll catch cold like that, young lady."

Margot made no reply.

"Where are you staying in Ilhéos?" the other asked. "At Machadão's place?"

"What business is it of yours?"

"Don't be stuck up, miss. It's off folks like us that you're going to make a living, ain't that right? Look, my friend Moura here can fix you up in fine style."

The short man tugged at his moustache. "And I'll come around, too, my dear. All you have to do is say the word."

They saw Juca Badaró approaching.

"Excuse me."

"Good evening, Juca." And the two of them slipped away. Juca nodded, then turned to Margot.

"It's time you were asleep, young lady. It's better to sleep than to stand here gabbling with everyone who comes along." He gazed resentfully at the backs of the retreating pair, but Margot stared straight at Juca.

"Who gave you the right to meddle in my life?"

"Better look sharp, young lady. I'm going below to see how my wife's getting along in the cabin; but I'll be back, and if I find you here, there's going to be a rumpus. A woman of mine does what I say." And with this he left.

"A woman of mine—" Margot repeated to herself contemptuously. Then, taking her time about it, she went down to her stateroom. As she passed, she heard the short man with the moustache saying:

"That fellow Juca Badaró has a good lesson coming to him."

Of a sudden she felt as if she were Juca's woman.

"Then why don't you teach it to him?" she asked.

12

A deepening silence lay upon the ship as it ploughed through the night sea. The harmónicas and guitars in third-class had stopped playing, and no voice sang the sad, sad songs of love and longing. Margot had gone to her cabin, and no musing passenger leaned on the ship's rail. The words of the poker-players were lost before they reached the sea. Suffused in the red and ominous light of the moon, the boat ploughed on, blanketed now in silence. The night aboard ship was filled with sleep—with sleep and dreams and the hopes of men.

The captain came down from the bridge, accompanied by the

first mate. Together they made their way through the cluster of first-class passengers, asleep beneath their blankets. Now and then one of the figures would mutter a word; he was dreaming of cacao plantations laden with fruit. The skipper and the first mate descended the narrow stair to third-class, where men and women lay huddled against one another for warmth. The skipper was silent. The second officer whistled a popular tune. Antonio Victor had a beatific smile on his lips, as he dreamed of an easy fortune won in the land of Ilhéos and of his return to Estancia in quest of Ivone.

The captain halted and looked at the sleeping mulatto.

"You see?" he said, turning to the mate. "He won't smile so much when he gets down there in the woods." And with his foot he pushed Antonio Victor's head. "I feel sorry for them."

They came up to the rail in the stern of the ship. The waves were tossing high and the moon was red. They were silent as the second officer lighted his pipe. It was the skipper who spoke at last.

"You know," he said, "there are times when I feel like the captain of one of those slavers in the old days." As the mate did not reply, he went on to explain. "One of those ships that brought blacks over to sell them as slaves." He pointed to the sleeping figures, to Antonio Victor, who was smiling still. "What difference is there?"

The first mate shrugged his shoulders, gave a puff on his pipe, but said nothing. He was gazing out over the sea, the immensity of the night, and the heaven of stars.

II

The Forest

~~~~~~

1

The forest lay sleeping its never interrupted sleep. Over it passed
the days and the nights. The summer sun shone above it, the
winter rains fell upon it. Its trees were centuries old, an unending
green overrunning the mountain, invading the plain, lost in the
infinite. It was like a sea that had never been explored, locked in
its own mystery. It was like a virgin whose flesh had never
known the call of passion. Like a virgin, it was lovely, radiant,
young, despite those century-old trunks. Mysterious as the body
of a woman that has not as yet been possessed, it too was now
ardently desired.

From the forest came the trill of birds on sunny mornings.
Summer swallows flew over its tree-tops, and troops of monkeys
ran up and down the trees and leaped crazily from bough to
bough. Owls hooted by the yellow light of the moon on nights of
calm. Their cries were not forebodings of evil, for men had not
yet come to the giant wood. Innumerable species of snakes
glided noiselessly among the dried leaves, and jaguars yowled
frightfully those nights when they were in rut.

The forest with its age-old trees lay sleeping, and its
interlacing lianas, its mire, and its prickly thorns stood guard
over it as it slumbered.

Out of the forest, out of its mystery, fear came to the hearts of men. As they arrived of an afternoon, after having made their way through mud and stream to open a trail, as they stood there face to face with this virginal growth, they were paralyzed with fright. Night came, bringing with it black clouds, heavy with June rains, and for the first time the owl's hoot was an augury of woe. The weird cry resounded through the forest, awakening the animals; snakes hissed, jaguars howled in their hidden lairs, swallows dropped dead from the bough, and the monkeys took flight. As the tempest fell, ghostly forms awoke. The truth is, they had come with the men, in their wake, along with the axes and the scythes—or can it be that they had dwelt in the forest since the very beginning of time? On this night they awoke: the werewolf and the goblin, the padre's she-mule, and the fire-breathing ox, the *boi tátá*.

The men huddled together in fright, for the forest inspired a religious awe. There was no trail here; here were only animals and ghosts. And so they came to a halt, fear in their hearts.

The tempest broke, lightning rent the skies, thunder crashed as though the deities of the wood were gritting their teeth at the threat that man brought with him. The lightning's rays illumined the forest from moment to moment, but all that the men could see was the dark green of the trunks as they listened intently to the sounds that reached their ears: the hiss of the fleeing snakes, the yowl of the terror-stricken jaguars, the terrifying voices of those shadowy shapes let loose in the wilderness. That fire which ran along the tops of the tallest boughs, that came without a doubt from the nostrils of the *boi tátá*. And that sound of hoofs which they heard, what was it if not the padre's she-mule scurrying through the undergrowth, once a beautiful maiden, who, in an access of love, had given herself to the sacrilegious embraces of a priest? They were no longer conscious of the howling of the jaguar. Now it was the ugly cry of the werewolf, a creature half wolf, half man, with enormous claws, and crazed by a mother's curse. The sinister goblin dance of the *caapora* on its one leg, with its one arm, as it laughed from a face that was cloven in two. There was fear in the hearts of men.

And the rain fell, in torrents, as though it were the beginning of another Deluge. Here everything was reminiscent of the beginning of the world. Impenetrable and mysterious, ancient as time itself and young as spring, the forest appeared to the eyes of men as the most formidable of ghostly habitations, home and refuge of the werewolf and the goblin. For them an unfathomable immensity. How small they were, there at its feet:

frightened little animals! From its depths came weird voices. But most terrifying of all was the sight, as the storm broke in all its fury, of the black heavens above, where not a single star shone to greet the newcomers with its light.

They came from other lands beyond the sea, where other forests once had been, felled now and conquered, cleared by fire, with roadways broken through them, forests from which the jaguars had disappeared and where the snakes were becoming rare. And here they stood again before another virgin wood, a trackless growth as yet untrodden by the foot of man, and with no stars in the storm-laden skies overhead. In their own distant land, on moonlit nights, old women had told gloomy tales of ghosts and sprites. In some far corner of the world, none knew where, not even the farthest-faring of travellers, not even those who went up and down the backland trails reciting prophecies—somewhere it was, in that far country, that the ghosts and goblins had their dwelling-place. Thus spoke the old women out of the wisdom of age and experience.

And then, of a sudden, on a stormy night, here on the edge of the forest, men discovered that awesome nook of the universe where the goblins dwelt. Here amid this tangled vegetation, amid the creeping lianas, in company with the venemous cobras, the fierce jaguars, the evil-auguring owls, those who had been transformed by a curse into fantastic animals were paying now for the crimes they had committed. It was from here, on nights without a moon, that they set out for the highways, to lie in wait for homeward-bound travellers and bring terror to men. And so now, amidst the tumult of the storm, the men stopped, feeling very small indeed, stopped and listened to the despairing ghostly cries that came from the forest. And when the lightning ceased, they beheld the flame-spitting mouths and caught a glimpse at times of the inconceivable countenance of the *caapora* as it did its horrible goblin dance. The forest! It is not a mystery, it is not a danger, a menace. It is a god!

No cold wind comes up from the sea, far away with its greenish waves. There is no cold wind on this night of rain and lightning gleams. Yet even so, men stand shivering, trembling with the cold as their hearts all but stop beating, the forest-god before them, and fear within.

They let fall their axes, their hand-saws, and their scythes. With lifeless hands they stand and gaze in terror at the sight of the forest. With eyes wide open, immeasurably wide open, they behold the furious deity there before them. Here are those animals which are man's enemies and which forebode him ill; here are those ghostly shades. It is not possible to go on; no human hand may be lifted against the god. They can but fall back slowly, fear in their hearts. The lightning flashes above the forest, the rain falls. Jaguars yowl, snakes hiss, as high above the storm come the lamentations of the werewolves, the goblins, and the padre's she-mules, defending the forest's virginity and its mystery. The giant wood before them is the world's past, the beginning of the world. They throw away their knives, their axes, their scythes, their saws. There is but one path for them, the backward-leading one, the one by which they have come.

2

The men are falling back. They have spent long hours, days and nights, in coming here. They have crossed rivers, made their way through all but impenetrable thickets, blazing trails, tramping through swamps; and one of them had been bitten by a snake and had been left buried at the side of the newly opened road. A rude cross, a mound of earth, was all that remained of the man from Ceará who had fallen thus. They did not put his name on the marker, for the reason that they had nothing with which to inscribe it. Along this highway in the land of cacao, this was the first of many crosses that later were to line the trails, serving to commemorate those who had perished in the conquest of the country. Another was seized with fever, bitten with that same fever which slew the monkeys. He has dragged himself along, and now he too falls back.

"It is the werewolf!" he cries, deliriously.

They are falling back. Slowly at first. Step by step, until they reach the broader path where the thorns and swamps are less numerous. The June rain falls upon them, drenching their clothes and causing them to shiver. But beyond lies the forest—the tempest, phantoms. They fall back.

They reach the trail now, a single-file passageway leading down to the banks of the river, where a canoe awaits them. They breathe a sigh of relief. The fever victim is no longer conscious of his fever; fear gives a fresh strength to his enfeebled body.

But there ahead of them, pistol in hand, his face contorted with rage, stands Juca Badaró. He too was at the edge of the forest, he too saw the lightning flashes and heard the thunder roar, he had listened to the yowling of the jaguars, the hissing of the snakes, and his heart also had contracted at the owl's ill-omened hoot. He as well as the others knew that this was the dwelling-place of spirits. But what Juca Badaró beheld was not the forest, not the beginning of the world. His eyes were filled with another vision. All he could see was that black earth, the best in the world for the planting of cacao. Before him he saw no longer a forest shot with lightning gleams, full of weird sounds, tangled with liana stocks and locked in the mystery of its age-old trunks, a habitation for the fiercest of animals and unearthly apparitions. What he saw was a cultivated field of cacao trees, trees in regularly planted rows, laden with their golden fruit, the ripe, yellow chocolate-nuts. He could see plantation after plantation stretching over this land where now the forest stood, and a beautiful sight it was. Nothing in the world more beautiful than a cacao plantation. Confronted with the forest and its mystery, Juca Badaró smiled. Here would be fruit-laden cacao trees, casting a gentle shade upon the ground; that was all there was to it. He did not even see his men as they fell back, terror-stricken.

When he did see them, he barely had time to run up and place himself facing them, at the entrance to the trail, pistol in hand and a look of stern resolve in his eye.

"I'll put a bullet in the first one who stirs a step!"

The men halted and stood like that for a moment, not knowing what to do. Behind them the forest, in front of them Juca Badaró, ready to fire.

"It's the werewolf!" cried the fever victim as he bounded forward.

Juca Badaró fired, a fresh gleam in the night. The forest echoed to the shot. The others stood about the fallen man, with bowed heads. Juca Badaró came slowly up to them, his pistol still in hand. Antonio Victor had stooped to ease the wounded man's head. The bullet had pierced the shoulder.

"I did not shoot to kill, but only to show you that I mean to be obeyed," said Juca Badaró, in a voice that was deadly calm. And he added: "Go get some water to bathe the wound."

He helped them care for the man; he himself adjusted a bit of cloth as a bandage and assisted in carrying him to the camp near the forest. The others were trembling as they went—but they went. The man was delirious as they laid him down. In the forest, goblins were loose.

"Come on!" said Juca Badaró.

The men looked at one another. Juca raised his revolver.

"Come on!"

31

Axes and pruning-knives then began to fall with a monotonous sound, awakening the forest from its sleep. Juca Badaró gazed straight ahead of him. Once again he could see all this black earth planted with cacao, plantation after plantation laden with the yellow fruit. The June rain fell on the men. The wounded man begged for water in a quavering voice. Juca kept his revolver in his hand.

3

The morning sun gilded the chocolate-nuts still green on the cacao trees as Colonel Horacio strolled slowly along between the evenly planted rows. These trees were five years old, and the plantation was now bearing its first fruits. Here, too, the forest lay beyond, threatening and mysterious as always. He and his men had cleared it, with fire, with sickle, with axes, and with scythes, felling the huge trees and routing the jaguars and the spirits. Then came the laying out of the groves, which was done most carefully in order that the yield might be the greater. And now, after five years, the trees were in bloom, and on this morning little nuts could be seen hanging from the boughs.

The first fruits. The sun touched them with gold as Colonel Horacio strolled on. He was about fifty years of age, with a heavy-featured, saturnine, pock-marked face. Holding a roll of tobacco and a jack-knife, he was engaged in making himself a *cigarro* with his big calloused hands, those hands which, long ago, had wielded the whip over the burros when he was still but a pack-driver employed on a Rio do Braço plantation. Later those same hands had learned to manage a repeating-rifle, when the colonel had become a *conquistador* of the land.

Many legends were current about him; not even the colonel himself was aware of all the tales that were told of him in Ilhéos and Tabocas, in Palestina and Ferradas, in Agua Branca and Agua Preta. The pious old ladies who prayed to St. George in the church at Ilhéos were accustomed to say that Colonel Horacio of Ferradas kept the Devil under his bed, imprisoned in a bottle. How he had come to make the capture was a long story, having to do with the sale of the colonel's soul one stormy day. And the Devil, having become his obedient servant, now waited on all his desires, increasing Horacio's fortune and aiding him against his enemies. But one day—and the old ladies crossed themselves as they said this—Horacio would die without confession, and then the Devil would leap out of the bottle and carry off the colonel's soul to the depths of hell. The colonel knew of this story and was in the habit of laughing over it, one of those short, dry laughs of his which were more frightening even than his shouts of rage on certain mornings.

There were other tales that came nearer to reality. When he was in his cups, Lawyer Ruy liked to recall the manner in which he had defended the colonel in a trial many years ago. Hóracio had been accused of three particularly brutal murders. According to the indictment, not content with having slain one of his victims, he had cut off the man's ears, nose, and tongue and had castrated him. Lawyer Ruy had been retained and was out for an acquittal. He put up a brilliant defence, making a plea in which he spoke of the "crying injustice" of the thing and of "slanders fabricated by nameless enemies without honour or self-respect." The result was a triumph; it was one of those pleas which gave him his reputation as a great trial-lawyer. In eulogizing the colonel, he spoke of him as one of the most successful planters in that region, a man who not only had been responsible for erecting the chapel at Ferradas, but even now was undertaking to build the church at Tabocas; he was a respecter of the laws, twice councilman at Ilhéos, and a Grand Master of the Masonic Lodge. Could a man like that be guilty of so heinous a crime?

Everyone knew, of course, that he *was* guilty.

It happened over a cacao contract. On Horacio's land the black man, Altino, together with his brother-in-law, Orlando, and a friend by the name of Zacarias, had entered into an agreement with the colonel to plant a grove for him. They had cleared the forest, had burned over the land, and then had planted cacao, sowing manihot and millet in between the rows in order that they might have something on which to subsist during the three years that it would take for the cacao trees to grow. When the three years were up, they came to the colonel to turn over the grove to him and to receive payment for it. Five hundred reis per foot of planted and matured cacao. With the money they planned to purchase a plot of ground for themselves, a bit of forest somewhere which they would clear and plant. They were very happy about it and went singing down the highway.

A week before, Zacarias had come to the plantation storehouse, bringing millet and manihot flour to exchange for dried beef, rum, and kidney beans. There he had met the colonel and had had a talk with him. Zacarias gave an account of how the cacao trees were doing, and his employer remarked that the three-year period was nearly ended. Afterwards Horacio had offered his visitor a drink on the veranda of the Big House and had questioned him as to what he and his companions were thinking of doing. Zacarias then told him of their plan to buy a piece of forest land and clear it for a cacao grove. The colonel not only approved of this, amiably enough, but even offered to assist them. Couldn't they see that he had the best forest land there was for cacao-planting? From all the region round about Ferradas, that enormous region which belonged to him, they might select any plot they liked. It would be better for him that way, since he would not have to lay out any money. Zacarias came back radiant to the bunkhouse.

When the time was up, they came to see the colonel, giving him an account of the number of feet of matured cacao and informing him of the plot of forest that they wished to buy. An agreement was reached and the bargain was sealed with several drinks of rum. Then Horacio spoke.

"You may as well go ahead with clearing the woods," he said. "One of these days, when I'm going in to Ilhéos, I'll let you know, you can come along, and we'll put it down in black and white at the registry office."

Something was said about a deed, but the colonel told them not to worry about that; they would be going in to Ilhéos in a month or so. With bows and polite expressions of regard the three thereupon took their departure; and the next day they set out for the forest and began cutting timber and erecting a bunkhouse. The days went by, the colonel had been to Ilhéos two or three times, they had already begun laying out the grove, and still they had nothing to show for it in writing. One day Altino plucked up courage and spoke to the colonel about it.

"You will pardon me, colonel, but we would like to know when we may have the deed to the land."

Horacio at first was indignant at this lack of confidence; but as Altino apologized, he went on to explain that he had already instructed Lawyer Ruy, his attorney, to take care of the matter. It would not be long now; one of these days he would send for them and they would hop in to Ilhéos and settle the thing. Time went by, however, and the first shoots of cacao, destined to become trees, had already begun sprouting on the newly planted land. Altino, Orlando, and Zacarias gazed at these sprigs lovingly. These were their trees, planted by their own hands, on a plot which they themselves had cleared. The sprigs would grow, bear golden-yellow fruit, fruit that meant money. They had forgotten all about the deed. Altino alone at times appeared to be thinking of it. He had known Colonel Horacio for a long while and did not trust him. Even so, they were all of them dumbfounded to learn one day that the Humming-Bird Plantation, which included their own plot, had been sold to Colonel Ramiro.

They decided to go and speak to Colonel Horacio about it. Altino and Zacarias went up to the Big House, Orlando remaining behind. They did not find the colonel; he was in Tabocas. They came back the next day; the colonel was in Ferradas. Then Orlando resolved to go himself. To him this plot of earth was everything, and he did not propose to lose it. He was told that the colonel was in Ilhéos. He nodded his head, but went on into the Big House, and there in the dining-room he found Horacio eating. The latter glanced up at his former workman.

"Want to eat, Orlando? Sit down, if you like."

"No, thank you, sir."

"What brings you here? Anything new?"

"Yes, sir, there is; some very ugly news. Colonel Ramiro was down at our place and he says our grove belongs to him; he says he bought it of you, Colonel."

"If Colonel Ramiro says so, it must be true. He's not the man to lie."

Orlando stood staring at him, but Colonel Horacio had resumed his meal. The visitor gazed at the colonel's big calloused hands, the face with its heavy features.

"So you sold it?" he said at last.

"That's my business."

"But don't you remember that you sold *us* that piece of forest? In place of money on the cacao contract?"

"Do you have it in writing?" and Horacio went on eating.

Orlando was twirling the enormous straw hat which he held in his hand. He realized the full extent of the misfortune that had befallen him and his companions. He realized that they no longer had any land, any cacao grove; they no longer had anything. A blood-red haze was dancing in front of his eyes, and he did not measure his words.

"It is no laughing matter, colonel. I am warning you that the day Colonel Ramiro sets foot in our grove, that day you're going to pay for everything. Think it over."

Saying this, he left the room, pushing aside with his arm the

35

Negro woman, Felicia, who was serving the colonel. Horacio went on eating as if nothing had happened.

That night he and his hoodlums came down to the grove that the three friends had planted. Making for the bunkhouse, the colonel announced that he himself would take care of these fellows. And afterwards, with a paring-knife, he had cut off Orlando's tongue, his ears, his nose, and then, taking down his victim's trousers, had castrated him. He then went back to the plantation with his men; and when later one of them was arrested by the police for drunkenness and accused him of the crime, Horacio gave his usual laugh. He was acquitted.

His *jagunços*, or hired ruffians, were in the habit of saying that Colonel Horacio was a real man and that it was worth while working for a boss like him. He would never let one of his men stay in jail; on a certain occasion he even left the plantation and made a special trip to free one of them who was in prison at Ferradas. Having taken the fellow from behind the bars, he had torn up the charge in the court clerk's face.

Yes, many were the tales that were told of the colonel. It was said that before becoming leader of the opposition political party, and in order to obtain that post, he had sent his thugs to lie in wait for the former party leader, a merchant of Tabocas, and they had done away with his rival for him. Later he had put the blame on his political enemies. Today the colonel was the undisputed lord of the region, the largest plantation-owner in those parts, and he was planning greatly to extend his holdings. What did it matter what stories they told of him? He was respected by landowners and labourers alike, by sharecroppers and those who worked the little groves; he had countless retainers.

And so on this particular morning he strolled along between the rows of young cacao trees bearing their first fruits. He had finished making his *cigarro* with his big calloused hands. He puffed on it slowly, thinking of nothing at all, neither of the stories they told of him nor even of the recent arrival of Lawyer Virgilio, the new attorney whom the party had sent down from Bahia to work at Tabocas. He was not even thinking of Ester, his wife, who was so young and pretty; educated by the sisters in Bahia, she was the daughter of old Salustino, an Ilhéos merchant, who had been only too happy to give her to the colonel as a bride. She was his second wife, the first having died while he was still a donkey-driver. She was slender, pale, and beautiful, with an air of sadness about her; she was, indeed, the

one thing in his life that could cause Colonel Horacio to smile in
a manner different from his usual one. But at this moment he
was not thinking of Ester. He was thinking of nothing; all that he
saw was the tiny fruit on the cacao trees, still green as yet, the
first which this grove had borne. With his hand he took one of
the pods and caressed it gently, voluptuously. Gently and
voluptuously as if he had been caressing Ester's young flesh.
Lovingly. With a boundless love.

4

Ester went over to the piano, the grand piano in a corner of the
big drawing-room. As she let her hands rest upon the keys, her
fingers mechanically began picking out a melody. An old waltz,
a scrap of music that brought back her school days and certain
festive occasions. It reminded her of Lucia. Where was Lucia
now, she wondered. It had been some time since her girlhood
friend had written her, since she had had from her one of those
extravagant but amusing letters. She had not even thanked
Lucia for those French magazines and the fashion-plates. There
they were on top of the piano, along with sheets of forgotten
music. Ester gave a sad little laugh and struck another chord. Of
what use were fashion-plates in this out-of-the-way place, here
in this wilderness? At the feast of St. Joseph in Tabocas, at the
feast of St. George in Ilhéos, the fashions were years behind the
times and she could never wear the clothes that her friend did in
Paris. Ah, if Lucia could but imagine what the *fazenda* was like,
this house lost amid the cacao groves, the hiss of frog-eating
snakes in the pools! And the forest—there behind the Big House
it stretched away interminably, with its maze of tree-trunks and
its tangle of lianas. Ester feared it as one might fear an enemy.
She would never become used to it, she was certain of that. This
was a despairing thought, for she well knew that her entire life
would be spent here, on this plantation, in this strange world
which held so much of terror for her.

She had been born in Bahia, in the house of her
grandparents, where her mother had gone to have her child and
had died in childbirth. Her father was in business in Ilhéos and at
that time was just entering upon his career. Ester accordingly
had remained with her grandparents, who had petted and
spoiled her, humoured her every whim, and devoted their lives
to her. Her father and his warehouse prospered at Ilhéos, and

from time to time he would put in an appearance, being accustomed to make two trips a year to the capital on business matters. His daughter attended the best school for young ladies that Bahia afforded, one kept by nuns. She had been a day pupil at first, and then, upon the death of her grandparents, she had become a dormitory resident. The old couple had died one after the other, the same month. Ester put on mourning, but at that moment she could not bring herself to feel that she was alone, for she had her schoolmates, and with them she read French novels and tales of princesses and dreamed of a life that was fair to behold. They had plans for the future, all of them, naïvely ambitious plans: marriages for riches and for love, fashionable clothes, trips to Rio de Janeiro and to Europe. All of them except Geny, who wanted to be a nun and spent the day praying. As for Ester and Lucia, being the best-dressed girls and the belles of the school, they gave free rein to their imaginations. They would hold conversations in the courtyard during recreation period, and in the silence of the dormitory as well.

Ester rose and left the piano, the last chord dying away in the forest. Ah, school days, those happy days! She recalled something that Sister Angelica, the friendliest and most understanding of all the nuns, had said to her when the girls were wishing that time would pass as quickly as possible so that they might begin to live life more intensely. Then it was that Sister Angelica had laid her delicate hands on her pupil's shoulders—and what thin shoulders they were!

"No time is better than this, Ester, when it still is possible to dream."

She had not understood then. Years had to pass before this remark came back to memory afresh, to be recalled after that almost every day. Ah, those happy school days! Ester went out to the hammock that was awaiting her on the veranda. From there she could see the main highway, where at rare intervals a workman passed, bound for Tabocas or Ferradas. She could also see the cluster of troughs where the cacao lay drying in the sun, trampled by the black feet of plantation labourers.

Upon completing her course at school, she had come to Ilhéos, without even waiting to be present at Lucia's marriage to Dr. Alfredo, the well-known physician. Her friend was now travelling abroad, Rio de Janeiro and then Europe, where her husband was specializing in celebrated hospitals. Lucia had realized her dreams: expensive clothes, perfumes, grand balls. How different was the destiny of each, Ester reflected. She herself had come to Ilhéos, another world. A small city that had barely begun to grow, with a population made up of labourers and adventurers, and where all that was talked of was cacao and deaths.

Her father lived on the second floor, above the warehouse, and from her window Ester could see the monotonous landscape of the city. A hill on every side. She found no beauty, either in the river or in the sea. For her, beauty lay in the life that Lucia was leading: those balls in Paris. Not even on the days when ships came in and all the city took on animation, when there were newspapers from the capital and the shops were filled with men discussing politics—not even on these occasions, which were almost like holidays, did Ester emerge from her sadness. The men admired and courted her from afar; and once during the carnival season a medical student had written her a letter and sent her some verses. But for Ester it was a time for weeping and for lamenting the death of her grandparents, which had obliged her to live in this out-of-the-way hole. The news of feuds and deaths frightened her, left her in an agony of apprehension. Little by little, however, she permitted herself to be overcome by the life of the city and gradually lost her preoccupation with that feminine elegance which had created such a stir (and a certain amount of scandal) upon her arrival there; and when one day her father, who was very happy over the matter, informed her that Colonel Horacio, one of the richest men in that region, had asked for her hand in marriage, all that she did was shed a few tears.

And now it was a festive occasion when she went to Ilhéos, even. The dream of great cities, of Europe, of imperial balls and Parisian gowns—all that was behind her. It all seemed very far away, lost in the mists of time, back in that time "when it still was possible to dream." Not a great many years had passed, but it seemed as though she had lived an entire lifetime with hallucinatory speed. The height of her dreams these days was a trip to Ilhéos, to take part in the church festival, a procession, or a fair with an auction of gifts.

She swung herself in the hammock slowly. There before her, as far as her eyes could reach, up hill and down, lay the cacao groves, laden with fruit. On the lawn about the house hens and turkeys were scratching. Negroes in the troughs were trampling the cacao. Coming out from behind a cloud, the sun burst forth, flooding the landscape.

Ester remembered her wedding day. The day they were

39

married, that very day, she had come to the plantation with her husband. She shuddered now as she thought of it, swaying in the hammock. It was the most horrible sensation she had ever experienced. She remembered that, upon the announcement of their engagement, the city had been filled with gossip and whisperings. A woman who never called upon her had appeared one day to tell her certain stories. Before that, some of the pious old ladies, well known in church circles, had informed her of the legends that were current regarding the colonel. But this woman brought a piece of news that was more concrete and more terrible still. She told Ester that Horacio had murdered his first wife, had beaten her to death with a whip when he found her in bed with another. That was back in the days when he was still a pack-driver, going up and down the recently opened trails in the mysterious forest. It was not until long afterwards, when he had grown rich, that this story began circulating in the streets of Ilhéos, in the land of cacao. Possibly just because the entire town was speaking of her with lowered voices, Ester, with a certain pride and a vast deal of contempt, went on with preparations for the wedding. Their "courtship," on those rare Sundays when Horacio came down to the city to dine at her father's house, had been made up of long silences. It was a courtship without kisses or subtle caresses, with no words of romance, so different from the wooing that Ester once upon a time had imagined in the quiet of the convent.

She had wanted a simple wedding, though Horacio had at first insisted on doing things in grand style: a banquet and a ball, Roman candles and a High Mass. She had had her way; it had been an intimate affair, and the two ceremonies, one with the priest and the other with the judge, had been performed at home. The priest had delivered a sermon; the judge, with the tired face of a heavy drinker, had wished them happiness; and Lawyer Ruy had made a pretty speech. They were married in the morning, and by early twilight, travelling on burros through the swamps, they had reached the Big House of the plantation. The labourers who had gathered on the lawn in front of the house shot off their rifles as the burros drew near. This was their way of welcoming the newly wedded pair, but Ester felt her heart contract at the sound of those shots in the night. Horacio had rum distributed to the help; and a few minutes later she found herself already alone as he went out to see how the groves were doing and to look over the cacao drying in the oven, to see how much they had lost on account of the rains. It was only when he returned that

40

the Negro women lighted the kerosene lamps. Ester was frightened by the cries of the frogs. Horacio had almost nothing to say, but waited impatiently for the time to pass.

"What is that?" she asked, as there came the cry of another frog from the pool.

"A frog in a snake's mouth," he answered her, indifferently.

Dinner was brought in, served by the Negro women, who cast suspicious glances at Ester. And then of a sudden, when dinner was barely over, came the tearing of clothes from her body and the brutal possession of her flesh in a manner that she had not expected.

She had grown accustomed to everything. She got along well enough with the Negro women now, and she had even come to like Felicia, who was a devoted mulatto girl. She had become used to her husband with his heavy silences, his sudden excesses of sensuality, his furious outbursts of rage, which left even the fiercest of the *jagunços* huddled in fright. She had become used to the shots in the night, along the highway, and to the corpses that from time to time went by in hammocks, to the mournful accompaniment of weeping women. The one thing to which she could not become accustomed was the forest at the back of the house, where at night, in the pool formed by the river, frogs cried despairingly in the mouths of assassin snakes.

At the end of ten months a son had been born. He was now a year and a half old, and Ester was horrified to see that Horacio had been born again in the person of his child. He was Horacio to the life; and Ester could not help thinking to herself that the fault was hers for not having collaborated in his conception; for she never gave herself, but was taken always, like an object or an animal. Even so, she loved the child dearly and suffered for him. She had become accustomed to everything; she no longer dreamed. The only thing to which she could not become accustomed was the forest and the forest night.

On stormy nights it was terrible: the lightning illuminated the tallest trunks, the thunder crashed, trees were uprooted. On such nights as these Ester would crouch in terror and weep for the fate that was hers. Nights of horror, nights of irrepressible fear, a fear that was like a concrete, tangible object. It would begin with the agonizing hour of twilight. Ah, those twilights, harbingers of the tempest to come! As the afternoon with its black, lowering clouds drew to a close, the shadows would become an unmistakable doom; there was no kerosene light that could frighten them off, prevent their seeking out the house and making of it, of the cacao groves, and of the wood one single entity bound by the dusk that was equal to night itself. The trees would assume gigantic shapes, growing in stature with the mysterious spreading of the shadows. Dolorous sounds would be heard, the cry of unknown birds and of animals, coming from—where? She did not know. And the hissing of the reptiles, the rustling of dried leaves where they crawled. Ester always had the feeling that one day the snakes would end by coming up on the veranda and making their way into the house, some stormy night, until they reached her own and her child's throat, which they would encircle like a necklace. She herself could never have told the horror of those moments, which lasted from the fall of twilight until the storm broke. And then, when at last it descended in all its fury and Nature appeared bent upon destroying everything, she would seek out those places where the light of the kerosene lamps was brightest. Even then the shadows cast by the light made her afraid and set her imagination to work, leading her to believe the most superstitious of the stories that the Negroes told.

There was one thing that she always remembered on these nights, and that was the cradle lullabies her grandmother had sung to her to calm her fears when she was a child, so many years before. And so now, beside her own child's cradle, she tearfully sang them over again, one after another, in a low voice, once more convinced of their magic efficacy. She sang them to her son as he looked up at her with his hard brown eyes, Horacio's eyes; but she sang them for herself as well, for she too was a frightened child. She sang in a low voice, lulling herself with the melody as the tears streamed down her face. She forgot the darkness of the veranda, those terrible shadows outside, the ominous hoot of the owls in the trees, the melancholy of the night, and the forest and its mystery. She sang the songs of long ago, simple melodies, efficacious against spells. It was as though her grandmother's protecting shade were hovering over her, lovingly and understandingly.

And then of a sudden the cry of a frog in the pool, killed by a snake, would come through the forest, through the cacao groves, and would enter the house; it was louder than the owls' hoot or the rustling of the leaves, louder than the whistling wind itself, as it came to die away in the lamp-lit room where Ester sat, her body all a-tremble. She sang no more. Closing her eyes, she could see—in every slightest detail—the slimy, repulsive reptile slithering along over the ground and among the fallen leaves, until it suddenly pounced on the innocent frog, as that despairing death-cry perturbed the calm waters of the little stream, filling with fear, with evil, and with suffering the menacing night-scene.

On such nights she beheld snakes in every corner of the house, crawling out from the chinks in the floor, from between the tiles, and entering at every opening of the door. One moment, with closed eyes, she would see them creeping up cautiously for the fatal pounce on the frogs; and the next moment she would be trembling as she reflected that one of them might be on the roof, slowly, stealthily, silently making for the rosewood bed, perhaps to strangle her as she slept. How many sleepless nights had she spent when she thought that a snake was coming down the wall! She had but to hear a noise as she dropped off to sleep; that was all that was needed to fill her with terror. She would throw back the covers, rise, and go over to her son's cradle. When she was convinced that he was sleeping peacefully, she would search the room thoroughly, a candle in her hand, her eyes wide-staring with fear. Horacio sometimes would awake and mutter something from the bed, but Ester would continue her fruitless search. She no longer slept, but waited and waited, terror-stricken, for *it* to come. Then it came, creeping toward her bed, and she was unable to move or cry out. She could feel it circling her neck, strangling her. She could see her young son dead, laid out in his sky-blue casket, the mark of venomous teeth on his face.

On one occasion she caught a glimpse of a piece of rope in the darkness, and gave a scream like that of the frogs, a scream that, crossing field and pool, died in the forest.

Ester remembered another night. Horacio was away on a trip to Tabocas, and she was alone with the child and the servants. They were all asleep, when there came a sound of someone pounding on the door. Felicia went to see who it was and then called loudly for her mistress. It was some of the plantation labourers, with one of their fellow workmen by the name of Amaro who had been bitten by a snake. Ester stole a glance through the door, but did not care to go any nearer. She could hear the men asking for medicine, and she heard the explanation that one of them was giving in a hoarse voice. "It was a bushmaster, a fire-quencher, poisonous as anything." They had bound Amaro's leg with a cord above the place where he had been bitten, Felicia brought a coal from the kitchen, and Ester watched as they placed it on the wound. The burnt flesh sizzled,

Amaro groaned, and a strange odour spread through the house. One of the workers had ridden off to Ferradas in search of an antitoxin, but the poison took effect very rapidly and Amaro died there in the presence of Ester, the Negro women, and the other workers, his face a greenish hue, his eyes protruding from their sockets. Ester could not tear herself away from the corpse; from that mouth, silent now forever, she had heard the same agonizing cries as those of the frogs killed in the pools. When Horacio came back from Tabocas in the middle of the night and gave orders for them to take the body to one of the workmen's huts, she had a fit of weeping. Sobbingly she begged her husband to take her away, to take her to the city, or she would die; the snakes would come, any number of them; they would bite her all over; they would kill the baby and end by strangling her with their clammy coils. She could feel the snake's cold, flaccid body on her bosom now; a shudder ran over her and she wept more loudly than ever. Horacio laughed at her fears; and when he decided to go out and join those who were sitting up with Amaro's corpse, she could not bring herself to remain alone, but accompanied him.

The men, seated around the cadaver, were drinking rum and telling stories. Stories of snakes, the story of José da Tararanga, who was forever drunk and who one night came home staggering, a lantern in his right hand and a flask of rum in his left hand. At the curve of the road the bushmaster made a leap for the lantern and bowled José over. As soon as he felt the snake's first bite, José opened the flask and drank everything that was in it. The next day, as the men went along to work in the groves, they found him asleep, and the bushmaster was sleeping, too, curled up on José's chest. After killing the snake, they found that José had seventeen bites in all, but he was none the worse for it on account of the rum. The alcohol had diluted the poison. The only thing was, he swelled up as big as a horse for a couple of weeks, but after that he was as right as ever.

They also told stories of "snake-charmers," those who were immune to the serpent's bite, who would even pick them up along the highway and remain unharmed. There was Agostinho, on the next plantation; he was a "charmer"; a snake would never do him any harm. Why, merely for the fun of it, he would put out his arm for them to bite.

Joanna, the pack-driver's wife, who drank as much as any of the men, then began telling of something that had happened on the backlands ranch where she had lived before moving to these parts, here in the south. The family had come down to the Big

House to spend their vacation; and one day a snake made its way into the house. They always came down at the end of the year; and this year they were very happy because a child had just been born to them, their first one, for they had been married only a little over a year and a half. But the snake came in and curled up in the baby's cradle. The baby was crying for its mother's breast, and so, in its innocence, it took the snake's tail in its mouth. They found the infant the next day, the tail of the sleeping serpent still in its mouth; but it was no longer sucking on it, for the poison had taken effect. The lady of the house then ran out through the fields, her golden hair flying in the wind, her feet bare and white—Joanna had never seen any feet as white as they were—as she ran along over the thorns and briers. They said that she was never quite right in the head after that, but became an idiot and grew ugly, lost all her beauty of face and figure. Before that, she had been like one of those foreign dolls, but afterwards she was nothing but an old hag. The Big House was always closed after that; the family never came back. The ivy grew all over the verandas, and weeds crept into the kitchen; and those who go by there today can hear the hisses of the snakes that make their nests inside the house.

Joanna ended her story, took another drink of rum, and spat, then turned around to look at Ester; but Ester was no longer there; she was running toward the house, to her own baby's cradle, as if she too had gone mad.

On the veranda now, with the bright sun playing about her, Ester remembered this and other nights of terror. From Paris Lucia had written her, letters that arrived three months later and brought news of another mode of life, other people, of civilization and festivities. Here was the forest night, the nights of storm and snakes. Nights for weeping over her own unfortunate lot. Twilights that clutched the heart, taking away all hope. Hope of what? Everything was so very, very definite in her life.

There were other nights also when she wept. When she saw Horacio leave at the head of a group of men on some expedition or other. She knew that on that night, somewhere, shots would ring out, that men would die for a plot of earth in order that Horacio's plantation, which was hers as well, might be augmented by another bit of forest. From Paris Lucia wrote, telling of balls at the Embassy, operas, concerts. And here in the plantation Big House the grand piano waited for a tuner who never came.

Ah, those nights when Horacio left with his men on armed

expeditions! Once, after he had gone, Ester tried to picture to herself what his death would mean. If he were to die—Then the plantation would be hers alone, she would turn it over to her father to manage, and she would go away. She would go to join Lucia. . . . But it was a shortlived dream. For Ester, Horacio was immortal; he was the master, the boss, the "colonel." She was certain that she would die before he did. He disposed of land, of money, and of men. He was made of iron, was never ill; it seemed as though bullets knew and feared him. For this reason she did not lull herself with the dream that was at once so wicked and so marvellous. There was no hope for her; she could not even lift a hand. Her life was what it was; this was her destiny. And to think that in Ilhéos many a young girl doubtless envied her! She was Dona Ester, wife of the richest man in the Tabocas region, the political leader, master of so many cacao plantations and so much virgin forest land.

She barely had time to dry her tears as Horacio came up to the hammock. In his hand was a small cacao pod, the first from the new grove.

"The grove is bearing already," he said, half smiling.

He stood there, unable to understand why she had been weeping.

"What the devil are you crying for?" he said angrily. "Is that all you do? What's the matter, don't you have everything you want? Is there anything you lack?"

"It's nothing," said Ester, stifling a sob. "I'm silly."

She took the cacao fruit because she knew this would please her husband. Horacio was smiling jovially now; he was happy in the possession of his wife as his eyes ran down her body. They were the only things in the world that he loved: Ester and cacao.

"Why are you crying, foolish girl?" he asked, seating himself beside her in the hammock.

"I'm not crying now."

Horacio was thoughtful for a moment; then he spoke, his eyes wandering in the direction of the groves as he held the cacao pod in his calloused hand.

"When the little fellow grows up"—he always referred to the child as "the little fellow"—"he's going to find all this full of groves, all under cultivation." He was silent for some time; then he added: "My son's not going to have to live stuck off here in the backwoods like us. I'm going to put him into politics; he's going to be deputy and governor. That's why I make money."

He smiled at Ester and let his hand run over her body.

"Dry those eyes, and go tell them to see that they have a first-rate dinner, for Lawyer Virgilio, the new attorney in Tabocas, is coming here today. And see that you put on your best clothes, too. We want to show that young fellow that we're not backwoodsmen."

He laughed that short laugh of his, and leaving Ester with the cacao pod, he went out to give orders to the workmen. She sat there thinking of the dinner they would have that night, with this what's-his-name of an attorney. Naturally, he would be like Lawyer Ruy, who got drunk and then stayed on after dessert to spit all over the floor and tell dirty stories. And from Paris Lucia had written letters telling of parties and theatres, gowns, and banquets.

5

The two men stood in the doorway; it was the black man who spoke.

"You sent for us, colonel?"

Juca Badaró was about to tell them to come in, but his brother made a gesture with his hand to indicate that they should wait outside. The men obeyed and sat down on one of the wooden benches that stood on the broad veranda. Juca was pacing up and down the room, from one end to the other, puffing on his cigarette. He was waiting for his brother to speak. Sinhô Badaró, the head of the family, was taking his ease in a high-backed chair of Austrian make, which contrasted strangely not only with the rest of the furniture, the wooden benches, the cane chairs, the hammocks in the corner, but also with the rustic simplicity of the whitewashed walls. Sinhô Badaró was thinking, his eyes half-shut, his black beard resting on his bosom. Raising his eyes, he glanced at Juca, pacing nervously with his riding-whip in one hand and the puffing cigarette in his mouth. Then he took his eyes away and let them rest on the single picture that hung on the wall, a chromolithograph depicting a European rural scene.

Sheep were feeding against a soothing dark blue background. There were shepherds playing a kind of flute, and a pretty, fair-haired country girl dancing among the ewes. An indescribable peace emanated from that chromo. Sinhô Badaró remembered how he had come to buy it. He had casually entered a shop kept by Syrians in Bahia to get a price on a gold watch.

He had caught sight of the picture, and had recalled Don' Ana's saying to him not long before that the drawing-room walls needed something to brighten them up a bit. For this reason he had bought it, but only now for the first time did he study it attentively. A peaceful country scene, with those sheep and their flute-playing shepherds and the dancing maiden with the golden hair. Blue, dark blue, almost sky-blue. Quite different from the fields around here, in this land of cacao. Why could not they be like this European one? But Juca Badaró was still striding up and down impatiently, waiting for his elder brother's decision. Sinhô Badaró hated to see blood flow. None the less, he had many times had to make a decision such as that which Juca expected of him this afternoon. It was not the first time that he had sent one or two of his men to take up their places in "ambush" and wait for someone to come along the road.

He gazed at the picture. A pretty young woman—rosy cheeks, heavenly eyes. Prettier even than Don' Ana. And the shepherds, they were quite different from the donkey-drivers here on the plantation, no doubt of that. Sinhô Badaró liked the land, liked planting the land. He liked breeding animals—big, gentle oxen, high-strung horses, and mild-bleating sheep. The thing he loathed was sending men to their death. For this reason he withheld his decision as long as possible and only gave it when there was no other way out. He was the head of the family, it was he who was engaged in building the Badaró fortune, he had to get over what Juca called his "weakness." He had never before studied that picture closely. That was a very pretty blue—even prettier than some of the calendars they sent out at the end of the year, and there were some very nice calendars.

Juca Badaró paused in front of his brother.

"I am telling you, Sinhô," he said, "there's nothing else to do. The fellow is stubborn as a mule. He won't sell the grove; it's not a matter of money, says he doesn't need money. And you know, Firmo always did have the reputation of being bullheaded. There's nothing else to be done."

Sadly Sinhô Badaró took his eyes off the chromo.

"It's too bad that he's a man who never did anyone any harm. If it weren't that this is the only way of extending the plantation on the Sequeiro Grande side— Otherwise, it will fall into Horacio's hands." His voice altered slightly as he uttered the hateful name. Juca nodded approvingly.

"If we don't do something about it, Horacio certainly will. And whoever gets Firmo's grove holds the key to the forest of Sequeiro Grande."

Sinhô Badaró was once more lost in contemplation of the picture.

"I don't need to remind you, Sinhô," Juca continued, "that no one knows cacao land better than I do. You came from outside, but I was born here, and ever since I was a child I've learned to know land that is good for planting. Why, I tell you, all I need to do is walk over it and I'll know what it's worth. It's something I have in the soles of my feet. And I can further tell you that there's no better land for cacao-raising than that of Sequeiro Grande. You know how many nights I've spent inside that jungle, looking it over. And if we don't get there pretty quick, Horacio will be there before us. He has a good scent, too."

Sinhô Badaró ran his hand over his black beard.

"It's a nasty business, Juca. You are my brother; your mother was the same aged Filomena who bore me, God rest her soul. Your father was the late Marcelino, who was my father as well. Yet the two of us are as different, one from the other, as any two persons in this world could be. You like to solve everything with bullets and with slayings; but there is one thing I wish you would tell me: Do you enjoy killing people? Don't you feel anything at all? Nothing on the inside? Nothing here?" And Sinhô put a hand to his heart.

Juca puffed on his cigar, struck his mud-spattered boot with his riding-whip, and resumed his pacing. Then he spoke.

"If I didn't know you as I do, Sinhô," he said, "and if I didn't respect you as my older brother, I'd be capable of thinking that you are a coward."

"You haven't answered my question."

"Do I like to see people die? I don't know, myself. When I'm angry with someone, I could cut him up piecemeal. As you know—"

"And when you're not angry?"

"Whenever anyone gets in my way, he's got to get out, so that I can pass. You are my older brother, and you are the one who settles family matters. Father left you in charge of everything— the groves, the children, me myself. It is you who are making the Badaró fortune. But I am telling you, Sinhô, that if I were in your place, we would have twice as much land as we do have."

Sinhô Badaró rose. He was almost six feet tall, and his black beard fell over his chest. His eyes gleamed, his voice filled the room.

"And when, Juca, did you ever know me to fail to do anything that was necessary? You know very well that I don't have the taste for blood that you do. But when did I ever fail to have some one put out of the way when it had to be?"

Juca made no reply. He respected his brother, who was perhaps the only person in the world whom he feared. Sinhô Badaró lowered his voice.

"It is only that I am not, like you, an assassin. I am a man who does things out of necessity. I have had people done away with, but, as God is my witness, I have only done it when there was no other way out. I know, that is not going to help me any when the day comes to settle accounts up there," and he pointed to the ceiling, "but it means something to me at least."

Juca waited for his brother to grow a little more calm.

"And all this on account of Firmo," he said, "a pig-headed idiot. You may call me what you like, it makes no difference to me; but I want to tell you one thing right now: there's no better land for cacao than that of Sequeiro Grande, and if you want those lands for the Badarós, there is nothing else to be done. Firmo won't sell his grove."

Sinhô Badaró made a gesture. Juca understood and called in the two men from the veranda. But before doing so, he said: "If you like, I'll explain everything to them."

Half closing his eyes, Sinhô sat down in the high-backed chair.

"When I make a decision," he said, "I assume the responsibility. I will speak to them myself."

He glanced up at the picture, that soothing blue. If the land in that chromo were only good for raising cacao, he, Sinhô Badaró, would not have to be sending out ruffians to lie in wait behind a tree and do away with those flute-playing shepherds, that rosy-cheeked girl dancing so merrily. . . . The men were waiting, and, with an effort, he forgot all about the scene in the picture (the young woman ceasing her dance with the bullet that he was sending) and began giving orders in his usual firm, calm, measured tone of voice.

6

Down the highway where the afternoon breeze was carrying a cloud of red dust the two men came, each with a rifle slung over his shoulder. Viriato, a back-country mulatto, was suggesting a wager.

"I'll bet you five milreis our man comes from my side."

As it happened, the highway forked near Firmo's little

plantation. That was why Sinhô Badaró had sent two men—one for each road. The Negro Damião, who was his trusted man, a crack shot and as devoted as a hound to his master, was to station himself along the path by which it was most likely that Firmo would come, since it was the shorter route and he would save time that way. Viriato was to wait on the highway, behind a guava tree, at a spot where others had fallen. And now Viriato was proposing a bet, and in spite of the fact that it was almost certain that Firmo would come along the side-road, Damião would not take him. Viriato marvelled at this.

"What's the matter with you, brother? Are you short of dough?"

But it was not because he lacked the five milreis, representing two days' pay, that Damião would not accept the wager. Many times he had bet more than that, on other similar expeditions, on other afternoons like this. Today, however, there was something that kept him from betting.

Night was falling as the two men went down the highway, where not a traveller was to be seen. The only person they met was a fellow on a burro, who looked at them long and hard and then spurred his mount in order to put as much distance as possible between himself and the pair from the plantation. For who was there in these parts that did not know Negro Damião, Sinhô Badaró's *jagunço*, his trusty? Damião's fame had long since spread far and wide, far beyond the confines of Palestina, of Ferradas, and of Tabocas. From the wine-shops of Ilhéos, where his exploits were retailed, it had travelled by small boats all the way to the capital, and a newspaper of Bahia had already published his name in big letters. Since it was an opposition newspaper, it had had some very bad things to say about him, had called him some ugly names. Damião recalled that day perfectly. Sinhô Badaró had sent for him to come up to the Big House at lunch time. There were a lot of people at the table, and the unstoppered bottles of wine revealed the presence of the judge. Lawyer Genaro, the Badaró's attorney, was there also; he was the one who had brought the newspaper. Lawyer Genaro was not so brilliant as Lawyer Ruy, he could not make speeches full of high-sounding words, but he did know, meticulously, all the intricate details of the law and how to get around it, and Sinhô Badaró preferred him to any of the various lawyers who were in practice at the bar of Ilhéos. Sinhô smiled at Damião and pointed him out to the others.

"Here's our wild man."

Seeing that Sinhô laughed, Damião gave a broad innocent grin, his perfect white teeth gleaming in his enormous black mouth. The judge, who had drunk his fill, laughed heartily also, but Lawyer Genaro barely smiled, and you felt that he was doing that out of politeness. Sinhô Badaró went on talking, speaking now to Damião.

"Did you know, Negro, that the newspapers in the capital are concerned over you? They say there's no better killer in the region than Damião, Sinhô Badaró's boy."

He said this with an air of pride, and it was with pride that Damião answered him.

"Yes, sir, that's right, that is. There's no boy who's a better shot than this Negro right here." And he grinned once more, with satisfaction.

Lawyer Genaro took a swallow and filled his glass. Sinhô Badaró burst out laughing, and the judge joined in the merriment. Then Sinhô had read the piece in the paper to Damião, who only half understood it, for there were many expressions in it that were too difficult for him. But he was pleased when he heard Sinhô call: "Don' Ana! Don' Ana!"

His daughter came in from the kitchen, where she had been supervising the serving of the lunch.

"What is it, Father?"

The judge looked at her with a show of interest in his eyes.

"Take fifty milreis from the strong-box," Sinhô Badaró directed, "and give them to Damião. His name is in the newspapers."

He then had dismissed the Negro, and the conversation around the lunch table had been resumed. As for Damião, he went off to Palestina to spend the money on whores. He drank all night long, telling everybody how a newspaper in Bahia had printed a piece about him, saying there was nobody who was as good a shot as he was.

This was why it was that the man on the burro had spurred his mount. He knew that a bullet from Negro Damião meant a coffin with a funeral to order, and he knew besides that Sinhô Badaró's boys were guaranteed protection; there was no police so far as they were concerned. Everybody knew that the judge was the Badarós' man; they even had planted a grove for him; the Badarós were riding high in politics and could depend on the courts. As he saw the man spurring his burro, Viriato smiled with amusement, but Negro Damião remained solemn-faced.

"What's the matter with you, brother?" Viriato repeated.

52

Damião himself did not know what the matter was. Many times before he had gone out to wait in ambush and kill someone; but today it seemed as if it were the first time.

At this point the road forked off.

"So you don't want to bet, black boy?"

"I've told you I didn't."

They separated, and Viriato went off whistling.

Night had fallen and the moon was rising. A good night for an ambush. You could see the road as plain as day. Negro Damião took the side-path; he knew of a tree that was just right for his purpose. It was a leafy breadfruit tree at the edge of the road and appeared to have been put there purposely for a man to hide behind and fire on some passer-by. "I never fired on anyone from behind this tree," Damião thought to himself. The Negro was sad, for from the veranda he had overheard the conversation of the Badaró brothers. He had heard what Sinhô said to Juca, and it was this that disturbed him tonight. His innocent heart was in agony. Damião had never felt like that. He could not understand it; his body did not pain him anywhere, he wasn't sick, and yet it was the same as if he were.

If before that anyone had told him that it was a terrible thing to waylay men in ambush, to kill them, he would not have believed it; for his heart was innocent and free of all malice. The children of the plantation adored Negro Damião, who played horse with the smaller ones, went to get nice soft breadfruit for them from the big breadfruit trees, brought them clusters of golden bananas from the banana groves where the snakes lived, saddled tame horses for the older ones, and took them all to the river to bathe and taught them how to swim. The children adored him, for them there was no one better than Negro Damião.

His profession was killing. Damião did not even know how it had all begun. The colonel sent him out; he killed. He could not have told you how many he had killed, for Damião could not count beyond five, and then only on his fingers. He had no interest in knowing. He did not hate anyone; he never did anyone any harm. At least he had thought so until today. Why, then, today was his heart so heavy, as though he were sick? He was very kind and thoughtful of others in his rude way. If there was a sick worker on the plantation, Damião would show up to keep him company, to teach him about herb remedies, and to go for Jeremias, the witch-doctor. Sometimes travelling salesmen stopping at the Big House would insist on his telling them of some of the men he had killed, and Damião would do so, in a calm voice, innocent of all evil.

For him an order of Sinhô Badaró's was something that admitted of no discussion. If Sinhô sent him to kill, he had to kill. Just as, when Sinhô sent him to saddle the black mule for a journey, Damião had to saddle it as quickly as possible. What was more, there was no danger of going to jail; for one of Sinhô Badaró's boys never was arrested. Sinhô could guarantee his men that; it was a pleasure to work for him. He was not like Colonel Clementino, who sent you out to do a job and then turned you in. Damião despised the colonel. A boss like him was no boss for a man of courage. Damião had worked for the colonel a long time ago, when but a youngster. It was there that he had learned to shoot, and it was for Clementino that he had killed his first man. And then one day he had had to flee the plantation, when the police came looking for him, without the colonel's even having warned him. He had taken refuge on the Badaró estate, and now he was Sinhô's trusty. If in his heart there was any ill will toward anyone, it lay in the profound contempt that he felt for Colonel Clementino. At times, when the colonel's name was mentioned in the workers' huts, Damião would spit and say:

"He's not a man. He's a bigger coward than a woman. He ought to wear petticoats."

He would say this and then laugh, laugh with his white teeth, his big eyes, his entire face. A happy, wholesome laugh, like that of a child. As he roamed the plantation, none could distinguish his laugh from that of the young ones with whom he played on the lawn beside the Big House.

Negro Damião had reached the breadfruit tree. Unslinging his rifle, he rested it on the tree-trunk. From his trousers pocket he took out a twist of tobacco and with his knife began cutting himself a *cigarro*. The moon now was round and enormous; Damião had never seen it so large. Inside himself he felt a huge hand, like one of his own great black hands, clutching at him. In his ears Sinhô Badaró's words were still ringing: "Do you enjoy killing poeple? Don't you feel anything at all? Nothing on the inside?" Damião had never thought that he could feel anything; but today the colonel's words were like a weight on his chest, a weight it was impossible even for a Negro as strong as Damião to remove. He had always hated physical pain. He bore it well, however. There was that time when he had cut a deep gash in his left arm with his knife as he was gathering cacao nuts in the grove. It was a cut that went almost to the bone, and he had loathed the pain of it; but nevertheless he had gone on whistling as Don' Ana Badaró poured iodine on the wound. Then there was that other time when Jacudino also had cut himself with a knife: three gashes in the leg. That sort of thing, that kind of pain, he could understand; it was, so to speak, something that was there in front of his eyes. But the pain he felt now was different. Things of which he had never thought before now filled his head, which was almost as big as that of an ox. Sinhô Badaró had put words into his head, and in their wake came images and sensations, old images long forgotten and new sensations, unknown before.

He had finished rolling his smoke. The light of a match glowed in the forest. He puffed on his cigarette. He could never imagine the colonel being remorseful. Remorseful was the word. Once a travelling salesman had asked him if he, Damião, never felt any remorse. He had asked what the word meant, the salesman had explained, and Damião had then replied, with the utmost innocence: "Why should I?"

The travelling salesman was astonished, and to this day still told the story in the cafés of Bahia when with some of his cronies he was discoursing largely on the subject of mankind, human life, and various philosophies of life. Some while after that, at Christmas time, Sinhô Badaró had procured a friar to say Mass at the plantation. They had set up an altar on the veranda—and a lovely altar it was; Damião smiled at the memory of it, smiled for the one and only time that night, as he waited there in ambush. Damião had been of great help to Don' Ana, to the late Dona Lidia, and to Don' Olga, Juca's wife, as they made preparations for the fête. The friar had arrived that night, and there was a dinner with any number of good things to eat: hens, turkeys, pork, mutton, game, and even fish, for which they had had to send to Agua Branca. There was something cold as a rock, which they called an "ice"; and Don' Ana, who was just coming into young womanhood, had given some of it to Damião. It had burnt his tongue, and Don' Ana had laughed heartily at the face which the Negro made.

Mass was said the next morning; and those on the plantation who were lovers were married and the young ones were baptized, the godfathers and godmothers being, always, members of the Badaró household. Then the friar had preached a sermon, better than any speech that Lawyer Ruy was capable of making, and he made some very fine ones to the juries in

Ilhéos. True, the friar's tongue got rather twisted, for he was a foreigner; but perhaps for that very reason, when he came to speak of hell and the flames that burned the damned forever and ever, he caused his listeners to shudder all the more. Even Damião was frightened. He had never thought much about hell before, and he seldom thought of it again afterwards. It was only today that he remembered the friar and the angry vehemence with which the latter had cried out against those who slay their fellow men. The friar had had much to say about remorse, which was hell in this life. Damião already knew what the word meant, but it made little impression on him at that time.

He was impressed, it is true, with the description of hell, a fire that never subsided but was endlessly burning human flesh. On his wrist Damião had the scar from a burn where a live coal had fallen on him one day while he was helping the Negro women in the kitchen. It had hurt frightfully. So he could imagine one's whole body being burnt, forever and ever and ever. The friar had said that all you had to do was to kill a man and you would be certain to go to hell. Damião did not even know how many men he had killed. He knew that it was more than five, because he could count, and had counted, up to five. After that he had lost count, but he had not thought it was of any great importance. But today, as he puffed on his cigarette there in ambush, he made a vain effort to remember them all. First there had been that pack-driver who had insulted Colonel Clementino. It was something wholly unlooked for. He had been going along with the colonel, both of them mounted, when they had met a pack-train on its way to Banco da Victoria. The pack-driver, the moment he laid eyes on Clementino, had lashed him across the face with his long burro-whip. Clementino was white with rage.

"Get him!" he had shouted to Damião.

Damião had drawn the revolver that he carried in his belt; he had fired, and the pack-driver had fallen, the burros passing over his body. Clementino had made for the plantation, the mark left by the whip still glowing red on his cheek. Damião had had no time to think it over, for the police had appeared, some days later, and he had had to flee. After that he had begun killing for Sinhô Badaró: Zequinha Fontes, Colonel Eduardo, that pair of thugs from Horacio's plantation, in the fight at Tabocas— that made five, didn't it? But then there was Silvio da Toca; Damião did not know how many that was. Not to mention the fellow who had been going to shoot Juca Badaró in the whorehouse at Ferradas—and if he didn't shoot him, it was

56

because Damião was quicker on the draw. And not to mention, also, the other killings that followed. Firmo—how many would he make? "I'm going to ask Don' Ana to teach me to count on the other hand." There were some of the workers who could count on their fingers and on their toes as well, but these were the more intelligent ones; they were not stupid like Negro Damião. But now it was necessary at least to learn to count on the fingers of the other hand. How many men had he killed already?

The moon above the breadfruit tree was casting its light on the path along which Firmo would come. It was a side-road, some two miles in length. Firmo would surely be in a hurry to get home, to take off his boots, and to be with Dona Tereza, his wife. Damião was acquainted with her. He had stopped sometimes in front of the house when he was passing, to ask for a jug of water. And Dona Tereza one day had even given him a drop of wine and they had exchanged a few words. She was pretty, and whiter than any writing-paper. Whiter than Don' Ana. Don' Ana was brown-skinned, sunburned. Dona Tereza looked as if she had never been in the sun, as if the sun had never touched her cheeks, her white flesh. The daughter of an Italian, she had come out from the city. She had a charming voice, and it sounded as if she were singing when she talked. Firmo surely would be in a hurry to get home, to be with his wife, to creep into that white flesh of hers. A woman was a rarity in these parts. Aside from the whores in the towns, four or five in each one, and they were a sickly lot, very few of the men had women. That was certainly true of the workers; but Firmo was not a worker; he had a little plantation of his own; he was up-and-coming and would end by being a colonel with a lot of land. Having laid out his grove, he had gone to Ilhéos to get him a wife. He had married the daughter of an Italian baker, a woman who was white and pretty—they even said that Juca Badaró, who was crazy over women, had cast an eye on her. Damião could not say for sure. But even if it was true, one thing was certain: she had not given him any encouragement. Juca had transferred his attentions elsewhere, and the gossip had ceased.

Yes, there was no doubt of it, Firmo would come by this road; he would not take a longer way home when he had a woman who was young and white waiting for him. The truth is, Negro Damião would have preferred that Firmo come by the highway. It was the first time that this had ever happened to him. Amid all the confused thoughts that were running through his head and the pain that he felt in his bosom, he was conscious at the same time of a certain humiliation. You would think he wasn't used to this sort of thing. You would think that he was Antonio Victor, that worker who came from Sergipe, and who, when he had killed a man in the fight with Horacio's gang at Tabocas, had afterwards trembled all night long and had even cried like a woman. He had got used to it after a while, and now he was Juca Badaró's killer, always at Juca's side when the latter went on a trip. Negro Damião was like Antonio Victor that first time; just as if he were not used to waiting up all night, lying for his man in ambush. The others would laugh at him as they had laughed at Antonio Victor that night of the row at Tabocas.

Negro Damião shut his eyes so that he might be able to forget all these images. He had finished his cigarette and he wondered if it was worth while rolling another. He did not have much tobacco, and he might have to wait a long time. Who could say when Firmo would come? He could not make up his mind, and was rather glad that now he had the problem of tobacco to occupy his thoughts. This was good backlands tobacco; the kind you got at Ilhéos was no good at all; it was terrible—too dry, it didn't last. But Tereza, what was she doing there? She was white. Damião had been thinking of his tobacco—how came Dona Tereza's white face to be there? Who had sent for her? Negro Damião was angry. A woman was always sticking her nose into things, coming when she wasn't called. But there was something else—why had Sinhô Badaró that afternoon spoken of those things to his brother? And why, if he had to speak of them, had he not at least sent him and Viriato out of earshot? As it was, Damião had overheard the entire conversation from the veranda.

"Do you enjoy killing people? Don't you feel anything at all? Nothing on the inside?"

Negro Damião knew now what it meant to feel things. He had never felt anything before. Possibly, had it not been Sinhô Badaró who spoke those words, had it been Juca instead, he would have thought nothing of it. But to Damião, Sinhô was a god. He respected him more than he did Jeremias, the witch-doctor who had cured him of bullet-wound and snake-bite. And Sinhô's words had stayed with him, weighing on his heart, running through his head. They brought him a vision of Dona Tereza's white face as she waited for her husband, repeating, meanwhile, Sinhô Badaró's words, the words of the friar also. Like the friar, she was half a foreigner. Only the friar's voice was full of anger as he told of terrible things to come, while Dona Tereza's was soft, like music.

He no longer thought of rolling himself a cigarette and puffing on it. What he was thinking of was Dona Tereza, waiting for Firmo and for love in the marriage bed. White flesh waiting for the husband. She had a kind face, too. Once she had given Negro Damião a drop of wine. And he had exchanged a few words with her, about the sun which was beating down on the highway that afternoon. Yes, she was a good woman, no foolishness about her. So good that she could even talk to a black assassin like Damião. She was mistress of her own cacao plantation and might have been stuck-up like so many other women. But instead she had given him wine and had spoken of the sun and how hot it was. She was not afraid of him as so many other women would have been. Many of the others were frightened when they saw Damião coming and would hide inside the house to wait for their husbands. Damião always laughed at this fear on their part; he was even proud of it: it showed how widespread was his fame. But today, for the first time, it occurred to him that what they were fleeing was not a brave black man, but a black assassin.

A black assassin. He repeated the words in a low voice, slowly, and they had a tragic sound to his ears. The friar had said that no one should kill his fellow men, for it was a mortal sin, and one would pay for it by going to hell. Damião had thought little of it. But today it was Sinhô Badaró who had said those same things about killing. A black assassin. And Dona Tereza was kind, pretty as could be, and whiter than any woman on the neighbouring plantations. She loved her husband, you could see that, loved him so much that she would have nothing to do with Juca Badaró, a rich man, whom women slobbered over. The women were afraid of him, of Damião, the assassin.

He recalled now a long train of incidents: women who disappeared from the lawns when he came in sight; others who timidly spied on him from their windows; that prostitute in Ferradas who would not sleep with him for anything in the world, in spite of the fact that he had shown her a ten-milreis note in his hand. She simply would not sleep with him. She would not say why, she pretended she was sick, but in her face Damião could see something else: fear. He had thought nothing of it, had given that deep, full laugh of his, and had gone off to look for another woman. But now that whore's refusal was an additional wound. Don' Ana Badaró alone was kind to him; she was not afraid of the black man. But Don' Ana was a brave woman, a Badaró. Children also had no fear of him; but children do not understand such things; they did not know that he was a killer who went out to wait for men in ambush, to bring them down with that sure aim of his. He liked children. He got along with them better than he did with grown-ups. He liked to play with the simple toys of the children in the Big Houses; he liked satisfying the whims of the wretched little ones in the workers' huts. He got along well with children.

And then, of a sudden, the terrifying idea shot through his head: supposing that Dona Tereza were pregnant, with a child in her belly? The child would be born without a father; the father would have been brought down by Negro Damião's aim. With a tremendous effort he drew himself up; his enormous head was as heavy as on those days when he was on a big drunk. No, Dona Tereza could not be pregnant; he had had a good look at her that day when they had exchanged a few words at the door of Firmo's house. She wasn't carrying any child; no, no, she wasn't pregnant. But that had been six months ago. How was she now? Who could say? Why, she might very well be about to have a child, a child in the belly. It would be born without a father; it would learn that its father had fallen on the highway one moonlit night, brought down by Negro Damião. And it would hate him; it would not be like the other children who came to play with him, who climbed up on his back before they were able to mount the tamest of the burros. It would not eat the breadfruit that Negro Damião had gathered, or the golden-ripe bananas that he had gone to pluck in the banana groves. It would look at him with hatred, for Damião would always be the one who had killed its father.

Damião was sad beyond words. The moonlight fell upon him, the breadfruit tree hid him from the road, his rifle was resting on the tree-trunk. Others were in the habit of carving notches on their gun-stocks for each man they killed. He had never done that, because he had not wanted to deface his rifle. He was fond of it. He always kept it hanging up above the wooden bunk where he slept without a mattress. Sometimes at night Sinhô Badaró would have to leave on a trip, and he would send for the Negro to accompany him. Damião would then take down his rifle and go up to the Big House. The burros would be already saddled, and when Sinhô mounted he did likewise, and would ride along behind his boss, his rifle resting on the pommel of his saddle. For they might come upon one of Horacio's men in hiding along the highway. Sometimes it happened that Sinhô would call to him, and he would come up and ride alongside, and Sinhô would talk to him about the groves, the crops, the condition of the soft cacao, and all sorts of things that had to do with the life of the plantation. Those were happy days for Negro Damião. He would be happy, too, when they arrived at the end of their journey, at Rio do Braço, Tabocas, Ferradas, or Palestina. The colonel would give him a five-milreis note, and he would go spend the rest of the night in bed with some woman. He always left his rifle at the foot of the bed; for Sinhô might take it into his head to return at any moment, and would send a boy from the town to run down and look for the Negro in the whorehouses. He would leap from the bed—one night he had even leaped off the body of a woman—would seize his rifle and set out once more. He loved the weapon and kept it bright and shining; he liked to look at it. Today, however, he did not enjoy looking at it, but sought for something else on which to fix his gaze. There was the moon high up in the sky. Why was it you could look at the moon, and yet there was not a pair of eyes that could bear looking at the sun? This problem had never occurred to Negro Damião. He became absorbed in it, his mind wholly bent on solving it. That way he did not have to see Dona Tereza, nor the child which she was about to bear, nor listen to Sinhô Badaró's voice as he put the question to Juca:

"Do you enjoy killing people? Don't you feel anything at all? Nothing on the inside?"

Why was it no one could look the sun straight in the face? There was no one who could. The same with the men he killed; Damião never looked at them afterwards. He had no time; he had to get away the moment the job was done. Neither had he ever had the misfortune of finding that his victim was still alive, as had happened to the late Vicente Garangau, whom people talked so much about—Vicente had been done in at the hands of a man on whom he had fired. He had not taken the trouble to find out if the man was dead or not, and so had ended up in that horrible fashion, carved into tiny bits. Damião also never went to look at anyone he had brought down. What did they look like, anyway? He had seen many a dead person, but those that he had killed—what were they like? What would Firmo be like, this very night? Would he fall forward over his burro, which would carry him along; or would he tumble to the ground, blood flowing from his bosom? They would take him home like that, with the gaping wound in his chest, would take him to the house where he, Damião, had been the other day. Dona Tereza would be there, worried because her husband was so late in coming home. And what would she say when she saw them bringing him in, already cold in death, slain by Negro Damião? The tears would fall, over her chalk-white face. She might even become ill on account of her pregnancy; she might have her child before her time. She might even die, for she was such a weak little thing, so slender in her whiteness.

Thus, in place of killing one, he would have killed two. He would have killed a woman, which was something a brave black man did not do. And the child? He had not reckoned on the child—Damião counted on his fingers—that made three. For there was no longer any doubt in his mind that Tereza was pregnant. To him it was a certainty. He was going to kill three persons that night, a man, a woman, and a child. Children were so pretty, so kind to Negro Damião, he liked them. And with that shot he was going to kill one of them. And Dona Tereza also, with her white flesh, now lying dead in her coffin. He could see the funeral procession setting out for the cemetery in Ferradas, which was the nearest one. It would take a lot of people to carry the three caskets. They would have to get people from round about; they might even come up to the Badaró plantation. And Damião would come and lift the little sky-blue casket of the child, dressed like an angel. It was almost always he who bore the caskets of the "little angels" when a child died on the plantation. Damião would arrange the wildflowers, strew them over the casket, and then lift it to his shoulder. But Firmo's child he would not be able to lift, for he was the one who had killed it.

Again Negro Damião drew himself up with an effort. His head would not do what he wanted it to—why was that? The truth of the matter was, he had not killed any child, he had not killed Dona Tereza, he had not even killed Firmo as yet. And it was at that moment that the idea of *not* killing Firmo entered Negro Damião's head for the first time.

It was no more than a rapid, fugitive thought, but it frightened him nevertheless. He really could not bring himself to think of it. How could he fail to carry out an order of Sinhô Badaró's? An upright man, Sinhô Badaró. What was more, he was fond of Negro Damião. He would talk with him as they rode along the highway; he treated him almost like a friend. And Don' Ana also. They gave him money. His wages were two and a half milreis a day, but as a matter of fact he had much more than that, and each man that he brought down meant an additional reward. Not only that, but he had very little work to do; it was a long time now since he had gone to the groves; he always stayed around the Big House, doing little chores, accompanying the colonel on his trips, playing with the children, waiting for orders to kill a man.

That was his profession: killing. Damião was perfectly aware of that fact now. He had always thought that he was a worker on the Badaró plantation, but now he saw that he was no more than a *"jagunço,"* a back-country ruffian. His profession was killing, and when there were no men to be brought down along the highway, he had nothing to do. If he accompanied Sinhô, it was to guard his boss's life; it was to kill anybody who tried to shoot the colonel. He was an assassin. That was the word which Sinhô Badaró had used in speaking of Juca in their conversation that afternoon. A word that fitted Damião, also. What was he doing now, if not waiting for a man, to fire on him? He was feeling something on the inside, something that was terribly painful. It hurt like a wound. It was as if someone had stabbed him. The moon shone upon the silent forest. And Damião remembered that he might be rolling himself a cigarette; that would be something to occupy his thoughts.

When he had finished lighting his cigarette, the idea came back to him once more; supposing he did not kill Firmo? It was now a definite idea, and Damião found himself thinking of it. No, that was out of the question. Damião knew perfectly well why Sinhô Badaró had to have Firmo put out of the way. It was in order that he might be able to get hold of Firmo's grove without any more trouble than was necessary, and so go on to the forest of Sequeiro Grande. Once the Badarós had that forest, theirs would be the biggest plantation in the world, they would have more cacao than all the rest of the folks put together, they would be richer even than Colonel Misael. No, not to do away, with Firmo tonight would be to betray the confidence Sinhô had placed in him. If Sinhô had sent him out, it was because he did have confidence in Negro Damião. He, Damião, had to kill. He clung to this thought. He had been killing all these years; why should it be so difficult today?

The worst was Tereza, the white-skinned Dona Tereza, with a child in her womb. She was certainly going to die, and the child as well. He could see her now. Before there had been but the whiteness of the moon; now it was the white face of Firmo's wife. He had not been drinking, either. Others drank before they came out to kill a man; he never needed to. He was always calm when he arrived, confident of his aim. He never needed to take a drink as the others did, to get drunk in order to kill someone. But today he felt as though he had been drinking a great deal and the rum had gone to his head. He could see Dona Tereza's white face there on the ground. Before, it had been the moon, the milk-white moon, spreading over the earth. And now Dona Tereza had come, her face so white and sorrowing, with a look of tragic surprise. She was waiting for her husband, waiting for love; and he would come to her dead, a bullet in his chest. From the ground she looked up at Negro Damião. She was begging him not to kill Firmo, for the love of God not to kill him. On the ground the Negro could see her face, perfectly plain. A shudder ran over his giant's body.

No, he could not listen to her, to Dona Tereza. Sinhô Badaró had sent him and there was nothing that Negro Damião could do about it. He could not betray the confidence of an upright man like Sinhô. Now, had it been Juca who had sent him—But it was Sinhô, Dona Tereza; this Negro can do nothing about it. Your husband is to blame, too. Why the devil wouldn't he sell the grove? Couldn't he see that he had no chance against the Badarós? Why wouldn't he sell the grove, Dona Tereza? Don't cry—Negro Damião is about to cry himself. He's a brave lad, and he mustn't cry, for that would ruin his reputation. Negro Damião swears to you that if he had his way about it, he would not kill Firmo; he would do what you want him to do. But it was Sinhô who sent him, and Negro Damião has nothing to do but to obey.

Who was it said that Dona Tereza was kind? It is a lie! She is opening her mouth now, and in that musical voice of hers she is repeating Sinhô Badaró's words:

"Do you enjoy killing people? Don't you feel anything at all? Nothing on the inside?"

Her voice is musical, but terrible at the same time. It is like a curse uttered in the forest, in the Negro's frightened heart. His cigarette goes out, and from fear of awakening the spirits of the wood he has not the courage to strike a light. It is only now that he thinks of them; for Dona Tereza's face, projected there on the ground—that is certainly witchcraft. Damião knows that many people have called down a curse upon him. Relatives of those he has slain. Horrible curses, uttered in the hour of suffering and hatred. But all this was far in the past; Damião had barely heard tell of them. Not so now. Now it is Dona Tereza who is here, with her sorrowful eyes, her white face, her voice that is musical and terrible. Calling down curses on Negro Damião's head. Demanding to know if he feels nothing inside, there in the bottom of his heart. Yes, he does, Dona Tereza. If Negro Damião had his way, he would not kill Firmo. But there is nothing else to do; it is not because he wants to do it, no.

But what if he were to say that he had missed his aim? It was a fresh idea that flashed through Damião's mind. For a second he beheld the moonlight where Tereza's face had been. His reputation would be ruined; the other lads did not miss their aim, much less Negro Damião! He was the best shot of all, in all that cacao region. He never had to fire a second time in order to kill a man. The first was always enough. He would be ruined; everybody would laugh at him, even the women, even the children; and Sinhô Badaró would give his place to another. He would become a worker like the others, gathering cacao, driving donkeys, treading cacao seeds in the trough. Everyone would laugh at him. No, he could not do it. Moreover, he would be betraying Sinhô Badaró's confidence. The colonel needed to have Firmo put out of the way; the one who was to blame was Firmo himself, for being so bull-headed.

Dona Tereza knows everything, she must be a spirit herself, for here she is reminding the Negro, from the ground where her face has once more replaced the moon, that Sinhô had been undecided about it that afternoon and had only sent his men out because Juca had forced him to do so. Damião shrugs his shoulders. Sinhô Badaró, is he the man to decide upon a thing merely because Juca insisted? Anyone who thinks that does not know him. It is plain to be seen that Tereza does not know him—yet here she is recalling details of that conversation, and Damião is beginning to waver. Supposing that Sinhô himself did not want Firmo killed? Supposing that he too was sorry for Dona Tereza and for the child in her belly? Supposing that he too had felt something inside, like Negro Damião? Damião put his hands to his head. No, it was not true. It was all a lie on Dona Tereza's part—Dona Tereza, with her sorceries. If Sinhô Badaró had not wanted Firmo put out of the way, he would not have sent him. Sinhô Badaró only did what he wanted to do. That was why he was rich and the head of the family. Juca was afraid of him, in spite of all his boasting and strutting. Who was there who was not afraid of Sinhô Badaró? Only himself, Negro Damião. But if he did not kill Firmo, he was going to be afraid all his life long; he would never be able to look Sinhô Badaró in the face again.

From the ground Dona Tereza's voice is laughing up at the Negro: "So it is only out of fear of Sinhô Badaró that he is going to kill Firmo? Out of fear of Sinhô Badaró? And this is Negro Damião, who is said to be the bravest lad in these parts?" Dona Tereza laughs, a crystal-clear and mocking laugh that shakes the Negro's nerves. He is trembling all over, inside. The laugh comes from the ground, comes from the forest, the highway, the sky, from everywhere; they are all saying that he is afraid, that he is a coward—he, Negro Damião, whose name is in the newspapers.

Dona Tereza, don't laugh any more, or I'm capable of putting a bullet into you. I never fired on a woman; a man doesn't do that. But I'm capable of firing on *you* if you don't stop laughing. Don't laugh at Negro Damião, Dona Tereza. This Negro is not afraid of Sinhô Badaró. He respects him; he does not want to betray the confidence that Sinhô has in him. I swear to God, that' so. Don't laugh any more, or I'll let you have a bullet. I'll put a bullet into that white face of yours.

They are clutching at his bosom now. Something is pressing down upon him from above; what is it? This is witchcraft; it is a curse that they are calling down on him. A woman's curse on the head of a Negro. There comes from the forest a voice repeating Sinhô Badaró's words:

"Do you enjoy killing people? Don't you feel anything at all? Nothing on the inside?"

The entire forest is laughing at him, the entire forest is screaming those words at him, the forest is clutching his heart, dancing in his head. There in front of him is Dona Tereza—not all of her, only her face. This is witchcraft, a curse they are calling down on his Negro head. Damião well knows what they want. They want him not to kill Firmo. Dona Tereza is pleading with him, but what can he do? Sinhô Badaró is an upright man. Dona Tereza has a white face. Someone is weeping. But who can it be? Is that Dona Tereza's face there on the ground, or is it Negro Damião? Whoever it is, is weeping. It hurts worse than a knife-cut, worse than a sizzling coal on black flesh.

They have seized his arms; he cannot kill. They have seized his heart; he cannot kill. Down Damião's black cheeks tears are flowing from Dona Tereza's blue eyes. The forest is shaking with laughter, shaking with groans; Damião is surrounded by the witchery of the night. He sits down on the ground and weeps, softly, like a punished child.

The sound of a burro's hoofs grows louder along the highway. They are coming nearer, nearer every moment, and

Firmo's face appears beneath the light of the moon. Negro Damião shakes himself and rises, a knot in his throat, his hands trembling on his rifle. The forest screams at him from round about. Firmo is coming nearer.

7

"Baccarat cyrstal," announced Horacio, tapping the goblet with his finger as little clear-ringing sounds were heard about the table. "It cost me a pretty penny," he went on. "I got it when we were married. Sent to Rio for it."

Lawyer Virgilio—"Dr. Virgilio"—raised his glass, where the drops of Portuguese wine had stained the transparent crystal a blood-red.

"It is the very refinement of good taste," he said, holding the goblet level with his eyes.

His remark was addressed to all of them, but his gaze was fixed on Ester. It was as if he were trying to tell her that he knew perfectly well that the good taste was hers. His voice was orotund and well modulated, and he picked his words as carefully as if he had been engaged in an oratorical contest. He sipped his wine like a connoisseur, as if endeavouring to estimate the worth of the vintage. His fine manners, his languid gaze, his blond hair, all were in contrast to the room. Horacio sensed this vaguely, and Maneca Dantas was aware of it. But for Ester the room did not exist. In the presence of the young attorney, she had been suddenly snatched away from the plantation, carried back to bygone days. It was as though she were still in the convent school, on one of those holidays at the end of the year when she and her schoolmates danced with the finest and most distinguished youth of the capital. She smiled at everything, and she too affected an over-refinement in her words and manners as a gentle melancholy that was almost happiness took possession of her. "It was the wine," she thought. Wine went to her head very easily. So thinking, she drank some more, and all the while she was drinking in Virgilio's words.

"It was at a party in honour of Senator Lago—a ball in celebration of his election, as a matter of fact. And what a party, Dona Ester! You really cannot imagine it. It was all so very aristocratic. The Paiva sisters were there." Ester knew them, for they had been schoolmates. "Mariinha was charming in blue taffeta, like a dream."

"She is pretty," Ester agreed, but there was a certain reserve in her voice that did not escape Virgilio.

"Ah, but not the prettiest girl in school, in her day," said the young lawyer, correcting himself. Ester blushed, and took another sip of wine.

Virgilio went on discoursing. He spoke of music, mentioned a certain waltz by name, and Ester remembered the melody. At this point Horacio spoke up.

"Ester is a first-rate pianist, eh!" he said.

Virgilio's voice at once took on a suppliant tone.

"Well, then, after dinner we shall be happy to listen to her. Surely, she will not deny us that pleasure."

But Ester said no, she had not touched the piano for a long while, her fingers had lost their suppleness, and moreover the piano was in a terrible condition—all out of tune, as there was no one to look after it here in this God-forsaken place.

Virgilio, however, would not accept any excuses. Turning to Horacio, he begged him to "insist that Dona Ester stop being so modest and consent to fill the house with harmony." Horacio dutifully insisted.

"Stop beating around the bush and play for this young man. I want to hear you, too. After all, I put a nice little sum of money into that piano, the best they had in Bahia. It was a devil of a job getting it out here, and what use is it? Money thrown away—six *contos de reis*." He repeated the phrase, as if unburdening himself of something that was on his mind. "Six contos thrown away." He glanced at Maneca Dantas. The latter should be capable of understanding how he felt. Maneca decided that he must lend his support.

"Six contos is a lot of money. It's a cacao grove."

Virgilio, on the other hand, was incorrigible.

"What are six *contos de reis*, six miserable contos, when they are laid out to give happiness to one's wife, colonel?" As he said this, he raised a finger close to the colonel's face, a finger with a well-manicured nail and with an advocate's ring, the ruby of which gleamed showily. "You may say what you like, colonel, but I will guarantee you never spent six contos that brought you as much satisfaction as when you purchased that piano. Isn't that so?"

"Well, I was glad to do it, of course. She had a piano at home, you know, but it was a cheap and flimsy little affair and I didn't want to bring it out here." This was said with a sweeping gesture of contempt. "So I bought this one. But she almost never touches it. Once in a lifetime—"

68

Ester listened to all this, a mounting hatred inside her, a hatred greater even than that she had felt on her wedding night, when Horacio had torn her clothes off and had hurled himself upon her body. She was slightly under the influence of wine, intoxicated also by Virgilio's words, and her eyes once more held the restless dreams of the schoolgirl that once had been. In those eyes Horacio was transformed into a filthy pig, like one of those on the plantation that wallowed in the mudholes down by the highway. Virgilio, by contrast, appeared a wandering knight, a musketeer, a French count, an admixture of the characters in the novels she had read in school, all of them noble, daring, and handsome. In spite of it all, in spite of the hatred that she felt—or because of that hatred, perhaps?—the dinner was delicious. She sipped another goblet of wine.

"Very well, then," she announced with a smile, "I'll play." She had spoken for Virgilio's benefit. Then she turned to Horacio. "You never ask me," she said. Her voice was mild and gentle, but her hatred was satisfied because she now realized that she had a means of revenge. Wishing to hurt him as deeply as possible, she went on: "I thought you didn't like music. Now that I know you do, that piano's never going to have a rest."

But it was lost on Horacio. For him these were not feigned words. This was not the Ester he had known; this was another, one who thought of him and his desires. He felt a glow of kindliness breaking through the many layers with which his heart was covered and laving him with goodwill. Possibly he had been unjust toward Ester; he had not understood her; she was from another world. He felt that he must promise her something very fine and generous, something that would make her very happy.

"For the holidays," he said, "we're going up to Bahia." He was speaking to her and to her alone, taking no account of the others at the table.

Thereupon the conversation resumed its normal course. A brilliant one it was, limited almost exclusively to Ester and Virgilio and consisting of descriptions of parties and a discussion of fashions, music, and novels. Horacio was lost in admiration of his wife, but Maneca Dantas looked on with wary eyes.

"I like Georges Ohnet," Ester was saying. "I wept when I read *Le Grand Industriel.*"

"Perhaps," said Virgilio, and his tone was slightly melancholy, "because you found in it something of the autobiographical?"

Horacio and Maneca Dantas got nothing of this, and even Ester was a bit slow in comprehending. But when she did understand, she put a hand to her face and shook her head nervously.

"Oh, no, no!"

"Ah!" sighed Virgilio.

Ester felt that he was going a little too far.

"That is not what I meant to say."

But Virgilio paid no heed. He was beaming, his eyes glowing.

"And Zola? Have you read Zola?" he finally asked.

No, she had not read him; the sisters at the convent would not permit it. Virgilio opined that, really, he did not think it the proper thing for young ladies. But a married woman—he had a copy of *Germinal* at Ilhéos; he would send it to Dona Ester.

The Negro women had finished serving the endless desserts, and Ester suggested that they take their coffee in the drawing-room. Virgilio quickly rose, drew back her chair, and stood aside for her to pass. Horacio looked on with a certain distant envy, while Maneca Dantas admired the attorney's manners. As he saw it, education was a great thing; and he thought of his own sons and imagined them, in the future, as being like "Dr. Virgilio." Ester left the room, the men following.

It was raining outside, a fine drizzle shot through with moonbeams. There were many stars, with no other light to dim their heavenly lustre. Virgilio went over to the door and stepped out on the veranda. Felicia came in with the coffee tray and Ester began serving the sugar. Virgilio returned from the veranda and observed, as if he were declaiming a poem:

"It is only in the forest that one sees a night as lovely as this."

"It's pretty, yes," agreed Maneca Dantas, mixing chicory with his coffee. "Another little spoonful, if you please," he said, turning to Ester. "I like my coffee sweet." Then he addressed the lawyer once more. "A very pretty night, and this shower makes it all the prettier." He had to make an effort to keep up with the rhythm that Virgilio and Ester gave to the conversation; but now he was content, for he had the feeling that he had made a remark that was comparable to theirs.

"And you, doctor? How many?"

"Just a little, Dona Ester. That will be enough. Thank you very much. And do you not find, senhora—you, too—that progress slays beauty?"

Ester handed the sugar-bowl to Felicia and paused a moment before replying. She was grave and pensive.

"I think that progress may also be very beautiful."

"But in the great cities, with all their lights, one cannot even see the stars. And a poet loves stars, Dona Ester—those of heaven and those of earth."

"But there are other nights when there are no stars." Ester's voice now was deep; it came from her heart. "On stormy nights it is terrible."

"It must be terribly beautiful—" The sentence was left hanging in the air, dangling before them. "For there is a beauty that is terrible," he added.

"Perhaps," said Ester, "but on nights like that I am afraid." And she gave him a beseeching look, as if he were a friend of long standing.

Virgilio saw that she was not acting now, that she was pained, very deeply pained; and it was at that moment that he for the first time let his eyes rest upon her with real interest. Gone was his jovial and at the same time astute manner; its place had been taken by something more serious and profound.

Horacio now took a hand.

"Do you know what this foolish girl is afraid of, doctor? Of the cry of frogs when the snakes swallow them down there on the river bank."

Virgilio too had already heard that heart-rending cry.

"I understand," was all he said.

It was a blissful moment. Ester's eyes were now filled with a wholesome, unfeigned happiness. She was not acting. It was but a second, but that second was enough. Even her hatred for Horacio was gone.

She went over to the piano. Maneca Dantas, meanwhile, began to expound to Virgilio the business that they had in hand. It was an important "ouster," involving many *contos de reis*. Virgilio had to force himself to pay attention. Horacio from time to time put in a word out of his own experience. Virgilio cited a law. The first chords from the piano were vibrating in the room. The lawyer smiled.

"Now we are going to listen to Dona Ester," he said. "Afterwards we will see what we can do about increasing your plantation."

Maneca assented with a gesture, and Virgilio joined Ester at the piano. The waltz that she was playing was not confined to the drawing-room, but made its way outside, across the fields and all the way to the forest at the back of the house. On the sofa Maneca Dantas was conversing with Horacio.

71

"A fine lad, eh? And what ability! Why, they say he's even a poet. And how he can talk! He'll make a good lawyer for us. He's got brains in his head."

"And Ester?" said Horacio, "what do you have to say about her, my friend? Where in Ilhéos, or even in Bahia—even in Bahia," he repeated, "will you find a woman of such education? She knows all the tricks: French, music, fashions, everything. She has a head on her shoulders," and he tapped his own head with one finger. "She's more than just a pretty little thing." He spoke with pride, as an owner might of his property. His words breathed vanity. He was happy because he imagined that Ester was playing for him, playing because he had asked her. Maneca Dantas nodded his head. "She's an educated woman, all right, that she is."

At the piano, his eyes brimming with tenderness, Virgilio was humming the melody. When Ester finished and rose, he put out a hand to assist her. She remained standing there beside him as Virgilio clapped his hands in applause and whispered to her, for her alone to hear:

"You are like a little bird in the snake's mouth."

Maneca Dantas was enthusiastic; he wanted more. Horacio came over to them. With a supreme effort Ester restrained her tears.

8

At the edge of the forest Negro Damião was waiting for a man in ambush. In the light of the moon he was seeing hallucinatory visions, and he was suffering. At the edge of another forest, in the drawing-room of the Big House, Dr. Virgilio was putting his knowledge of the law at the service of the two colonels and their ambition and was discovering love in Ester's frightened eyes. Beside the forest that ran down the slope of the hill on the other side, on the Badarós' Sant' Ana da Alegria plantation, Antonio Victor also was waiting, his feet dangling in the river water. The stream at this point was a small one, and its calm, clear waters were strewn with a mixture of fallen leaves from the cacao trees on the one side and those trees which stood on the opposite bank, huge trees that the hand of man had not planted. These waters formed the boundary between the forest and the groves, and Antonio Victor, as he waited, was thinking that it would not be long before fire and ax would have laid low this wood. It would soon be all cacao groves, and the river would no longer mark any separation. Juca Badaró was talking of felling the forest this very year, and workmen were getting ready to burn it over; the cacao saplings that were to fill the space now occupied by the wood were already being prepared.

Antonio Victor was fond of the forest. His home town of Estancia, so distant now even in his thoughts, was situated within a wood, with two rivers encircling it, and the trees overran its streets and public squares. He was better accustomed to the forest, where all the hours were hours of twilight, than he was to the cacao groves, glowing so brightly with their ripened fruit the colour of old gold. He had formed the habit of coming here during his first days on the plantation, when his work in the groves was ended. Here it was that he took his rest. Here it was that he remembered Estancia, still present in his recollections, and recalled Ivone, whom he had left behind on the bridge over the Piauhitinga River. It was here that he suffered the gentle pangs of melancholy.

It had been hard for him at first. In addition to the gnawing pain of homesickness, the work was heavy, a great deal heavier than it had been on the little millet plot that he had cultivated with his brothers before coming to these lands in the south. Here on the plantation they rose at four o'clock in the morning to prepare the dried beef and manihot flour for their noonday lunch; and then, after gulping down a pot of coffee, they had to be at the grove, gathering cacao, by five, just as the sun had barely begun to appear above the hill at the back of the Big House. Then it began beating down on the bare backs of Antonio Victor and the other workers, especially those who had come down with him from Bahia and were not used to it. Their feet would sink into the mire, the viscous molten cacao would stick to them, and then from time to time there would come a rain that would leave them in even a sorrier plight than they had been before, for, having been blown in over the tufted groves, it brought with it bits of brushwood, insects, and filth of all sorts. At midday—they could tell it by the sun—work would stop, and after eating their lunch they would shake down a soft breadfruit from some breadfruit tree for their dessert. But the foreman astride his burro would already be shouting to them to take up their scythes again; and they would begin once more and keep it up until six o'clock in the evening, at which time the sun abandoned the groves.

After that came night, mournful and filled with weariness,

without a woman with whom to stay, without Ivone to caress on a non-existent bridge, without the fishing parties such as they had in Estancia. People talked about the money to be made in the south. Heaps upon heaps of money. But here all that they got for all this work was two and a half milreis a day, to be wholly spent at the plantation store, a miserable wage at the end of the month when accounts were settled. Night came, bringing with it far-off longings, and thoughts as well; and Antonio Victor would come down to the edge of the forest, to dip his feet in the river, shut his eyes, and give himself over to his memories. The others would remain in the mud huts, having flung themselves down on the wooden bunks to sleep the sleep of utter exhaustion. Others would sing *tiranas*, love-songs filled with longing, and the guitars would moan as the airs of other lands were sung, bringing memories of a world left behind. It was enough to tear one's heart out.

Antonio Victor would then come down to the forest, his memories accompanying him. Once again, for the hundredth time, he would possess Ivone on the Estancia bridge. Yet when it was over, there would remain the same soft and viscous cacao caught on the soles of his feet and growing greater in bulk all the time, like some weird kind of shoe.

After that, Juca Badaró had taken a liking to him. First of all because, when they were engaged in felling the wood where the Border Line Grove now stood, he had not been afraid as the others were when they arrived there at night in the midst of a storm. It was, in fact, he, Antonio Victor, who had chopped down the first tree. Now that place was the Border Line Grove, where the cacao saplings were beginning to turn into trunks and were already near to their first flowering. And then later, in that row at Tabocas, Antonio Victor had brought down a man—his first one—in order to save Juca's life. It was true he had wept much and despairingly upon his return to the plantation; it was true that for night after night he had seen that man as he fell, a hand to his bosom, his tongue lolling out. But that had passed also, and Juca had taken him out of the groves for the much pleasanter job of "*capanga*"—bodyguard and killer. He now accompanied Juca Badaró when the latter went out to pay off his men, and on the trips he was constantly making to the near-by towns and to the city; he had exchanged the scythe for the rifle. He knew the prostitutes in Tabocas, Ferradas, Palestina, and Ilhéos; he had had an ugly disease and a bullet in his shoulder. Ivone was now a vague and distant shadow,

Estancia a memory that was all but lost. But he kept up his custom of coming down at night to the edge of the forest, to dangle his feet in the river.

And to wait there for Raimunda. She would come for pails of water, for Don' Ana Badaró's bedtime bath. She would come down singing; but no sooner did she catch sight of Antonio Victor than her song stopped, her face growing hard as a look of abhorrence came over it. She would give a surly reply to his greeting, and the one time he had tried to take her and press her to him, she had pushed him into the river; for she was as strong and resolute as a man. But, for all that, he did not stop coming down there every night; only he never again tried to take advantage of her. He would say good evening and receive her grumbling response as she went on humming the air she had been singing on the way down. She would fill her kerosene can with water at the river's brink, and he would help her put it on her head. And Raimunda then would be lost among the cacao trees, with her great black feet, much blacker than her mulatto face, sinking into the mud of the trail. He would thereupon leap into the water, and then finally he would go back through the cacao grove to receive Juca Badaró's orders for the following day. Sometimes Don' Ana would send him out a glass of wine. Antonio Victor could hear Raimunda's steps in the kitchen, could hear her voice answering Don' Ana's call:

"I'm coming, godmother."

For Raimunda was Don' Ana's godchild, although the two were of the same age. She had been born on the same day as Don' Ana, being the daughter of black Risoleta, the cook in the Big House, a pretty Negro girl with round hips and firm, hard flesh. Nobody knew who Raimunda's father was, seeing that she had been born a light-skinned mulatto with hair that was almost straight; but there were many who whispered that it was none other than old Marcelino Badaró, the father of Sinhô and Juca. These whisperings, however, were no reason why Dona Filomena should send her cook packing. On the contrary, it was Risoleta who suckled at her big black breasts the "little darling" who had just been born, the aged Badarós' first grandchild. Don' Ana and Raimunda had grown up together in their early years, one on each of Risoleta's arms, one at each of her breasts. On the day that Don' Ana was baptized, the little mulatto girl, Raimunda, was baptized also. It was black Risoleta herself who picked the godparents: Sinhô, who was then a lad of a little more than twenty; and Don' Ana, who was only a few months old. The priest had made no protest; for even then the Badarós were a power before which the law and religion alike bent the knee.

Raimunda had grown up in the Big House, for she was Don' Ana's "milk sister." And since Don' Ana had come unexpectedly to enliven the household as the grandparents were nearing old age, and thirty years after the last little Badaró girl had beguiled them with her childish ways, the entire family put themselves out to satisfy her every whim. And Raimunda got what was left over of this affection. Dona Filomena, who was a good, pious woman, was accustomed to say that, since Don' Ana had taken Raimunda's mother, the Badarós had to do something for the little mulatto girl. It was the truth: black Risoleta had eyes for only one thing in the world, and that was "her white daughter," her "little darling," her own Don' Ana. For this reason, when Don' Ana was small, Risoleta had even raised her voice against Marcelino when the elder Badaró was about to punish his lively and disobedient young granddaughter. She became a wild woman when she heard Don' Ana sobbing, and had come in from the kitchen with blazing eyes and wrathful face. Juca was then a small boy, and it was one of his favourite diversions to make his little niece cry so that he might witness Risoleta's outburst of fury. Risoleta had no respect for him; she called him the "demon," and even went so far as to tell him that he was "worse than a Negro."

"That youngster is a little pest," she would say to the other women in the kitchen as she dried her tears.

For Don' Ana the kitchen was always a place of refuge. Whenever she had been naughtier than usual, she would flee there, to the skirts of her "black mammy," and neither Dona Filomena nor the aged Marcelino nor even Sinhô would come to look for her; for on such occasions Risoleta would prepare herself as if for battle.

As for Raimunda, she performed little household tasks and learned to cook; but at the Big House they also taught her to sew and to embroider, taught her the A B C's and how to sign her name, and how to do simple sums in addition and subtraction. By this the Badarós believed that they were paying their debt.

Risoleta had died with Don' Ana's name on her lips, gazing at her foster-child, who gave her so much pleasure by being with her in her final hour. Old Marcelino Badaró was already dead and buried for two years; and the following year his daughter, who was married to a merchant in Bahia, had died there, not having been able to get used to the city and to living so far from the plantation. She had gone into a decline and had caught consumption. Dona Filomena had finally taken Raimunda out of the kitchen and had definitely assigned her to work in the Big House; and she always acted as the mulatto girl's protector as long as she lived. Later Sinhô's wife had also died of consumption, and there were left but her godparents, Sinhô and Don' Ana; but in any event Raimunda led a life that was much the same as that of the other "fillies" in the house: washing, mending clothes, going to the river for water, and making sweetmeats. The only difference was that at holiday time Don' Ana would make her a present of a new dress and Sinhô would give her a pair of shoes and a little money. She never asked for the latter; for of what use was money to her, seeing that she had everything, here in the Badarós' house? When Sinhô, at the feast of St. John and at Christmas time, gave her ten milreis, he would always say: "Put that away for your hope-chest."

It never occurred to him that Raimunda might want for anything. But meanwhile, from her infancy, Raimunda's heart had been filled with unsatisfied desires. At first it was the dolls and toys that came from Bahia for Don' Ana and that she was forbidden to touch. How many drubbings had she had from black Risoleta for wanting to lay hands on the playthings that belonged to her "sister of the cradle"! Later it had been the desire to mount a well-harnessed horse like Don' Ana's and gallop away over the fields. And finally she desired to have, like Don' Ana, some of those things that were so pretty: a necklace, a pair of earrings, a Spanish comb for her hair. She had fallen heir to one of the last mentioned articles when she had found a comb in the dust-bin where Don' Ana had tossed it as useless, since all of its teeth save two or three were missing. In her little room at night, by the light of a lamp, she would stick the comb in her hair and smile at herself. This might be the first time that day that she had smiled; for Raimunda had a serious, cross-looking face, a surly face for everybody. Juca, who never let a woman go by him, whether it was a prostitute or a married woman in the city, the mulatto girls in the grove, or even the Negro women, none the less steered clear of Raimunda. Possibly it was because he found her ugly, with her pug nose that contrasted so sharply with the light skin of her face.

Yes, she was ill-tempered; Don' Ana herself had noticed it, and it was generally said about the plantation that she was "mean," that she was not good-hearted. She appeared to care for no one, but lived her life in silence, doing as much work as four women and taking what was offered her with murmured thanks. Thus she had grown up into young womanhood. More than one had wanted to marry her, being certain that Sinhô Badaró would not fail to help out anyone who took his godchild, Don' Ana's "milk sister," for a wife. The employee at the plantation store, a young simpleton who had come down from Bahia and who knew how to do sums and read books—he, too, had wanted her; but he was thin and weak and wore glasses, and Raimunda would not have him. She had wept when Sinhô had brought up the subject, saying that no, no, she could not. Sinhô had shrugged his shoulders to indicate that his interest in the matter was at an end.

"If you don't want to, that settles it. Nobody's forcing you."

Juca then had put in his word.

"But that's a match for you—a white lad, with schooling. You'll never get another one like him. I don't know what he sees in this girl."

Raimunda, however, had appealed to Sinhô, and he let it be understood that the subject was closed. It was he who informed the young fellow of Raimunda's refusal, and Juca at the same time had asked what it was about that mulatto's cross-looking face that had attracted the clerk; surely she was not pretty.

Then there had been Agostinho, the Badarós' foreman; he too had wanted Raimunda, but she had met his advances in the same unfriendly fashion. Don' Ana had an explanation for it all.

"Raimunda," she said, "simply does not want to leave us. I know she has that cross-looking face, but she likes us just the same."

And Don' Ana would suddenly become tender as she thought of Risoleta. At such times she would give the girl an old dress or a bit of cheap jewelry. But these conversations on the subject of Raimunda were rare occurrences; the Badarós did not always have time to think of the "sister of the cradle."

Antonio Victor did his best to catch Raimunda's eye. Here on the plantation a woman was an object of luxury, and his young body craved one. Making love with the whores, on his trips to town, was not enough. He wanted a body that would warm his own on those long nights during the winter months, from May to September, that constituted the rainy season.

. And so he waited for her at the edge of the forest. And it would not be long before he would hear Raimunda's voice preceding her down the path. Her face might not be a beautiful one, but what Antonio Victor was thinking of was her big buttocks, her firm breasts, her shapely legs. From the twilight skies night was about to fall. The river was flowing calmly. Perhaps it would rain tonight. Already the crickets were beginning their song in the forest. Leaves were drifting down to settle on the water. People talked about the big money that was to be made in the south. Antonio had promised to come back one day, rich, with fine clothes and polished boots; but now those thoughts no longer existed in his mind. Now he was Juca Badaró's *capanga*, known for the rapidity of his rifle-fire. The memories of Estancia, of Ivone giving herself on the bridge, were blurred for him. Dreams no longer filled his head as they had that night aboard ship. He knew but one desire now: to marry the mulatto girl, Raimunda, and to have a clay hut for the two of them. To marry Raimunda and have a body on which to repose after a hard day's work, after a long trip over bad roads, after the death of someone whom he had brought down. To rest upon her body—a body on which to repose his dreamless head.

Raimunda's voice on the path. Antonio Victor half rises, ready to aid her in filling the water-pail. Night wraps the forest. The river flows tranquilly.

9

The men came to a stop in front of the Big House of the plantation known as the Monkeys.

The official name was much prettier than that: Auricidia Plantation, a tribute from Maneca Dantas to his wife, a fat, sluggish matron whose sole interests in life were her children and the sweets she knew how to make as no one else did. To the colonel's great sorrow, however, the name had not stuck, and everyone insisted on calling the place the Monkeys, which had been the name of the original grove, carved out of the forests of Sequeiro Grande between the great Badaró estate and that of Horacio, where bands of monkeys were to be seen scampering through the woods. It was only in the official deed to the land that the name "Auricidia" appeared; and it was only Maneca Dantas who was wont to say: "Down there, at Auricidia—" Everyone else referred to it by its popular appellation.

The men came to a stop and set down the hammock they carried slung to a pole. In it a corpse was making its last earthly journey. From within the dimly lighted parlour Dona Auricidia called out, as she lazily set her mountainous flesh in motion:

"Who is it?"

"We come in peace, lady," one of the men replied.

A child had run out to the veranda and now came back with the news: "Mamma, there is two men with a dead man—a skinny dead man."

Before permitting herself to become alarmed, Dona Auricidia, who had been a schoolteacher, gently corrected her young son.

"Don't say: 'There is two,' Ruy. 'There *are* two,' is what you should say."

She then moved toward the door, the child clinging to her skirts. The smaller children were already asleep. On the veranda the men had sat down on a bench, while the hammock with the corpse sprawled open on the floor.

"May Jesus Christ give you good evening," said one of them, an old man with a white woolly head.

The other took off his hat with a polite greeting. Dona Auricidia replied, then waited expectantly.

"We're bringing him from the Baraúnas Plantation," the young man explained. "He worked there. We're taking him to the cemetery at Ferradas."

"Why don't you bury him in the forest?"

"Well, he has three daughters in Ferradas, you see. We're taking him to them. If you don't mind, we'd like to rest a little while. It's a long way, and Uncle here is about all in," pointing to the old man.

"What did he die of?" asked the lady of the house.

"Fever." It was the old man who spoke. "That pesky fever that you get in the forest. He was cutting timber when it laid hold of him. That was only three days ago. There was nothing to be done for him."

Dona Auricidia drew back her child and fell back a few steps herself. She was thinking, as that emaciated cadaver—he was an old man, too—lay there in the hammock on her veranda.

"Take him to one of the workmen's huts," she said; "you can rest there. But not here. Just go a little farther on and you'll come to the huts. Tell them I sent you. But you mustn't stay here, on account of the children."

She was afraid of contagion, afraid of that fever for which no remedy was known. Only years afterwards were men to learn that it was the typhus, then endemic throughout the cacao region. Dona Auricidia watched the men as they lifted the hammock, placed the pole on their shoulders, and departed.

"Good night, lady."

"Good night."

She stood staring at the spot where the corpse had lain. And then, of a sudden, that mountain of flesh was in motion again. Shouting to the Negro women within, she directed them to get soap and water at once and, in spite of the fact that it was night-time, to scrub the veranda thoroughly. Taking her child with her, she proceeded to wash his hands until he almost cried. And that night she did not sleep, but rose from hour to hour to see if Ruy was not feverish. As luck would have it, Maneca was not at home; he was dining at Horacio's.

The men with the hammock paused in front of one of the workers' huts. The old man was tired.

"He's heavy, eh, Uncle?" the young fellow said.

This idea of taking the body to Ferradas had been the old man's. He and the dead man had been friends. They must turn the remains over to the daughters for "Christian burial," he had insisted. It was a journey of ten or twelve miles, and they had been trudging along the moonlit highway for hours. Once more they put the hammock down, the young man wiping the sweat from his forehead as the old one knocked with his staff on the rude planks of the half-closed door. Inside the hut a lamp was lighted.

"Who is it?"

"We come in peace," was the old man's answer, as before.

But even so the Negro who opened the door held a revolver in his hand, for in this country you could not be too careful. The old man told his story and ended by saying that it was Dona Auricidia who had sent them.

"So, she don't want him up there," said a lean-looking individual who had appeared from behind the Negro's back. "He might give her kids the fever. But it makes no difference to us, ain't that so?" and he gave a laugh.

The old man thought that they were about to be sent on their way a second time. He began an explanation, but the lean man interrupted him.

"That's all right, Dad. You can come in," he said. "We don't catch the fever here. A worker's got a tough hide."

They went in. The other men who were asleep in the hut now woke up. There were five of them in all. The hut had but one room, with mud walls, a zinc roof, and an earthen floor. This was at once parlour, bedroom, and kitchen. Their toilet was the out-of-doors, the groves, the forest. They placed the body on one of the wooden bunks where the men slept, and remained standing around it. The old fellow then took a candle from his pocket, lighted it, and placed it at the head of the deceased. It was already half burned down, having served as illumination for the dead in the early part of the night, as it was to do again when they reached the house where the daughters lived.

"And what do they do?" the Negro asked.

"What does anybody do in Ferradas?" said the old man. "They're all whores."

"All three of them?"

"Yes, sir, all three."

There was a moment's silence as they stood around the emaciated corpse with its growth of beard streaked with white.

"One of them was married," the old man went on. "Then her husband died."

"He was pretty old, too, wasn't he?" said the Negro, pointing to the dead man.

"He was all of seventy."

"Old enough to be our grandpappy," said one of them who had taken no part in the conversation before. But no one laughed.

The lean man found the bottle of rum and a bowl that passed from hand to hand. Another of those who lived in the hut, and who had arrived at the plantation that very day, wanted to know what kind of fever it was that had caused the man's death.

"No one knows, to tell you the truth. It's a forest fever; you catch it and you're a goner in no time. There's no remedy that will do you any good—not even a regular doctor. Not even Jeremias and his herbs."

The Negro then explained, for the benefit of the newcomer from Ceará, that the witch-doctor lived all by himself in the forests of Sequeiro Grande, in a ruined shack stuck off among the trees. It was only in cases of great emergency that anyone went to look for him there. Jeremias subsisted on the roots of trees and on wild-growing fruits. He knew how to cure bullet-wounds and snake-bites. In his shack the snakes ran around loose, and every one of them had its name just like a woman. He had remedies for bodily ills and for lovers' ailments as well. But he could do nothing about this fever.

"I heard of it in Ceará, but I never believed it. They tell so many stories about this country; you hear some whoppers."

The lean-looking worker asked what it was they said: "Is it good or bad?"

"Both good and bad, but more bad than good. They say there's a mint of money to be made here, and they tell how so-and-so got rich the minute he stepped off the boat; they say the streets are paved with it, that it's as common as dust. On the bad side they say there's the fever, the *jagunços*, the snakes—a lot of bad things."

"And yet you came down here."

The man from Ceará did not reply to this; it was the old man who spoke.

"Having money may be a bad thing in itself," he said, "if that's all that you think of. A man is a worm if all he can see in life is money; he becomes blind and deaf when he hears them talk of it. That's why there's so much trouble in these parts."

The lean man nodded his head. He too had left father and mother, sweetheart and sister, to come after money in this land of Ilhéos. The years had gone by, and he was still gathering cacao in Maneca Dantas's groves.

"There is a heap of money here," the old man continued, "but what folks can't see—"

The candle was casting its light on the dead man's thin face. He appeared to be listening attentively to the conversation round about him. The bowl of rum was passed another time. It had begun raining outside and the Negro closed the door. The old man gazed long and hard at the corpse with its bearded face.

"Do you see him?" he said, and his voice was weary and hopeless. "He worked for more than ten years at Baraúnas for Colonel Teodoro. He had nothing, not even his daughters' company. He spent ten years of his life in debt to the colonel all the time. Then the fever took him off, and the colonel would not even give a penny to help the girls bury him."

His companion took up the tale at this point: "He even said that he was doing a lot by not sending the daughters a bill for what the old man owed him. He said a whore made a lot of money."

The lean man spat disgustedly. The big ears of the deceased appeared to be listening. The man from Ceará was a little alarmed by it all. He had arrived that day; one of Maneca Dantas's foremen had hired him in Ilhéos, along with a number of others who had come down by the same boat. They had reached the plantation that afternoon and had been assigned to the various workers' huts. The Negro now undertook to enlighten the new arrival, draining the bowl of rum as he did so.

"You'll see, tomorrow."

The old man who had helped carry the body then went on: "I never knew anybody who was worse off than a worker in a cacao grove."

The lean man thought this over.

"The *capangas* are better off," he said. "If you are a good shot," he added, turning to the native of Ceará, "your fortune's made. Down here the only folks that have money are those that are good at killing, the assassins."

The newcomer from the north opened his eyes in astonishment. The dead man frightened him, vaguely; here was concrete proof of what they were talking about.

"Good at killing?" he repeated.

The Negro laughed.

"A lad who's a dead shot," the lean man went on to explain, "can live like a lord. He can hang around town with the women, he always has money in his pocket, and he never fails to collect his wages. But the worker in a grove—well, you'll see tomorrow."

He was the second man who had spoken of "tomorrow," and the one from Ceará was by this time curious to know what was going to happen then. Any one of them could have told him, but the lean man went on.

"Bright and early tomorrow," he said, "the clerk down at the store is going to send for you to make up your kit for the week. You haven't any tools to work with, so you'll have to buy some. You'll have to buy a scythe and an ax, a knife, and a pickax; and all that's going to set you back something like a hundred milreis. Then you're going to have to buy flour, beef, rum, coffee, for the whole week. You're going to have to lay out another ten milreis for food. At the end of the week you'll have fifteen coming to you in wages—" the man from Ceará did a mental sum, six days at two and a half, and agreed—"that'll leave a balance of five milreis, but you won't get it; you'll have to leave it there to apply on what you owe for the tools. You'll be a whole year paying off that hundred milreis without seeing so much as a penny of your wages. Oh, maybe at Christmas time the colonel will advance you ten milreis to go spend with the whores in Ferradas."

The lean man said all this in a jesting manner, but his tone was half cynical, half tragic and discouraged. Then he asked for some rum. The man from Ceará was silent and sat staring at the corpse.

"A hundred milreis," he said at last, "for a knife, a scythe, and a pickax?"

"In Ilhéos," the old man told him, "you can get an 'alligator knife' for twelve milreis. At the plantation stores you can't get one for less than twenty-five."

"A whole year," the man from Ceará repeated. He was calculating as to when the rain would fall once more on his drought-ridden native province. He had planned to go back as soon as the rains came to the parched earth, planned to return with money enough to buy a cow and a calf. "A whole year." He stared at the dead man, who appeared to be smiling.

"There's something else for you to think about. Before you get through paying off what you owe, your debt will have increased. You will have had to buy a pair of work-pants and a shirt. You'll have had to buy medicine, which God knows is dear enough. You'll have to buy a revolver, which is the only money well laid out in this man's country. And you'll never get out of debt. Down here,"—and the lean man made a sweeping gesture with his hand which took in all those present, both those that worked at the Monkeys and the pair that had come with the corpse from Baraúnas—"down here everybody's in debt; no one has anything coming to him."

There was fear now in the eyes of the man from Ceará. The candle was burning low, casting a reddish light on the corpse's face. It was raining outside.

"I was a lad in the days of slavery," the old man said as he rose. "My father was a slave, my mother also. But it wasn't any worse then than it is today. Things don't change; it's all talk."

The worker from Ceará had left his wife and daughter there. He had been going to return as soon as word came of the first showers, his pockets bulging with money from the south, money to begin life anew in his own country. But now he was afraid. The candlelight was increasing and diminishing the dead man's smile. The lean man agreed with the old fellow.

"There's no difference," he said.

The old man put out the candle and stuck it in his pocket; then slowly they lifted the hammock, he and his younger companion. The lean man opened the door for them.

"And what about his daughters," the Negro inquired, "the whores?"

"Yes?" said the old man.

"Where do they live?"

"In the rua do Sapo. It's the second house."

Then the old fellow turned to the man from Ceará:

"Nobody ever goes back from here. You're tied to the store from the day you come. If you want to leave, go this very night; tomorrow will be too late. If you want to go, come along with us; maybe you'll be good enough to help us carry him. Afterwards it will be too late."

The newcomer was still in doubt. The old man and the youth were standing there, the hammock slung over their shoulders.

"And where will I go? What will I do?"

No one had an answer for him; that question had not occurred to any of them. Not even the old man, nor the lean man with the cynical, jesting voice. Nor the young man, either. They stood staring at the door. The Negro crossed himself out of respect to the corpse, but at that moment he was thinking of the three daughters, the three whores. Rua do Sapo, second house. He would go around there the next time he was in Ferradas. The man from Ceará stared after the pair as they were swallowed up in the night.

"I'm going, too!" he suddenly exclaimed.

Feverishly he began throwing his things together and, sobbing a farewell, he ran out. The lean man closed the door behind him.

"And where's he going to go?" Seeing that no one replied to his question, he answered it himself: "To another plantation, where it will be the same thing as here."

He, blew out the light.

10

Some while before, from the door of his bedroom, Horacio had bidden Lawyer Virgilio good night; the latter was sleeping in the front room.

"Sleep well, colonel," came the sonorous and fastidiously polite response.

In the silence of the room Ester was opening and closing her hands upon her bosom, as though to stifle the beating of her heart. From the drawing-room came Maneca Dantas's measured snores. Their friend, having yielded to the attorney the guest-room which he usually occupied, was lying in a hammock that had been strung up in the parlour. From the darkness Ester followed the movements of her husband. She was experiencing a very definite sensation, the feeling of Virgilio's presence in the other room. Horacio was undressing in the dark, and she could hear the sound made by his boots as he dropped them to the floor. Seated on the edge of the bed, he was in a joyful mood; he had been almost childishly happy ever since Ester, at the table, had consented to play the piano at his request. From where he sat he could hear his wife's breathing. Taking off his shirt and trousers, he put on his nightgown with little red flowers embroidered on the front of it.

Then he rose to shut the door that led from the bedroom to the room where the child slept, watched over by Felicia. Ester had been strongly opposed to this arrangement and had insisted that the door must remain always open; for she was afraid that during the night snakes might come in and strangle the little one. But Horacio was now slowly closing it. With eyes wide open in the dark, she continued to follow his movements.

She knew that he was going to take her tonight; he always closed the door between the two bedrooms when he wanted to possess her. But tonight—and this was the strangest of all the strange things that had happened that evening—for the first time Ester did not have that obscure feeling of repulsion which was renewed in her whenever Horacio sought to make love. Other times she would unconsciously huddle in the bed as a shudder ran over her, along her belly, up and down her arms, and around her heart. She would feel her body closing to him in anguish. But tonight she felt nothing of all this. Was it, possibly, for the reason that, while her eyes from the darkness of the room might be spying on Horacio, her mind was in the front bedroom, where Virgilio was sleeping? But was he sleeping? Perhaps he was not; perhaps he was thinking of her, as his own eyes pierced the darkness and the door, made their way down the corridor and through the other door, for a glimpse of her body beneath the cambric nightgown. She shuddered at the thought of it. The very presence of Virgilio in the other room gave her an expansive feeling. She smiled, and Horacio thought that her smile was for him. He too was happy tonight. For him it was a new dawn, an unhoped-for spring, a happiness to which he had never dared look forward. He was holding her lovely head in his hands, when suddenly there was a knocking at the front door. Pausing in his caress, Horacio listened attentively. He could hear Maneca Dantas rising as the knocks were repeated, could hear the bolt being drawn and the door opened as his friend inquired who was there. Ester's head was in his hands, and her eyelids now slowly parted. Maneca's footsteps were drawing near, and Horacio was compelled to abandon his wife's body and its pleasing warmth. His eyes grew small with a sudden anger at this unfortunate interruption on Maneca's part. From the corridor the latter's voice could be heard.

"Horacio! Friend Horacio!"

"What is it?"

"Come here a minute. It's something serious."

From the other room came Virgilio's voice: "Am I needed?"

"You can come, too, doctor," Maneca told him.

"What is it, Horacio?" Ester asked, in a choking voice, from the bed.

Horacio turned to her. Smiling, he put a hand to her face.

"I'm going to see. I'll be back."

"I'll go, too."

As he left, she rose from the bed and slipped on a dressing-gown. It had occurred to her that she would thus be able to have another glimpse of Virgilio this evening. Horacio went out the way he was, the lighted lamp in his hand, clad in the voluminous nightshirt that came all the way to his feet, with the funny little flowers down the front of it. Virgilio was already in the drawing-room with Maneca Dantas when Horacio came in. Horacio at once recognized the third person present—he was Firmo, who had a grove near the forests of Sequeiro Grande, and he was obviously tired as he sat there in a chair with his mud-spattered boots and his face streaked with grime.

Hearing Ester's steps, Horacio said: "Bring us something to drink."

She barely had time to note that Virgilio did not sleep in a nightgown as the other men did. He was clad in very fashionable pyjamas, and was smoking with beautiful self-assurance. Maneca Dantas took advantage of Ester's absence to draw on a pair of trousers over his nightshirt, but the effect was all the more comical, with the tail of the gown sticking out from behind. Firmo was explaining things to Horacio.

"The Badarós," he was saying, "tried to have me done away with."

Maneca cut a ridiculous figure in that get-up, with his anxious manner, but the question that he now asked revealed a profound knowledge of the *capangas* employed by the Badarós.

"And how does it come that you are still alive?"

Horacio also was waiting for an answer to this question, and Virgilio was eyeing him: the colonel with his wrinkled forehead looked enormous in that funny nightgown.

"The Negro," said Firmo, "became frightened and missed his aim."

"But are you sure it was one of the Badarós' men?" Horacio wanted to be certain.

"It was Negro Damião."

"And he missed?" Maneca's voice was full of incredulity.

"He missed. He must have been drinking. He came out and ran down the road like a crazy man. There was such a fine moon, I could see his black face."

"Well, then," said Maneca, speaking slowly, "you had better have them light some candles in the church. To escape a bullet of Negro Damião's is a miracle, and a big one I should say."

They were all silent as Ester came in with the rum-bottle and the glasses. She served them, and Firmo gulped his drink down at once and asked for another, which he consumed with equal promptitude. Virgilio was admiring the back of Ester's neck, where the furrow showed white beneath her loosened hair as she bent over to serve Maneca. He watched Horacio as the latter stood there in the act of taking a glass from his wife's hand. He felt a desire to laugh, the colonel was so ridiculous; he was like a circus clown in that embroidered nightgown of his, with his pock-marked face. At the table he had been a timid fellow who had failed to understand the major part of what Virgilio and Ester were saying. He had been more comic than anything else, and the young attorney had felt himself the master of this woman whom chance had stranded there in an environment that was not her own; despite his gigantic frame, the cacao-planter had given an impression of weakness; he was a person of no importance, incapable of proving an obstacle to the plans already forming in Virgilio's mind. It was Firmo's voice that brought the lawyer back to reality and the present scene.

"That's why you see me drinking like this. I might be lying there stretched out in the road."

Ester shuddered, the bottle trembling in her hand. Virgilio, also, was now suddenly a part of the scene. There before him was a man who had just escaped death. It was the first time he had come into direct contact with one of these occurrences of which his friends had spoken to him in Bahia as he was preparing to leave for Ilhéos. Even so, he did not quite grasp the significance of it. He assumed that Horacio's wrinkled forehead and the anxious look on Maneca Dantas's face merely reflected their emotions at seeing a man who had almost been assassinated.

During the relatively short time that he had been in the cacao country he had heard much talk of such things, but he had not as yet encountered anything concrete. The row at Tabocas between Horacio's men and those from the Badaró estate had occurred while he was back in Bahia on a vacation. When he returned, there was still much gossip, but he had had his doubts about a number of things. He had heard people speak of the forest of Sequeiro Grande, had heard it said that both Horacio and the Badarós coveted the woods in question, but he never had attached any particular importance to it all. Moreover, the Horacio whom he now beheld, in that outlandish sleeping-garment, was a clown, a comic figure serving to round out the impression formed of him at the dinner table and later in the drawing-room. If it had not been for Firmo's manner, the drama of the situation would have been lost on Virgilio. He was, accordingly, surprised when Horacio turned to Maneca Dantas and said:

"There's nothing else to be done. They're asking for it; we're going to let them have it."

That firm and energetic voice was something Virgilio had not expected. It was out of keeping with his previous impression of the colonel. In response to his questioning glance Horacio went on to explain how matters stood.

"We'll be needing you very much, doctor. When I asked Seabra to send me down a good attorney, I already could see that this was going to happen. We're the under-dog in politics down here, we can't depend on the courts, and so what we need is someone who knows the law. I don't have confidence in Doctor Ruy any more; he's a drunkard, and he's quarrelled with everybody, even with the judge and the notaries. He makes a good speech, but that's all he's good for. What we need down here is an attorney with a head on him."

The frankness with which Horacio spoke of attorneys and their profession and of courts of justice, his strong words masked by a certain air of contempt, was a fresh shock to Virgilio. His picture of the colonel as an amusing dull-witted clown was spoiled for him.

"But what is it all about?" he asked.

The men formed a strange group standing there, all of them, around Firmo, whose clothes were wet with rain and who was still panting from his hard ride: Horacio, enormous in his white nightgown; Virgilio, smoking nervously; Maneca Dantas, pale-faced and unaware of the shirt-tail sticking out of his trousers. Ester, who had sat down, had eyes only for Virgilio. She too was pale, for she knew that the struggle for the possession of Sequeiro Grande was about to begin. More important than this fact, however, was Virgilio's presence, the new pulse-beat of her heart, the inner happiness of a kind she had never known before.

"Let's sit down," said Horacio as Virgilio put his question.

There was in his voice a note of authority that was also new, as if an order of his admitted of no discussion. Virgilio now recalled the Horacio of whom they gossiped in Tabocas and in Ilhéos: his many killings; the old wives' tale of the Devil in a bottle. He now found himself wavering between two images: one, that of a strong and powerful man, a lord and master; the other, of an ignorant and unprepossessing clown who was a very weak creature indeed. From his chair Horacio spoke, and the image of the clown disappeared.

"This is what it's all about," he began. "This forest of Sequeiro Grande is good cacao land, the best in the country. No one yet has gone into it to do any planting. The only person who lives there is a crazy man who works cures. On this side of the forest is my property, and I've already bit off a chunk of it. On the other side is the Badaró plantation, and they've done the same. But very little on either side. That forest means everything, doctor. Whoever gets it will be the richest man around Ilhéos. He will also be master, at the same time, of Tabocas, of Ferradas, of trains and ships."

The others were drinking in his words, Maneca Dantas nodding his head. Virgilio was beginning to grasp it. Firmo had recovered from his fright.

"Here on this side of the forest, between my place and the Badarós', is friend Maneca and his plantation. Farther up is Teodoro das Baraúnas. But there are only the two big estates. The rest are small groves, like Firmo's, a score of them or so. And all of them nibbling at the forest, without the courage to go in. For a long time I've planned to cut down the Sequeiro Grande. The Badarós know it very well. They're butting in because they mean to—"

He stared straight in front of him. The last words he had spoken sounded as though they presaged an irremediable disaster.

"They're riding high in politics," explained Maneca Dantas. "That's why they dare—"

There was one thing that Virgilio wanted to know.

91

"But what has Firmo to do with all this?"

"His grove," said Horacio, "happens to lie between the forest and the Badarós' property. They tried to buy it of him some time ago, even offered him more than it was worth. But Firmo is my friend; he's been a political follower of mine for many years; and so he consulted me about it, and I advised him not to sell. I knew what a temptation it was to the Badarós to set foot in that woods, but I never dreamed they would try to have Firmo put out of the way. That means they've made up their minds. Well, they're asking for it."

His voice held a threat, and the other men lowered their gaze. Horacio laughed that ingrowing laugh of his. Virgilio saw him now as a giant of inconceivable strength. At the sound of his imperious tones the funny flowers in his nightgown vanished. The colonel made a gesture and Ester served another round of rum.

"Do you think, doctor," he said, "that Seabra is going to win the election?"

"I am certain of it."

"That's good—I believe you." He spoke as if he had taken a definite resolve, as was apparent when he rose and went over to Firmo.

"What do you say?" he inquired of the latter. "And you, my friend," turning to Maneca Dantas. "Do you think there's any grove-owner on the edge of the forest who won't be with me?"

Firmo was the first to speak.

"They will all be with you."

Maneca felt called upon to qualify that statement.

"I can't vouch for Teodoro das Baraúnas. He hangs around the Badarós a lot."

It did not take Horacio long to reach a decision.

"You, Firmo, will go back this very minute. I'll send a couple of men with you. You talk to the others, to Braz, to José da Ribeira, to the widow Miranda, to Coló—talk to them all. And don't forget our friend Jarde; he's a fellow with nerve. Tell them all to come over for lunch tomorrow. The lawyer's here and we'll put it all down in black and white. I take the forest all the way down to the river, and the rest of it, what's on the other side, you can divide among you. And that goes for the land we take as well. Is that agreed?"

Firmo assented; he was already on his feet, preparing to leave. Virgilio had a giddy feeling. He glanced at Ester, who was white as could be—pale was not the word for it. She had not spoken a syllable. Horacio was now talking to Maneca Dantas, giving orders; he was the lord and master.

"And you, my friend, you go talk to Teodoro. Explain the matter to him. If he wants to come along tomorrow, let him come. I'll make an agreement with him. But if he's not willing, let him get ready, for it's going to rain lead for fifty miles around."

He went out on the lawn. Virgilio gazed after him, his eyes big with astonishment. Then, turning timidly to Ester, he found her distant, all but unattainable. Outside, Horacio was shouting orders in the direction of the labourers' huts.

"Algemiro! Joe Littlefinger! Red John!"

In response to his call they all came up to the veranda. Out in front the burros were saddled, the men armed. They set out together, Maneca, Firmo, and the three *capangas*, the hoofs of the cavalcade echoing in the early dawn. Virgilio and Ester went back into the room, and she came up to him. Her face was livid. She spoke rapidly, as though the words were torn from her heart.

"Take me away from here—far, far away."

Before Virgilio could reply they heard Horacio's footsteps. The colonel came in.

"That forest," he said, speaking to his wife and the attorney, "is going to be mine, if I have to drench the earth in blood. You may as well get ready, doctor; the row's about to start." Then, discovering Ester's fear: "You can go to Ilhéos; that'll be better." But it was the things that were happening that held his interest. "Doctor, you're going to see how we get rid of a bunch of bandits. For that's all the Badarós are, bandits."

Taking Virgilio by the arm, he led him out to the veranda. In the nearing dawn the earth was suffused in a dim and mournful light.

"Over there, doctor," said Horacio, pointing to the far-distant horizon, which was barely visible, "over there lies the forest of Sequeiro Grande. One day it's all going to be in cacao. I'm as certain of that as I am that my name is Horacio da Silveira."

11

As the dog howled on the lawn, Don' Ana Badaró, who was seated in the hammock, shuddered. It was not fear; in the city and in the neighbouring towns people were in the habit of saying that the Badarós did not know what fear was. But she was worried; for she had felt certain, all afternoon, that they were keeping something from her, that between her father and her uncle there was a secret of which the women of the household were ignorant. Noting the absence of Damião and Viriato, she had asked Juca about it, and he had replied that the men had "gone on an errand." She could tell by the sound of his voice that he was lying, but she said nothing. There was something serious in the wind, she could feel it, and it made her restless. The dog was howling again, baying the moon with the anguish of the male on a night when he is in rut. Don' Ana glanced at her father's face. With half-closed eyes he was waiting for her to begin reading. Sinhô Badaró was calm; there was a deep serenity in his eyes and in his beard and in his big hands resting on his thighs; everything about him spoke of peace and assurance. Had it not been for Juca fidgeting in his chair, the howling of the dog would not, perhaps, have had the effect that it did upon Don' Ana.

They were in the parlour, and the hour for Bible-reading had come. This was a custom of many years' standing, dating back to the time of Dona Lidia, Don' Ana's mother. She had been a religious woman and had loved to look in the Bible for some word of advice in connection with her husband's business affairs. After her death, Sinhô had kept up the custom religiously. No matter where he might be, at the plantation, in Ilhéos, or even in Bahia on business—no matter where he was, someone had to read to him every night scattered passages from the Bible, in which he sought for counsel or for words of prophecy that would throw some light on his undertakings. Following Lidia's death Sinhô had grown constantly more religious, now mixing his Catholicism with a little spiritualism and a great deal of superstition. Above all, this habit of Bible-reading had become a deeply rooted one with him. There was much wagging of tongues about it in Ilhéos, and there was a story going the rounds of the cafés to the effect that, one night in Bahia, Sinhô had decided to go to a house of prostitution, but that, before staying with the whore, he had taken the old, well-thumbed Bible out of his pocket and had made her read him a few verses. It was on account of this yarn that Juca Badaró had had a fight in Zeca Tripa's place and had smashed in the face of the apothecary, Carlos da Silva, who had related the anecdote amid loud guffaws.

After Dona Lidia died, Don' Ana became the Bible-reader.

94

Whether at the plantation or in Ilhéos, she had to leaf through the soiled and frequently torn pages of this ancient copy of Holy Writ, a copy that Sinhô Badarô refused to exchange for another, being certain that this one held the magic power to guide him. Nor was he shaken in this resolve when Canon Freitas, who was sleeping at the plantation one night, called his attention to the fact that it was a Protestant Bible, and that it was not becoming in a Catholic to be reading an "anathematized" book. Sinhô Badaró did not know the meaning of the word "anathematized," and asked for no explanation. He merely replied that it made very little difference, that he had always got along well enough with this one, and that, moreover, "a Bible was not something that you changed every year like an almanac." At a loss for arguments, Canon Freitas deemed it best to remain silent; after all, he concluded, it was quite a marvellous thing for a "colonel" to be reading the Bible—any Bible—every night.

There was another point on which Sinhô was firm. He would not permit Don' Ana to direct the reading, as she had endeavoured to do when she had first taken Lidia's place as housekeeper. She had suggested starting with the first page and reading through to the end, but Sinhô had protested; he felt that the Bible should be opened at random, since for him it was a magic book and the passage that was thus found was the one that held a message for him. When he was not satisfied, he would ask his daughter to open to another, and another, and another, until he came upon one that appeared to have some bearing on the business in hand. He would listen most attentively to the words—many of which he did not understand—seeking to find a meaning in them and interpreting them after his own fashion, in the light of his own needs and desires. More than once he had carried through a business deal or had failed to carry it through in accordance with the sayings of Moses and of Abraham, and he would declare that never once had they failed to stand him in good stead. Woe to that person, relative or guest, who, coming in at the Bible-reading hour, should venture to discuss the matter or voice a protest. Sinhô Badaró then would lose his calm and there would be an outburst of wrath. Not even Juca dared object to this custom, which to him was extremely annoying. He had to force himself to pay attention, finding amusement in those passages which had to do with sexual matters—he was the only one who understood certain words, whose real meaning escaped Sinhô and Don' Ana alike.

The latter gazed at her father as he sat there so serenely in his high-backed chair. Through half-shut lids he appeared to be studying the picture on the wall, that picture which he had picked up in Bahia when he remembered that the parlour needed something to brighten it up. She too looked at the chromo and could feel all the peace that emanated from it. Juca, meanwhile, was becoming more and more fidgety, having lost interest in the newspaper he was reading, a paper from Bahia that was two weeks old. The dog howled again.

"The next time I come back from Ilhéos," said Juca, "I'm going to bring along a bitch. Pery feels the need of one."

To Don' Ana these words had a false ring, as if Juca were merely trying to conceal his agitation with the sound of his own voice. They were not deceiving her; there was something up, something serious. Where were Damião and Viriato? Many times before, Don' Ana had been conscious of this air of perturbation in the house, this secretive atmosphere. Sometimes it was not until days afterwards that she would hear that a man had been killed and that the Badaró estate had been increased in size. She was terribly hurt by their hiding things from her as if she were a child.

Taking her eyes from her uncle, whose statement had met with no response, she began envying the calm manner in which Olga, Juca's wife, sat crocheting in a chair at her husband's side. Olga spent very little time at the plantation; and when, upon Juca's compulsion, she took the train from Ilhéos to spend a month with Don' Ana, she would arrive in tears and full of self-pity. Her life was wrapped up in the gossip of Ilhéos, and she loved to play the martyr for the benefit of the pious old ladies of the town and her women friends by complaining day and night of her spouse's amorous escapades. At first she had actively resented his successive infidelities and had sent some rowdies to threaten the women who were involved with him. She once had had these ruffians assault a young mulatto girl whom Juca was keeping; but his reaction to this had been so violent—the neighbours said that he had beaten her—that she afterwards had been compelled to be content with gossiping and with complaining to everyone she met, as she put on the air of a victim resigned to her fate, whose only consolation lay in the feast-days and rites of the Church. This was her very life; she enjoyed nothing so much as bemoaning her lot and listening to the pious dames, with their mutterings and lamentations. It is quite possible that she would have felt that she had been cheated, had Juca of a sudden been converted into a model husband.

Olga loathed the plantation, where Sinhô turned a deaf ear to her wailings, and where Don' Ana, busy all day long, had little time to condole with her. The latter, moreover, had the Badaró view of things and found nothing wrong in Juca's adventures so long as he gave his wife everything she needed. That was the way it had been with her father, that was the way it was with all men, Don' Ana reflected. Then, too, Olga had not the faintest interest in any of the family problems; hating the country, she was wholly ignorant of everything that had to do with cacao-raising. In short, she impressed her sister-in-law as being an utter stranger, a person who was at once distant and dangerous, one who breathed a different atmosphere from that which she, Sinhô, and Juca did. Nevertheless, at this moment she eyed Olga with a certain envy for the calm indifference that Juca's wife was displaying in the presence of this mystery with which the room was laden. Don' Ana felt that something very serious was taking place, and she was both grieved and angry that they should be keeping the secret from her instead of according her the place that was rightfully hers in the Badaró family councils. She delayed the Bible-reading as her eyes wandered from face to face.

Raimunda then came in, her kitchen tasks having been completed. Sitting down on the floor behind the hammock, the mulatto girl with crackling fingers began searching for imaginary lice in her mistress's braids; but not even this playful caress could soothe Don' Ana's restlessness. What secret was it that Sinhô and Juca were keeping? Where were Viriato and Negro Damião? Why was Juca so nervous; why did he keep looking at his watch every other minute? The dog's howl rent the anguished night.

Slowly Sinhô opened his eyes and fixed them on Don' Ana.

"Why don't you begin, daughter?"

She opened the Bible, Olga looking on with no show of interest, as Juca spread the newspaper over his knees. Don' Ana began:

And they went out, they and all their hosts with them, much people, even as the sand that is upon the seashore in multitude, with horses and chariots very many.

It was the story of Joshua and his battles, and Don' Ana wondered that Sinhô did not tell her to turn to another page. On the contrary, her father was paying very close attention, and so she tried to make out the meaning of the verses as she read them, in an effort to find what they had to do with the secret that was bothering her. Sinhô had turned his head and was gazing at her, his beard in his lap as he bent forward to catch every word. She went on, slowly; for she, too, was endeavouring to solve a world of doubts.

There was one verse that Sinhô asked her to read over again:

So Joshua took all that land, the hills and all the south country, and all the land of Goshen, and the valley, and the plain, and the mountain of Israel, and the valley of the same.

Don' Ana's voice fell silent as her father made a gesture for her to stop. He was thinking deeply as to whether or not the divine benediction on his family and their plans was clear. A great peace then came over him, a feeling of absolute assurance.

"The Bible," he said, "does not lie. I never went wrong in following it. We are going to get that forest of Sequeiro Grande, for it is God's will. I had my doubts about it today, but I don't have any longer."

And then, suddenly, Don' Ana understood, and she was happy; she now knew that the forest of Sequeiro Grande was going to belong to the Badarós, that on that land the cacao saplings would be growing, and that, as Sinhô had promised her, she would have the privilege of naming the new plantation. Her face lighted up with joy.

Sinhô Badaró rose, majestically. He had the appearance of a prophet of old, with his long hair, which was beginning to turn white, and his black beard, which fell down over his bosom. Juca looked at his elder brother.

"I always told you, Sinhô," he said, "that we had to go into that forest. And once we get our hands on it, there's nobody who's going to be able to cope with the Badarós."

Don' Ana's smile grew more expansive at her uncle's words.

"So it's going to begin all over again!" said Olga in a frightened voice. "If that's the way things are, I'm going back to Ilhéos. I don't want anything to do with this kind of a life, killing people."

At that moment Don' Ana hated her. The look that she gave her uncle's wife was filled with contempt, contempt and indignation. This was someone from another world, a futile, apathetic world, Don' Ana thought to herself.

The clock was striking the hour.

"Go on to bed, Don' Ana," said Sinhô to his daughter. "It is time. And you, too, Olga—I want to talk to Juca."

All the happiness vanished from Don' Ana's face. Olga and Raimunda had already risen, but she herself was searching for words with which to persuade Sinhô to let her stay. At this point, however, the barking of the dog on the lawn showed that there was someone outside. They all stopped short. A few seconds later Viriato appeared in the doorway of the veranda, followed by the dog, which, having recognized him, was no longer barking.

"Well, how did it go?" said Juca, coming forward.

The mulatto dropped his eyes. He spoke hurriedly:

"He came by the side-road. He didn't come on my side. If he had, I'd have got him."

"But what is it, anyway?" said Sinhô. "Something happened to Damião? Speak up."

"He missed his aim."

"That's not possible!"

"Missed?" echoed Juca, in astonishment.

"Yes, sir, that's what I thought myself. I don't know what got into him. He was acting funny from the time we left here. I don't know what was the matter with him. It wasn't rum; for I know—"

"Just what is it that you know?" asked Sinhô.

The mulatto again stared down at the floor.

"Firmo wasn't even wounded. Everybody in the neighbourhood knows that by now. They're saying that Damião went crazy. Nobody saw which way he ran."

"And Firmo?" said Juca. "What about him?"

"I met a couple of men carrying a corpse. They told me that Firmo had passed them, on the way to Colonel Horacio's house. He was riding at a gallop and only stopped long enough to tell them that you had sent to have him done away with and that Damião had missed him. That was all they could get out of him, for he was in a terrible hurry—I just happened to run into them. There was a lot of people standing around talking about it."

The women did not move. With the Bible clasped in her hand, Don' Ana followed the conversation with eager eyes. She understood everything now and was able to grasp the full import of what had happened. She realized that the future of the Badarós was at stake that night. Sinhô crossed the room with long strides.

"What could have got into that Negro, anyhow?"

Viriato attempted an explanation: "He must have been scared by something."

"I'm not asking you."

The mulatto shrank back, as Juca rubbed his hands together to conceal his nervousness.

"Now we have to go through with it," he said. "And we'd better start before Horacio does. For this is going to be war."

Frightened at her husband, Olga started to make a gesture and stopped. Sinhô sat down again. There was a moment's silence; he was thinking of the Bible passages that his daughter had read to him. It had been clear enough, but—

"Read some more, Don' Ana."

Still standing, she once more opened the book at random. Her hands were trembling but her voice was steady as she read:

And if any mischief follow, then thou shalt give life for life. Eye for eye, tooth for tooth, hand for hand, foot for foot.

Sinhô threw back his head; he no longer had any doubts. With his hand he motioned for the women to leave the room. Olga and Raimunda had already started to leave, but Don' Ana did not stir. The two others were out in the hallway, yet she still stood there, the book in her hand, gazing at her father. Juca was anxious for her to leave so that he could talk freely with Sinhô.

"I told you to go to bed, Don' Ana," her father said. "What are you waiting for?"

She then began reciting from memory, without looking at the book, her eyes fixed on his:

"Intreat me not to leave thee, or to return from following after thee; for whither thou goest, I will go; and where thou lodgest, I will lodge."

"This is no business for a woman," Juca began; but Sinhô interrupted him.

"Let her stay. After all, she's a Badaró. One day it's going to be her children, Juca, who will gather the cacao from the Sequeiro Grande groves. You may stay, my daughter."

Juca and Don' Ana sat down near him. They then began drawing up their battle plans for the possession of the Sequeiro Grande forest. Don' Ana Badaró was happy; her tawny face was lovelier than ever; her eyes were dark and glowing.

12

Round about the forest on this night of ambitions, longings, and the unleashed dreams of men, lights were glowing: kerosene chandeliers in Horacio's house, lights in the home of the Badarós. There was the lighted candle that Don' Ana had placed at the feet of the Virgin on the altar of the Big House to implore her assistance in the days to come. There was that other candle which illumined the way for the dead, as the two men bore their burden to the daughters in Ferradas. Lights on the Baraúnas plantation, where Juca Badaró and Maneca Dantas arrived at almost the same time for a talk with Teodoro. The light of red and smoky oil lamps in the workers' huts, as the inmates awoke earlier even than was their wont to hear the story of Negro Damião, who had missed his aim and who had run away none knew where. A light in Firmo's house, where Dona Tereza was awaiting her husband, her white body ready for love in the rosewood bed. Lights in the houses of the small grove-owners, awakened by the unexpected arrival of Firmo with Horacio's men, come to invite them to lunch that day. Round about the forest of Sequeiro Grande glowed the light of lanterns, chandeliers, hanging lamps, and lamps of a humbler kind. They served to mark the boundaries of the giant wood to the north and to the south, to the east and to the west.

From time to time men on horseback would cut through small stretches of the forest to reach the main road. They were those who were riding from plantation to plantation, from grove to grove, bearing the invitation to come and talk matters over. On every hand human ambition was kindling lights and galloping along the highway. But neither the lights nor the sound of beating hoofs could rouse those slumbering boughs and trunks from their sleep of centuries. The jaguars, the snakes, and the monkeys were at rest, and the birds had not as yet awaked to greet the dawn. Only the glowworms, spirit lanterns, lighted up with a greenish brightness the dark, dense green of the trees. The forest of Sequeiro Grande was asleep, as round about it men avid of money laid their concerted plans for its conquest. And there at the forest's heart, where the vegetation was thickest, with only the uncertain, wavering light of the glowworms for illumination, in his wretched hut Jeremias, the witch-doctor, also slept.

Like the trees and the animals, he was unaware that the forest was menaced, that it was being encircled by human ambition, and that the days of giant trunks, wild beasts, and ghostly shades were drawing to a close. He slept, as did the wood and the beasts. How many years was it that black Jeremias had been there, with his white woolly mop of hair, his eyes, which had long since lost their lustre and were all but blind, his bent and fleshless frame, his wrinkled face, his toothless mouth, and his voice that was but a murmur at the meaning of which one had to guess? There was no one for half a hundred miles around who could have told you. To all of them he was a woodland being, quite as much to be feared as were the jaguars and the snakes, as the trunks with their tangle of liana stalks, as the very spirits themselves, whom he directed and let loose. He was the lord and master of the forest of Sequeiro Grande, the possession of which Horacio and the Badarós were disputing. From the seashore, from the port of Ilhéos, all the way to the more distant town or village along the backlands road, people spoke of Jeremias the witch-doctor, who cured diseases, who fortified men's bodies against bullets and snake-bites, who provided remedies, also, for the ills of lovers, who knew the charms that would make a woman cling to a man as not even the viscous breadfruit did. His fame had gone through the cities and through the towns he had never seen, and the afflicted came from afar to consult him.

It had been on a day many years before, when the forest covered a great deal more of the land than it did now, when it extended in all directions and men had not thought of felling it to plant the cacao tree, which had not as yet been brought from Amazonia—it was then that Jeremias had taken up his abode in the wood. He had been a young Negro, fleeing from slavery. The "bush captains" had been on his trail, and he had come into the forest where the Indians dwelt and had never more emerged. He had come from a sugar plantation where his master was in the habit of having him flogged. For many years he bore upon his back the mark of the lash. Not even when his scars had at last disappeared, not even when they told him that the freeing of the slaves had been decreed, would he consent to leave the woods. All that had been long, long ago; Jeremias had lost track of time; he had also lost all recollection of those events. The only memory he had not lost was that of his Negro gods, whom his ancestors had brought with them from Africa and for whom he had been unwilling to substitute the Catholic divinities of his plantation masters. Here within the forest he lived in the company of Ogún, of Omulú, of Oxossi, and of Oxolufã, while from the Indians he had learned the secret of medicinal herbs. With his own black deities he was in the habit of mingling those of the aborigines, invoking now one and now another on those days when someone made his way to the heart of the forest to ask his advice or to seek a remedy of some kind. And many of them did come; they even came from the city; and before long the feet of the ailing and the anguish-ridden had beaten a path to his door.

He had seen the white men draw near this forest, he had seen other forests felled, he had seen the Indians flee to take refuge at a safer distance, he had witnessed the sprouting of the first cacao shoots, he had seen how the earliest plantations were formed. And all the while he had retired deeper and deeper within the wood; for there was a fear that lay heavy on his heart: the fear that one day they would come to cut down the forest of Sequeiro Grande also. For that day he had prophesied woes unending. To all who came to see him he would say that this forest was the abode of the gods, that each tree was sacred, and that if men dared to lay a hand upon it, the gods would exact a merciless vengeance.

He lived on herbs and roots, drank pure river water from the stream that ran through the forest, and in his hut he kept two tame snakes that greatly frightened his visitors. Not even the most feared of the colonels, not even Sinhô Badaró himself, who was the political chieftain and highly respected; not even Horacio, of whom they told all those stories; not even Teodoro das Baraúnas, who had a terrible reputation as a "bad man"; not even Brasilino, the very symbol of courage—none of them in all the São Jorge dos Ilhéos region inspired as much awe as did Jeremias the witch-doctor. For the powers at his command were supernatural ones; they could avert the course of bullets, could stop the assassin's upraised dagger, could turn into harmless water the poison of snakes deadlier, even, than the rattlesnake.

In his hut Jeremias the witch-doctor lay sleeping. His ears, however, which were attuned to all the noises of the forest, had caught, even in sleep, the sound of running feet. Opening his tired eyes, he raised his head from the earthen floor. In an effort to pierce with his vision the half-light of dawn, he drew his body, clad in tatters, to a sitting posture. The footfalls were coming nearer every moment; someone was running along the path that led to the hut. Someone in search of a remedy or of counsel, or who came with despair in his heart. Jeremias was long skilled in recognizing the anguish of human beings from the degree of rapidity with which they made their way through the woods. This one was despairing; he was running along the path; he must be bringing with him a heart laden with grief. As the witch-doctor squatted down to wait, the dim light filtering through the boughs fell upon a snake crawling over the floor of the hut. He waited. The one who was coming brought no light to show him the way; his suffering was sufficient guide. Jeremias muttered some words that were unintelligible.

And then, suddenly, Negro Damião burst into the hut, dropped to his knees, and began kissing Jeremias's hands.

"Father Jeremias, something terrible has happened to me. I can't tell you, I don't know how to begin. Father Jeremias, I'm ruined."

The Negro was trembling all over; his enormous body was like a fragile bamboo stalk whipped by the wind on the river bank. Jeremias laid his fleshless hands on Damião's head.

"My son, there is no trouble that cannot be cured. Go ahead and tell me, and this old black man will give you a remedy." His voice was weak, but his words carried the strength of conviction. Negro Damião drew nearer, dragging his knees along the earthen floor.

"My father, I can't tell you how it happened. Nothing like that ever happened to Negro Damião before. Ever since you gave me a charm against bullets, I never once missed a shot, I never was afraid of bringing down some poor fellow. I don't know how it happened, Father Jeremias, I was bewitched."

Jeremias waited for the story in silence. Putting his hands on Damião's head was the only gesture that he had made. The snake had now stopped crawling and had curled up in the corner where the witch-doctor slept. Damião trembled as he went on, speaking now in a hurried voice and now slowly, as if searching for words.

"Sinhô Badaró sent me out to do away with a man. It was Mr. Firmo, the one who has the grove not far from here. I was in hiding along the side-road, and I saw a ghost, my father, I saw a ghost. It was his wife, Dona Tereza, and she put me out of my head."

He paused. His heart was not big enough to contain the emotions that filled it to overflowing, emotions that were so new, so unfamiliar.

"Go on and tell me, my son."

"I was waiting for him, and his wife came along; she had a kid in the belly, and she told me the child was going to die and that

Negro Damião would be the death of all three of them. That made me soft, it got me, it put something into my head, it took the strength out of my hand, it took the aim from my eye. It was witchcraft, father; Negro Damião missed his shot. And now what is Sinhô Badaró going to say? He's a good man, good and kind to Negro Damião, and I betrayed him. I didn't kill the man, it was witchcraft. Give me a charm, father!"

Jeremias stood there, his body rigid, his half-blind eyes staring into space. He realized that behind Negro Damião's story there was another one that was far more important, that beyond the fate of this black man lay that of the entire forest of Sequeiro Grande.

"Why did Sinhô want to have Firmo done away with?"

"Mr. Firmo wouldn't sell his grove, so that Sinhô could get into the forest, father. And I betrayed him, I didn't bring the man down, his wife's eyes took the courage out of my bosom. That's the truth, father, I swear it is; it's no lie this Negro's telling you."

Jeremias drew himself erect. He needed no staff now to support his centenarian's frame. In two strides he was at the door of the hut, where his half-seeing eyes had a view of the forest in all its splendour. At the same time he beheld the path that led from those distant days of the past down to this morning which was to mark his end. He knew that men were coming into the woods, knew that they were going to fell them, that they were going to kill off the animals and plant cacao on the land where the forest of Sequeiro Grande once had stood. He could see the smoke from the flames writhing among the lianas, licking the treetrunks, could hear the howls of the jaguars as they fled, the hiss of the burning snakes. He could see the men with their axes and their pruning-knives completing the work of the flames, stripping the earth, laying it bare, digging up even the deepest roots of the trees. What he did not see was Negro Damião, who had betrayed his employer and was kneeling there, weeping for his treason. He saw, instead, the devastated wood, felled and burned over, he saw the cacao trees springing up, and a tremendous hatred took possession of him. When he spoke, it was no longer to mutter as he always did, nor did he address himself to Negro Damião, who was trembling and weeping, waiting for the words that should dispel his suffering. Jeremias's words were addressed to his gods, to his own gods, those gods that had come from the jungles of Africa—to Ogún, Oxossi, Yansan, Oxolufã, Omolú—and to Exú, as well, who was the

Devil himself. He was calling upon them now to unloose their wrath upon those who were coming to disturb the peace of their dwelling-place.

"Piety is dried up, and they are eyeing the forest with the eye of the wicked. They shall enter the forest, now; but before they enter, they shall die, men and women and little ones, even unto the beasts of the field. They shall die, until there is no longer any hole in which to bury them, until the buzzards have had their fill of flesh, until the earth shall be red with blood. A river shall flow in the highways, and in it relatives, neighbours, friends shall be drowned, and not a one shall escape. They shall enter the forest, but it shall be over the bodies of their own dead. For each tree, each sapling that they fell, a man shall be felled, and the buzzards shall be so many in number as to hide the sun. Human flesh shall be the fertilizer that they spread for their cacao shoots, and every shrub shall be watered with their blood—with the blood of all of them, all, all—for none shall escape, not a man, woman, child, or beast."

Once again he called upon the names of his beloved deities. He called upon Exú as well, entrusting to him the vegeance that he sought, as his voice rang out through the forest, awakening the birds, the monkeys, the snakes, and the jaguars. Then one last time he shouted, and this time it was a curse, a flaming curse:

"Each son shall plant his cacao tree on the banks of a river flowing with his father's blood."

He then gazed fixedly at the dawn, which was greeted by the trill of birds above the forest of Sequeiro Grande. His body was giving way; the effort he had made had been en enormous one. His body was yielding, his eyes were closing wholly now, his legs bent beneath him, and he sank to the earthen floor, his feet touching Negro Damião, who was beside himself with fear. Not one sigh, one moan, came from his lips, but in his death-agony Jeremias strove to repeat his curse, his mouth still writhing with hatred. In the trees the birds were warbling their early morning song. The forest of Sequeiro Grande was flooded with the light of dawn.

III
The Birth of Cities

◆◆

1

Once upon a time there were three sisters: Maria, Lucia, and Violeta. Three sisters who were as one in the lives that they led and in their light-hearted laughter. Lucia of the black braids, Violeta of the lacklustre eyes, and Maria who was the youngest of the three. Once upon a time there were three sisters who were as one in the fate that awaited them.

They cut off Lucia's braids, her breasts grew round, and her cinnamon-coloured thighs were like two brown columns. The boss came and took her. A cedarwood bed and a feather mattress, bolsters and coverlets. Once upon a time there were three sisters.

Violeta's eyes were wide-opened on the world, her breasts were pointed, her big, youthful buttocks were waves as she walked. The overseer came and took her. An iron bed and a horsehair mattress, sheets, and the Virgin Mary. Once upon a time there were three sisters.

Maria, youngest of the three, had tiny breasts and a belly that was sleek and smooth. Came the boss; he did not want her. Came the overseer; he did not take her. There was left Pedro, a worker on the plantation. A cowhide bed without sheet or coverlets, no cedarwood, no feathers. Maria and her love.

Once upon a time there were three sisters: Maria, Lucia, Violeta. Three sisters who were as one in the lives that they led and in their light-hearted laughter. Lucia with her boss, Violeta with her overseer, and Maria with her love. Once upon a time there were three sisters whom destiny had parted.

Lucia's braids grew again, her rounded breasts sank in, and her column-like thighs were covered with black-and-blue marks. The boss rode away in an automobile, taking with him the cedarwood bed, the bolsters, and the coverlets. Once upon a time there were three sisters.

Violeta's wide eyes were closed from fear of looking at the world about her, her breasts were flaccid, and she had a child to suckle. On his sorrel horse the overseer left one day, never to return. The iron bed went also. Once upon a time there were three sisters.

Maria, youngest of the three, went with her husband to the field, to the cacao plantations. When she came back from the field, she was the oldest of the three. Pedro went away one day, for he was neither a boss nor an overseer; he went away in a casket, a plain wooden box, leaving behind him the cowhide bed and Maria with her love. Once upon a time there were three sisters.

Where now are Lucia's braids, Violeta's breasts, Maria's love?

Once upon a time there were three sisters in a cheap whorehouse. Three sisters who were as one in their suffering and in their despair. Maria, Lucia, Violeta: three sisters who were as one in the fate that awaited them.

2

At the door of the clay-walled house, a house without paint or whitewash, the three men stopped. The young man and the man from Ceará were carrying the hammock with the corpse while the old man rested, leaning on his staff. They stood there for a minute or so. It was early morning, and there was no sign of life in the street of whorehouses.

"What if they're sleeping with customers?" the young one asked.

The old fellow threw up his hands. "We'll have to wake them just the same."

They pounded on the door, but there was no response from

within. All was silent in the street outside. A street on the outskirts of the town of Ferradas. Small houses of beaten clay, some of them roofed with straw, some with tiles, the majority with zinc. Here lived the town whores, and here, on feast-days, came workers from the plantations in search of love-making. The old man pounded on the door with his staff from time to time. At last someone shouted from inside the house:

"Who is it? What the devil do you want?" It was a woman's sleepy voice. A masculine voice then added: "Be on your way. We're full up here." This was accompanied by a satisfied laugh.

"They've got company, all right," the young man observed. He could not see how they were going to deliver the dead man to his daughters if they were sleeping with customers.

The old man was lost in thought for a moment.

"We've got to do it," he said. "We've got to deliver him, anyway."

"Wouldn't it be better to wait?" said the man from Ceará.

"And what are we going to do with him?" the greybeard demanded, pointing to the corpse. "He's been out of the ground a long time already. The poor fellow needs a rest." And with this he called again: "Lucia! Violeta! Lucia!"

"What do you want?" It was a man's voice again.

The old man then called out the third daughter's name: "Maria! Oh, Maria!"

At the door of the neighbouring house an old woman appeared, still half asleep. She was about to protest against the noise when she caught sight of the corpse.

"Who is it?" she asked.

"He's their father," the man from Ceará replied, pointing to the house in front of him.

"Did they kill him?" the old woman wanted to know.

"He died of fever."

The woman left her doorsill and came up to the men. She looked the body over with an air of nausea.

"Are they at home? Nobody answers the door."

"They had a jamboree last night. It was Juquinha's birthday, the one who's sweet on Violeta. They kept it up until morning. That's why you can't wake them." She them chimed in with the old man in calling: "Violeta! Violeta!"

"Who is it? What the devil do you want?"

"It's your father!" the woman screeched.

"Who?" There was a note of surprise in the speaker's voice.

"Your father!"

There was a silence broken only by the stirring of the people inside the house. The door opened and Violeta stuck her head out. As her eyes fell on the little group, she craned her neck, and then, recognizing the corpse as that of her father, she screamed. The commotion on the inside grew louder. The entire street was astir now. Women came running out of the houses, followed at a more leisurely pace by the men who had been spending the night with them. Most of them were scantily clad in their sleeping-garments; only a few had thrown a nightgown over their nakedness. Standing around the body, they conversed with lowered voices.

"It was the fever."

"You can't do anything for it."

"But it's catching, isn't it?"

"They say you can get it from the air."

"They'd better bury him, then."

"He hadn't seen his daughters for years. He was sore at them because they went wrong."

"They say he never came to Ferradas, out of shame."

Women with battered faces, mulatto women, Negro women, here and there a white woman. Their legs and arms and frequently their faces as well bore scars. The atmosphere was heavy with stale alcohol mingled with cheap perfume. One woman whose uncombed hair formed an enormous top-knot now went over to the corpse.

"I slept with him once. It was in Tabocas."

This remark was greeted by silence. Violeta still stood in the doorway without the courage to come closer.

"Take him inside." It was a mulatto girl who gave the order.

Lucia and Maria had now come out. Lucia was weeping. "My father, my father." Maria slowly approached the body, a frightened look in her eyes. Several men had followed them out.

"Juquinha, your father-in-law's kicked the bucket," said one of the women with a smile.

"Please have some respect for the dead," the old man begged her.

"You're nothing but a dirty whore," said one of the other girls.

Lifting the hammock, the bearers carried it into the house, the entire crowd following at their heels. Some of the men had just finished buttoning up their trousers; the women went as they were, half-clad. The latter appeared to be all of the same age and the same colour—a sickly hue. These were the dregs of life, the

110

lower depths. Inasmuch as the house did not afford a parlour, there being merely five small cubbyholes for the five women inmates, they left the dead man in Violeta's bed, which was in the front room. The old man took out the stub of a candle, now almost wholly burned away. Above the bed was the picture of a saint, Senhor do Bomfim, the saint who presides over a "good end." A magazine page showing a blonde nude had also been tacked to the wall. Lucia was sobbing, Maria was standing beside the body, and Violeta had gone to look for another candle. The bystanders were scattering through the hallway. Juquinha then came in with a bottle of rum and began serving the men who had carried the corpse. Maria picked up the guitar that was standing at the head of the bed.

Speaking to the man from Ceará, the old man pointed to Maria as she passed, guitar in hand.

"I knew her when she was a little thing. She was cute as could be. And afterwards she grew up to be one of the prettiest gals you ever saw—when she married Pedro. You wouldn't think it to look at her now."

"You can see she was good-looking once."

"Ah, but this whore's life does away with their good looks in a couple of days' time."

The young man was eyeing Maria with interest.

A number of the women had retired to put on more clothes. Before leaving, one of the men offered Lucia some money. Violeta and Juquinha were calculating the cost of a casket and a burial. It came high. They now returned to the room where Lucia and Maria were with the body, and all four of them began discussing the matter. Juquinha, who was like one of the family, did the figuring. No, it would not be possible for them to buy a casket. Even a plot in the cemetery was very dear.

"We'll have to bury him in the hammock," said Lucia. "We can put a sheet over him."

After her first screams Violeta had been calm enough.

"I don't know," she said, "why we don't bury him in the street and get it over with. He never had anything to do with us."

"You've got no heart," Maria broke in. "I'm sure I don't know why you screamed like that when you first saw him. It was all put on. He was a good man." Violeta was about to retort, but Maria went on: "He was ashamed of us because we led a fast life, that was all. He had some feelings. It wasn't that he didn't like us."

Outside in the hallway the old fellow who had brought the

corpse was telling the visitors how the man had died, how the three days' fever had carried him off.

"There was no remedy that would do him any good. We had a lot of medicine from the store on the Baraúnas plantation, but it didn't help any."

Back in the room Lucia, who was very religious, was suggesting that they send for Friar Bento to say some prayers. Juquinha doubted that he would come.

"He wouldn't set foot in a place like this."

"Who told you he wouldn't?" said Violeta. "When Isaura died, he came. The only thing was it cost a lot." Not wishing to be taken for her father's enemy, she said no more; it was Juquinha who took up where she left off: "He'll only come for a big fee—not less than twenty milreis."

Lucia was ready to give up the idea: "If that's the way it is, we won't send for him."

She stood there gazing at the dead man's emaciated face, his greenish countenance, which appeared to be smiling in this, his last affliction. She was deeply grieved, heart-broken, at the idea of their putting her father away like that.

"They're going to bury him without so much as a prayer, poor fellow!" she stammered between her tears. "He never did anyone any harm. He was a good man. And now there's no one even to pray for his soul. I never thought—Oh, my father—"

Violeta took her sister by the arm, which was the most affectionate gesture that she knew. "We'll pray ourselves. I still remember a prayer."

But the mulatto girl who had slept with the dead man once upon a time, and who had overheard this conversation from the hallway, now took twenty milreis from her stocking and, coming into the room, handed the money to Lucia.

"Don't leave him without a prayer," she said.

This gave Juquinha the idea of taking up a collection, and he went about among those present to get their contributions. One man who had nothing to give volunteered to go for Friar Bento, and set out at once; it was his way of collaborating.

Lucia then remembered the rites of hospitality. "We must give these men some coffee," she said, alluding to the three who had brought the body.

Maria went out to the back of the house; and when she called for the old man, the young man, and the man from Ceará to come, the others all accompanied them to the kitchen. In the room with the dead there remained only Violeta and the mulatto girl who had given the twenty milreis. The latter had never before beheld in the peaceful repose of death a man with whom she had slept. She was greatly impressed, and looked upon him as her own, as a near relative.

In the kitchen, over the coffee, the old man sought to change the subject.

"Did you know," he was saying, "that the Badarós sent out to have Firmo killed yesterday?"

They all pricked up their ears at this.

"What's that you're saying?"

"Did they kill him?"

"No, the shot missed him. And it's a wonder, too, for it was Negro Damião."

One of the listeners whistled in astonishment.

"And Negro Damião missed his aim?" Another man put the question. "Well, it's the end of the world, that's all I've got to say."

The old man was flattered at having aroused so much interest. Employing a fingernail as a toothpick, he extracted a shred of manihot and then continued:

"Firmo passed us on the road, riding like the very devil. He was making for Colonel Horacio's house. They say there's going to be hell to pay."

Forgetful of the dead, they crowded about the speaker, some of them sprawling over the tiny kitchen table in order not to lose a single word, as others raised their heads to see over those in front of them. Their eyes were bulging with curiosity. The old man was explaining what they all knew:

"It's on account of the forest of Sequeiro Grande."

"It's going to start now."

The speaker asked for silence and then went on:

"Yes, it's already starting. Farther along we ran into Firmo again, coming back with a couple of Colonel Horacio's lads, and Colonel Maneca Dantas was with them. They took the short-cut to the Baraúnas place. They were riding at a gallop."

Juquinha, who was one of the Badarós men, put in a word here.

"Colonel Horacio thinks Teodoro's going to side with him. You can fool him as easy as a baby with a stick of candy. He can't see that Colonel Teodoro is hand in glove with the Badarós."

Lucia broke in at this point.

"He's a wretch," she said, "that's what he is, a bandit. He'll go with whichever side offers him the most."

113

"You ought to know," said one of the women, with a smile, "seeing as how you was his sweetie and he was the one that first had you."

Lucia drew herself up, her eyes flashing. "That was the worst thing that ever happened. He's the meanest man there is."

"But he's got nerve," said one of the men who were present.

"Oh, he's got that, all right, especially when he's with a woman; but when he's after one of them, he can be as tame as a little bird. I remember how he was with me. He used to come around with a present every day—a new dress, a pair of shoes, an embroidered handkerchief. And the promises that he made! Why, he promised me a house in Ilhéos, he promised me clothes, he even promised me a diamond ring for my finger. He promised everything, until he'd had me—and then the promises flew out the window and I ended up here in this street, without my father's blessing."

They were all silent; the man from Ceará looked frightened. Lucia glanced around and saw that they were waiting for more:

"And do you think I was the only one? When he'd had his fill of me, he began making eyes at Violeta; and if it hadn't been that Ananias, the overseer, was there before him and had already laid a leg with her—if he didn't go after Violeta, it was because he was afraid of Ananias."

The old man now spoke up. "A black man who has a daughter," he said, "is only bringing her up for the white man's bed."

But Lucia had more to tell.

"And when Pedro died," she went on, "the one that was married to Maria, the very night after he was buried the colonel came to the house to offer his help. He didn't even respect the poor girl's grief, but climbed into the bed which was still warm from her husband's body. There's nothing lower than that."

There was another silence. The young man who had helped carry the corpse had had his eyes on Maria ever since he came; it was obvious that he desired her. Had it not been a day of mourning, he would have suggested going to bed with her. It was two months now since he had known what a woman was like, and the remnants of Maria's good looks had at once attracted his attention. Of all the conversation, only that part about Colonel Teodoro's possessing her on the day of her husband's burial had interested him.

The old man, who had lost his prominence in the gathering, thanks to Lucia's interruption, once more brought the conversation back to the events of the night.

"A *jagunço*," he said, "is going to be worth his weight in gold now. If the fracas is starting, the man who's a good shot is going to get rich. He can get himself a cacao grove."

"I'm with the Badarós," said Juquinha. "They've got the upper hand in politics, and I'm sure they're going to win. Sinhô and Juca are a couple of real men."

"They're no match for Colonel Horacio," said one of the others.

One man rose and left the room.

"Chico is going to offer his services already," Juquinha remarked. "There's no rumpus that he's not mixed up in it. He's Colonel Horacio's man."

A number of the other visitors now took their departure, being anxious to spread the news the old man had brought. They scattered out through the streets of Ferradas, which were not many in number, going from one acquaintance to another. The man from Ceará did not know what to make of it all.

"In this country," he said, "all they talk about is death."

"Death comes cheap here," declared the old man sententiously. "You ought to be thankful you're getting out in time."

"Are you running away?" asked one of the women.

"I'm getting out while I can."

Juquinha laughed: "You're leaving just when things are getting good."

The women who had gone home to put some clothes on now returned to the house. One of them brought some withered flowers which a man who occasionally came to see her had given her a couple of days before; she deposited them at the foot of the corpse. More men came in also, eager to hear the news; for word had gone through the town and the tale had grown with the telling. It was said that the corpse was that of one of the lads who had accompanied Firmo and that he had died of a bullet intended for the latter. By a miracle Firmo had escaped a shot fired by Negro Damião. Others, again, asserted that it was Firmo's own body that had arrived.

Friar Bento now came into the house of prostitution, and one of the women who had nothing on but a nightgown ran out hastily in search of a more suitable garment.

"God be with you," said the man of God from the doorway, in his foreign-sounding voice. He then came down the hall, for first of all he wanted to know the news. After the old man had repeated the entire story in a humble voice, the friar went into the front room where the body was. Violeta with some embarrassment explained to him their money troubles, then made the necessary arrangements with the sacristan, giving him the twenty-milreis note, which had been the mulatto girl's contribution, and a few additional coins. Friar Bento thereupon began the prayers for the dead, men and women muttering the responsories:

"*Ora pro nobis.*"

Lucia wept softly as the three sisters stood huddled together. The young hammock-bearer still had his eyes on Maria. Was it not possible that she would consent to sleep with him this very day, after the burial? Had she not slept with Colonel Teodoro on the night after Pedro's funeral? Mechanically he repeated with the others:

"*Ora pro nobis.*"

The friar was running through the litany when from the doorway someone shouted:

"There comes Juca Badaró!"

They all ran out to the street, where Juca, accompanied by Antonio Victor and two other lads, was galloping by in a cloud of dust, along the road to Tabocas. Practically all of them, even to the sacristan, hastened out for a glimpse of the cavalcade. Friar Bento, leaning over the corpse and craning his neck, looked on from the window, without stopping his prayers. Only the three sisters and the young man who desired Maria remained with him beside the body. Juca Badaró and his *cabras* were by this time on the far side of town; and as they passed the big warehouse where Horacio's dried cacao was stored, they fired their rifles in the air as those in the street turned and fled to the safety of the house. The prayers for the dead were lost in a babble of voices. The young man was drawing near to Maria.

3

Years afterwards, when someone was passing through the town of Ferradas in the company of an old inhabitant, a first settler who knew the tales of the land of cacao, the latter would be almost certain to remark, as he pointed to the houses and to the streets whose mud had disappeared beneath the cobblestone pavement:

"This place was once the worst bandits' den in the country. A lot of blood flowed here in Ferradas back in the early days, when they were just starting to raise cacao."

The town of Ferradas was Horacio's fief, being situated in the middle of his plantations. For some years it marked the boundaries of the cacao country. When men began planting the new crop at Rio do Braço, they little thought that it would end by doing away with the sugar plantations, the rum stills, and the coffee groves that were then to be found in the neighbourhood of Rio do Braço, Banco da Victoria, and Agua Branca, the three settlements that stood on the banks of the Cachoeira River, which empties into the ocean at Ilhéos. The cacao not only did away with the rum stills, the small sugar plantations, and the coffee groves; it even invaded the forest. And in its path sprang up the town of Tabocas and, farther along, that of Ferradas, when Horacio's men had felled the woods on the left bank of the stream.

For some time Ferradas was the most distant of the settlements from Ilhéos. It was from here that the *conquistadores* of the new land set out. Now and then, breaking a path through the forest, travellers would come from Itapira, from Barra do Rio de Contas, which lay just beyond the cacao region. Ferradas became a business centre, small in size but full of stir and bustle. Its growth, however, was destined to stop with the conquest of the forest of Sequeiro Grande, on the edge of which the town of Pirangy was to rise, a city built in two years' time. Long afterwards, with the rapid spread of cacao as a crop, Baforé, then a hamlet on the backlands trail, was to grow into a town and to exchange its name for the more euphonious one of Guaracy. But at the time of the conquest Ferradas was important, possibly even more important than Tabocas. There was talk to the effect that a branch line of the railroad was to be extended there, a project that occasioned much discussion in the taverns and in the apothecary's shop. But the railroad never came; for Ferradas happened to be in Horacio's political domain; he was its absolute ruler; and inasmuch as he was a *seabrista*—that is to say, a partisan of Seabra's—he found himself in the opposition, and the government, accordingly, would not approve the plan of the English to build a branch line to the town. And when Seabra finally did come to power and Horacio was on top, he was by that time much more concerned with having the railroad extended to Pirangy, on the edge of Sequeiro Grande.

Ferradas remained but a frontier outpost, but in those days its streets were thronged, it did a thriving trade, it was known to the big exporting houses in Bahia and was on the itinerary of the travelling salesmen. The latter would arrive on horseback, their sample-cases being carried by a train of burros; and for some days thereafter their white linen suits would stand out among the khaki ones worn by the natives, or *grapiúnas* as they were called. The salesmen would make love to the unmarried girls of the town, would dance when dances were held, would sip lukewarm beer while complaining loudly about the lack of ice, and would do a big business. And later, upon their return from their travels, in the cafés of Bahia, they would tell wild yarns of this town that was populated with adventurers and *jagunços*, where there was only one hotel, where the streets were paved with mud, but where every barefoot inhabitant had a pocketful of money.

"I never saw so many five-hundred-milreis notes in my life as I did in Ferradas," they would say.

This was the highest-denomination banknote at that time. No one in the town, to hear the visitors tell it, had any change, and small coins were practically nonexistent. And they told other foolish stories, as travelling salesmen do.

"When anyone comes to Ferradas, Chico Martins, who runs the hotel, puts sugar in the bed where the guest is going to sleep."

The listener would be duly astonished at this: "Sugar? But what for?"

"To attract the ants, and the ants eat the bedbugs."

Smallpox and typhoid were endemic, and the best house in Ferradas was not, properly speaking, in the town, but rather in the forest. This was the pesthouse where smallpox patients were quarantined. It was said that no one ever came back from there. The infirmary was kept by an aged Negro who had had the black-pox and had been cured of it. No one would set foot in the strip of forest where the pesthouse stood. To the entire population it was terror-inspiring.

Ferradas had grown around the cacao warehouse that Horacio had built there. He needed a depository for the crop from his various plantations. And so dwellings had sprung up beside the warehouse, and in a short time a street with two or three intersecting lanes had been opened through the mud, and the first prostitutes and the first salesmen had begun to arrive. A Syrian had opened an inn, and a couple of barbers had come from Tabocas to set up shop, a fair was held on Saturdays, and Horacio would kill a pair of oxen and send their flesh in to be sold. Pack-drivers who came with a load of dried cacao from outlying plantations would spend the night in Ferradas, keeping close watch on their burros on account of the danger of cacao thieves.

But it was in connection with the appointment of a local police officer that the town first really came into the pubic eye. The prefect at Ilhéos, upon the insistence of Juca Badaró, had appointed a deputy for Ferradas, which was in itself an insult to Horacio, since it represented an interference with his jurisdiction. The authorities insisted that this was a town, and it made no difference if it did happen to lie within Horacio's domain. The administration of justice must be established there and an end must be put to all the assassinations and robberies that were constantly occurring. The deputy arrived one afternoon, accompanied by three sorry, anaemic-looking police troopers. They were mounted when they came, but they went back that night on foot and minus their clothes, after having received a terrific beating.

In connection with this incident the pro-government newspaper in Ilhéos printed an attack on Horacio, whereupon the opposition paper demanded to know "why a deputy should be appointed for Ferradas, when nothing was done about paving the streets or lighting the street corners." Such improvements as the town possessed had been due to Colonel Horacio da Silveira. If the government wished to intervene in local affairs, why then did it not make some contribution toward the betterment of the community? Ferradas was a law-abiding place and had no need of a police officer; what it needed was paving, lights, and a water system.

But the arguments brought forward by the opposition press, representing Horacio's interests, proved unavailing. The prefect, who all the time was being spurred on by Juca, appointed another deputy. In this instance it was an individual who was known as a "bad man"—Vicente Garangau, long one of the Badarós' *jagunços*. He arrived with a dozen soldiers and much loud talk of what was going to happen. The next day he arrested one of Horacio's labourers who had kicked up a rumpus in a whorehouse. Horacio sent word demanding the fellow's release, and Vicente replied that Horacio himself should come and free the man. Horacio came, the man was freed, and Vicente Garangau was killed along the Macados road as he sought to hide on Maneca Dantas's plantation. They stripped him of his skin, cut off his ears and testicles, and forwarded these mementoes to the prefect in Ilhéos. From that time forth there was no police officer in Ferradas, for the very good reason that Juca Badaró could not find anyone who would take the job.

Horacio had had a chapel built and had brought down a friar

to officiate in it. Friar Bento was more by way of being a *conquistador* of the land than a servant of Christ. His one passion was the nuns' school for girls which was being built under tremendous difficulties at Ilhéos, and all the money that he could scrape together he sent on to the sisters for the good work. For this reason he was not well liked in the town. His parishioners would greatly have preferred that he pay more attention to Ferradas; according to them, he should have been thinking of building a better church than the one at Tabocas, to take the place of the chapel. But all that Friar Bento could think of was the school, which was to be a monumental affair on Conquista Hill, in the city of Ilhéos. It was his own pet scheme, and he had had much trouble in persuading the Archbishop of Bahia to send the nuns down. If he had accepted the chaplaincy at Ferradas, it was merely with the object of raising all the money he could there. He was horrified by the indifference which the colonels displayed toward the upbringing of their daughters. They gave much thought to the education of their sons in medicine, the law, or engineering, the three professions that had come to take the place of the nobility of old; but as for their daughters, it was enough for them to learn to read and to sew.

The short of the matter was, Ferradas could not forgive Friar Bento for his utter lack of interest in the place. They accordingly began telling stories about him, one of which was to the effect that he slept with his cook, a young mulatto girl who had come from Horacio's plantation. And when she gave birth to a child, despite the fact that everybody knew that its father was Virgulino, who worked for the Syrian, they all stoutly maintained that it was Friar Bento's bastard. The friar knew of these tales, but he merely shrugged his shoulders; the thing that he was after was money for his school. Secretly he had a contempt for his parishioners, one and all, whom he looked upon as hopelessly lost, a lot of thieves and assassins, lawless folk with no respect for God or man. According to him, there was not a single inhabitant who had not long ago won for himself an eternity in hell. And he was in the habit of saying as much in his sermons at Sunday morning Mass, to the scant congregation that saw fit to attend.

This opinion held by the friar was more or less general throughout the cacao region, where Ferradas had become a synonym for violent death. But if the brand of Catholicism represented by the monk had little appeal for the residents of the town, spiritualism on the other hand flourished. The "believing ones" were in the habit of meeting at the house of Eufrosina, a medium who had begun to acquire a reputation in those parts; it was there that they assembled to listen to messages from dead relatives and friends. Seated in her chair, Eufrosina would begin stammering unintelligibly, until one of those present recognized the familiar voice of the dead. It was said that long ago the spirits—and especially the spirit of an Indian, who was Eufrosina's "guide"—had predicted the trouble that was to occur over the forest of Sequeiro Grande. These prophecies were much talked about, and no one in Ferradas was surrounded with so much respect as was the mulatto with the skinny figure as she made her way through the muddy streets.

Her "séances" having proved so successful, Eufrosina then began treating diseases by spiritualism, with comparative success. This was an encroachment on the domain of Dr. Jessé Freitas, the physician at Tabocas, who came over to Ferradas once a week to look after the sick and who was also called in on nights of gun-play; and he now joined forces with Friar Bento against Eufrosina. For she was taking his patients away; fever-sufferers were now going to the medium instead of the doctor. Friar Bento took the matter up with Horacio, but the latter did nothing about it. It was for this reason, so they said, that the friar had made up that story about Horacio and the spiritualist séance; for the monk—according to Ferradas—had a venomous tongue. Anyway, it was after this that he began spreading the story.

At a certain séance in Eufrosina's house, so ran the tale, they had sought to summon the spirit of Mudinho de Almeida, one of the earliest *conquistadores* of the region and the most terrible of them all, whose fame, though he had been dead for years, persisted—they still spoke of him as the very symbol of wickedness. Eufrosina had done all she could to "materialize" him, but without success. It was a long and exhausting struggle, with the medium making a tremendous effort and fairly splitting herself with her tremblings and her trances. Fianlly, after more than an hour of these exertions, when those present had grown weary of so much concentration, Mudinho de Almeida appeared, very tired and in a great hurry. Let them tell him what it was they wanted and be quick about it, for he had to return at once.

"But why all the rush, brother?" inquired the medium in a dulcet tone.

"We're very busy in hell these days; everybody's very busy," was the spirit's churlish response; and by his crustiness the older ones vowed that they did indeed recognize him as none other than Mudinho de Almeida.

"But why are you so busy?" Eufrosina insisted, giving voice to the general curiosity.

"We're piling up firewood all day long. Everybody's working, sinners and devils alike."

"And why so much firewood, my friend?"

"We're making a bonfire for the day when Horacio arrives."

Such were the tales told in the town of Ferradas, Horacio's fief, the bandits' den. From here it was that the grubbers of the land set out for the forest. It was a world of its own, a primitive and a barbarous one, whose sole ambition was money. Every day strangers arrived in quest of a fortune. From Ferradas the newly opened highways spread out over the cacao country. From Ferradas Horacio's men set out to enter the forest of Sequeiro Grande.

On this particular day the town was abuzz with the news that the old man with the corpse had brought. Juca Badaró had already passed through on his way to Tabocas, but he would not be able to return by that route; he would have to take another road home. For from morning to afternoon Ferradas had put itself upon a war footing. *Jagunços* were pouring in to guard Horacio's warehouse; and in the taverns men drank more rum than usual. Early that night Horacio came.

He came with a great retinue, a score of horses, and a burro train to carry the luggage. They were on their way to Tabocas, where the following day Ester was to take the train for Ilhéos. She was mounted after the fashion of the time, on a side-saddle with silver mountings, and she carried a silver-headed riding-whip in her hand. At her side rode Virgilio on a mottled-grey horse. Behind them, at Horacio's side, his low, squat figure weighing heavily on his mount, his face marked by a long knife-scar, came their friend Braz, owner of a grove at the edge of the Sequeiro Grande forest and respected throughout the cacao region. He carried a repeating-rifle on the saddle in front of him, and his hand that held the reins rested on it. Bringing up the rear were a number of plantation lads and pack-drivers, rifles on their shoulders, revolvers in their belts, and, last of all, Maneca Dantas.

Maneca had failed in his mission to Colonel Teodoro

Martins, owner of the Baraúnas plantation; the latter was siding with the Badarós.

They came riding in a closely compact group, raising a cloud of red dust in the road. With pack-drivers shouting at their beasts of burden and all the other noise and stir, one might have thought that this was a small detachment of an army invading the town. They came in at a gallop; and at the head of the street Horacio rode up to the front, his horse pawing the earth as the colonel drew up sharply before the house of Farhat, the Syrian, where they were to spend the night. The pawing steed, rearing on his hind legs and lifting his rider from the saddle, as the latter, whip in hand, reined him in—all this gave the effect of an equestrian statue of some ancient warrior. The plantation lads and the pack-drivers now scattered out through the town, which was agog with excitement. There was little sleep in Ferradas that night. It was like a bivouac before the morrow's battle.

4

With their long whips cracking on the ground, the pack-drivers made their way through the mud-laden streets of Tabocas as they shouted at their beasts to keep them from wandering off along the side-lanes and down the newly opened thoroughfares.

"Hey! Diamante! Dianho! Get up, there! Straight ahead, you damned burro, you!"

Leading the procession, with tinkling bells and showy breast-trappings, came the burro that best knew the road, the "little mother of the troop." The colonels made a point of decking out these "little mothers" as an emblem of their wealth and power.

"Whoa, Piranha! Get up, Borboleta! The Devil's in that mule—"

And so their long whips would crack in the air and on the ground as the animals with their sure, slow pace stirred up the mud of the street. From a doorway some acquaintance would call out the most overworked gibe that the town knew:

"How goes it, wife of a donkey-driver?"

"I'm on my way to see your mother right now."

Now and then herds of lowing oxen would come in from the backlands and would either remain in Tabocas to be sold for slaughter or continue on to Ilhéos. The leather-clad cowboys would then dismount from their high-mettled ponies and would mingle with the donkey-drivers as they drank rum in the taverns or went to the houses of prostitution in search of a woman's caress. Horsemen with revolvers in their belts would from time to time gallop through the town, and children playing in the mire would scamper for safety. A thousand times a day that mire was stirred up as cacao and still more cacao was brought in to be deposited in the enormous warehouses. That was the kind of town Tabocas was.

It had had no name at first, consisting as it did of four or five houses on the bank of the river. Afterwards it became the town of Tabocas as more houses were built, one after another, and streets without any sort of symmetry were opened by the hoofs of burros bringing in the dried cacao. A railway branch line had been extended to the village from Ilhéos, and this led to the building of still more houses. Nor were these houses, like those in Ferradas, Palestina, and Mutuns, mere unpainted huts of beaten clay with wooden planks for windows, flimsy structures thrown up in haste and serving rather as shelters than as dwellings. In Tabocas there were brick houses and houses of stone and plaster with tiled roofs and glass windows, while a part of the main street had been paved with cobblestones.

The other streets, it is true, were mudholes pure and simple, daily churned by the pack-trains that came in from the entire region round about, bearing hundred-pound bags of the precious crop to be stored in numerous warehouses that had been constructed. A number of export firms already had branches in Tabocas, where they bought cacao directly from the planters; and if a branch of the Bank of Brazil had not as yet been installed, there was at least a banking representative who spared many of the colonels the trouble of a train trip to Ilhéos to deposit or withdraw their money. In the middle of a large grass-planted square the Church of St. Joseph, patron saint of the region, had been erected, while almost directly opposite, in one of the few two-story buildings that the town boasted, was the Masonic Lodge, which numbered among its members the majority of the plantation-owners and which gave balls and maintained a school.

Houses were also springing up on the other side of the river, and already there was talk of building a bridge to connect the two portions of the "city"; for the one thing upon which the inhabitants of Tabocas strenuously insisted was that their village be elevated to the rank of a city and become the seat of government and of the administration of justice, with a prefect of its own, a judge, a prosecutor, and a police deputy. A name had even been suggested for the new municipality: Itabuna, which in the Guarani Indian tongue means "black rock," allusion being to the big rocks that stood on the banks and in the middle of the river, upon which the washerwomen spent the day at their labours. But inasmuch as Tabocas lay within Horacio's bailiwick, he being the largest landowner in the vicinity, the government of the state had paid no heed to the inhabitants' appeal. The Badarós asserted that it was all a plot on Horacio's part to seize political control of the region. Accordingly, Tabocas continued to be a borough of the municipality of São Jorge dos Ilhéos. Nevertheless, many of the residents, in writing letters, referred to it not as Tabocas, but as Itabuna. And when one of them who happened to be in Ilhéos was asked where his home was, he would reply, in a tone of great pride: "I am from the city of Itabuna."

There was, as a matter of fact, a police officer in Tabocas, who represented the highest authority in the town—nominally, that is, for the supreme authority was in reality Horacio. This officer, a former army corporal, was a small, lean fellow, but a nervy one, and had managed to hold on to his job in spite of all the threats of Horacio's ruffians. He was clever, too, being careful not to abuse his authority; he never interfered in a row unless there was serious bloodshed or someone had been killed. Horacio got along well enough with him, and had even, more than once, backed the corporal against his own *jagunços*. Whenever the colonel came to Tabocas, Corporal Esmeraldo always went around to have a little chat with him, and at such times he never failed to bring up the subject of a possible reconciliation with the Badarós. Horacio would laugh that ingrowing laugh of his and would clap the corporal on the shoulder:

"You're a straight-spoken fellow, Esmeraldo. Why you keep on working for the Badarós is more than I can understand. But any time you need a friend, I'm at your service."

Esmeraldo, however, had a deep veneration for Sinhô Badaró, a feeling that dated back to the days when they had roamed the forest together, here in this land of cacao. In these parts it was said that Sinhô's men were loyal to him out of friendship, and that anyone who went to work for him never left him; he was not like Horacio, a man to betray his friends.

125

In Tabocas whoever was a friend and political follower of Horacio's was careful to maintain an attitude of hostility toward the Badarós and their henchmen. Invariably at election time there were rows, gun-fights, and killings; and Horacio always won and always lost, for the votes were fraudulently counted in Ilhéos. They voted the living and the dead, and many of the former cast their ballots under threat from Horacio's ruffians. Tabocas in those days was full of *jagunços*, who stood guard over the homes of the local bigwigs: that of Dr. Jessé, who was Horacio's perpetual candidate; that of Leopoldo Azevedo, leader of the government party; that of Dr. Pedro Matta; and now that of Lawyer Virgilio, the new attorney, as well. Each party had its own apothecary's shop, and no patient who voted for the Badarós would think of patronizing Dr. Jessé, but went to Dr. Pedro instead. The two physicians continued to maintain personal relations, but said terrible things about each other when their backs were turned. Dr. Pedro alleged that Dr. Jessé neglected his patients, being a good deal more concerned with politics and with his cacao grove. Dr. Jessé on the other hand asserted, and the population bore him out, that Dr. Pedro had no respect for women, and that no husband or father of a family was safe in trusting his wife or daughter to him for an examination. There was likewise a dentist for each faction. In brief, the entire town was thus divided, with the two parties exchanging gross insults in the newspapers of Ilhéos. Horacio, now, had already sent for a printing press, with the object of starting a weekly in Tabocas, which Lawyer Virgilio was to edit.

The attorneys of the town were numerous, six or seven of them, and all earned their living out of the scandalous "ousters"; for this form of "legal" process flourished here even more than it did in Ilhéos. Men who for years had owned land and plantations would lose them overnight, thanks to a well-drawn "ouster." There was not a colonel who would do business without first consulting his lawyer, by way of assuring himself against the possibility of a future eviction of this sort.

There was a Negro in Tabocas, one Claudionor by name, who raised his two or three thousand pounds of cacao, and who once worked an "ouster" of a little different sort that made him famous—he was even mentioned in the Bahia papers. The victim was Colonel Misael, whose fortune even in that day was a matter of legend. A cacao-planter who raised many thousands of pounds, he was at the same time a banker in Ilhéos and a stockholder in the railroad and in the docks; he was, in short, a power to be reckoned with economically, and he had a son-in-law who was a lawyer. In spite of all this, however, the Negro Claudionor got the better of him. In the seclusion of his own little plantation Claudionor had thought the thing out, and Lawyer Ruy helped him to carry it through.

Appearing one day before Colonel Misael, Claudionor asked him for the loan of seventy *contos de reis* with which to buy a grove. Swearing roundly, Misael advanced him the money on a short-term loan: six months in which to pay; for the colonel had a plan of his own, which was to take Claudionor's plantation when the latter failed to meet his obligation. Being illiterate, the Negro signed his name with a mark to the promissory note. Then, on his way home, he stopped off at Tabocas and contracted for the services of a primary-school teacher. Taking the latter with him, he set himself to learn to read and to sign his name. Six months later, when the note fell due, Claudionor denied that he owed the money; he had never had any loan from Misael; it was all a trick on the colonel's part. The best proof of this, so his attorney, Lawyer Ruy, argued, was that Claudionor could read perfectly well and was able to sign his name. Colonel Misael accordingly lost the seventy *contos de reis* and Claudionor increased his own holding and was able to make an extra contribution at the feast of St. Joseph that year.

The truth of the matter was, it could not properly be said that there were only six or seven lawyers in the town, for that number merely included those who resided there. But those who lived in Ilhéos also practised in Tabocas, while those in Tabocas had clients in the city. It was only a ride of three hours and a half by train, and one day it would be no more than forty-five minutes, when, as the region grew more prosperous, the new graded road-bed should have been constructed.

And so, amid "ousters," political struggles, intrigues, holy days of the Church, and Masonic festivals, Tabocas continued to live its life—a town that had not even had a name, and which now thought of calling itself Itabuna. Many a time was the blood of men slain in brawls mingled with the mire of its streets, to be churned under by the slow-paced burros. There were even occasions when Dr. Jessé, upon arriving with his instrument-case, would be unable to locate the wound on account of the mud with which the victim's body was covered. Even so, the fame of Tabocas was widespread; men spoke of it in the remote backland regions, and a certain newspaper in Bahia had referred to it as a "centre of civilization and progress."

5

Raising her hand, Margot pointed to the bit of street that was visible through the open window, by which she meant to indicate the entire town of Tabocas.

"This is the most out-of-the-way place in the world. It's a cemetery."

As Virgilio drew her to him, she poutingly left her chair and came over to seat herself upon his knees.

"You're a bad little girl."

Angrily she bounded to her feet.

"That's what you always say—I'm always the one that's to blame. You knew what this place was like before you came down here. I remember Juvenal's telling you that you ought to go to Rio if you wanted to make a name for yourself. I don't know why you chose to come here instead."

Virgilio opened his mouth as if about to speak, then stopped, deciding that it was not worth while. Had it been the month before, he undoubtedly would have spent an enormous amount of time in explaining to Margot that his future lay here, that if the opposition party won the election—and everything pointed that way—he would be the candidate for deputy from this region, the most prosperous in the state of Bahia. He would have tried to explain that the road to Rio was much more easily travelled by the highways of the cacao country than by a coastwise voyage in a seagoing liner. Tabocas was the land of money; within a few months' time he had made more there than he would have made in years of practice in the capital.

He had explained all this to her more than once; but Margot was always longing for the festivals, the cafés and theatres of Bahia. In a way he understood the sacrifice she was making. It had all begun when he was in his fourth year in school. He had made Margot's acquaintance in a house of assignation, had slept with her a few times, and she had soon become smitten with him. And when he had been on the verge of abandoning his studies, owing to the death of his father, who had left the family affairs in bad shape, she had offered him everything she possessed and in addition her earnings each night. He had been deeply touched by this; and after one of the political leaders had found him a place in the party office and on the staff of the opposition newspaper, he had kept up his relations with Margot for her own sake alone; he had formed the habit of paying her room rent, had slept with her every night, and they had even gone to the theatre together.

The only thing was he had not lived with her openly, for this would have created a scandal that might have had a bad effect upon his career. But nevertheless it was in Margot's room that he, Juvenal, and other classmates had planned the student campaign that was to make him class orator, and it was at her side that he had written his baccalaureate address.

When upon the advice of the opposition leader he had accepted the post of attorney for the party at Tabocas, Virgilio had spent hours in endeavouring to convince Margot that she should come with him. She had been unwilling, had not wished to leave the merrymakings and all the life and movement of Bahia. She had always thought that upon graduation he would go to Rio de Janeiro, and Virgilio himself had thought the same in his student days. The party chieftains, however, had succeeded in convincing him that, if he wanted a career, he ought to spend a few years in the new cacao country. He accordingly had gone there, in spite of Margot's declaration that all was over between them. It had been a painful night, that last one in the American House. She had wept and clung to him and had accused him of abandoning her—he did not love her any more. The truth was that Margot was afraid.

"You'll go down there and marry some rich backwoods girl and leave me stuck off in the bushes. I'm not going."

"You don't love me. If you did, you'd come."

He had possessed her amid all the anguished quarrelling of that night, which they had thought would be their last together. They had refined upon their love-making, each being desirous of preserving a cherished memory of the other.

He had come down alone; but only a few weeks had gone by when she unexpectedly put in an appearance, scandalizing Ilhéos with her gowns, which were in the latest fashion, with her broad-brimmed hats and painted face. The night of her arrival the streets of the town were filled with amorous sighs. She had gone with him to Tabocas and at first had behaved well enough. She seemed to have forgotten the gay and brilliant life of Bahia; she even gave evidence of becoming a housewife by caring for his clothes and superintending the preparation of meals in the kitchen. She was, in short, wholly devoted to him. She now paid a little less attention to her toilet, let her hair fall to her shoulders, and even failed to complain about the lack of hairdressers capable of fashioning those complicated structures which she formerly had worn upon her head.

Again they lived apart in order to avoid offending local

prejudices. After all, he was the legal representative of a political party; he had his responsibilities. And so Margot lived in a pretty little cottage with a girl who was being kept by a merchant of the town. There Virgilio spent a great part of the day. At times, in case of emergency, he would even receive his clients there. He ate there, slept there, and it was there that he drew up his briefs for the cases that he had to try in the court of Ilhéos.

Margot appeared to be happy; her ultra-fashionable gowns were forgotten in the wardrobe, and she no longer spoke of Bahia. But she was little by little growing tired of it all, as she came to realize that the time she would have to spend here was longer than she had thought. Moreover, Virgilio as a rule avoided taking her to Ilhéos on his repeated trips, in order not to arouse malicious gossip. When she did go, it was in another train, and in the city she saw little of him. But worst of all, she had caught a glimpse of him once or twice engaged in conversation with marriageable young women, the daughters of wealthy planters. At such times Margot would bring the roof down with her screams; it was no use Virgilio's telling her that he had to do this in order to further his career; she was unimpressed by such arguments. They would then have a passionate quarrel, with Margot throwing up to him the sacrifice she was making for his sake, stuck off there as she was in the sticks when she might be in Bahia living on the fat of the land; for surely there must be some rich business man or politican who had already made a success in life, and who would be only too glad to set her up in a little place of her own. Many had asked her already, but she had left everything to come running after him. She was a fool, that was what she was.

"Cléo was right when she said I shouldn't come down here—that this was the way it would be."

These quarrels always ended with the opening of a bottle of champagne and with the sound of kisses in a night of delirious love-making. But Margot would find herself left each time with an ever greater longing for the merry life of Bahia, strengthened by the certainty that Virgilio would never leave this country. For one reason or another their quarrels grew more frequent, coming every few days now as she began complaining about the lack of dressmakers and similar inconveniences: she was losing what hair she had, she was getting fat, and she had forgotten how to dance, it had been so long since she had had an opportunity.

But this afternoon things were more serious. When he had

announced that he was going to Ilhéos for a couple of weeks or more, she had been very happy about it. Say what you might, Ilhéos was a city; she would be able to dance in Nhôzinho's café, and there were a few women there with whom it was possible to hold a conversation—they were not like these filthy whores in Tabocas, most of whom came from the groves, having been deflowered by the colonels or their overseers, after which they had fallen in with the life of the town. Even the woman with whom she lived, the merchant's mistress, was a mulatto girl who could not read, with a pretty figure and an idiotic laugh; a planter's son had been her downfall, and the merchant had then taken her out of the rua do Poço, which was the street where the women of easy virtue lived. In Ilhéos there were girls who had been to Bahia and Recife and even to Rio, and with them one could talk about clothes and ways of doing one's hair. It was not strange, then, if she was overjoyed when Virgilio had spoken of a stay in Ilhéos. Running up to him, she threw her arms about his neck and kissed him time and again on the mouth.

"How nice! How nice!"

But her happiness was of short duration, as he informed her that he could not take her with him. Before he had a chance to explain, she had burst out weeping and sobbing.

"You're ashamed of me!" she screamed. "Or else you've got somebody else in Ilhéos. You're quite capable of taking up with some brazen hussy. But I'm telling you, I'll scratch her eyes out, I'll make such a scandal that all the world will know about it. You don't know what I'm like when I'm angry."

Virgilio let her scream. When her tears and sobs had at last subsided, he began explaining, in a voice that he strove to make as caressing as possible, why it was that he could not take her. He was going on business, important business, and there would be no time for him to look after her. Surely she knew of the ugly situation between Horacio and the Badarós over the forest of Sequeiro Grande? She nodded her head; yes, she knew. But she could not see that that was any reason for his leaving her behind. As for his not having time to spend with her, that did not matter. He would not have to work all night long, and at night she could go to the café with him while they were in Ilhéos.

Virgilio was still seeking for arguments. He sensed that there was a reason for her attitude; the note of distrust that had crept into her voice, her vague accusations with regard to another woman, the half-angry, half-frightened look that she gave him—all of these signs were not lost upon him. If he was not taking her with him on this trip, it was not because he was going to be occupied solely with Horacio's affairs; he was also planning to have some time for Ester. For he was unable to put Ester out of his mind. He could still hear, day and night, that murmured plea for help, while her husband was on the veranda:

"Take me away from here—far, far away."

Virgilio knew that if Margot were in Ilhéos, it would not be long before she heard some bit of malevolent gossip, and then his life would be a hell; for she was capable of making a scandal that might involve Ester. Ester and Margot: he could not think of the two of them together; their names were not to be uttered in the same breath. The one had been the sweetheart of his wild student days. The other was the love that he had found among the forests, the love that comes one day and is stronger than the world. No, he did not want Margot with him, his mind was made up as to that. But he did not wish to hurt her, for he could not hurt a woman. Like a despairing man, he sought for some argument that would clinch the matter; and he believed that he had found it when he told Margot that if he did not want to leave her alone during the day in Ilhéos it was because he was jealous; Machadão's house, where she always put up, was the one most frequented by the wealthiest of the colonels. Yes, that was the reason that he was not taking her: he was jealous. As he said this, he endeavoured to put into his voice all the conviction that he could muster. Margot now was smiling through her tears, and he felt that he had won. He hoped that the matter was settled as she came over and seated herself in his lap.

"So you're jealous of your little girl?" she said. "Why? You know very well that I never pay attention to any propositions that are made to me. If I let myself be stuck away out here, it is for your sake. What reason, then, would I have for deceiving you?" Kissing him again, she went on: "Take me with you, honey; I swear I won't put my foot out the door except to go with you to the café. I won't leave my room; I won't talk to any man. While you're busy, I'll spend the day shut up in my room."

Virgilio felt himself weakening. He decided to change his tactics.

"I don't know what you find so terrible about Tabocas that you can't spend ten days here without my company. You only want to be in Ilhéos."

It was then that she rose and pointed to the street. "It's a cemetery."

With this she began talking once more about what a mistake

it was, his sacrificing his own future and her life like this. Again Virgilio thought of attempting an explanation; but he realized that it was of no use, that his affair with Margot had come to an end. Ever since he had known Ester he had had eyes for no other woman. Even in bed with Margot he was not the lover of old, sensual and passionately desirous of her body. Already he looked upon her charms with a certain indifference: the rounded thighs, the virgin breasts, all the little tricks that she knew by way of rendering the hour of love more pleasurable. His bosom was filled with desire, but it was desire of Ester; he wanted her, the whole of her: her thoughts, her body, her heart—everything. That was why it was he had remained open-mouthed, as if about to say something. Margot waited, and when he did not speak but merely raised a hand, as much as to say it was not worth the effort, she returned to the charge.

"You treat me like a slave, taking yourself off to Ilhéos and leaving me here. And now you come around with this story about being jealous. It's all a lie. I'm the one that's being made a fool of. But I'm not going to be one any longer. The next time anyone wants to take me to Ilhéos or Bahia, I'm going to clear out."

Virgilio was losing his temper. "So far as I'm concerned, my dear, you can go ahead. Do you think I'm going to die of a broken heart?"

She was furious. "Oh, what a fool I am! And with all the men there are running after me. Juca Badaró is just waiting for me to say the word. And here I am, making a fool of myself over you, while all you think about is traipsing off to Ilhéos. You've got some rich girl that you're marrying for her money, I'm sure of that."

Virgilio rose from his chair, his eyes flaring with anger. "Shut your mouth!"

"I won't shut my mouth! It must be true, all the same. You're out to pull the wool over some country girl's eyes and get your fingers on her money."

With the back of his hand Virgilio struck her on the mouth. As the blood spurted from her lip, a look of fright and astonishment came over Margot's face. She was about to hurl an insult at him, then broke into sobs.

"You don't love me any more or you wouldn't have struck me."

He too was disturbed by what he had done; he could not understand how he had come to do a thing like that. It occurred

133

to him that the very atmosphere of this country must be getting into his blood, must be changing him. He was not the same man who had arrived some months before from Bahia, every inch the gentleman, who never would have thought of striking a woman. Upon him, also, a civilized being from another region, the land of cacao had begun to weigh heavily. He hung his head in shame, gazing regretfully at his hand, then went up to Margot, took out his handkerchief, and wiped the drop of blood from her lip.

"Forgive me, my dear. I lost my head. I have so much on my mind, it makes me nervous. And then your talk about leaving me for Juca Badaró, about going away with another man. I didn't mean to—" She sobbed, and he added: "Don't cry any more; I'll take you to Ilhéos with me."

Margot raised her head; she was smiling already, for she believed that it was out of jealousy that he had struck her. She felt more his than ever now: Virgilio was her man. She huddled against him, making herself very small. And then, filled with desire, she drew him with her to the bedroom.

6

The shouts of the tailors reached Dr. Jessé as he went down the street: "Doctor! Dr. Jessé! Come here!"

The four tailors stood in the doorway of the Parisian Shears, the best tailor-shop in Tabocas, owned by Tonico Borges, who at the moment held the pieces of a pair of trousers in one hand and a needle and thread in the other. The Parisian Shears was not only the best tailor-ship in Tabocas; it was also, as everyone admitted, the headquarters for the most malicious local gossip. Here everything was known, even to the food that was eaten in private homes, and everything that happened was duly discussed. On this particular day the Parisian Shears was buzzing with excitement on account of the news that had just arrived from Ferradas in the wake of Horacio and his retinue. It was for this reason that Tonico Borges was shouting at the top of his voice for Dr. Jessé. The latter's presence was urgently needed by way of throwing light on a number of matters.

Short, squat, and puffing, his hat on the back of his head, his spectacles falling down over his nose, his boots thoroughly splashed with mud, the physician came up to them and inquired what it was they wanted of him. One of the tailors hastened to bring him a chair.

"Make yourself comfortable, doctor."

Dr. Jessé sat down, depositing his instrument-case on the brick floor. That case was famous in the town, for in it was to be found the most diverse collection of objects imaginable: everything from a bistoury to dried cacao seeds, from injections to ripe fruit, from medicine phials to rent receipts for the houses that the doctor owned. Tonico Borges, who had gone to the rear of the shop, now returned with a big, ripe avocado.

"I was saving that for you, doctor," he said.

Jessé thanked him and stowed the fruit away in his case. The tailors formed a circle about him, having drawn up their chairs as close to him as possible at a point that afforded them at the same time a view of the entire street.

"Well, what's new?" said Dr. Jessé.

"That's for you to tell us, doctor. You're the one that knows."

"Knows what?"

"Well, they're saying around here that things are getting hot between Colonel Horacio and the Badarós," one of the other tailors began.

"And that Juca Badaró is lining up people for his side." Tonico completed the sentence for him.

"You call that news?" said the doctor. "I could have—"

"But there's one thing I'll guarantee you don't know, doctor."

"Let's hear it."

"That Juca Badaró has already sent for an engineer to survey the forest of Sequeiro Grande."

"What's that you say? Where did you hear it?"

Tonico made a mysterious gesture. "A little bird told me, doctor. Is there anything in Tabocas that everybody doesn't know? When they have nothing to talk about, they make something up."

But Dr. Jessé was not satisfied with this. "Seriously speaking," he said, "who was it that told you?"

Tonico Borges lowered his voice: "It was Azevedo, who runs the hardware store. It was in his place that Juca wrote out the telegram sending for the man."

"That I didn't know. I'll have to get a message to friend Horacio this very day." The tailors glanced at one another; they did not like the look of things.

"They say," Tonico went on, "that Colonel Horacio has sent Dona Ester to Ilhéos, so that she will not be in danger on the plantation. They say he means to go into the forest this week, that he has an agreement with Braz, with Firmo, with José da

Ribeira, and with Jarde for the division of the timberland. He is to take half, and the rest is to be divided among them. Is that true, doctor?"

"It's news to me," replied the latter evasively.

"But, doctor," and Tonico Borges rolled his eyes, "it is even known that it was Lawyer Virgilio who drew up the contract, with a seal and everything. Ah! and Maneca Dantas, he's in on it, too. Everybody knows it, doctor; it's an open secret."

Dr. Jessé finally owned up, confessing, even, that he himself was to get a slice of the forest.

"So you have a finger in the pie, do you, doctor?" said Tonico, jestingly. Have you bought your Colt 38 yet? Or maybe you'd like an old-fashioned horse-pistol? I have one that I'll sell you, in good condition."

Dr. Jessé joined in the laugh that greeted this remark: "I'm pretty old to start out being a bad man."

They all laughed loudly, for Dr. Jessé's cowardice was proverbial. And the astonishing part of it was that, in spite of this, he was looked upon with respect in the land of cacao. For the one thing that would utterly ruin a man in the region that extended from Ferradas to Ilhéos was a reputation for being a coward: such a man was one without a future in these towns and highways. If there was one virtue that was required of any male who undertook to live in southern Bahia in this period of the opening up of the country, it was that of personal courage. How otherwise venture among these *jagunços* and *conquistadores*, these unscrupulous lawyers and remorseless assassins, unless one had a complete disregard as to whether one lived or died? The man who did not react to an insult, who fled from a row, who did not have some tale of personal bravery to relate—such a man was not taken seriously by the *grapiúnas*.

Dr. Jessé was the one exception to this rule. A physician in Tabocas, a councilman in Ilhéos, Horacio's perpetual candidate and one of the political leaders of the opposition, he was the sole person who could still retain the public's esteem in spite of the fact that all knew him to be chicken-hearted. His cowardice was indeed proverbial, being employed as a standard of measurement for that of others: "He's almost as big a coward as Dr. Jessé" or "He's a bigger coward than Dr. Jessé ever thought of being." This was not, as might be imagined, a gibe levelled at him by his political enemies; the members of his own party knew that they could not count on him when a row was brewing. Stories that went to prove the doctor's lack of courage were told even in the wine-shops and the houses of prostitution.

For example, in connection with another brawl here in Tabocas, comparable to the one between Horacio and the Badarós, it was related how Dr. Jessé had gone down to a whorehouse and hidden himself underneath a bed. Then there was that rally in Ilhéos during the last campaign for the election of senators and deputies. There had come down from Bahia, as the opposition candidate for this region, a young fellow, son of a former Governor of the state, who was just beginning his political career. He was frightened out of his wits; for he had been told terrible things about this country, and he expected every minute to receive a bullet or a dagger-thrust. Horacio had sent his lads over to keep order at the meeting, and they had taken their places about the speakers' platform, revolvers in their belts, ready for anything. The Badaró ruffians, meanwhile, had scattered out through the crowd, being anxious to hear the young fellow from Bahia, who had the reputation of being a good speaker. Half drunk as always, Lawyer Ruy had opened the meeting, with a few digs at the federal government. Then came Dr. Jessé, whose business it was to introduce the candidate to the voters; and finally the visitor himself. The latter walked to the front of the small platform, which had been hastily improvised out of planks and packing cases and which swayed beneath the weight of the speakers, and cleared his throat by way of claiming the attention of his hearers. A dead silence fell.

"Senhoras, senhores, and senhoritas," he began. "I—"

That was as far as he got. There being no senhoras and no senhoritas present, some rowdy cried out: "Your mother was a senhorita!" There was a laugh at this, while others called for silence. The speaker then said something about "lack of breeding," and in the hullabaloo that followed, the lads from the Badaró estate drew their guns and began firing, with Horacio's men answering in kind. It was at this point, as the tale had it, that the youthful candidate tried to crawl under the platform in order to escape the bullets that were whirring about his head, but he found the space already occupied by Dr. Jessé, who not only refused to make room for him, but who reproved him severely.

"If you don't want to ruin yourself forever, sir, you'd better get back up there. I'm the only one around here who has a right to hide, for everybody knows that I'm a coward."

The youth from Bahia, however, could not see it that way, and when he forcibly insisted on crawling under the platform, a tussle ensued. This was said to be the one and only time that Dr.

Jessé had ever been known to get into a brawl, and the bystanders, who were in a position to take it all in, asserted that it was the funniest sight they had ever seen—like a hair-pulling match between two women trying to scratch each other's eyes out.

Tonico Borges drew up his chair to the doctor's side. "Do you know who came to town this morning?"

"Who?"

"Colonel Teodoro. They say he's siding with the folks up at the plantation."

Dr. Jessé was astonished. "Teodoro? What has he got to do with it?"

Tonico could not tell him. "All I know is, he came in with a lot of *jagunços*. What he's up to I couldn't say. But he's got nerve, eh, doctor?"

"I'll say he has," put in another of the tailors, "coming into Tabocas like that, with so many of Colonel Horacio's men here. And then that answer he sent back—how did it go, Tonico?"

Tonico knew it by heart: "The answer he gave Maneca Dantas was: 'You can tell Horacio that I'm not joining up with anybody like him, that I don't do business with muledrivers.'"

Such was the response that Maneca had received when, in Horacio's name, he had gone to invite Teodoro to join them in the conquest of the Sequeiro Grande forest. Dr. Jessé was fairly agape by this time.

"Why," he said, "you know everything. Life is cheap here, and no one escapes."

One of the tailors laughed. "It's a great sport down this way, doctor."

Tonico Borges then wanted to know if Horacio had given any orders concerning Teodoro, in case the latter came to Tabocas.

"I don't know—I don't know anything." And the doctor picked up his case and hurriedly rose, as if he had remembered something urgent that he had to do. But before he left, Tonico had a final bit of gossip for him:

"They tell me, doctor, that Lawyer Virgilio is hanging around Dona Ester."

Dr. Jessé's manner was grave, as he paused with one foot in the door.

"If you want the advice of a man who has lived in these parts for going on twenty years," he said, "here it is: say anything you want to about anything and anybody, say anything you want to

138

about Horacio, even, but don't ever say anything about that wife of his. For if he hears of it, I wouldn't give a penny for your life. That's a friend's advice."

With this he went out, leaving Tonico Borges ghastly pale with fright.

"Do you think he will tell Colonel Horacio?" Tonico asked the others.

Despite their assurances that Dr. Jessé would not do so, that he was a good fellow, Tonico could not rest until he had gone around to the physician's consulting-room and had asked him not to tell the colonel; for that story had been told him "by the woman who lived with Margot, and who had overheard a quarrel between Virgilio and his girl about some wench or other, who, she thought, might be Dona Ester."

"This is a terrible place, doctor," he concluded. "They talk about everybody. No one can escape their tongues. But my mouth is sealed from now on. You won't hear a peep out of me. I was only telling *you*, doctor."

"Don't let it worry you," said Dr. Jessé soothingly. "So far as I am concerned, Horacio will never know anything about it. But now the best thing for you to do is to keep quiet. Unless you're thinking of committing suicide."

He opened the door, Tonico went out, and a woman came in. The doctor at once began rummaging in his surgical case for a stethoscope. In the waiting-room men and women sat conversing. One woman with a child by the hand, upon catching sight of the tailor, left her chair and came up to him.

"How are you, friend Tonico?" she inquired with a smile.

"Very well, Dona Zefinha. And you, senhora?"

She made no reply, for she was in a hurry to tell him what she knew.

"Have you heard of the scandal?"

"What scandal?"

"Colonel Totonho of Riacho Doce has left his wife and family to go chasing after a hussy, some flighty young thing from Bahia. They got on the train together, in plain sight of everybody."

Tonico made a gesture of boredom. "That's old, Dona Zefinha," he said. "But I have some news that I'll guarantee you haven't heard, senhora."

The woman was bursting with curiosity; her body was trembling all over from nervousness. "What is it, friend

Tonico?" Tonico hesitated a moment, as Dona Zefinha waited anxiously. "Go ahead and tell me." He glanced around in all directions, then drew her down the hall.

"They're saying around here," he began in a low voice, "that Lawyer Virgilio—" He whispered the rest in the old lady's ear.

"Can it be possible!" exclaimed the latter. "Now, who would have thought of anything like that!"

"I haven't said a word, remember," Tonico admonished her. "I'm only telling *you*, senhora."

"Now, friend Tonico, you know very well that my lips are sealed. But who would have thought it? She always seemed such a perfect lady."

Tonico disappeared through the doorway. Returning to the waiting-room, Dona Zefinha looked the other patients over. There was no one there worth her while, so she decided to let her grandchild's injection go until the next day. Saying good afternoon to the others, she remarked that it was getting late and she could not wait any longer, as she had an appointment at the dentist's. She went out dragging the child behind her. The tidbit she had just heard was burning her tongue, and she was as happy as if she had held the winning ticket in the lottery. With all speed she set out for the home of the Aventinos, three old maids who lived near St. Joseph's Church.

7

Dr. Jessé examined the patient, mechanically tapped his chest, front and back, listened to his breathing, told him to say "thirty-three." But the truth was his mind was far away, occupied with other things. His office had been full of people today. It was always like that. Whenever he was in a hurry or distracted, his waiting-room would be filled with patients who had nothing whatsoever the matter with them, who just came to take up his time. Telling the man to put his clothes on, he scrawled a prescription.

"Have that made up for you at St. Joseph's Pharmacy; they will give you a better price there." This did not happen to be the truth, but St. Joseph's Pharmacy belonged to a member of the opposition party, whereas the Springtime was the property of one of the Badaró followers.

"Nothing serious, is it, doctor?"

"It's nothing. Just a little catarrh from the forest rains. Take the medicine and you'll be all right. Come back in a couple of weeks."

"But I can't do that, doctor. I lose money, you know, leaving the grove to run down here. The place where I work is a long way off."

Dr. Jessé sought to cut the conversation short.

"All right, come back when you can. You've got nothing serious the matter with you."

The man paid his fee and the doctor pushed him toward the door. Another patient then came in, an aged plantation labourer with bare feet and clad in working-clothes. He had come for medicine for his wife, who "has a fever that comes and goes and lays her flat on her back every month." As the man told his long-drawn-out story, Dr. Jessé was thinking of what he had heard in the tailor-shop. There had been two pieces of disagreeable news. First there was Teodoro's coming to Tabocas. What the devil was he up to? He must know that Tabocas was not a healthy place for him. But Teodoro was a man of courage, who liked to kick up a row. If he came to Tabocas, he was certainly up to no good. Dr. Jessé should have got a message to Horacio, who was in Ilhéos, but the worst of it was, the train had already left and he would not be able to do anything until the next day. In any case, he must talk to Lawyer Virgilio at once.

And then he recalled the second piece of news: the gossip that was going around town about Virgilio and Ester—the latter and Horacio had been the godparents of one of the doctor's numerous progeny—he now had nine all together, like stairs, each being a year older than the preceding one. Dr. Jessé did some thinking. He remembered. Ester had spent four days in Tabocas while waiting for Horacio to arrange his affairs so that he might accompany her to Ilhéos. During those four days Virgilio had frequently been at the doctor's house, where the colonel was a guest. He and Ester had spent an enormous amount of time together in the parlour, talking and laughing. Jessé himself had had to put a stop to the servants' chattering. But worst of all had been that party at the home of Rezende, a merchant whose wife was having a birthday. There had been refreshments; and afterwards, since they had a piano in the house and young ladies who played it, they had got up a dance on the spur of the moment. Now, in Tabocas a married woman did not dance. Even in Ilhéos, when one who was "more modern" ventured to do so, was with her husband. Hence the scandal when Ester stepped out on the floor to dance with Virgilio. Dr. Jessé recalled that Virgilio had asked Horacio's permission to dance with her, and the latter had granted it, being proud to see his wife shine in company. But the people of the town did not know this and went on gossiping. It was bad business. As bad or even worse than Teodoro's coming to town. Dr. Jessé scratched his head. Ah, if Horacio should come to hear of it! There would be the devil to pay. The patient had now finished telling of his wife's troubles and was waiting silently for the doctor's diagnosis.

"You don't think it's the ague, do you, doctor?"

Dr. Jessé gave him a startled look. He had forgotten all about the man's being there. He had him repeat the details.

"Yes, it's swamp fever," he agreed.

He prescribed quinine and recommended St. Joseph's Pharmacy; but his thoughts were once more with Tabocas and the complications of life. So the wicked tongues—and who in Tabocas did not have a wicked tongue?—were meddling with Ester's personal affairs? Bad business, that was what it was. To hear these folks tell it, there was not a married woman who was respectable. There was nothing that the town so enjoyed as a scandal or a tragedy growing out of a love-affair. And then, on top of it all, that news about Teodoro. What the devil was he up to, anyhow?

Slipping on his coat, Dr. Jessé went out to call upon two or three of his patients. In each house he was obliged to enter into a discussion of the looming row over the forest of Sequeiro Grande. Everybody wanted the latest news; and seeing that the doctor was Horacio's intimate friend, he ought to be in a position to give it to them. After that he went down to the school, of which he had been superintendent ever since a preceding government, that of his own party, had been in power. He had never been dismissed from the post, for that would have created too much of a scandal, in view of the fact that it was he who had had the new building erected, while the teachers, all of whom were women, strongly supported him. Entering the courtyard, he made his way through an outer room. By this time he had forgotten all about Ester, and all about Teodoro as well. He had forgotten all about the forest of Sequeiro Grande. He was thinking of the celebration the school was planning for Arbour Day, later in the week. The children playing in the courtyard came running up to clasp the doctor's short, stout legs, and he now dispatched two or three of them to go in search of the assistant superintendent and the teacher of Portuguese. Then he crossed another classroom, the pupils rising as he came through. Making a sign for them to be seated, he went on to where the assistant superintendent and a number of the other teachers were waiting for him.

Dropping into a seat, and placing his hat and medicine-case on a table, he took out a handkerchief and wiped the sweat that was streaming from his fat face.

"The program is all prepared," the assistant superintendent informed him.

"Let's hear about it."

"Well, first we'll have the meeting here, a speech—"

"Dr. Virgilio cannot be present, for he's going in to Ilhéos tomorrow on business for Colonel Horacio. Estanislau will speak, of course."

Estanislau was a teacher in a private school and an obligatory speaker at any affair in Ferradas. In each address that he made, whatever the occasion, he invariably employed the same figures of rhetoric, the same metaphors, until the town had come to know by heart what they called "Estanislau's speech."

"That's too bad," said one of the teachers, regretfully. She was a thin little creature who was a great admirer of Virgilio. "He makes such a nice speech and he is so good-looking."

The others laughed. Dr. Jessé was still mopping the sweat.

"What can I do for you?" he asked.

The assistant superintendent went on outlining the arrangements.

"Well, then: first the formal meeting in the school; a speech by Professor Estanislau" (she corrected the name on the program as she read); "then a recitation by the pupils; and in conclusion they will all sing the 'Arbour Day Song.' After that they will form in line and march to Church Square. There they will plant a cacao tree, Dr. Freitas will give his talk, and Professora Irene will read a poem."

"Very good, very good," said the doctor, rubbing his hands. Opening his satchel, he took out a number of sheets of manuscript paper, folded in half lengthwise. This was his speech, which he now began to read to the teachers. As he read, in a loud and ringing voice, he grew more and more enthusiastic and rose to his feet so as to be better able to make all the appropriate gestures. The children crowded about the door and, in spite of repeated "shushes" from the assistant superintendent, could not

143

keep silent. It made little difference to Dr. Jessé, however, for he was intoxicated with his own eloquence, as he read, with emphasis:

"The tree is a gift of God to men. It is our vegetable brother, which gives us cooling shade, luscious fruit, and wood that is so useful in the construction of furniture and other objects that go to increase our comfort. Out of the trunks of trees were built those caravels which led to the discovery of our beloved Brazil. Children ought to love and respect trees."

"Very nice, very nice," the assistant superintendent applauded; and the others chimed in: "Very pretty—it will be a big success."

Dr. Jessé was sweating at every pore. Running his handkerchief over his face, he gave a bark at the children who were still standing in the door and who now scurried away.

"So it's good, eh?" he said, seating himself once more. "I dashed it off last night. I wasn't able to work on it these past few days, for my friend and his wife were at our house and I had to do the honours."

"If what I hear is true," said one of the teachers, "that shouldn't have been necessary in Dona Ester's case. They say Dr. Virgilio does them all day long."

"Oh, they talk about everybody," the thin-looking one protested. "That always happens in a backward place like this." She came from Bahia and could not get used to the ways of Tabocas.

Another teacher, who was a *grapiúna*—that is to say, a native—took offence at this. "I don't know what you call backward," she said, "unless you think that certain shameless carryings-on that I could mention are a sign of progress. Maybe it's progress to stand in the doorway until ten o'clock at night hanging on to young men. If so, then thank God Tabocas *is* backward."

This was an allusion to a love-affair that the skinny teacher was having with a lad who also came from Bahia and who was employed by an export house. The entire town was scandalized by it. But the object of their gossip stood her ground.

"Is it me you're talking about? Very well, then, I'll have you know that I will do what I please. I don't care what anybody thinks about it. My life's my own; why should others meddle with it? I'll stand there talking until any hour I see fit. I prefer that to being an old maid like you. I wasn't born to be a dried-up heifer."

Dr. Jessé took a hand at this point.

"Be calm now," he said, "be calm. There are things that are talked about for good reason, and there are other things that are exaggerated for no reason at all. Just because a young man calls upon a married lady and lends her a few books to read, is that any cause for making a scandal? That really is backward."

They all agreed that it was. Moreover, according to the assistant superintendent, that was as far as the talk went. People merely had noticed that the young attorney was in the habit of spending practically the entire day at the doctor's house, talking to Dona Ester in the parlour. The teacher who had protested when the skinny one spoke of Tabocas being a backward place now added a further comment:

"That Dr. Virgilio doesn't even respect the family life of the town. Why, he keeps a fast woman in a respectable street, and it's a scandal every time they say good-bye to each other. They stand there hugging and kissing so that everybody can see."

The other teachers gave an excited little laugh at this, and Dr. Jessé himself was anxious for more details. The moralistic one, who lived near Margot, thereupon grew expansive.

"It's immoral, that's what it is. As I was saying to Father Tomé, one can sin without meaning to; one can sin with one's eyes and with one's ears. With a woman like that coming to the door in a dressing-gown that's open half-way down the front—almost naked—and hanging on to Dr. Virgilio's neck as they stand there kissing and slobbering over each other, worse than a couple of dogs, and saying all kinds of things."

"What do they say?" the teacher from Bahia wanted to know. Her body was twitching nervously and there was a convulsive look in her eyes as she listened to the description of the scene.

The other teacher now had her revenge. "Wouldn't it be backward for me to tell you?"

"Don't be a fool. Tell us."

"It's 'my little puppy-dog' here and 'my little kitty-cat' there, 'my pretty little poodle,' and—" here she dropped her voice and covered her face with her hands, at thought of the doctor's presence—"and 'my bounding little filly.'"

"What was that?" said the assistant superintendent, blushing furiously.

"Just what I told you. It's immoral."

"And in a family street," put in another.

"Yes, in broad daylight the people come from other streets to look on. It's a free show, like being in a theatre," she added by way of summing it all up.

Dr. Jessé clapped a hand to his head; he had remembered something.

"Theatre— There's a rehearsal today; I had forgotten all about it. I shall have to snatch a bite and run or I'll hold up everything."

Almost on the run now, he made his way out of the empty building, through the deserted classrooms and silent courtyards. The voice of the teachers, still discussing Lawyer Virgilio, followed him all the way to the street entrance; it was the only sound to be heard.

"It's indecent. . . ."

Dr. Jessé had a hasty meal, and then, after answering his wife's questions about the health of one Ribeirinho, a patient who was a friend of theirs, and pulling one of his children's ears, he set out for the Lauro home, where he was to direct the Tabocas Amateur Group, which was giving a performance soon. Already there was being circulated through the town all the way to Ferradas a hand-bill announcing:

SATURDAY, JUNE 10

ST. JOSEPH'S THEATRE

WILL PRESENT AN OUTSTANDING DRAMA IN FOUR ACTS

SOCIAL VAMPIRES

Watch for Announcement

TABOCAS AMATEUR GROUP

BIG DRAMATIC EVENT!

There was politics, there was his family, there was his medical practice, there were his groves and his houses to rent, there was the school—there were all of these things with which to occupy his mind, but Dr. Jessé Freitas's one real and grand passion was

146

the Tabocas Amateur Group. It was something that he had dreamed of for years, but difficulties had always arisen. First of all, he had had to engage in a stubborn struggle to overcome the refusal of the young ladies of the town to take part in a theatrical performance. If he finally had succeeded, it had been owing to the word put in for him by the daughter of a rich merchant of Tabocas who had just come back from Rio, where she had been in school. She had urged the others to "stop being so silly" and to go ahead and join the Amateur Group. Even so, Dr. Jessé had had to obtain the consent of the fathers, and this had not been easy: "I only permit it because it is you who ask it, doctor." Others had refused outright: "This business of the theatre is not for any self-respecting young girl."

The group, none the less, had been formed at last and had given its first performance, a drama written by Professor Estanislau entitled *The Fall of the Bastille*. It had been an enormous success. The mothers of the actors had hardly been able to contain themselves with pride, and there were even a few quarrels started as to whose daughter had played her part the best. Dr. Jessé had promptly begun directing another play, this time one of his own, based upon a theme from national history having to do with Pedro II. It had been given for the benefit of the church building fund; for the church was then in process of construction. In spite of a regrettable incident that had occurred upon the stage between two of the performers, this piece likewise had been a success and had definitely established the prestige of the Tabocas Amateur Group. That organization had now become the pride of the town, and each time that a resident of Tabocas went in to Ilhéos, he did not fail to speak of the "Amateurs," if only to annoy the city folk, who, while they had a very good theatre, did not have a company of their own. Dr. Jessé was counting upon the success of the *Social Vampires*—a work that was also from his pen—in his effort to persuade the mothers to allow their daughters to go to the city and give a performance there.

He spent long hours directing them. He would make the young women and the young men repeat their lines over and over again, with prolonged gestures, tremulous voice, and an affected style of delivery. He would applaud one, correct another, mop the perspiration from his brow, and beam with happiness.

It was only as he left the rehearsal that he once more remembered the forest of Sequeiro Grande, Teodoro, Ester, and

147

Lawyer Virgilio. Taking up his medicine-case, where the original manuscript pages of the play were mingled with phials and dressings, he hastened to the attorney's home. Not finding him there, he set out for the house where Margot lived. The church bell had just sounded the hour of nine and the streets were deserted. The Amateurs were on their way home, the young ladies being accompanied by their mothers. A drunkard on the corner was muttering to himself. In a wineshop men were discussing politics. The kerosene street-lamps were pale in the light of the moon.

Lawyer Virgilio was in his pyjamas and Margot's voice could be heard from the bedroom, inquiring who was there.

"Did you know that Colonel Teodoro has been in town?" asked Dr. Jessé as he deposited his case on a chair in the parlour. "You had better get word to our friend Horacio. Nobody seems to know what he's up to."

"He's looking for trouble, that's certain."

"And there's something still more serious."

"Go ahead. What is it?"

"They are saying the Juca Badaró has sent for an engineer to survey the forest of Sequeiro Grande so that he can take out a title to the property."

Virgilio gave a self-satisfied laugh. "What do you think my business is as a lawyer? Doctor, that forest has already been entered, with a survey and everything, in the office of Venancio, the registrar, as the property of Colonel Horacio, Braz, Maneca Dantas, the widow Merenda, Firmo, Jarde, and—" here he raised his voice slightly—"Dr. Jessé Freitas. You will have to go down and sign the papers tomorrow."

As the attorney went on to explain the "ouster" that had been effected, the physician's face expanded in a grin.

"Congratulations, doctor. That's a master stroke."

Virgilio smiled modestly. "It cost a couple of *contos de reis* to convince the registrar. The rest was easy. We'll see what they do now. We've stolen a march on them."

Dr. Jessé was silent for a moment. It was a master stroke, no doubt of that. Horacio had got there ahead of the Badarós, and he was the owner of the forest—he and his friends, among whom was Dr. Jessé. He rubbed his fat hands together, one inside the other.

"It's a good piece of work. There's not another lawyer around here like you, sir. Well, I'll have to be going; I'll leave you two"—and he pointed to the bedroom where Margot was

148

waiting—"alone. This is no time to talk. Good night, doctor."

At first Dr. Jessé had thought of sounding Virgilio out on the subject of the gossip that was going around about him and Ester. He had even thought of advising the lawyer, while in Ilhéos, not to be seen too often at Horacio's place. Tongues in the city were quite as malicious as they were here in town. But now he decided to say nothing; he was afraid of offending the attorney, of hurting him, and not for anything in the world would he have done that today to one who had given the Badarós so serious a set-back.

Virgilio accompanied his guest to the door. As he went down the street, Dr. Jessé encountered no one whom he felt to be deserving of such a piece of news. Legally the Badarós were done for. What could they do now, anyway? Upon reaching the wine-shop, he glanced inside the door.

"Will you have something, doctor?" asked one of the pair who stood there drinking. Here, too, there was no worthy audience. The doctor accordingly countered with a question: "Do you know where Tonico Borges went?"

"He's gone to bed," said one of the men. "I met him a short while ago; he was headed for the whorehouse."

Dr. Jessé made a face to show his annoyance. He would have to keep the big news until the next day. He walked on, with the short, light step of the heavy man. But before coming to his own house he paused for a moment to make out whose cacao it was that was being brought into town by a troop of fifteen burros, to the jingling of bells and the shouts of a pack-driver that woke the neighbourhood:

"Whoa, there, you damned burro, you! Get up, there, Jack-knife!"

8

The man was out of breath as he burst into the hardware store.

"Friend Azevedo! Friend Azevedo!"

The clerk came up to him. "Azevedo's in the back, friend Ignacio."

The man went on to the rear of the shop, where Azevedo, engaged in balancing his books, was leafing through a big ledger. He turned as the other came in. "What is it, Ignacio?"

"Then you haven't heard, sir?"

"Speak up, man. What is it? Something serious?"

Ignacio paused for breath; he had been running, almost.

"I just heard it, this very minute. You can't imagine—it will bowl you over."

Azevedo put aside pencil, paper, and his ledger and waited impatiently.

"It's the biggest 'ouster' that you ever heard tell of. Lawyer Virgilio has greased Venancio's palm and has entered title to the forest of Sequeiro Grande in the name of Colonel Horacio and five or six others—Braz, Dr. Jessé, Colonel Maneca, I don't know who all."

Azevedo rose from his chair: "And the survey? What about that? Their title is no good."

"Oh, it's all legal, right enough, friend Azevedo. It's all as legal as can be, down to the last comma. That young fellow is a crackerjack of a lawyer. He's looked after everything. There has already been a survey made, an old one, for Mundinho de Almeida while he was still alive, the time he was starting to open up a grove in that region. It was never registered because Colonel Mundinho cashed in his checks. But Venancio has the documents."

"I didn't know that."

"Don't you remember Colonel Mundinho's sending for a surveyor from Bahia, an old fellow with a beard who could outdrink the colonel himself?"

"Ah, yes, I remember now."

"Well, Lawyer Virgilio dug up that old survey, and the rest was easy; all he had to do was to change the names and enter it at the registry office. They say that Venancio got ten contos for his trouble."

Azevedo realized what all this meant.

"Ignacio," he said, "I'm much obliged to you. This is a favour I won't forget. You're the kind of a friend to have. And now I must get word right away to Sinhô Badaró. He will be grateful to you, you know that."

Ignacio smiled. "Tell Colonel Sinhô that I'm at his service. So far as I'm concerned, he's the only leader in these parts. So the minute I heard of it, I came straight here."

As Ignacio went out, Azevedo stood for a moment deep in thought. Then, taking up his pen, he bent over the table and in a laboured hand wrote a letter to Sinhô Badaró; after which he sent the clerk for a man to take it to its destination. The messenger came a few minutes later. He was a dark-skinned mulatto, barefoot but wearing spurs, and with a revolver sticking out from under his ragged coat.

"You sent for me, Mr. Azevedo?"

"Militão, I want you to get on my horse, ride as fast as you can to the Badaró plantation, and give this letter to Sinhô. Tell him it's from me and that it's urgent."

"Shall I go by way of Ferradas, Mr. Azevedo?"

"It's a lot shorter that way."

"They say Colonel Horacio has ordered them not to let any Badaró people through there."

"That's all talk. You're not afraid, are you?"

"Did you ever know me to be afraid? I just wanted to make sure."

"All right, then. Sinhô will pay you well, for it's an important piece of news."

The man took the letter. "Any answer?" he asked before leaving to go for the horse.

"No."

"Well, then, see you later, Mr. Azevedo."

"Good luck, Militão."

At the door the man turned his head: "Mr. Azevedo."

"What is it?"

"If I should be left in the street in Ferradas, you'll look after my wife and kids, won't you?"

9

Don' Ana Badaró stood on the veranda of the Big House conversing with a man who had just dismounted.

"He's gone to Ilhéos, Militão."

"And Mr. Juca?"

"He's not here, either. Is it something urgent?"

"I think it is, miss. Mr. Azevedo told me to lose no time in getting here and to come by way of Ferradas because it's a shorter road—and they're ready for war there."

"How did you make it?"

"I cut in behind the pesthouse—no one saw me."

Don' Ana turned over the letter in her hand.

"So you think it might be urgent?" she asked again.

"I think so, Don' Ana. Mr. Azevedo told me it was very important and couldn't wait. He even sent me on his own horse."

Don' Ana came to a decision, opened the letter, and proceeded to decipher Azevedo's scrawl. Her face grew hard. "Bandits!" She started into the house, the letter in her hand, then remembered the bearer. "Raimunda! Raimunda!" she called.

"What is it, godmother?"

"Serve Militão some rum, here on the veranda."

Entering the parlour, she began pacing up and down from one side of the room to the other. She had the appearance of one of the Badaró brothers when they were thinking things out or engaged in a discussion. She ended by seating herself in Sinhô's high-backed chair, her face still set in hard lines, her mind wholly taken up with the news she had received. Her father and uncle were in Ilhéos, and this was a matter that could not wait. What ought she to do? Send the letter on to her father? It would not get to Ilhéos until the next day, and that would mean too great a delay. Then, suddenly, she remembered; and rising, she returned to the veranda. Militão was sipping his rum.

"Are you very tired, Militão?"

"No, miss. It was a short twenty miles or so."

"Very well, then, I want you to ride on over to the Baraúnas. I want you to take a message to Colonel Teodoro. Tell him he should come here and talk to me at once. And you come back with him."

"At your service, Don' Ana."

"Tell him to come as quickly as he can. Tell him it's serious."

Militão mounted his horse once more. "Good afternoon, miss," he said, as he patted the animal's neck. She remained on the veranda gazing after him as he rode off. She surely was taking responsibilities upon herself. What would Sinhô say when he knew? Once more she read over Azevedo's letter and then decided that she had done the right thing in sending for Teodoro."

"Bandits!" she muttered. "And that little wretch of a lawyer—he deserves a bullet."

The cat came up and rubbed against her legs, and Don' Ana put her hand down and stroked it gently. Her face, with its deep, dark eyes and sensual lips, was no longer hard; there was a tinge of melancholy to it, that was all. Glimpsed thus on the veranda, Don' Ana Badaró might have been a timid little country girl.

10

At the school things were going very well. Dr. Jessé had succeeded in persuading a number of merchants to close their shops and stores in honour of Arbour Day. Outside of teachers and pupils, the audience at the school building, where Professor

Estanislau read his speech and some of the children gave recitations, was a small one; but Church Square was filled. The doctor presided at the indoor session and was presented with a flowering tree bough. Then they all marched to the square, where the pupils from the town's two private schools were lined up and waiting for them. These other institutions were conducted, respectively, by Estanislau and by Dona Guilhermina, a teacher noted for the stern discipline that she enforced. Dr. Jessé walked at the head of the children from the public school, holding the bough in his hand.

The square, as had been said, was full of people. Women in holiday garb, young girls glancing about for their sweethearts, and merchants and clerks from those business houses which had closed for the day—all were there to avail themselves of this unlooked-for diversion, this variation in the dull rhythm of small town life. The public-school children drew up in front of those from the private institutions; and Professor Estanislau, who had a long-standing difference with Dona Guilhermina, now came forward to impose silence on his young wards—he wanted them to behave at least as well as those of his rival, standing there quiet and sober-faced beneath the schoolmistress's shrewish eye. Beside a hole that had recently been dug in the middle of the square they had placed a young cacao tree, a little more than a year old. This was the tree that was to be planted as the climax of today's ceremony. The Badarós had been called away to Ilhéos, and the police deputy with them, and for that reason the police force—consisting of eight troopers—did not put in an appearance; but the Euterpe Third of May Band, which was outfitted with Horacio's money, was there with its musical instruments. It was the band that inaugurated the ceremonies, by playing the national anthem, and the men removed their hats and silence fell as the children sang the verses. The sun was burning hot and a number of parasols had been opened as a protection against its rays.

As the band ceased playing, Dr. Jessé stepped well into the centre of the square and began his speech. On all sides there were calls for silence as the teachers went among the pupils in an effort to quiet them. With no great results, however; the only ones who were quiet were those from Dona Guilhermina's school, as that lady herself, in a white stiffly starched dress, stood there grimly with her hands folded over her bosom. Almost no one was able to hear what the speaker was saying, and very few had even a glimpse of him, since there was no raised platform and he had to speak from the ground level. Nevertheless, when he had finished there was much applause, and a number of men who had ridden up on horseback came over to compliment him. He modestly grasped their outstretched hands with a show of deep emotion. And then, in turn, he was the first to call for silence so that they might be able to hear Professora Irene's poem. In a thin, piping voice, the teacher began reading:

"Blessed be the seed that renders fertile the earth—"

The children were calling, all but shouting, to the sweetmeat-venders, as they laughed, chatted, quarrelled, and exchanged kicks, the teachers meanwhile threatening dire punishments for the next day. Professora Irene raised an arm, lowered it, raised the other arm:

"O blessed tree that gives us shade and fruit—"

The number of horsemen in the vicinity had been increasing, and they now came bursting into Church Square. It was Colonel Teodoro das Baraúnas at the head of a band of armed men. They came in firing shots in the air as their horses trampled down the grass. Riding into the midst of the scampering children and the fleeing men and women, Teodoro reined up in front of the group that was clustered about the tree. With arm still upraised, Professora Irene gulped back the verse that she was about to recite next.

"What nonsense is this?" said Teodoro, revolver in hand. "Are you planting a tree here in the square?"

Jessé, his voice trembling, explained the nature of the ceremony. Teodoro laughed; he appeared to fall in with it.

"Go ahead and plant it," he said. "I want to watch you." Saying this, he aimed his revolver and the lads who were with him levelled their rifles. Assisted by a couple of men, Dr. Jessé did as he was told. The ceremony, surely, was turning out quite differently from the way he had planned it. There was no dignity to it at all; they merely stuck the cacao tree in the ground as quickly as they could and covered the roots over with the earth heaped at the side of the hole. There were very few people left in the square; most of them had run away.

"Are you through now?" asked Teodoro.

"Yes, we have now—"

"All right," laughed Teodoro, "I'll give it a little dew." And, seated in the saddle, he opened the flap of his trousers and proceeded to urinate on the tree. His aim was not very good, however, and he bespattered everybody. Professora Irene covered her eyes with her hand. Before Teodoro had finished, he turned around and splashed Dr. Jessé. Then, calling to his men, he set off at a swift gallop down the main street. Those who had not been able to flee stood motionless, gazing at one another. One of the teachers wiped a drop or two from her face. "Did you ever see anything like it?" said another in amazement.

Still firing in the air, Teodoro rode down the street. Finally he and his men drew up at the corner of an alleyway, in front of Venancio's registry office, where they all dismounted. Venancio and his clerks barely had time to scamper out through the rear. Calling to one of his followers, Teodoro had him bring a bottle, and he then began sprinkling kerosene on the floor and on the files crammed with papers, after which he tossed the bottle away.

"Set fire to it," he ordered.

The man struck a match, and flame ran over the floor and up one of the filing-cases, until it encountered a sheaf of papers, whereupon it began to fatten on the documents and archives that the place contained. Teodoro and the man then ran out to where the others were standing guard on the corner, waiting for the fire to take hold. The colonel wore a white coat over khaki trousers, and on his little finger he sported a diamond solitaire. Red tongues of flame were now running over the building, as the street rapidly filled with people. Teodoro ordered his men to mount, and with their horses' hoofs the plantation lads now dispersed those who in their curiosity had drawn too near.

At this moment a band of Horacio's armed men made their appearance, and Teodoro, rounding the corner with his *capangas*, made for the Mutuns road. The crowd began surging into the street and Venancio appeared, tearing his hair, as Horacio's retainers came riding up. From the corner the latter opened fire on the fleeing band and Teodoro's men fired back, galloping headlong all the while through the throng that had come running down the alley to see the blaze. Before the master of Baraúnas was lost from sight at the end of the street, one of his *jagunços* had fallen, his riderless horse still galloping along with the others. Horacio's bucks then went up to the fellow and finished him off with a knife.

IV
BESIDE THE SEA

~~~~~~

1

The man in the sky-blue vest did not answer. He was a little runt
of a man, and that enormous vest of his hung down over his
brown canvas trousers, browner still from stains.

The night outside was a lyric one, and the poetry of the night
penetrated even to the tallow-smelling bar of the wine-shop, by
way of a bit of moonlight on the cobblestones of the street, a
glimpse of stars through the half-opened doors, and a woman's
languorous, mournful voice singing a song of lost love and the
days of long ago. More disturbing than the moonlight and the
stars, the sinful scent of jasmine from next door, or the glow of
lights from the ship—most disturbing of all, perhaps, to the tired
hearts of the men drowsing on packing-cases or sprawled over
the bar, was that melancholy song in the night.

The man with the big imitation ring repeated the question
when the one in the sky-blue vest failed to reply.

"And you, you old snail, you, didn't you ever have a
woman?"

It was the blond-haired one, however, who replied: "Now, if
it's a woman you're talking of—there are dozens of them in every
port. A woman is something that a sailor never has to go
without. For my part, I've had them by the dozen," and he made
a gesture with his hands, opening and closing his fingers.

The prostitute spit between her rotting teeth and eyed the blond sailor with interest.

"A sailor's heart," she said, "is like the waves of the sea that come and go. There was José de Santa—I knew him well. One day he went off without saying a word, on a boat that wasn't even his."

"Well," continued the sailor, "a seagoing man can't cast anchor anywhere, not even in a woman's flesh. One day he's off, the dock's empty, and then another comes along and throws out a grappling-line. A woman, my dear, is more treacherous than a gale at sea."

A ray of moonlight had now forced its way through the door and fell on the flooring of rough wooden planks. The man with the imitation ring prodded the sky-blue vest with a carving-knife.

"Speak up, you snail—ain't that right, that you're a snail? Did you fellows ever see anyone who looked more like it? I'm asking you, did you ever have a woman?"

The prostitute burst out laughing and put her arm around the blond sailor's neck; they both laughed together. The man in the sky-blue vest drank what was left of his rum and wiped his mouth with his coat-sleeve.

"You wouldn't know where it was," he began. "It was a long way from here, in another port, in a country that was a lot bigger than this. It was in a wine-shop—I remember the name: New World."

The man with the imitation ring pounded on the table for more rum.

"I was acquainted with the girl who was with her—there were two of them and some fellow. I was having a drink with a buddy of mine, and we were sitting there talking about our troubles. They say there's no such thing as love at first sight, that it's all a lie."

The prostitute leaned her head on the blond sailor and tightened her grip on his brawny arm. Suddenly the squalor of the wine-shop was drenched with song—a woman's voice, singing:

"He went away, never more to return...."

They sat listening. The man with the imitation ring was sipping his rum as if it were a rare liqueur, as he waited with an anxious look on his face for the man in the sky-blue vest to continue.

158

"But what difference does it make?" said the latter; and again he wiped his mouth with his sleeve.

"Just look at the moon, how big and pretty it is," whispered the prostitute, drawing nearer to her blond. "It's been a long time since I saw it like that."

"Go ahead! Tell us the rest of it!" said the man with the imitation ring.

"Well, then, as I was saying, there I was sitting with a friend, having a little drop. He was complaining about what a hard life it was. He was in the dumps, and I was, myself, when she came in. She came in with another girl—did I tell you that?"

"Yes, you told us that," said the blond sailor, who was becoming interested in the story. Even the Spaniard who kept the shop leaned on the bar to listen to the tale. The woman's voice, singing, came faintly out of the mysterious depths of the night. The man in the sky-blue vest made an appreciative gesture toward the sailor, and went on:

"Well, then, that's how it was. She came in with the other girl and some fellow. I knew the other girl; I'd been out with her—but, mates, I'm telling you, I didn't even see her, you might say—all I could see was the other one."

"Was she brown-skinned?" asked the man with the imitation ring, who had a fondness for that kind.

"Brown-skinned? No, she wasn't brown-skinned, nor blonde either, but she was pretty—she was like a foreigner, someone from another country."

"I know how it is," said the blond sailor, who came from a seagoing vessel. The man with the sky-blue vest made another gesture of appreciation.

The prostitute was snuggling up against her new-found friend.

"You know everything," she whispered to him, with a smile. "Just look at the moon—big, big—and so yellow."

"As this lad says," and the man in the sky-blue vest pursed his lip at the sailor, "you would have thought she had just got off a boat that came from some place far away. I don't even know how I happened to sit down with her—it must have been my buddy who struck up a conversation with the other one, and she told her friend who we were and we got to talking. What we talked about I couldn't tell you—all I could do was look at her, and she had nothing to say. All she did was laugh, with her white teeth, whiter even than sand on the beach. It was my friend all the while who was doing the talking, telling them all about his troubles. The girl I knew, she talked, too—I think she was trying to cheer him up, but to tell you the truth, I couldn't say. The strange girl and the fellow who was with them didn't say a word—she just laughed." He smiled at the memory, and then went on: "—such a short, sharp little laugh—I never heard anyone laugh the way she did. And her eyes—" He paused at the recollection. "I can't say what her eyes were like." He spread out his hands. "She seemed to me like a woman in a story which black Asterio used to tell on board that Swedish ship, the one that went down on the Coqueiros Reef."

The man with the imitation ring put his foot out into the moonlight, and spit.

"And the guy she had with her," he asked, "was he the skipper of that likely little craft?"

"I can't say. He didn't appear to be. He seemed more like a friend, but I couldn't be sure. All I know is that she laughed and laughed, with those white teeth and her white face, and her eyes."

He now put his fingers into the pockets of his sky-blue vest, being without anything else for his hands to do, seeing that he had drained his glass.

"And what happened?" said the man with the ring.

"They paid and the three of them left. I did the same; but I went back to that wine-shop so many times! Once I saw her again. She came from some place far away. I'm certain of that. From very far away—she wasn't from this country."

"The moonlight's so pretty," said the prostitute, and the sailor noticed that her eyes were sad. There was something that she wanted to say, but she could not find the words.

"—from far away—who knows? From beyond the sea, maybe? All I know is that she came and went. That's all I know. She took no notice of me; but to this day I remember that way she had of laughing, and her teeth, and how white she was. And the dress she wore!" He almost shouted with joy at recalling this fresh detail—"that dress with the open sleeves."

He drained his cup and stuck out his lip; he was cheerful no longer. The woman's voice singing in the lyric night came to them languorously:

"He went away, never more to return...."

"And then?" said the man with the imitation ring once more. The man in the sky-blue vest made no reply; the prostitute could not tell whether he was gazing at the moon or at something which she could not see, beyond the moon and the stars, beyond the sky, even, beyond the night that was so calm and still. She did not know, either, why it was she felt like weeping. But before the tears would come, she had left with the blond sailor to make the most of the moonlit night.

The Spaniard was leaning on the bar to hear the adventures that the man with the imitation ring might have to relate, but the one in the sky-blue vest was once more indifferent as he gazed up at the yellow disk above. In the midst of a story about a wench he had known, which he was telling with sweeping gestures, the man with the ring stopped. Turning to the proprietor and pointing to the blue vest, he said:

"I'm asking you, now: doesn't he look just like a snail?"

2

While men sat talking on the wharves that night, the city of Ilhéos was tossing in a restless sleep, its slumbers being interrupted by rumours that kept arriving from Ferradas, from Tabocas, and from Sequeiro Grande. The struggle between Horacio and the Badarós had begun. The two weekly papers that were published in the town were exchanging violent insults, each one praising its own party leaders and dragging those of the opposition through the mire. The best journalist was the one who could think up the most outrageous invectives. Nothing was sacred, including the private and family lives of the individuals involved.

Manuel de Oliveira, editor of *O Comercio*, the Badarós' paper, was watching the poker game from a seat behind Juca. The other players were Colonel Ferreirinha, Teodoro das Baraúnas, and João Magalhães. Ferreirinha, who had met the captain on the boat coming down from Bahia, had introduced him to Juca Badaró.

"An educated chap," he had said, "very rich, travels for the pleasure of it, a retired captain, an engineer."

Juca had come in to the city on a matter having to do with the forest of Sequeiro Grande. But as it happened, Dr. Roberto, the surveyor, was not in Ilhéos; he had left on a trip to Bahia; and Juca was in a hurry to have the surveying done so that he could register the property. Accordingly, when he had heard that there was an engineer in town, he had felt that his problem was solved.

"It's a great pleasure to know you, captain. I have a business proposition by which you might be able to make some money, sir."

João Magalhães was interested. Who could say?—this might be the opportunity he had been waiting for. He had come to Ilhéos in search of money, but big money, not just what he might be able to pick up at the poker table. He tried to be as polite as possible to Juca.

"The pleasure is all mine. I believe, though, that I know you, sir, at least by sight. We came down on the same boat from Bahia, but we did not have a chance to get acquainted."

"That's right," Ferreirinha remembered, "you did come down on that boat, Juca. Only you were too busy thinking about some woman that was on board," and he slapped his friend jovially across the stomach and laughed.

After expressing his regrets that he and the captain had not met before, Juca then plunged into the subject that was uppermost in his mind.

"Captain," he began, "this is the way it is. Our plantation borders on a forest which doesn't belong to anybody but which comes nearer to being ours than anyone else's, seeing that we were the first to go into it. It's the forest of Sequeiro Grande that I'm referring to. Well, now we want to fell it and plant it in cacao; but there is a leader of a band of ruffians down here, one Horacio da Silveira, who wants to take it over; he has dug up some old survey and has had it registered in his own name and those of some of his friends. But it won't do him any good, because we put a stop to that ouster in short order."

"So I've heard. A fire in the registry office," and Captain João Magalhães accompanied his words with expressive gestures. "Was that your work, sir? If so, my congratulations. I like men who know their own minds."

"No, that was my friend Teodoro, the master of Baraúnas; he's a dashing fellow, with plenty of nerve."

"Yes, you can see that."

"Well, then, what we're looking for is an engineer to survey that forest for us. But unfortunately Dr. Roberto is away on a trip, and he's the only one around here that would do it. The others are a pack of cowards; they don't want to get mixed up in it. And so, when I heard that you, sir, are an engineer, I thought I would consult you and see if you would care to undertake it. We will pay well. And as to any vengeance on the part of Horacio, you needn't be afraid of that; we will guarantee you protection."

Captain João Magalhães gave a superior laugh.

"Come, now, for the love of God—you speak of fear to me? Have you any idea how many revolutions I've taken part in, colonel? More than a dozen. The only thing is I don't know if I am legally in a position to—" he paused—"make the survey. You see, I'm not a surveyor; I'm a military engineer. I don't know if I have the right—"

"Before coming here," said Juca, "I consulted my lawyer, and he says that you can do it, sir, that military engineers may practice—"

"I'm not so sure of it, all the same. What's more, I'm not registered at Bahia, but in Rio. The registry office wouldn't accept my survey."

"That's of no importance. We can fix matters with the registrar. Don't let that worry you."

But João Magalhães was still doubtful. He was neither a military personage nor an engineer. He could play any kind of game, could do tricks with a deck of cards and win the confidence of others; but he wanted wider opportunities, he wanted to make big money and not go on living forever dependent upon the card table, one day with a roll of money and the next day without a cent. After all, what risk was he running? The Badarós were on top in politics, they had every chance of winning the struggle, and if they did win out, the property rights to the forest of Sequeiro Grande would never be questioned. And even supposing it was found that the survey was illegal, done by a charlatan, he would be far away by that time, enjoying the money he had got, in another part of the country. It was worth taking a chance. He thought it over, his eyes on Juca Badaró, as the latter stood there impatiently before him, tapping his boot with his riding-whip.

"The truth of the matter is, I'm an outsider here and don't like to get mixed up in local squabbles. On the other hand, I have a very warm feeling toward you, sir, and toward your brother. Especially after the firing of the registry office. Deeds of courage like that impress me very much. In short—"

"We will pay well, captain. You won't regret it, sir."

"I'm not speaking of money. If I did it, it would be out of friendship."

"But we want to show our appreciation just the same. Business is business, aside from the debt of gratitude that we will always owe you."

"That's true."

"How much would you ask to do the job, sir? It would mean spending a week at the plantation."

"What about the instruments?" The captain asked this question by way of gaining time while he calculated how much he should ask. "Mine are in Rio, you know."

"That makes no difference. I'll get Dr. Roberto's from his wife."

"Well, in that case—" The captain was still thinking. "Very well. I didn't come here to work, but for a holiday. Let's see: a week at the plantation—that means I'll have to miss Wednesday's boat." He dropped his voice to a murmur again. "I may not be able to close that lumber deal in Rio in time—that's too bad. Well, then—" and he addressed his remarks to Juca, who was waiting nervously, tapping harder than ever on his boot. "Twenty contos—I don't think that is too much."

"It's a lot of money," said Juca Badaró. "A week from now and Dr. Roberto will be back; he would do it for three contos."

João Magalhães made a facial gesture to indicate his complete indifference, as much as to say, very well, then, let him wait.

"It's a lot of money," Juca Badaró repeated.

"Look, my friend: three contos is your surveyor's fee; but he's registered in Bahia, he lives here, although he's out of town—won't be back for a week at least; whereas, I'm risking my professional reputation. I might be prosecuted and lose my right to practise or even my diploma. And then, as I was saying, I am on vacation, I'm going to miss my boat and possibly lose out on a big business deal that will cost me hundreds of contos. If I agree, it is more out of friendship than for the money that's in it."

"I realize that, captain, but it's a lot of money just the same. If you would take ten contos, sir, it's a bargain; we'll go out tomorrow morning, bright and early."

João Magalhães thereupon suggested that they split the difference: "Fifteen contos."

"Captain, I am not a Syrian or a pedlar. If I pay ten contos, it is because I am in a hurry to have the job done. If you like, sir, you can have your money today, and we'll set out tomorrow."

João saw that he would not get any further by arguing the matter. "Very well, then, just as a favour to you. It's agreed."

"I'll be indebted to you all my life, captain. I and my brother. You can count on us, sir, whenever you need us." And before leaving he had inquired: "Do you want the money at once? If so, come around to the house."

"Now, now, what do you take me for? Whenever you care to pay, sir. There's no hurry."

"Then we can meet tonight."

"Do you play poker, sir?"

Ferreirinha applauded this idea enthusiastically: "A good idea. We'll get up a little game at the café."

"All right," said Juca. "I'll bring the money along, and afterwards I'll win it back from you at poker, and you'll do the survey free of charge."

João fell in with his jesting mood: "What you mean is, I'll win another ten big ones to cover the twenty that I asked. You'd better come with your pockets well lined, Mr. Juca Badaró."

"We need a fourth hand," Ferreirinha reminded them. Juca solved the problem: "I'll bring Teodoro."

And so here they all were, in the back room of Nhôzinho's café, sitting in a poker game. Juca Badaró was taking more and more of a liking to the captain all the time. João Magalhães was the type that appealed to him: a lively conversationalist who had had a wide experience with women and knew how to tell a spicy story. The winnings were divided between them; Ferreirinha and Teodoro lost, the latter heavily. The ante was steep—so steep that Manuel de Oliveira had gone into the ballroom to summon Astrogildo, another planter, to come and see how high the bets were. The two of them now were looking on.

"Your hundred and sixty and raise you three hundred and twenty," said Teodoro.

"He's already lost more than two contos," whispered Manuel de Oliveira to Astrogildo. "I never saw anything like it."

Juca Badaró paid to see. Teodoro held nines, Juca tens. "Too bad, my friend," and Juca raked in the chips.

Nhôzinho came in at this point, bowing, scraping, and cracking jokes, a whisky tray in his hands. Manuel de Oliveira took a glass from the tray. It was for windfalls like this that he hung around: a whisky, a bite of supper, and whatever he might be able to pick up in the way of a stray chip at bacarat or roulette.

"Good whisky," he remarked. Captain João Magalhães smacked his tongue approvingly. "Better even than what they sell me in Rio—it's contraband stuff, you know—tastes like nectar."

Teodoro called for silence. Everybody said that he was a poor loser, which was too bad, considering that he was so fond of trying his luck at every kind of game. It was likewise said that he

165

could have been a rich man had it not been for his vice of gambling. On days when he won he bought drinks for the house, threw his money away on women, and gave champagne suppers at the café; but when he lost, he was impossible and would insult his best friend.

"You don't talk when you're playing poker," he protested.

Ferreirinha dealt the cards, and they all stayed. Manuel de Oliveira, sitting behind Juca Badaró's chair, was sipping his whisky; he was not even following the game, but gave his entire attention to his drink. Astrogildo, on the other hand, standing behind Teodoro, was observing the hands closely. From his face, where disapproval showed, João Magalhães could tell what kind of cards Teodoro held. The latter drew two, and Astrogildo made a face expressive of disgust. João stayed with what he had, although it was but a lonesome pair. Teodoro then spread out his cards on the table.

"Every time I try a bluff, I always run into that!"

The others threw down their hands also and João took the pot. Nhôzinho now appeared, to inquire if they wished anything else.

"Go to hell," said Teodoro.

He stayed in every hand and invariably lost. Finally, when the colonel broke a pair of aces to draw to a flush. Astrogildo was unable to contain himself.

"As long as you play them like that," he said, "you're bound to lose. That's not poker; that's throwing your money away. Breaking up your hand—"

Teodoro bounded from his chair; he was looking for a fight.

"And what business is it of yours, you son of a bitch? Is it my money or yours? Why don't you attend to your own affairs?"

"You're a son of a bitch yourself!" and, drawing his revolver, Astrogildo was on the point of firing. Juca Badaró and Ferreirinha at once leaped in and strove to quiet the two men. João Magalhães did his best to appear calm and not to show how frightened he was. Manuel de Oliveira did not budge from his chair, but went on sipping his whisky with an air of indifference; he even took advantage of the confusion to pour into his own glass half of Ferreirinha's drink, which the latter had not touched. When both Astrogildo and Teodoro had been disarmed, Juca Badaró sought to restore amity.

"What kind of foolishness is this?" he said. "Two friends fighting like that. Save your bullets for Horacio and his kind."

Teodoro sat down again, still grumbling about the "ganders"

watching the game. They brought him bad luck, he said. Astrogildo, a trifle pale, had sat down also, this time beside João Magalhães. They played a few more hands, and then Ferreirinha suggested that they go and dance a little in the front room. Upon counting the chips, it was found that João Magalhães had won three contos and Juca Badaró one and a half. Before they left the room, Juca made another appeal to Teodoro and Astrogildo.

"That's enough now. It's all in the game, you know. People get hot-headed—"

"But he insulted me," said Astrogildo. Teodoro put out his hand and the other grasped it. They then went into the front room, but Teodoro did not stay long; saying that he had a headache, he went home.

"He's going to get himself killed one of these days," remarked Ferreirinha, "acting like that. Somebody will put a bullet in him before he knows what's happened to him."

Juca was for excusing him. "He has his faults, but he's a good fellow."

The dance hall of the café was animated. An aged Negro was pounding on a piano that was older than himself, while a blond-haired individual was doing his best with a violin.

"Lousy orchestra," said Ferreirinha.

"Terrible," Manuel de Oliveira agreed.

The couples on the floor, tightly clasped, were dancing a waltz, and women of varying ages were scattered about at the tables. Most of the customers were drinking beer, but here and there was a party with whisky and gin glasses. Nhôzinho came up to serve them, for Juca had a dislike for the two waiters because they were pederasts, and so the proprietor himself always waited on him. And inasmuch as Juca Badaró was in the habit of spending large sums, Nhôzinho was extremely respectful, putting himself out to be of service. Ferreirinha had left the table to dance with a very young girl—she did not look a day over fifteen. She could not have been a prostitute for long, and Ferreirinha was crazy over young ones like her, "so green and tender," as he put it to João Magalhães. A woman who was getting along in years came over to sit down beside Manuel de Oliveira.

"Will you buy me one, Manú?" she asked, pointing to the whisky. Manuel glanced at Juca and, when the latter nodded approval, called Nhôzinho over.

"Bring a whisky for the lady and be quick about it," he said in an authoritative tone of voice.

The orchestra had stopped playing, and Ferreirinha, who was back at the table again, had begun telling of something that had happened to him a long time ago.

"Down here, captain, you have to be a little of everything. You, sir, are a military engineer, and here you are, going to do a surveyor's job. And I, who am only an ignorant farmer, have already had to play the part of a surgeon."

"A surgeon?"

"Yes, a surgeon. One of the labourers on my plantation swallowed a rabbit bone, and it got lodged in the poor fellow's stomach and was killing him—he couldn't even do his duties. There wasn't time to send to the city for a doctor, and so there was nothing for it but for me to operate myself."

"But how did you manage it?"

"I rigged up a long, heavy piece of wire and made a hook on the end of it. I washed it in alcohol first, of course. Then I turned the poor wretch on his face and dug the wire into him. It worked. A lot of blood came out and the bone with it, and he's alive and well to this day."

"Remarkable, eh!"

"Oh, I tell you, that fellow Ferreirinha—"

"The worst of it was, captain, the reputation that it got me. People came from miles around wanting me to treat them. If I had cared to open an office, I'd have been the ruin of many a good doctor." He laughed and the others joined in.

"That's right," said Juca Badaró, "you do have to be a jack of all trades in these parts. You'll find a backwoodsmen here, captain, who can give lessons to a lawyer."

"It's the coming country, no doubt of that," said João, with befitting admiration.

Manuel de Oliveira was making a date with the aged prostitute, but Juca had eyes only for Margot, who was seated at a table with Virgilio. Astrogildo followed his friend's gaze; he thought that Juca was looking at the lawyer.

"There's that so-and-so of a Dr. Virgilio who entered that survey for the ouster."

"Yes, I know. I'm acquainted with him."

João Magalhães also glanced in Margot's direction and gave her a nod.

"Do you know her, sir?"

"Do I know her? Why, she used to be around all the time with a little thing that I had in Bahia, by the name of Violeta. She's been with Dr. Virgilio for two years now."

"She's pretty," said Juca, and João knew that he was interested in the woman; he could tell that by the look in his eyes, the tone of his voice. The captain was wondering what he could get out of it for himself.

"She's a nice little piece—great friend of mine." Juca turned to look at him as João went on, very casually: "She's stopping at Machadão's place. Tomorrow, when she's alone, I shall drop around and see her. I don't like to go when the doctor's there, for he's very jealous. She's a good sort, very affectionate."

"But you can't go tomorrow, captain. Early tomorrow morning we're leaving for the plantation, on the eight o'clock train."

"That's right. Well, then, when I come back."

"She's some woman!" was Astrogildo's comment.

At the next table Margot and Virgilio were engaged in an animated conversation. She was greatly agitated and kept moving her arms and head.

"They're quarrelling," said Juca.

"That's all they do," said the old woman who was with Manuel de Oliveira.

"How do you happen to know?"

"Machadão told me. It's a scandal."

They ordered another round of whisky. The orchestra struck up, and Margot and Virgilio went out on the floor; but they did not talk as they danced. In the middle of the piece she dropped his arm and went over and sat down. He stood there for a moment, not knowing what to do, then called the waiter, paid his bill, took up his hat from a chair, and left.

"They're quarrelling all right," said Juca.

"This time it appears to be serious," the woman said.

Margot was now looking around the room, endeavouring to appear indifferent. Juca leaned forward in his chair and whispered to João Magalhães: "Do you want to do me a favour, captain?"

"At your service."

"Introduce me to her."

João Magalhães gave the planter a deeply interested look. He was laying his plans. He would leave this land of cacao a rich man.

3

In the lyric, moon-drenched night Virgilio was walking along the railroad track. His heart was bounding but not at memory of the violent scene with Margot in the café. When he thought of the incident for a moment, it was to shrug his shoulders with indifference. It was better that it should end this way, once and for all. He had wanted to take her home, had told her that he had a business engagement that would keep him out until very late and accordingly would be unable to spend the night with her. Margot, who was already distrustful, with a flea in her ear, would not accept his excuses: either he would accompany her home, or she would remain in the café and all would be over between them. Without knowing just why he did so, he had sought to convince her that he really had an engagement and that she ought to go home to bed. She had refused, it had ended in a quarrel, and he had left without even saying good night. Even now, perhaps, she was seated at Juca Badaró's table, in the company of the man with whose rivalry she had threatened him.

"What difference does it make to me? I'm not hard up for a man. Just look at the eyes Juca Badaró is making at me."

This did not trouble him. It was better that she should be with another; indeed, it was the best possible solution. When he thought of it, he smiled. How times had changed! A year ago, at the thought of Margot with another man, he would have been altogether likely to lose his head and do something foolish. Once at the American House in Bahia he had created a scandal, had got into a fight, and had ended up at the police station, all because some young fellow had made a slighting remark to Margot. Now he actually felt relieved at knowing that Juca Badaró was interested in her, that he coveted her flesh. Virgilio smiled at the memory. Juca had good reasons for hating him, Horacio's lawyer, and yet, without knowing it, was doing him a big favour.

But as he walked along the railroad track, endeavouring to adapt his stride to the space between the sleepers, Virgilio was not thinking of Margot. Tonight his eyes were drinking in the beauty of the world: the full moon bending over the earth; the star-filled sky above the city; the crickets chirping in the underbrush near by. A freight train whistled in the distance and he stepped off the track. He was going along the back of a row of houses with their big silent gardens. In a gateway a couple were making love. He hurried on so that they might not recognize him. At another gate, farther on, Ester would be waiting.

The house that Horacio had recently built in Ilhéos, the "mansion," as everybody called it, was in the new town that had sprung up in the fields where cocoa trees not so long ago had stood. The rear of all of these dwellings looked out on the tracks. A company had been organzied to buy up the land, which, after the trees had been felled, had been subdivided and sold as building-lots. It was here, after his marriage, that Horacio had erected his town house, one of the best in Ilhéos, being constructed of specially made brick from his own kiln at the plantation, with furniture and hangings from Rio. At the back of the house Ester would be waiting, tremulous with fear, anxious with love.

Virgilio quickened his step. He was already late, the quarrel with Margot having detained him. The freight train passed by, its powerful headlights illuminating the scene. He stopped to let it pass and then once more began walking along the ties. He had had difficulty in convincing Ester that she should wait for him at the gate, so that they might be able to have a quiet talk. She had been afraid of the servants, of the gossiping tongues in Ilhéos; she was afraid that one day Horacio would come to know of it. As yet the affair between them had not progressed beyond a distant infatuation, consisting as it did of hastily whispered words, a long and ardent letter that he had written, and a note from her in reply—two or three words only: "I love you, but it is impossible"—a clasp of hands at the door, glances filled with desire. All this to them seemed so little; it did not occur to them that, little as it was, the whole town was talking about them and, looking upon them as lovers, was laughing at Horacio. After the exchange of letters, when Horacio had gone back to the plantation, he had called upon Ester. This had truly been an act of madness, thus to defy the power of gossip. Ester had told him so, begging him to go away; and in order to persuade him to go, she had promised to meet him here, the next night, at the garden gate. He had tried to kiss her, but she had fled.

Virgilio's pounding heart was that of a lovesick youth, as he drank in the loveliness of the night with all the intensity of youth. Here was the gate at the back of Horacio's house. Virgilio was trembling, deeply moved, as he approached it. The gate was ajar, and laying a hand on it he pushed it open. Under a tree, wrapped in a cape, bathed in moonlight, Ester was waiting. He ran to her, took her hands in his. "My darling!" Her body was quivering as they embraced; the words of love are useless in the light of the moon.

"I want to take you with me, away from here, far away, away from everybody, to build a new life."

She was weeping gently, her head on his bosom. From her hair came a fragrance that completed the beauty and the mystery of the night. The wind brought the murmur of the sea to mingle with her weeping.

"My darling!"

"It is impossible, Virgilio. I have my child to think of. We can't do that."

"We will take him with us. We will go far away, to another country, where no one knows us."

"Horacio would come after us; he would follow us to the end of the world."

But more than words love's maddening kisses proved convincing as a lovers' moon bent over them. Stars were born in the heavens above Ilhéos, and Ester could not help thinking of Sister Angelica: the time when it still was possible to dream had come again. Dreams did come true. She closed her eyes as she felt Virgilio's hands upon her nude body, beneath her cape. A bed of moonlight, the stars for coverlet, and the moans and sighs of love's extremity.

"I'll go with you, my darling, wherever you wish—" And as she felt herself dying in his arms—"even to death."

4

Captain João Magalhães was smiling from the other table, and Margot smiled back. The captain rose, went over, and shook hands with her.

"Lonesome?"

"Well—"

"Have a quarrel?"

"It's all over."

"Really? Or is it like the other times?"

"I'm through this time. I'm not the woman to put up with such treatment."

João Magalhães assumed a conspiratorial air: "Well, then, as a friend, Margot, let me tell you something. I've got something good for you. There's someone here, with more money than he knows what to do with, who's crazy over you. Right now—"

"Juca Badaró," she interrupted him.

The captain nodded. "You've got him hooked."

Margot was tired of hearing him run on. "I knew that. On the boat coming down he was all over me. The only thing was I was tagging after Virgilio then."

"And now?"

Margot laughed. "Now it's another story. Who knows?"

The captain then proceeded to give her some fatherly advice: "Stop being a fool, my dear; put away all the money you can in your stocking while you're young. This business of having a poor man for a lover is all right for a woman with a rich husband."

She was permitting herself to be persuaded. "I *was* a fool. In Bahia I had—I can't tell you how many rich men running after me," and she made a gesture with her fingers. "You know how it is." The captain nodded. "And there I was, like an old hag, hanging on to Virgilio. And what did he do but stick me off down here in the woods, to spend my life mending socks in Tabocas. But it's over now, I'm through."

"Do you want me to introduce you to Juca Badaró?"

"Did he ask you to?"

"He's dying to meet you." Turning in his chair, the captain beckoned, and, buttoning his coat, Juca rose and came over, a smile on his face. As he left the table where he had been sitting, Astrogildo made a comment to Manuel de Oliveira and Ferreirinha: "This is going to end in a row."

"Everything in Ilhéos ends in a row," was the journalist's reply.

João was about to introduce the pair, but Margot did not give him time: "We know each other already. The colonel once gave me a pinch that left me with a black-and-blue mark."

Juca laughed with the others: "And then you ran away and I never laid eyes on you again. I heard that you had gone to Tabocas; I was down there, but I didn't see anything of you. They told me you were married, and so I respected—"

"They're divorced," João Magalhães announced.

"Have a quarrel?"

Margot did not care to go into explanations. "He left me to keep a business engagement," she said, "and I'm not the woman to be brushed aside for a matter of business."

Juca Badaró laughed once more. "All Ilhéos knows what his business is."

"What do you mean?" asked Margot, puckering up her face.

Juca Badaró had no reins on his tongue. "It's Horacio's wife, Dona Ester. The little lawyer chappie is getting mixed up with her."

Margot bit her lips. There was a silence, of which the captain took advantage to retire to the other table.

"Is that the truth?"

"I'm not the man to lie."

She gave a prolonged laugh. "Aren't you offering me anything to drink?" she asked in an affected voice. Juca called Nhôzinho over. "Bring some champagne."

"Do you remember," he said to Margot as their glasses were being filled, "I once made you a proposition—on the boat, coming down here?"

"Yes, I remember."

"Well, I'm making it once more. I'll set you up in a house and give you everything you want. But you've got to remember that a woman of mine is mine and nobody else's."

She looked at the ring on his finger, took his hand. "It's pretty."

Juca Badaró took off the ring and placed it on Margot's finger. "It's yours."

More than a little tipsy, the two of them left at dawn. With them went Manuel de Oliveira, who, the moment he had spied the champagne glasses, had come over to their table, where he had drunk more than both of them together. It was cold in the early morning along the wharves of Ilhéos, but Margot was singing and the journalist was joining in the chorus. As for Juca Badaró, he was in something of a hurry, for he had to catch the eight o'clock train. The fishermen were already returning with their deep-sea haul.

5

A municipal ordinance prohibited burro trains bearing cacao from coming into the centre of the city. The principal streets of Ilhéos were all of them paved, two of them with brick, a token of progress of which the inhabitants were inordinately proud. The burros would come to a halt in the streets next to the station, and the cacao would then be brought into town in horse-drawn carts, to be stored in the big warehouses near the harbour. However, only a small portion of the crop that was sent to Ilhéos for shipment was any longer carried on the backs of burros; mostly it came by rail or was transported in barges from Banco da Victoria by way of the Cachoeira River, which emptied into the sea at this point.

The harbour was the chief concern of the city's residents. At that time there was only one wharf at which ships were able to moor, and when more than one came in on the same day, the other cargoes had to be unloaded in small boats. A company had accordingly been incorporated for the purpose of improving and exploiting the port, and there was talk of building more wharves and big docks and of dredging the harbour entrance, which was dangerously shallow.

Ilhéos had sprung up on a cluster of islands and stood on a point of land between two hills, known as União and Conquista; and it had also invaded the neighbouring islands, on one of which was situated the suburb of Pontal, where the wealthy had their summer homes. The population of the place had grown astonishingly since the raising of cacao had become general in the region, for practically the entire crop from the southern part of the state of Bahia was shipped to the capital from there. There was but one other port, Barra do Rio de Contas, and it was a very small one, where only sailing vessels could anchor. The citizens of Ilhéos dreamed of exporting cacao directly abroad some day, without having to ship it by way of Bahia. This provided a constant theme for editorials in the local press: the need of deepening the harbour so that ships of greater tonnage might pass. The opposition newspaper would take advantage of the topic to attack the government, while the government organ also alluded to it from time to time, printing items to the effect that "our most worthy and hard-working municipal prefect is engaged in negotiations with the state and federal governments with a view to a final solution of the harbour question." But the fact of the matter was that nothing ever came of it, as the state government consistently put obstacles in the way, in order to protect the income of the port of Bahia. The subject none the less, phrased in almost identical words, served to fill out the platforms of both political parties and the speeches of both candidates for the prefecture. If there was any difference, it was a slight stylistic one, the platform for the Badaró candidate having been written by Lawyer Genaro, while that of Horacio's man came from the far more brilliant pen of Lawyer Ruy.

In Ilhéos the fortune of a colonel was measured by the houses that he owned, each one seeking to put up a better one, until little by little their families became used to spending more time in town than they did at the plantation; but still these houses remained closed a good part of the year, being occupied chiefly at Church festival time. The town was without diversions. The men, it is true, had the café, and there were the wine-shops where the Englishmen connected with the railroad drowned their sorrows in whisky and shot dice, where the *grapiúnas* exchanged revolver bullets; but for the womenfolk there remained nothing but visiting between families, gossiping about the private lives of others, and the enthusiasm that was awakened in them by the feast-days of the Church. Then, when work on the nuns' school had been begun, a few of the ladies had banded themselves together to raise money for the building fund by staging fairs and balls.

The Church of St. George, patron saint of the region, was a large, low structure wholly lacking in architectural beauty, but with an interior that was rich in gold-work. It overlooked a square that had been laid out as a garden. There was also the Church of St. Sebastian, next to the café and facing the sea; and on Conquista Hill, opposite the cemetery, was the Chapel of Our Lady of Victory, dominating the city from a height. In addition there was a Protestant church for the Englishmen from the railroad, which had won a few local adherents as well. And finally, in the matter of religion, there were various "spiritualistic séances" in the side streets, becoming more numerous every day. All in all, the city of Ilhéos with its outlying boroughs and its cacao plantations was in ill repute with the Archdiocese of Bahia, where much was made of the lack of religious sentiment among the inhabitants, the absence of menfolk from Mass, the widespread prostitution—in short, it was a terrible place, a land of assassins. The number of priests that the city proper or the municipality as a whole could boast was small indeed in comparison with the number of lawyers and doctors; and as for the few padres that there were, many of these, as time went on, became cacao-planters with little interests in the salvation of souls.

A case in point was Padre Paiva, who carried a revolver under his cassock and who was not in the least perturbed if a row was started in his presence. He was the political leader for the Badarós at Mutuns, and at election time he brought in swarms of voters—it was said that he promised them a veritable slice of heaven and many years of heavenly life on this earth if they cast their ballots the way they should. He was a councilman at Ilhéos, but was not in the least interested in the religious life of the city.

The only cleric who had such an interest was Canon Freitas, who on one memorable occasion preached a sermon in which he contrasted the amount of money spent by the colonels at the café and on prostitutes with the small amount he was able to collect for the building fund of the school. It was a violent, passionate sermon, but it had no practical result whatsoever. The Church continued to live off the womenfolk, and they lived for it, for the Masses, the processions, and the feasts of Holy Week; and so, exchanging juicy morsels of gossip, they went on decorating the altars and making new tunics for the holy images.

The city lay between the river and the sea, a truly lovely site, with cocoa palms growing all around. A poet who once had come to Ilhéos to give a lecture had referred to it as "the city of palms in the wind," a bit of imagery that the local papers were fond of quoting every so often. And in truth all the palms did was to grow and be tossed by the breeze. The shrub that really influenced Ilhéos life was the cacao tree, even though not a single one was to be seen inside the city itself. But it was there, behind all the life that went on in São Jorge dos Ilhéos. Behind every business deal that was made, behind every house that went up, behind every shot that was fired in the street—it was there. There was no conversation in which the word "cacao" did not play an essential part. Over warehouses, railway trains, ships' holds, wagons, and citizenry there hovered, ever, the odour of chocolate, which is the odour of dried cacao.

Another municipal ordinance forbade the carrying of weapons, but very few persons ever knew that it existed and those who were aware of it never thought of respecting it. Men were to be seen going through the streets clad in boots or shoes of coarse leather, khaki trousers, and a cassimere coat, with a revolver under the last mentioned garment. Men with rifles slung over their shoulders crossed the town and no one paid the slightest attention to them. As a consequence, in spite of its pretentious dwelling-houses, its stone mansions and paved streets, Ilhéos still had something of the appearance of an armed camp. At times, when ships crowded with immigrants from the backlands of Sergipe and Ceará arrived and the inns near the station were filled to overflowing, tents would be set up facing the harbour, kitchens would be improvised, and the colonels would come down there to pick workers for their plantations. Lawyer Ruy once pointed out one of these camps to a visitor from the capital. "There is the slave market," he said. He said it with a certain air of pride mingled with contempt; for he really loved this city which had sprung up overnight around the harbour, which had grown with the cacao region, and which was now rapidly becoming the most prosperous of any in the state.

There were few of those who had been born there who were of any importance in the life of the town. Almost all the planters, doctors, lawyers, surveyors, politicians, journalists, and contractors had come from the outside, from other states, but they nevertheless had a deep affection for this land which was so rich and so full of adventure. They all called themselves *"grapiúnas,"* and when in Bahia were readily recognizable everywhere by the pride with which they spoke. "That fellow is from Ilhéos," the Bahians would say. In the cafés and business houses of the capital they made a swaggering display of their wealth, spending their money without thought as to value received, never haggling over the price of anything, and always ready to start a rumpus without knowing what it was all about. In the houses of prostitution at Bahia they were looked up to, feared, and anxiously awaited. In the offices of those wholesale firms which did business in the interior of the country, merchants from Ilhéos were always shown the highest consideration and enjoyed an unlimited credit.

From the whole of northern Brazil people came down to this land of southern Bahia. Its fame had travelled far; it was said that money rolled in the streets there and that no one thought anything of a two-milreis piece. Ships came choked with immigrants, bringing adventurers of every sort, including women of all ages, for whom Ilhéos was either the first hope or the last. In the city all mingled together; for the poor man of today might be the rich man of tomorrow, the pack-driver might be a big plantation-owner, and the worker who did not know how to read might one day be a respected political leader. Cases in point were cited, and they never failed to mention Horacio, who had begun as a mule-driver and was now one of the largest planters in the region. And the rich man of today might be the poor man of tomorrow, if another richer than he, with the aid of a lawyer, worked a clever "ouster" and succeeded in taking his land away from him. What was more, any of today's living might tomorrow be lying dead in the street, a bullet-hole in his chest. For over and above the court of justice, the judge, the prosecutor, and the citizen jury was the law of the trigger, which in Ilhéos was the court of final appeal.

At this particular time the city was beginning to deck itself out with gardens and the municipality had sent for a famous gardener from the capital. For doing this it was attacked by the opposition paper, which asserted that "what Ilhéos needs more than gardens is streets." But all the same, the *opsicionistas* were very proud as they pointed out to visitors the flowers growing in public squares, which before had been planted in wild grass. As for streets, men and burros were opening those as they brought in their cacao to the harbour, where the seafaring ships were riding at anchor. And so it was about this time that the port of Ilhéos began to show on the latest economic maps with a cacao tree to mark its location.

6

The opposition newspaper, known as *A Folha de Ilhéos*, came out every Saturday; and on this particular week-end the issue was one marked by an unheard-of violence. The paper was edited by Filemon Andréa, a former tailor who had come down from Bahia to Ilhéos and had there abandoned his trade. It was well known about town that Filemon was incapable of writing a line, that even the articles that bore his signature were written by others. He was, in short, a blockhead, and how he had come to be the editor of a newspaper no one could say. He had previously done political chores for Horacio; but when the latter bought a printing press and type-cases to set up a weekly, everybody was surprised at his choice of editor.

"Why, he can hardly read."

"But," explained Lawyer Ruy, "he has a reputation for being an intellectual—a very good reputation. It is a question of aesthetics," and he puffed out his cheeks as he uttered the word. "Filemon Andréa! The name of a great poet!" he concluded.

The residents of the town generally held Lawyer Ruy himself responsible for the editorial articles that appeared in *A Folha de Ilhéos*; and as election time drew near and the two papers began their wordy warfare, hurling insulting adjectives at each other, the entire populace was divided into hotly wrangling groups. On the one side there was Lawyer Ruy with his verbose style, his rounded periods and redundant phrases, and on the other side was Manuel de Oliveira, with Lawyer Genaro at times to assist him. Manuel was a printer by trade who had worked on various newspapers in Bahia. Juca Badaró had made his acquaintance in the cafés of the capital and had there hired him to come down and direct the destinies of *O Comercio*. He was more clever and more direct than his rival and always came off with the greater laurels.

As for Lawyer Genaro's articles, they were filled with judicial citations. The attorney for the Badarós, he was commonly looked upon as the most cultured person in the city, and his fellow townsmen spoke admiringly of the hundreds of books that he possessed. He led a very reserved life, making his home with his two children, and almost never left the house. He was abstemious and was never seen in the wine-shops or the café; and as for women, it was rumoured that Machadão was in the habit of going to his house twice a month to sleep with him. She was an old woman by now, having come to the city when it was barely beginning to expand—she had been the feminine sensation of Ilhéos twenty years before. Now she kept a house for girls, but no longer practised prostitution herself. The one exception she made was Lawyer Genaro, who, as she put it, could not get used to sleeping with another woman.

Possibly it was for this reason that the leading editorial in *A Folha de Ilhéos*, which on this particular Saturday took up practically the entire front page of the small opposition weekly, referred to Lawyer Genaro as a "Jesuitical hypocrite"; and in this issue he was let off the easiest of all the Badarós' friends. The editorial in question dealt with the firing of Venancio's registry office at Tabocas, which *A Folha de Ilhéos* violently condemned as an "act of barbarism against the laws of a civilized community and harmful to the reputation that the municipality of Ilhéos enjoys in the mind of the country at large." As for Colonel Teodoro, his name called forth whole columns of abuse, a magnificent collection of insulting nouns and adjectives: "Bandit," "habitual drunkard," "a natural-born gambler who has made a profession of it," "a sadistic soul," "unworthy of living in a civilized community," "blood-thirsty," and so forth. But with all this, enough was left over for the Badarós. Juca appearing as one noted for his "cheap conquests among women of easy virtue," and for being a "shameless whoremaster and protector of bandits," while against Sinhô the usual accusations were levelled: he was a "master hand at an ouster," a "*jagunço* leader wallowing in his ill-gotten gains" and "responsible for the death of dozens of men," an "unscrupulous political boss," and so on.

The editorial demanded justice. Legally, it stated, there could be no question as to the property rights to the forest of Sequeiro Grande. That forest had been surveyed and the title entered at the registry office. It was not the property of any one individual, but of a number of cacao-planters, among them one or two outstanding ones, it was true, but the majority, so the editorial asserted, were small cultivators. What the Badarós were after was to obtain for themselves sole possession of this tract, thus not only defrauding the legitimate owners of their rights, but interfering with the development of the region as well; for "the trend of the century was toward the subdivision of large estates, as could be seen in the case of France." The article went on to state that Colonel Horacio, a progressive-minded, forward-looking individual, upon resolving to fell the forest of Sequeiro Grande and plant the land in cacao, had not been thinking of his own interests alone, but of those of the municipality, having associated with him in his undertaking all the small planters whose groves bordered on the forest. This was what you called being a good and useful citizen. How compare a man like that with the Badarós, who, "ambitious and unscrupulous," were thinking only of enriching themselves? *A Folha de Ilhéos* ended its editorial by announcing that Horacio and the other lawful owners of Sequeiro Grande meant to have resort to the courts; and as to what might happen afterwards, should the Badarós attempt to prevent the felling of the forest and the planting of the land, the latter alone would be responsible. It was they who had first employed violence, and the blame would be theirs for whatever might ensue. The article ended with a Latin quotation: *"Alea jacta est."*

Those who were accustomed to following these newspaper polemics were greatly excited by all this. In addition to the fact that the present exchange of insults bade fair to be an unprecedentedly violent one, it was noted that the editorial in *A Folha de Ilhéos* was not the work of Lawyer Ruy, with whose style the readers were long familiar. He was a good deal more rhetorical; he could make a very good speech to a jury, but in the columns of the paper he was not so forceful. This editorial showed more energy, better reasoning powers; and the adjectives were sharper-pointed. It was not long before it was known that the author of the piece was Lawyer Virgilio, the attorney for the opposition, who lived in Tabocas, but was in Ilhéos at the moment. It was Lawyer Ruy himself who, when someone congratulated him upon the article, had revealed its author's identity. It was further recalled that Virgilio was directly involved in the matter, inasmuch as he had been the one to enter the survey at the registry office which Teodoro had burned. And the gossiping tongues went on to recall the fact that he was also interested in Horacio's wife. Undoubtedly in its edition the following Wednesday *O Comercio* would have something to say about this phase of the lawyer's private life and that of Horacio, and the public was looking forward to it with relish.

To every one's surprise, however, *O Comercio* in its reply to the opposition editorial—a reply that was by no means overly calm—proceeded to ignore the subject about which the whole town was talking. To begin with, the paper informed its readers that it would not employ the "language of the gutter" like that "clown" who had so vilely attacked the Badarós and their political associates. Neither did it propose to delve into the private life of anyone, as was the custom of the "filthy organ of the opposition." It must be said, however, that this latter promise was hardly fulfilled, since the article took pains to go into the entire past life of Horacio, "that ex-mule-driver who has got rich no one knows how." Mixing public with private matters, the writer on the one hand recalled the colonel's trial for the slaying of three men, and how, "owing to the chicanery of lawyers who are a disgrace to the profession, he had escaped a just sentence but had not escaped the public's condemnation"; and on the other hand there were some extremely personal remarks about the death of Horacio's first wife, with an allusion to "those mysterious instances, with which we are all familiar, of members of the family who have suddenly disappeared and been buried at night." Neither did *O Comercio* wholly keep the promise it made with respect to language. Horacio was referred to as a "low-life assassin," while Lawyer Ruy was the "inveterate drunkard," the "dog that barked but did not bite," the "disgraceful father of a family who spent his life in the wine-shops and gave no thought to his wife and children."

The individual who evoked the most violent adjectives of all, however, was Lawyer Virgilio. Manuel de Oliveira began that portion of his article dealing with the attorney—his "biographical sketch" of the latter—by stating that he "would have to dip his pen in the gutter to write the name of Dr. Virgilio Cabral." It proved to be something more than a "sketch," for the author went back to Virgilio's student days in Bahia—"the best-known face in all the brothels of the capital"—and spoke of the financial difficulties he had encountered in completing his course, "having had to live off the crumbs fallen from the table of that old buzzard Seabra." Margot also entered the picture, even

182

though her name did not appear. The paragraph referring to her ran as follows:

Meanwhile, it was not only politicians of ill repute who filled the belly of this disorderly young loafer during his student days. A fashionable cocotte was also the victim of his blackmailing habits. Having deceived the young beauty, this bounder of a student proceeded to live at her expense, and it was with the money that she earned in bed that Dr. Virgilio Cabral managed to obtain his law degree. It is hardly necessary to add that, after having been trained in the service of the mule-driver, Horacio, the wretch abandoned his victim, that beauteous and kind-hearted creature who had aided him in buffeting the odds of fortune.

Despite the fact that *O Comercio* was a good deal larger paper than *A Folha de Ilhéos*, the article filled a page and a half. It went into the firing of Venancio's office in great detail, explaining to the public what an "indescribable kind of ouster" it was to undertake to register title to a property on the basis of an old survey that had no legal validity whatsoever, in connection with which, moreover, an erasure had been made, the names of Horacio and "his henchmen" having been substituted for that of Mundinho de Almeida. As for the burning of the registry office, it was Venancio himself who was the guilty party—"that false servant of justice who, when Colonel Teodoro asked to see the survey, preferred to set fire to the place, thereby destroying the proofs of his own villainy." The Badarós, on the other hand, were pictured as saints, incapable of harming a fly. As for the "wretched insults" hurled by the "clownish spokesman for the opposition," they were powerless to impugn the good name of persons so well thought of as the Badaró family, Colonel Teodoro, on "that illustrious luminary of science and the law, Dr. Genaro Torres, the price of all cultured *grapiúnas*." Finally reference was made to the "threats of Horacio and his hound-dog followers." The public in the days to come would remember who it was that had first threatened bloodshed, and would weigh the moral responsibilities "in the scales of popular justice." Nevertheless, let Horacio know that he was not frightening anyone with his "ridiculous fanfaronades." The Badarós knew how to employ the weapons of justice and the law, but they also, *O Comercio* promised, would be able to make use of any other one that their "disloyal adversary" might select.

183

On whatever terrain, they would see to it that "conscienceless bandits of that stripe and their unscrupulous lawyers" received their just deserts. And in conclusion, replying to the *"Alea jacta est"* of the opposition, the editorial in *O Comercio* likewise had recourse to a Latin quotation: *"Quousque tandem abutere, Mule-driverus, patientia nostra?"* This last represented Lawyer Genaro's contribution to Manuel de Oliveira's article.

Ilhéos, on the street corners, revelled in it all.

7

When, with mud-spattered boots and a growth of beard, João Magalhães had returned from the forest of Sequeiro Grande, he had been conscious of various conflicting emotions within himself. He had come down to spend a week at the Badaró plantation and had already been there two weeks now, having stayed on after there was no further need for his services. He had contrived to make out somehow with the surveyor's instruments—with the theodolite, the chain, the goniometer, and the marker—instruments on which he had never before laid eyes in the whole of his professional gambler's life. The actual surveying of the land had been done largely by the workmen who had accompanied him and by Juca Badaró; he himself did very little more than ratify their findings by scribbling a few calculations of squares and triangles. They had spent twó days in the forest, the Negroes carrying the instruments. Juca, meanwhile, was displaying his knowledge of the soil.

"Captain," he said, "I will stick my hand in the fire, if you can find anywhere in all the world any land that is better than this for the raising of cacao."

João bent over and took up a handful of moist earth. "It's first-rate, that it is. A little fertilizer and it will be of the best."

"It doesn't need any manure," Juca replied. "This is virgin soil, captain, and fertile as any there is. The groves here are going to bear as no grove ever did before."

João Magalhães continued to nod approval; he did not care to go into the subject any more deeply than necessary, from fear of exposing his ignorance. And so they had made their way into the giant wood, with Juca singing the praises of a land where trees such as those about them grew wild.

But what interested the captain a good deal more than the high quality of the land was the brown-skinned Don' Ana

Badaró. Already, in Ilhéos, he had heard of her, had heard that it was Don' Ana who had given the order to Teodoro to set fire to Venancio's registry office. In the city she was spoken of as a strange girl, little given to gossiping with other women or to taking part in the feasts of the Church (in spite of the fact that she had had so religious a mother); nor on the other hand was she fond of balls and sweethearts. Very few persons could recall ever having seen her dancing, and no one could mention the name of a single young man of hers. She was much more interested in horseback riding, shooting, and fathoming the mysteries of the plantation and the countryside. Olga was in the habit of telling her neighbours how disdainful Don' Ana was of the gowns which Sinhô had had sent down for her from Bahia or from Rio, expensive ones, the creations of well-known designers. Don' Ana scarcely gave them a thought, but was concerned, rather, with the new colts that had been born; she knew the names of all the animals the family owned, including even the pack-burros. She had taken upon herself the keeping of the Badaró accounts, and she it was to whom Sinhô turned whenever he was in need of information. Juca always said that "Don' Ana should have been born a man."

João Magalhães would not have agreed with him on this. It was possibly her eyes—eyes that recalled another adored pair—that first attracted him. Striving to be exquisitely polite in words and manner as he addressed her, he was lost in contemplation of those lovely eyes, which of a sudden would light up with an intense glow, like the others which, once upon a time, had gazed at him with so much contempt. Later he came to forget those of the girl he had left behind in Rio de Janeiro, as the days went by and he became better acquainted with Don' Ana.

In the Badaró household the sole topic of conversation was the forest of Sequeiro Grande and the plans of Horacio and his friends. They made guesses, suppositions, reckoned the possibilities. What would Horacio do when he learned that the Badarós were surveying the forest and were going to have it registered and take out title to the property? Juca had no doubts in the matter. Horacio would attempt to go into the wood immediately, while filing suit in the court at Ilhéos for possession of the land, basing his claim upon the survey entered in Venancio's office. Sinhô, however, was not so sure of this. He felt that, since Horacio was without government support, being in the opposition, he would first attempt to legalize the situation by an ouster of some sort before having resort to force.

From Ilhéos Juca had brought back the latest news: the scandalous affair of Ester and Virgilio—the whole town was talking about it. Sinhô was not inclined to believe this.

"That's just talk on the part of people who have nothing else to do."

"But Sinhô, he has even left the woman he was keeping—what do you say to that? It's a fact, as I have reason to know." And glancing at João, he laughed as he thought of Margot.

The captain took part in all these conversations and discussions as if he were one of the Badarós, just as Teodoro das Baraúnas did the night he slept there. He felt like a relative; and each time that Don' Ana looked his way and respectfully asked "the captain's opinion," he would be lavish in his insults for Horacio and those associated with him. Once when he noted that those eyes were a little more interested and tender than usual, he had gone so far as to place at the disposition of the Badarós his "military knowledge, as a captain who had taken part in eight revolutions." There he was, at their orders. If there was to be a fight, they could count on him. He was a man for anything, come what might. As he said this, he smiled at Don' Ana, and the latter, grown suddenly timid and overcome with blushes, fled into the house as Sinhô Badaró was thanking the captain for his offer. Sinhô was grateful, but he hoped the captain's services would not be needed, that everything could be settled peaceably, without need of bloodshed. It was true, he said, that he was preparing for any eventuality, but in the hope that Horacio would give up the idea of disputing possession of the forest with him. As for abandoning the stand that he himself had taken, he could not do that; he was the head of the family and had his responsibilities; moreover, he had an agreement with his friends, with people who, like Teodoro das Baraúnas, were making sacrifices for him. If Horacio wanted to go ahead, he, Sinhô, would do the same. But he still had hopes—Juca shrugged his shoulders; he was quite certain that Horacio would attempt to go into the forest by force, and that much blood would flow before the Badarós would be able to plant their cacao trees in peace on that new land. This was the cue for Captain João once more to volunteer his services.

"Anything that I can do—I don't like to boast about my bravery, but I'm used to these little fracases."

He did not catch sight of Don' Ana again that day until the

186

hour for Bible-reading came. As she entered the room, she was greeted with a burst of laughter from Juca, who pointed a finger at her.

"What have we here? Is the world coming to an end?"

Sinhô looked at her also. Don' Ana was serious-faced and stern of mien. With the assistance of Raimunda, she had laboured to effect a head-dress of the kind that Ester had worn one feast-day in Ilhéos, and now they were laughing at her. She was wearing, too, one of her party gowns, which gave her a strange appearance here in the parlour of the Big House. Juca continued to laugh, while Sinhô could not understand what had happened to his daughter. João Magalhães alone felt happy. If he perceived clearly enough the ridiculousness of the situation, with Don' Ana dressed as for a ball, he none the less preserved his gravity and gave the young woman a languishing glance. She, however, was not looking at any of them; all she could think of was that they were making fun of her. But when at last she raised her eyes and met the captain's tender gaze, she found the courage to retort to Juca.

"What are you laughing at?" she said. "Do you think that your wife is the only one who can dress well and do her hair?"

"My daughter," Sinhô reproved her, "what kind of talk is that?" He was astonished even more by her vehemence than by her clothes.

"This dress is my own. It was you who gave it to me, sir. I'll put it on whenever I want to, and nobody's going to laugh at me."

"You look like a scarecrow," said Juca jestingly. At this point João Magalhães resolved to take a hand.

"It's very fashionable," he said. "You look like a *carioca*; that's just the way the girls in Rio dress. Juca was only joking."

Juca gave the captain a look. His first impulse was to start a quarrel. Was that fellow trying to give him a lesson in good breeding? Then the thought occurred to him that, as a guest, the captain was under obligation to be polite to the young lady.

"There's no accounting for tastes," he said with a shrug. Sinhô Badaró put an end to the discussion.

"Read, my daughter."

But she ran out of the room so that they might not see her weeping.

In Raimunda's arms she gave vent to her stifled sobs. And that night it was João Magalhães, deeply thoughtful, who read the Bible passages for Sinhô Badaró as the latter watched him closely out of the corner of his eye, as if studying and measuring him.

The next day, when the captain upon rising went out for his early morning stroll, he met Don' Ana in the stable-yard, where she was helping to milk the cows. He went over and spoke to her, and she, leaving off milking for a moment, raised her face.

"I made a fool of myself last night," she said to him. "You must be thinking all sorts of things about me, sir. It's always like that when a country girl tries to be a city girl," and she laughed, showing her white perfect teeth.

Captain João seated himself on the gate.

"You looked very pretty," he said. "If it had been at a ball in Rio, you would have been the prettiest woman there, I swear it."

She stared at him. "Don't you like me better the way I am every day?"

"To tell you the truth, I do," and it *was* the truth that the captain spoke. "I like you as you are now, that's pretty enough for me."

With this Don' Ana drew herself erect, picking up her milkpail as she did so.

"You're a straight-spoken man, sir. I like anyone who tells the truth." And the glance that she gave him was her manner of declaring her love.

Raimunda came running up, laughingly—a little laugh of complicity—to take the pails from her mistress, and they both went away.

"It would seem," said João Magalhães in a low voice, addressing the cows in the barnyard, "it would seem that I am going to be married." And he glanced around him at the Big House and the lawn about it and the cacao groves in the distance with an air of proprietorship. Then he remembered Juca, Sinhô and the *jagunços* on the plantation and he shuddered.

Today there was more stir and bustle than usual. Every morning workers would set out for the groves to gather cacao, while others trod the vats or the dried product in the troughs; and as they laboured they would sing their mournful songs:

> A Negro's life is a hard one,
> Hard as hard can be.

Laments that the wind carried away, the moanings of those who, from morning to night, beneath the blazing sun, had to toil in the grove.

This night I want to die,
Far away in some hidden place;
Lashed by the hem of your garment,
I would die for your sweet face.

The workers sang their mournful songs as they went to their labours, songs of servitude and of unrequited love.

But at the same time there was a population of a different sort on the plantation. In physical appearance and the sound of their rude voices, in their manner of speaking and their clothes, they resembled the workers; but these men who now came daily to the place, filling the huts to overflowing and sleeping even in the warehouses or sprawled out on the veranda of the Big House—these were the *jagunços* who had been rounded up by Juca or who had been sent over by Teodoro, by Corporal Esmeraldo of Tabocas, by Azevedo, or by Padre Paiva of Mutuns to guard the Badaró plantation and wait for what might happen. Some of them came mounted, but they were few in number; most of them came on foot, their rifles over their shoulders, their knives in their belts. They would come up to the veranda and wait for orders from Sinhô Badaró, meanwhile sipping the rum that Don' Ana had sent out to them. They were as a rule men of few words, of an indefinable age, black men and mulattoes, with here and there a blond head among them standing out in contrast to the others. Sinhô and Juca knew them all, and so did Don' Ana. This happened every day; João Magalhães estimated that as many as thirty men must have arrived since he had been there. He could not help wondering what would come of it all and what preparations were afoot at Horacio's place. He felt interested, for he had come under the spell of this land, as if he had suddenly sunk roots there. Far away now were his plans for travel. He could not see how he was going to be able to leave Ilhéos, nor could he see why he should do so.

Filled with thoughts such as these, he returned to the city. On the train, seated beside Sinhô Badaró, who slept all the way, he had ample opportunity for reflection. The night before, he had said good-bye to Don' Ana on the veranda.

"I am leaving in the morning."

"Yes, I know. But you will come back, won't you?"

"If you wish me to, I will."

She had looked at him and nodded her head and then had run into the house without giving him time for the kiss that he so desired and for which he had hoped. The next morning he saw nothing of her, but Raimunda gave him a message:

"Don' Ana wanted me to tell you that she will be in Ilhéos for the feast of St. George," And she had also given him a flower, which he carried in his bill-fold.

On the train he did his best to think seriously of the matter, and the conclusion that he came to was that he was in beyond his depth. In the first place there was that business of his having surveyed the land and signed the documents. He was neither an engineer nor a captain, and he might be prosecuted for it and go to prison. It would be better for him to take the first boat out; he had got hold of sufficient money to last him for a number of months without his having to worry. But the worst of it was this crush he had on Don' Ana. Juca already suspected something, had laughed and made a few jokes—he seemed to approve. He had warned him, moreover, that whoever married Don' Ana would have to go straight or he would get into trouble with his wife. And Sinhô had eyed him and studied him closely; and one night he had asked him all kinds of questions about his family, his relationships in Rio, and the state of his business.

As a result Captain João Magalhães had let himself in for a monumental series of lies. And now, on the train, he was frightened as he thought of all this, his eyes every so often instinctively seeking out the barrel of the six-shooter that was visible under Sinhô's coat. Upon thinking it over well, he decided that what he really ought to do was to leave; he ought to take a boat for Bahia, and even there he ought not to remain long, on account of that business of the survey. He would not be able to return to Rio, but he had the whole of the north country from which to choose; the sugar-mill owners of Pernambuco, the rubber-planters of Amazonia. In Recife, in Belém, or in Manáus his ability at poker would stand him in good stead and he might go on living his life with no greater complications than the occasional accusations of a suspicious player, his expulsion from a gambling-house, or an inconsequential summons to the police station. And so on the train João Magalhães made up his mind that he *would* catch the next boat. He had fifteen or sixteen hundred contos that he could lay his hands on and that would enable him to enjoy life for some little while.

But when Sinhô Badaró awoke and the captain had a glimpse of his eyes, which reminded him of Don' Ana's, he remembered that the young lady had something to do with the case. He had always endeavoured to force himself to view their relationship in a cynical light, by seeing in it merely a possibility of getting into the Badaró family through marriage and getting at the Badaró fortune; but he now realized that there was more to it than this. He was feeling the absence of Don' Ana, with that brusque way she had and her manner that was sometimes tender and sometimes austere, as she lived her virgin's life apart, without kisses and without dreams of love. She had sent word to him that she would be in Ilhéos for the feast of St. George. It was not far off. Why not wait until she came and then decide what he should do? There would be no danger in that. The only danger was in Sinhô Badaró's sending to Rio for information concerning him, in which case he most assuredly would not escape the vengeance of these rude but sensitive folk, and he would be lucky if he got off with his life. Once more he eyed that pistol-barrel. But there were Sinhô's eyes, and Don' Ana was seated beside him. Captain João Magalhães did not know what to do. The train whistled as it pulled into the Ilhéos station.

That night he went to call on Margot, with a message from Juca for her. She had moved from Machadão's place and was living alone in a small cottage with a maid to do the cooking and tidy things up. She had sent for her things from Tabocas and now, in her fashionable gowns, she paraded down the streets of Ilhéos with her lace parasol, amid the whisperings of the populace. Everybody knew by this time that she was Juca Badaró's woman, but opinions were divided as to just how matters stood. The Badaró adherents asserted that Juca had taken her away from Virgilio, while Horacio's friends maintained that Virgilio had already left her. Ever since the article in *O Comercio* had appeared, the whisperings had increased, and the Badaró faction would point her out in the street as "the woman who paid for Lawyer Virgilio's schooling." It was a triumph for Margot. Juca had had credit accounts opened for her in the stores, and the merchants bowed before her and were honey-sweet in their words.

Margot offered him a chair in the dining-room and the captain sat down. He accepted the coffee that the maid brought in and proceeded to deliver Juca's message: he would be in to see her the following week and wished to know if she needed anything. Margot then pumped the captain as to what was happening at the plantation, for she, too, had a feeling of proprietorship in the Badaró estate. She appeared to have almost entirely forgotten Virgilio, and only spoke of him once, when she inquired if João had read the article in *O Comercio*.

"When anybody does me dirt, they pay for it," she said. She

went on to praise Manuel de Oliveira: "a sharp fellow, with brains in his head." And she added: "What's more, he's a good sport, very amusing. He always comes here to keep me company. He's so nice."

Captain João Magalhães at once became suspicious: was Margot "staying" with the journalist? There was no telling. But inasmuch as he was conscious of a certain kinship with her, both of them being adventurers and strangers in a strange land, he felt called upon to give her a bit of advice, as on a previous occasion.

"Well you tell me one thing?" he asked. "You're not playing around with this fellow Oliveira, are you?"

She denied it, but not very vigorously. "I don't see—"

"Well, let me give you a word of warning. You don't need to tell me; it makes no difference; I don't care to know. What I want to say to you is: be careful with the Badarós. They're nobody to fool with. If you value your hide, never think of trying to deceive one of them. No, you can't fool with them." He was speaking to Margot, but he appeared to be endeavouring to convince himself. "It's better to give up everything than to think of trying to pull the wool over their eyes."

8

Down by the harbour, in a two-story building, was the export house of Zude Brothers and Company. The lower floor was a cacao warehouse, with the offices of the floor above. This was one of three or four firms that for some years past had been going in for the exportation of cacao. Previous to that time the local crop had been a small one, limited to home consumption; but as cacao-raising became more extensive, a number of Bahia merchants and a few foreign ones, Swiss and German, had founded enterprises to deal in the new commodity. Among these houses was that of Zude Brothers, who had formerly been engaged in exporting coffee and tobacco. They had now added a branch for the cacao trade, had opened an office in Ilhéos, and had sent down as branch manager Maximiliano Campos, an aged white-haired clerk of long experience. In those days it was the exporters who catered to the colonels, the managers and clerks fairly bending double in an effort to be courteous, while the heads of the firms provided luncheons for the planters when the latter were in the capital, and took them out to cafés and houses of prostitution. The firms that dealt in cacao exclusively were small ones as yet; for the most part the business was handled by the branches of the large tobacco, coffee, cotton, and cocoa houses.

And so it was that when Sinhô had finished climbing the stairs of Zude Brothers and Company and pushed open the door of the manager's office, Maximiliano Campos hastily rose and came forward to grasp his hand.

"What a surprise, colonel!" He offered his visitor the best chair in the room, his own, and seated himself on one made of cane. "It's been some time since I saw you. Not since I was down at your place, negotiating for your crop."

"That's where I've been—hard at work."

"And how are things going, colonel? What do you think of the crop this year? Strikes me as being a good deal better than last year's, eh? We've bought more cacao here in the last month than we did in twelve months last season. And this in spite of the fact that some of the big planters like yourself, sir, have not sold as yet."

"That's what I came to see you about," said Sinhô. Maximiliano Campos at once became even more courteous than he had been before.

"You have made up your mind, then, not to wait for a better price? I think you are doing the right thing, sir. I don't believe cacao is going to bring more than fourteen milreis the hundredweight this year—and mark you, at fourteen milreis, planting cacao is more profitable than saying High Mass." He laughed at his own figure of speech.

"Personally, friend Maximiliano, I think it is going to bring more—fifteen milreis at least, at the end of the season. Whoever is in a position to hold on to his cacao is going to make a lot of money. The production will not be up to the demand. They tell me that in the United States—"

Maximiliano Campos shook his head. "It is true we are able to place all the cacao we can get. But this business of prices, colonel, it is the gringos who determine that. Our cacao doesn't stand a chance compared to that from the Gold Coast. And it is England that fixes the price. When you gentlemen have brought this whole region under cultivation, when you have cleared all the jungle land that's still left around here, then it may be we shall be able to dictate prices to the United States."

Sinhô Badaró rose from his chair, his beard falling down over his cravat and shirt-front.

"That is just what I mean to do, friend Maximiliano. I am

going to cut down the forest of Sequeiro Grande and plant it in cacao. Five years from now I'll be selling you the crop from that land, and then we shall have our say as to what the price is to be."

This was no news to Maximiliano. Who in Ilhéos did not by this time know of the Badarós' plans with respect to that forest? But they also knew that Horacio had identical plans. Maximiliano now mentioned that fact.

"The forest is mine," Sinhô Badaró informed him. "This very day I intend to enter title to it in the registry office of Domingos Reis. And God help any man who meddles with it." He said this with an air of determination, and Maximiliano Campos fell back before his outstretched finger. Sinhô, however, laughed and went on to speak of the business in hand.

"I want to sell my crop," he said. "As of now I'm selling twelve thousand hundredweight. Today's price is fourteen milreis two hundred. That makes a hundred and seventy *contos de reis*. Is that right?"

Maximiliano did some figuring. "And how about payment?" he said as he looked up and removed his glasses.

"I don't want any money down. What I want is to open a credit account for myself. I am going to need an advance for the felling of the forest and the planting of the groves. I'll draw a little out every week."

"A hundred and seventy contos and four hundred milreis," announced Maximiliano as he completed his calculations.

They then went on to discuss the details. The Badarós had been selling their cacao to Zude Brothers and Company for a number of years, and for none of their clients in southern Bahia did the export house have so much respect as for the brothers Badaró. Sinhô now took his leave; he would be back the next day to sign the bill of sale.

"Yes," he said before leaving the office, "I shall be needing money to fell the forest and plant cacao—and to fight, also, if I have to, friend Maximiliano." His face was grave and there was a hard look in his eye as he stroked his beard with his hand. Maximiliano did not know what reply to make.

"And your daughter, Don' Ana, how is she?"

Sinhô's face instantly lost its hardness and expanded in a smile. "Ah, there's a girl for you! And pretty, too! It won't be long before she's married."

Maximiliano accompanied the colonel downstairs and into the street, where he left him with a prolonged handshake. "My very best wishes to all the family, colonel."

Sinhô Badaró went down the centre of the street, his hand constantly to his hat as he returned the greetings from all sides. Men even crossed the street to say how-do-you-do to him.

9

The bells were pealing out on the afternoon of St. George's Day. This was the major event of its kind in Ilhéos, being the feast-day of the city's patron saint. The prefect that morning, at the municipal building, had read a proclamation in which he recalled the memory of that Jorge de Figueredo Correia who had held the captaincy of Ilhéos and who had founded the first rude sugar-mills, which the Indians had later destroyed; and those who came after him, bringing the cacao shrub, were then duly commemorated. Lawyer Genaro had made a speech full of quotations in some foreign language that most of his listeners could not understand.

In these official ceremonies Horacio's supporters had taken no part; but they were all there, in their black Prince Alberts, going down the streets to the cathedral, from which the procession was to issue to wend its way through the city's principal thoroughfares. Canon Freitas always strove to remain above the battle in which the political quarrels of the big land-holding colonels were involved; he never got mixed up in them, but contrived to be on amicable terms with the Badarós and with Horacio, with the prefect of Ilhéos, and with Dr. Jessé. If there was a subscription under way for the nuns' school building fund, he would have two copies prepared, so that neither Sinhô Badaró nor Horacio would have to sign on the second line. The result was that each was quite pleased at being handed a blank sheet of paper, thinking that he was the first to put down his name, and this clever bit of strategy had the effect of bringing the government and opposition parties together around the Church.

Canon Freitas, for the matter of that, was quite liberal-minded. He never, for example, made any fuss over the fact that a majority of the wealthy planters were members of the Masonic Lodge. It is true, he had lent his aid to Sinhô Badaró when the latter opposed Masonry (because the lodge had elected Horacio as Grand Master), but he had done so without appearing in the picture, from behind the scenes always. The one open fight that he waged was against the religion of the Englishmen, the

Protestant Church. Otherwise he sought to preserve a nice balance. At the novenas to St. Anthony, if Horacio's lady served as patroness for one, it was Juca Badaró's wife and Don' Ana who did the honours for the other; and at night on such occasions the two rivals would try to outdo each other in a lavish display of rockets and Roman candles. In the month of May, similarly, he would assign one of them a High Mass and the other the care of the altar. Whenever he could, he played upon this rivalry; and when it was to his interest, he endeavoured to bring about harmony.

Lined up around the square stood the men, buttoned in their black Prince Alberts, while the women folk hurried into the church. Ester went by on Horacio's arm, looking very fashionable in her clothes, which reminded her of her school days with the nuns in Bahia. Seeing her, Virgilio removed his derby hat in greeting. Horacio waved his hand, and Ester nodded as the bystanders whispered to one another with sarcastic smiles. Sinhô and Juca Badaró came next, the former with his daughter and the latter with his wife. It was now Captain João Magalhães's turn to remove his top-hat and bow low in greeting. In somewhat scandalous defiance of custom he wore a grey Prince Albert. Sinhô raised his hand to his hat-brim and Don' Ana buried her face in her fan.

"Hello, there, captain!" Juca shouted to him.

"They're sweeties," said a girl standing near.

Dr. Jessé came along, perspiring freely and almost on the run. He paused for a moment to speak to Virgilio, then hurried on. Lawyer Genaro followed, grave and solemn-faced, walking with measured stride, his eyes on the ground. The prefect passed, followed by Maneca Dantas, Dona Auricidia, and the young ones. Teodoro das Baraúnas was dressed in his everyday clothes, with the exception that, in place of khaki breeches he wore a pair of perfectly starched white ones, while on his finger gleamed his enormous solitaire.

Margot also put in an appearance. She did not go into the church, however, but stood in a corner of the square conversing with Manuel de Oliveira. The women bystanders shot her glances out of the corner of their eyes as they remarked on her dress and behaviour.

"She's Juca Badaró's new sweetheart," one of them said.

"They say she used to be Lawyer Virgilio's."

"He's got something better now." They all laughed.

Men in bare feet stood at the edge of the crowd, which was now overflowing the church and the square and spreading out through the streets. Canon Freitas and two other priests came out the door and began organizing the procession. First came the bier with the Christ Child, a small image. It was borne by white-clad children, selected from among the best families, one of them being Maneca Dantas's son. The procession then started off down the street with a band at the head of it. The Christ Child was followed by school children in uniform, under the eyes of their teachers. As soon as there was room, the bier with the Virgin Mary emerged, carried by young women of the city, one of them Don' Ana Badaró. As she passed, she glanced at João Magalhães and smiled, and the captain could not help thinking that she resembled the Virgin, despite the fact that she was brown-skinned while the image was of blue porcelain.

As the band and the school children proceeded on their way, the men stood silently, hat in hand, along the line of march. Also dressed in white, with the blue ribbons of religious confraternities about their throats, the nuns' school pupils took their places behind the Virgin. Then came the ladies: Juca's wife on the arm of her husband; and Ester with a woman friend, Maneca Dantas's wife, Dona Auricidia, who thought that everything was just too lovely. Finally space was made so that the litter bearing the image of St. George, a large and richly adorned one, could join the procession. The saint, a huge figure, mounted on his horse, was engaged in slaying the dragon. The litter was drawn by Horacio and Sinhô Badaró in the front shafts, while the rear ones were manned by Lawyer Genaro and Dr. Jessé. These latter two were conversing like friends, but not so Horacio and Sinhô—they did not so much as glance at each other, but went along with serious mien, careful to keep in step, but gazing straight ahead. The four litter-bearers wore red robes over their black Prince Alberts.

Bringing up the rear came Canon Freitas with a priest on either side of him and all the important personages of the city: the prefect, the deputy, the judge, the prosecutor, a number of lawyers and doctors, the surveying engineers, the colonels, and the merchants. Maneca Dantas and Ferreirinha, Teodoro, and Lawyer Ruy were among this number. And last of all the crowd fell in: pious old ladies, women of the town, fishermen, street labourers, and men and women in their bare feet, the women carrying their shoes in their hands in fulfilment of vows made to the saint.

The band struck up and the procession got under way, slowly and in orderly fashion.

Almost at the same moment Lawyer Virgilio and Captain

João Magalhães left their places on the sidewalk and joined the throng behind the Virgin's bier. Juca Badaró and Virgilio had just exchanged a cool greeting when the captain came up, proffering some sweets that he had bought. Upon hearing his voice Don' Ana threw the bier off balance as she turned to glance back at him. The other women laughed softly.

A group of men had gathered around Margot to watch the procession pass.

"Well, what do you know about that?" said one of them. "Colonel Horacio and Sinhô Badaró side by side! And Dr. Jessé with Lawyer Genaro. It's a miracle, that's what it is!"

For the moment Manuel de Oliveira forgot that he was the editor of the Badarós' newspaper.

"And each of them," he remarked caustically, "is praying to the saint to help him kill the other one. They're praying and threatening each other."

Margot and the others laughed. Then they too joined the procession, which, like an enormous serpent, was crawling slowly through the narrow streets of Ilhéos. Rockets were bursting in the air.

V
THE STRUGGLE

❈❈❈❈❈❈❈❈❈❈❈❈❈❈❈❈❈❈❈❈❈❈❈❈❈❈❈❈❈❈❈❈❈❈

1

Whence came those strains of a guitar on this night without a
moon? The song was a mournful one, a nostalgic melody that
spoke of death. Sinhô Badaró ordinarily did not spend any time
in reflection on the sad-sounding words and music of the airs
that were sung by Negro, mulatto, and white workers here in the
land of cacao; but tonight, jogging along on his black horse, he
could feel the sadness laying hold of him; and for some reason,
he could not have told you why, he thought of the figures in the
picture on the parlour wall of the Big House. That music must be
coming from a grove, from a house somewhere, hidden away
among the cacao trees. It was a man's voice, and Sinhô
wondered why the Negroes should spend a good part of the
night strumming their guitars when the time that they had for
sleeping was so short. Still that air accompanied him at every
turn of the road, at times but a murmur and then suddenly
swelling as if it were very near:

> *Mine is a hopeless life,*
> *Working night and day....*

Behind him Sinhô Badaró could hear the hoofs of the burros
ridden by his *capangas*. There were three of these men: the

mulatto, Viriato; Telmo, a tall, skinny fellow with an effeminate voice, but a dead shot with a rifle; and Costinha, the one who had killed Colonel Jacinto. They were talking as they rode along, and fragments of their conversation were borne to Sinhô on the night breeze:

"The fellow put his hand on the door—there was a rumpus."

"Did you shoot?"

"There wasn't time."

"You always get in trouble when you get mixed up with a woman."

Had Negro Damião been there, Sinhô would have called to him and had him come up and ride alongside him; he would have told him of some of his plans and the Negro would have listened in silence, nodding his enormous head in approval. But Damião now was a half-witted creature, wandering along the highways, laughing and crying like a child, and Sinhô had had a hard time in preventing Juca from having him put out of his misery. On one occasion, weeping and wailing, he had come near the plantation, and those who had seen him said that they would not have recognized him, he was so skinny and all covered with woolly hair, while his eyes were sunken in his head, as he went around muttering things about dead children and the white bellies of angels. He had been a good Negro, and to this day Sinhô Badaró could not understand how he had come to miss his aim that night he had fired on Firmo. Could he have been out of his mind even then? The song, reaching him once more at the bend of the road, brought back the memory of that afternoon, and Sinhô again recalled the picture on the parlour wall: the flute-playing shepherds and the countryside, the blue peace of the sky. It must have been a merry tune, with gentle words of love. A tune to dance by, for the lass had a foot in the air. Not a mournful tune such as the one that came to him now, which was more like a funeral chant:

> My life is a burden and I am tired;
> I came her and my feet were mired,
> Shackled with cacao....

Sinhô Badaró looked about him on both sides of the road. That song must be coming from some worker's hut in the vicinity. Or could it be someone going along the side-road, a guitar slung over his shoulder, and killing the tedium of his journey with music? For a quarter of an hour now the singer had been keeping up with Sinhô's party, lamenting the life that he was compelled to lead in this land, singing of toil and death and the fate of those who were caught in the cacao country. But accustomed as they were to the darkness of night, Sinhô's eyes could not make out any light in the vicinity. All that they encountered was another pair of eyes, belonging to an owl that was hooting ominously. Yes, it must be someone coming along the side-road; but if music was rendering his journey shorter, it was making Sinhô's homeward-bound one seem all the longer.

For these were dangerous roads, now that there was no longer any tranquility round about the forest of Sequeiro Grande. That afternoon when he had given orders for Negro Damião to do away with Firmo, he had still had hopes. But now it was too late. War had been declared, and Horacio was already going into the forest, was getting his men ready, and had filed suit in Ilhéos for possession of the land. On that afternoon, with the European shepherd lass doing her dance, Sinhô Badaró had had his hopes. Again that man's voice, singing. It surely must be someone approaching along the side-road, for the song was growing in volume and in mournfulness:

> *When I die,*
> *They'll carry me in a swaying hammock.*

Many hammocks would be going along the roads now; it was a scene that would be repeated on many nights. And blood would drip from those hammocks to sprinkle the earth. This was no land for rosy-cheeked shepherd lasses, rustic dances, and sky-blue backgrounds. This was a black land—but good for cacao-planting, the best in the world. The voice was coming closer still, singing its song of death:

> *When I die,*
> *Bury me beside the road....*

There were many nameless crosses along the side of the road, marking the graves of men who had died from bullets or of fever—and from the thrust of a dagger, too—on nights of crime or when the plague was stalking the countryside. But still the cacao trees grew and bore fruit, and friend Maximiliano was saying that, on a day when all the forests should have been felled and the land planted, they would dictate their own price to the North American dealers. They would have more cacao than the

English, and in New York Sinhô Badaró's name would be known as that of the proprietor of the cacao plantations of São Jorge dos Ilhéos. He would be richer than Misael. And Horacio would be left beside the road, while nameless crosses would mark the last resting place of Firmo and Braz, of Jarde and Zé de Ribeira.

They had willed it that way. Sinhô Badaró himself would have preferred things as they were in that chromo, with everyone dancing merrily to flutes on a field of heavenly blue. It was all Horacio's fault. Why did he have to come meddling with land that was not his, that could only belong to the Badarós, that no one would think of disputing with them? Horacio was the one who had willed it like that; Sinhô would have preferred a holiday, a lass with her foot in the air beginning a dance over the flowering greensward. Some day it would be like that here, the way it was in Europe. And a smile spread over Sinhô Badaró's face, above his beard, as if, like a prophet or a fortune-teller with cards, he were reading the future.

At the bend where the side-road forked off from the highway the man with the guitar appeared:

> When I die,
> Bury me 'neath a cacao tree....

But the sound of hoofs drowned out the song, and Sinhô was suddenly conscious of its absence. He was no longer seeing a country maiden dancing in the land of cacao, but planted forests and prices dictated from Ilhéos. He saw the man with fingers on his guitar as his feet plodded down the muddy road. Emerging upon the highway, he stood aside to permit Sinhô Badaró and his lads to pass.

"Good evening, boss."

"Good evening." And the *cabras* replied in chorus: "Pleasant journey."

"May Our Lord go with you."

The song died away in the distance as the man strumming his guitar was left farther and farther behind, until soon his voice was no longer audible as he went on singing his mournful refrains, as he went on lamenting the life that he had to lead and asking to be buried beneath a cacao tree. The saying was that it was the cacao slime that trapped men's feet and held them here. Sinhô Badaró did not know of a single one who had gone back. He knew many who mourned their fate, just as this Negro did, who mourned it day and night, in the huts, in the wine-shops, in the offices, in the café—many who said that this was an ugly country and an unlucky one as well, a world's end of a place, with no amusements and no pleasure to be had, where people killed for the sake of killing, and where one was rich today and tomorrow poorer than Job. Sinhô Badaró knew many of this kind; he had listened to such talk dozens of times; he had seen men sell their groves, get their money together, and swear that they were leaving never to return. They would set out for Ilhéos expecting to catch the first boat that left for Bahia. Bahia was a big city; they had everything there: fine stores, comfortable houses, theatres, everything a man could wish for; you had money in your pocket and could enjoy life. But before the boat had sailed the man would be back, the viscous cacao would have clung to his feet and held him, and he would once more sink his money in a piece of land and start planting. Some who did succeed in going, after having made the trip by sea, when they arrived in Bahia were unable to talk of anything but the land they had left behind, the Ilhéos country. And it was certain, as certain as his name was Sinhô Badaró, that after six months or a year had passed, the same individual would return, minus his money, to start the same life again. They said that the cacao clung to a man's feet and he could never leave. That was what the songs said, the songs that were sung on plantation nights.

Sinhô and his men were now among the cacao trees; for this was the Widow Merenda's grove, on the edge of the forest of Sequiero Grande. Sinhô Badaró had heard that she had made an agreement with Horacio; but this would not prevent his taking advantage of the side-road that shortened his journey by something like a mile. If she was with Horacio, so much the worse for her and for her two sons, for then these groves would be added to the new ones that the Badarós meant to plant on the land where the forest stood now. Within five years Sinhô would be entering the offices of Zude Brothers and Company to sell them the cacao from these new plantations. He had said it, and so it would be; for he was not a man to go back on his word. That shepherd lass who was just beginning her dance in the picture on the parlour wall—she would be dancing over a field of golden-yellow with ripened cacao, which was much prettier than that blue in the chromo. Much prettier.

The first shot was accompanied by many others. Sinhô Badaró barely had time to rein back his horse, which received the bullet in its belly and fell over on one side. His *jagunços* were dismounting and taking shelter behind their kneeling burros. Sinhô meanwhile was striving to free his leg, which had been caught beneath his dying mount. His eyes sought to pierce the darkness, and even from where he lay he was able to make out Horacio's ruffians lying in ambush behind some breadfruit trees near the road.

"There they are, behind that tree," he said.

Following the first shots there was a dead silence as Sinhô still tried to work his leg free. Having succeeded in doing so, he rose to his full height and a bullet tore through his hat. Firing his pistol, he shouted to his men: "Come on, we'll finish them off!"

The head of one of the attacking party appeared from behind the breadfruit tree as the fellow took aim. Telmo was standing at Sinhô's side. "I'll take care of him, boss," he said in his effeminate voice. With this he raised his rifle and the man's head tossed and dropped like an overripe fruit. Sinhô advanced, firing as he went. He and his men were now sheltered by a cluster of cacao trees, from where they had a sight of the enemy in his hiding-place. There were five of the latter all together, counting the one who had been killed. The Widow Merenda's two boys and three more of Horacio's *capangas* were there. Sinhô levelled his weapon and fired from behind Viriato. Meanwhile they were advancing through the trees, for Sinhô's plan was to fall upon their opponents from the rear. The latter, however, perceived this manoeuvre and in order to avoid it deemed it best to retire a short distance. As they did so, Sinhô got another of them. The man fell writhing, one hand and a foot in the air, and Viriato disposed of him.

"That will be enough, you son of a bitch. This is no time for dancing."

In the midst of all the fracas Sinhô remembered the girl in the picture, with one foot upraised. This was no time for dancing. Viriato was right. They went on. A bullet caught Costinha in the shoulder and the blood spattered down on the tip of Sinhô Badaró's boots.

"It's nothing," said Costinha, "only a scratch." And he kept on firing.

They continued circling around, and the three men left in the hiding-place, seeing that the game was up, took to their heels through the grove. Sinhô fired his pistol in the direction in which they had fled and then went over to the black horse he had ridden and laid his hand on the animal's neck, which was still warm. The blood was flowing from its belly, making a little pool on the ground. Telmo came up and began removing the saddle, as Viriato went in search of his burro, which had strayed some little distance while the shooting was going on. Sinhô now mounted the donkey and Telmo put the horse's harness on his own burro. Viriato rode on Costinha's beast, with the wounded man on the crupper behind, holding a hand to his shoulder to stop the blood.

Thus mounted they went on down the road, Sinhô still grasping his pistol. There was an almost mournful look in his eyes as he endeavoured to penetrate the darkness round about him. But there was no music now, no voice singing of the troubles of this land. There was no faintest bit of moon to light the corpses beside the cacao trees. Behind him Telmo, with his high-pitched voice which was like a woman's, was boasting vaingloriously:

"I got the bastard, right through the head."

A candle, which pious hands had placed there, was casting its light on a newly made cross beside the road; and Sinhô Badaró reflected that, if they were to illuminate like this all the crosses that would be raised there from now on, the highways of the land of cacao would be brighter even than the streets of Ilhéos. He felt sad about everything. "This is no time for dancing, my lass, but it is not my fault. No, it isn't."

2

The fracases that began that night were not to stop until the forest of Sequeiro Grande had been transformed into cacao groves. The people of the region from Palestina to Ihéos, and even those of Itapira, were later to reckon time with reference to this struggle.

"That happened before the fracases of Sequeiro Grande."

"That was after the struggle for Sequeiro Grande had ended."

It was the last great struggle in connection with the conquest of the land, and the most ferocious of them all. For this reason it has remained a living reality down the years, the stories concerning it passing from mouth to mouth, from father to son, from the old men to the young. And at the fairs in the towns and cities blind musicians sing of these gun-frays which once upon a time drenched with blood the black land of cacao:

> *It was a sorcerers' curse,*
> *On a night when witches rode....*

For the blind are the poets and chroniclers of this country. They it is who, strumming on their guitars, keep alive with their wheedling voices the traditions of the region. And the crowd at the fairs—men come to sell their flour, their millet, their bananas, and their oranges, and those who have come to buy—all gather around these blind bards to listen to the stories of the time when cacao was in its infancy and the century likewise was young. They will toss small coins into the cups at the beggars' feet as the guitar-strings moan and a quavering voice sings of those long-past fatal affrays of Sequeiro Grande:

> *Never was seen so much shooting,*
> *So many dead in the street....*

Men will squat on the ground, a smile on their faces, while others lean on their staffs to listen attentively to the blind man's tale. The verses are accompanied by the music of the guitar; and as the song goes on, there arise before these men of the present the men of another day, who cleared the jungle and felled the forest as they killed and died and planted cacao. Many who took part in the clashes of Sequeiro Grande are living still, and some of them figure in the verses that the blind men sing; but the hearers never think of associating the planters of today with the *conquistadores* of yesterday. It is as if the latter were beings of another world, so greatly have times changed. Where before was the forest, locked in the mystery of its century-old trunks, today stand open cacao groves with their fruit the colour of gold. The blind men go on singing, and their stories are terrifying ones:

> *I am going to tell you a tale*
> *Will make your blood run cold....*

A tale to make your blood run cold—the tale of the forest of Sequeiro Grande. On the very night that the brothers Merenda and Horacio's three *cabras* attacked Sinhô Badaró on the side-road, that same night Juca set out at the head of a dozen men and committed a series of outrages in the neighbourhood. They began by slaying the two Merenda brothers in the sight of their mother, so it was said, as an object-lesson. Then they went on to Firmo's grove, where they set fire to his manihot

206

plantation; if they did not kill Firmo himself, it was because he happened to be in Tabocas.

"That's twice he's got away," said Juca. "He won't get away the third time."

After that they proceeded to Braz's place; but here there was a fight, for Braz and his men put up a resistance and Juca was compelled to retire, leaving one of his lads behind, while it was not known how many had fallen on the other side. One thing was certain: it was Antonio Victor who had brought the man down, for Juca had seen the fellow tumble. Antonio asserted that he had got another one, but they were not sure of this.

A score of years later the blind singers visiting the fairs in the new towns of Pirangy and Guaracy which had sprung up on the site of the forest of Sequeiro Grande would narrate the details of the feud:

> It was a pity, it was a shame,
> So many the folks that died;
> Horacio's men and the Badarós, too,
> On the ground lay side by side.
> Oh, it was enough to break your heart,
> All the killing that was done,
> And all the folks that lost their lives
> Each day from sun to sun.

The men of the old days, it appeared, had gone around drumming up those *jagunços* who were known for the sureness of their firing-aim and whose courage had been tested. It was said that Horacio had sent into the backlands for famous "bad men," and that the Badarós were unstinting of money when it came to paying a rifleman who was a dead shot. The nights were filled with fear, with mystery, and with surprises. Whatever road one might take, however long and roundabout, was not a safe one for travellers. Even those who had nothing whatsoever to do with the forest of Sequeiro Grande, with Horacio or with the Badarós, did not dare to venture along those highways of the cacao country without being accompanied by at least one *cabra*, one professional killer. The hardware merchants, who also dealt in weapons, grew rich in those days. All of them, that is to say, except Azevedo in Tabocas, who bankrupted himself furnishing repeating-rifles to the Badarós. If he had been able to save anything out of the ruins of his business, it was owing to his political dexterity. Later he kept a small shop in Ilhéos, and he too, in his poverty-stricken old age, would tell stories of the same sort to the young students of the city.

> They threw away scythe and ax,
> Slung the rifle over their backs....
> The weapon-dealer, he got rich,
> For they bought guns by the stacks.
> Indeed, I think, when all is told,
> Well-nigh a million must have been sold.

So sang the blind beggars a score of years afterwards, as they told of the deeds and courage of the Badarós, of Sinhô and of Juca:

> Sinhô was a mighty fellow;
> Leader of the Badarós was he....
> One time he finished off five men,
> All alone, so they tell me.
> And Juca, he was also brave;
> His courage was known to all;
> He was not afraid of any man,
> Either great or small.

But they also sang of the courage of Horacio and his followers, and especially of Braz, the bravest of them all, who, though three times wounded, kept on fighting and killed two men:

> Braz, by name Brasilino
> José dos Santos, in full,
> Even as he lay dying,
> On the ground, the trigger did pull;
> For of fighting he'd not had his fill,
> And though wounded, he knew how to kill!

They also gave a picture of Horacio on his plantation, giving orders to his men and sending them out along the roads that surrounded the forest of Sequeiro Grande:

> Horacio gave the orders,
> For he was the master there,
> And his cabras rode down the highway,
> Bringing death with them everywhere....

But the popular ballads inspired by the struggle of Sequeiro Grande not only etched in the figures and pictured the exploits of the protagonists; they also touched on the troubled lives that people in those days led. For instance:

> *A married woman did not exist,*
> *"Unless in Bahia it be." . . .*
> *For down this way they would insist:*
> *"One married woman like any other*
> *—Even though she be a grandmother—*
> *Tomorrow's widow is she."*

The men at the fairs as they listened to all this, a score of years later, in towns that had been reared upon the site where the forest of Sequeiro Grande once had stood, would give vent to exclamations of amazement, laugh heartily, and comment on the narrative in short, sharp sentences. Thanks to the blind man's voice, that entire year and a half of struggle had passed before them, with men slaying, dying, and fertilizing the earth with their blood. And when the blind beggar had ended his song:

> *And now I have truly told you a tale*
> *To make your blood run cold!*

they would toss a few more coins into his cup and go off muttering to themselves: "It was sorcery, that is what it was." For that was what the ballad said, and that was what the men of today said as well. It was sorcery, on a night when witches rode. The curse of black Jeremias had been laid upon the land in those days, being carried from plantation to plantation by the voice of Negro Damião, a lean and filthy figure of a man, a harmless half-wit who wandered, weeping and wailing, down the highways and the by-ways of the cacao country.

3

The excited gossip over the attempt on Sinhô Badaró's life, from ambush, and the death of the Merenda brothers had not yet died down when Ilhéos was stirred by the incident in the café between Lawyer Virgílio and Juca Badaró. For the matter of that, events this year and a half followed one another with such rapidity that

Dona Yayá Moura, the old maid who took care of one altar in the Church of St. Sebastian, was led to complain to her friend Dona Lenita Silva, who had charge of the opposite one.

"So many things are happening, Lenita," she said, "that we really don't have time to discuss them the way we should. Everything moves so fast."

The truth was that both Horacio and the Badarós were anxious to have it over with. Each of them wanted to fell the forest and start setting out cacao trees as soon as possible. The struggle was running into money; the *jagunços* had to be paid by the day and the Saturday payrolls were unprecedentedly high, while the cost of weapons was going up. For this reason neither the Badarós nor Horacio cared to waste any time; and so it was these months were so laden with events worth gossiping about that the good Church ladies actually lost count of them; they had not yet done talking of one when another would come along to claim their attention.

The same was true of the newspapers. Manuel de Oliveira would be writing an article tearing Horacio to shreds over some depredation when word would reach him of another much more important one. The violence of *O Comercio* and *A Folha de Ilhéos* knew no bounds this year. There were no insulting adjectives that were not hurled; and it was a red-letter day in the editorial room of *O Comercio* when Lawyer Genaro received his copy of the big Portuguese dictionary that he had ordered from Rio because the book-stores in Bahia did not carry it. This was a work published in Lisbon and specializing in sixteenth-century terms; and it was then that *O Comercio*, to the delight of the admiring citizenry, began alluding to Horacio and his friends as "knaves," "coxcombs," "varlets," "villains," "filibusterers," and the like. *A Folha de Ilhéos* replied by falling back on the national argot, on which Lawyer Ruy was an authority.

As for the court suit Horacio had filed, it continued to drag along, with no end in sight. "Pending in the courts" was the most inadequate of judicial expressions where a lawsuit by the opposition against those of the government party was concerned, as was the case in this instance. The judge was there to protect the interests of the Badarós, and if he did not make a good job of it, the least that was likely to happen to him was to be transferred by the Governor of the state to some little town in the backlands where there were no modern conveniences and where he would be absolutely lost and forgotten by everybody, with nothing to do but vegetate year after year. On the other hand, the bench of Ilhéos was a stepping-stone to the state supreme court, where one might exchange the title of judge for that of justice, a more sonorous one and much better paid. And so it was in vain that Lawyer Virgilio and Lawyer Ruy bombarded the court with petitions, applications, requests for a writ of inquiry, and so on. As Horacio put it, things were going "at a snail's pace" so far as the suit was concerned. He did not have much faith in legal measures himself, but relied rather on taking the land by force; and here he saw to it that, in contrast to the court proceedings, no time should be lost. The Badarós, likewise, wanted as much speed as possible. An election was due to be held the following year, and many people were saying that a break between the state and federal governments was almost certain, over the question of the presidential succession. Should the state government fall, the Badarós would then find themselves in the opposition, in which case there was no counting on the judge—Horacio's case would then do something more than "pend."

All this was the subject of much talk in the wine-shops, on the street corners, and in the homes of Ilhéos, and even on the boats that lay anchored in the harbour, among the stevedores and the sailors. And in distant cities, in Aracajú and in Victoria, in Maceió and in Recife, people discussed the affrays in Ilhéos just as they did those of the famous Padre Cicero in Joazeiro do Ceará.

Virgilio had gone to Bahia and had secured from a justice who was a supporter of the opposition a court ruling favourable to Horacio in the matter of the rights to the Sequeiro Grande tract. This had been added to the other documents in the case, and Lawyer Genaro had had to cudgel his brains over the law-books in an effort to "quash the ruling" and soothe the feelings of the judge, who was terrified by this intervention of a supreme court justice in a case still in its initial stage. However, what undoubtedly provoked Juca Badaró more than anything else, more than the obtaining of this writ, was the series of articles that Virgilio had written for the opposition paper in Bahia regarding the Ilhéos disorders. The Badarós were not in the least concerned with what *A Folha de Ilhéos* printed, but these articles in a daily paper published in the capital had repercussions outside the state; and though the government dailies had defended Sinhô Badaró, the Governor himself had let it be understood that it would be well to avoid publicity having to do with "such incidents" at a moment when the state government was not on the best of terms with the federal authorities. Horacio had learned of this, and Virgilio had walked the streets of Ilhéos like a conqueror.

One night he went to the café. He had not been there for a long time; his nights were spent in Ester's arms, mad, delirious nights of love; for Ester's flesh had been awakened to the delights of sensuality, and she was being educated in the refinements he had learned with Margot. But tonight Horacio was in Ilhéos, and Virgilio had no place to go. He had grown accustomed by this time to being out of an evening and so decided to drop in at the café for a whisky. He was accompanied by Maneca Dantas, who had come to town with Horacio. It was Virgilio who extended the invitation.

"Shall we step over to the café?" he suggested.

Maneca laughed. "Do you want to lead the father of a family off the straight and narrow path, doctor? I have a wife and child; you know I don't go to places like that," he jestingly remarked.

They both laughed and went up the stairs. In the back room Juca Badaró was playing cards with Captain João Magalhães and other friends. Nhôzinho informed the newcomers that "it was a terrible game, with an ante the highest he had ever seen." Virgilio and Maneca went on into the dance hall, where the pianist and violinist were playing the current melodies. Seating themselves, they ordered a whisky, and Virgilio then noted that Margot was at a table with Manuel de Oliveira and other friends of the Badarós. The journalist nodded to the lawyer, for he never quarrelled with anyone; he was, he maintained, "a professional newspaper man; what he wrote in the paper was the Badarós' opinion and had nothing to do with his own private one—they were two distinct things." Virgilio replied to his nod, exchanging greetings with the others as well. Margot smiled at him; he looked handsome tonight, she thought to herself, and, as she remembered other nights, her lips parted in an initial gesture of desire. Nhôzinho came in with a bottle of whisky.

"This is good stuff—Scotch—I only serve it to a few select customers. It's not for everybody."

"What's the proportion of water?" asked Maneca, who was still in a bantering mood.

Nhôzinho swore that he was incapable of mixing his whisky—above all, one like this, a real whisky—and he blew a resounding kiss from the tips of his fingers by way of indicating how good it was. Then he inquired why it was that Virgilio had not been around for some time. He had missed him.

"Busy, Nhôzinho, busy!" Such was his brief summary of his motives for staying away.

Nhôzinho retired, but Manuel de Oliviera, who had caught sight of the whisky bottle, came over to ask Virgilio for news of another newspaper man, a friend of both of them, who was working on the opposition daily in Bahia.

"Did you see Andrade when you were up there, doctor?" he asked, after having shaken hands with Virgilio and Maneca Dantas.

"We had dinner together once."

"And how is he?"

"Oh, the same as ever. Drinking from the moment he wakes up until he goes to bed. The same old habits. He's amazing!"

"Does he still write his articles while he's drunk?" Manuel de Oliviera was becoming reminiscent.

"He's staggering all the time."

Maneca ordered another glass and served the journalist. Thanking him for his kindness, Manuel continued:

"He's a colleague of mine, colonel. The best writer in Bahia—an all-around newspaper man. But he drinks something terrible. The minute he opens his eyes, before brushing his teeth, he has his little 'snifter' as he calls it, a glass of rum. At the office nobody ever saw him when he could stand perfectly straight. But he has a head on him, colonel, always keeps his wits about him. Can write on any topic—a brilliant fellow." With this he drained his glass and changed the subject: "Good whisky."

He accepted another drink and with his full glass took his leave and went back to his own table. Before doing so, he turned to Virgilio.

"There is a lady friend of yours over at our table who sends you her greetings," and they both glanced in Margot's direction. "She says she would enjoy a waltz with you." And as he walked away, he added with a wink: "Once a king, you know, it's always Your Majesty."

Virgilio laughed at this. At bottom he was wholly uninterested. He had come to the café for a drink and a chat, not to go chasing after a woman, much less one who was at present Juca Badaró's mistress, being kept by him. Moreover, he was afraid that Margot, to whom he had not spoken since the night of their quarrel, would begin her recriminations again. He was not interested in her, so why dance with her? Why renew an attachment that had been severed? He shrugged his shoulders and took a drink of whisky. Maneca Dantas, on the other hand, was quite concerned with the episode. He would enjoy having the people in the café see Virgilio dancing with Margot. That way every one would know that she was still infatuated with the young attorney and that she had only gone with Juca because Virgilio had left her. They would no longer be able to say that Juca had stolen her from her former lover.

"The young lady can't take her eyes off you, doctor," said Maneca.

Virgilio glanced around and Margot smiled, her eyes fixed on him.

"Why don't you have one dance with her?"

But Virgilio was still thinking: "It's not worth the trouble." He moved back in his chair and Margot at the other table thought that he was coming for her and rose to her feet. This obliged him to make up his mind. There was nothing else to do but dance. It was a dreamy waltz, and as the two of them went out on the floor, everybody watched them and the prostitutes began gossiping. At the table where Margot had been sitting, a man started to rise from his seat; there appeared to be a discussion going on between him and Manuel de Oliveira. The journalist was trying to convince him of something; but the man, after listening to him, brushed Oliveira's hand off and went out into the gaming-room.

The pianist was pounding out the slow-dragging waltz on his ancient instrument, and Virgilio and Margot were dancing without saying a word to each other, but her eyes were closed, her lips parted. At this moment Juca Badaró came in from the back room, followed by the man who had summoned him and by João Magalhães and the other players. From the doorway between the two rooms Juca stood gazing at the couple, his hands in his pockets, his eyes sparkling dangerously. As the music died down and the dancers clapped their hands for an encore, he darted across the room, seized Margot by her arm, and dragged her back to the table. She struggled a little, and Virgilio stepped forward. He was about to say something, but Margot stopped him.

"Please don't get into this."

He stood for a moment undecided, eyeing Juca, who waited expectantly. Then he remembered Ester. What did Margot mean to him?

"Thank you, Margot," he said with a smile to his ex-mistress, and returned to his own table, where Maneca Dantas was standing, revolver in hand, anticipating a row.

Juca and Margot, meanwhile, back at their table, were quarrelling in a loud voice, so that all could hear. Manuel de

Oliveira tried to interfere, but Juca gave him one look and the newspaper man decided it was better to keep still. The argument between the pair was growing heated. She wished to get up from her chair, but he pushed her back violently. At the other tables there was a complete silence, even the piano-player being engaged in watching the scene. Juca whirled on the musician.

"Why the hell don't you play that God-damned piano!" he shouted, and the old fellow threw himself on the keyboard, and the couples once again went out on the floor. Juca at once took Margot by the hand, forcing her to come with him. As they passed the table where Virgilio and Maneca sat, Juca turned to the girl, whom he was almost dragging.

"I'll teach you to respect a real man, you filthy whore. This must be the first time you ever lived with one."

This was said for Virgilio's benefit; and he, losing his head for the moment, was on the point of rising from the table, but Maneca Dantas held him back, for he knew that the lawyer would die at Juca's hands if he so much as made a move. Juca and Margot went on down the stairs, and from inside the room they could hear the slaps that he was giving her. Virgilio was pale, but Maneca kept insisting that it was not worth while getting involved.

That was as far as the incident itself went, and by the next day Virgilio had entirely forgotten about it. He no longer gave it a thought, for Margot did not interest him. It was of her own free will that she had gone to live with Juca Badaró. His plan had been to send her back to Bahia with enough money to live on for a few months; but she had preferred to go with Juca the very night they had broken with each other; she had become Juca's mistress and had given to the Badarós' paper the details concerning her former lover's student life. She now had Juca, and if she could not dance with whom she pleased, that was her fault; he, Virgilio, had nothing to do with it.

In a way, he could not but feel that Juca was right. Had Margot been his own mistress, he would not have liked seeing her dance with a man who formerly had kept her. For much less than that he had kicked up a rumpus in a café in Bahia a few years before. He felt that he could even afford to overlook Juca's parting insult; after all, the colonel had simply been jealous and hot-headed. Virgilio was glad that Maneca Dantas had forced him to sit down when he himself was about to do something rash and get into a quarrel over Margot. He would not even snub Juca if the latter should speak to him in the street; he was not angry with him; he understood perfectly how it had happened. The thing was that he was not interested in quarrelling with anyone for Margot's sake.

But from mouth to mouth the tale grew with the telling. Some said that Juca had snatched Margot from Virgilio's arms and had struck the lawyer in the face, while others had a more dramatic version. According to the latter account, Juca had come upon Margot kissing Virgilio and had drawn his revolver. Virgilio, however, had not given him time to fire, but had grappled with him and they had struggled for possession of the girl. This version was the generally accepted one, but even those who had witnessed the incident became involved in glaring contradictions as they narrated it. According to some, Juca had left the café to keep Margot from dancing with Virgilio again and as he passed the table had begged the attorney's pardon. But the majority held to the contrary: that Juca had invited Virgilio to start something and the lawyer had shown himself to be a coward.

Despite the fact that he knew that the most unimportant happenings were magnified in Ilhéos, Virgilio was astonished at the seriousness with which Horacio viewed the thing. The colonel the following day sent him an invitation to come to dinner, and he was delighted to accept, since it meant an excuse for going to the house and thus being near Ester for a moment, feeling her presence, hearing her beloved voice. Arriving shortly before the dinner hour, he met Maneca Dantas at the door, for his companion of the evening had also been invited. Maneca embraced him, and Horacio did the same as the pair entered the house. It seemed to Virgilio that the other men were both very grave, and he imagined that something new must have happened in the neighbourhood of Sequeiro Grande. He was about to ask what the news was when the maid came in to announce that dinner was served. Virgilio at once forgot everything—he would be seeing Ester now. But she, to his surprise, greeted him coldly; and he noticed that her eyes showed the trace of recent tears. The first thing that occurred to him was that Horacio must know something about himself and Ester, and that the dinner was merely a subterfuge. Once more he looked at Ester, and then he realized that she was not merely sad, but offended; she was vexed with him. But Colonel Horacio was amiable enough, more so than usual. No, he was certain, it had nothing to do with Ester and himself. What the devil could it be, then?

Horacio and Maneca practically monopolized the conversation at the dinner table. Virgilio, meanwhile, could not help recalling another dinner, at the plantation, when he had met Ester for the first time. Only a few months had passed, and she was his; he knew all the secrets of that loved body; he had taken her for his own and had taught her all of love's sweetest mysteries. She was his woman. All he could think of was taking her far away from this land of bloody frays and sudden death, to Rio de Janeiro, where they would have a home of their own and live their own life. And it was not merely a dream. Virgilio was only waiting until he should have made enough money— waiting, too, for a reply from a friend in Rio who was endeavouring to procure him a place in some law office or a good job in the public service. He and Ester alone knew of this secret; they had talked it all over between kisses, in the huge bed that took up almost the entire room. They had dreamed of the day when they would belong to each other wholly, without their love, as at present, being tinged by the fear that the servants might suspect that he was in the house. They had dreamed of the time when they would go down the street together, her arm in his, or hand in hand, each belonging to the other forever. While Maneca Dantas and Horacio were talking about the crops, the price of cacao, the rainfall, the amount of soft cacao they had lost, Virgilio was recalling those moments in the bed, amid caresses, in which they had planned their flight to the last small detail, ending always with joyous, lingering kisses that kindled their flesh for love, until the dawn came to expel him and, with furtive steps, he would leave Horacio's house.

These reflections were broken off when, taking advantage of a momentary lull in the conversation between Horacio and Maneca Dantas, Ester spoke:

"They tell me that you were playing the knight errant last evening, Dr. Virgilio." She smiled, but her face was sad.

"I?" said Virgilio, his fork in the air.

"Ester is referring to the row in the café last night," Horacio explained. "I heard of it, too."

"But," replied Virgilio, "there was no row." He then went on to explain what had happened. He had had a bad case of the blues the evening before; he was restless for some reason—here he glanced at Ester—and, happening to meet Colonel Maneca, had invited him to the café for a drink.

"You mean you dragged me, doctor. Tell the story straight." And Maneca Dantas laughed.

Well, they had gone to the café and were having a whisky,

that was all, when Manuel de Oliveira came over to speak to them. At the table with him was a woman whom Virgilio had known in Bahia, in his student days. They danced a waltz together, and just as he was applauding for an encore, Juca Badaró had appeared and carried the woman off. He was not in the least interested in her, and the whole affair would have been of no importance whatsoever if Juca in passing had not made an insulting remark to him. Colonel Maneca Dantas had prevented him from avenging the insult, and he was grateful to the colonel, since otherwise he would have made a fool of himself over a creature who meant absolutely nothing to him. That was all there was to it—he called upon Maneca Dantas to bear him witness. But Ester was indifferent to explanations.

"What difference does it make, anyhow?" she said. "The café is the place where one would expect to find a young bachelor with no family ties. You have a perfect right to amuse yourself, and no one should reproach you for it. But our friend, Maneca here—that is a different story," and she pointed a threatening finger at the colonel. "He has a wife and children. I think I shall have to tell her about it, eh?" Her smile was a joyless one.

Laughing heartily, Maneca begged her not to say anything to Dona Auricidia. "She's terribly jealous." Horacio then closed the discussion. "That will be enough, my dear. Everybody has a right to amuse himself one way or another, to forget his troubles."

Virgilio was more at ease, for he now knew the cause of Ester's vexation, that forced air of indifference, that trace of tears. What gossip might she not have heard, coming from those incredible old maids of the city, those pious old ladies with nothing to do but pry into other people's lives? How he would love to take her in his arms and explain to her, amid a thousand caresses, that Margot meant nothing at all to him, that it was purely by accident that he had danced with her! A great feeling of tenderness came over him, and at the same time one that had in it a little of vanity, at knowing that she was sad because of jealousy. The maid was serving the coffee.

Horacio now invited Virgilio to step into his study, as there was something he wished to talk over with him. Maneca Dantas came also, and Ester remained behind with her crocheting. The study was a small room, the big iron safe being the most conspicuous piece of furniture. Virgilio sat down and Maneca took the armchair: "It's more my size." Horacio remained standing, rolling a straw *cigarro*. Virgilio waited, thinking the matter must have to do with some legal point in connection with the suit on which Horacio wanted his opinion. The colonel went on making his cigarette, rolling the tobacco slowly in his calloused hand and scraping the millet straw with a penknife. At last he spoke.

"I like the way you explained that to Ester," he said. "She would have been worried about it otherwise, for she thinks a lot of you, doctor. The poor girl has almost no one to talk to, for she is much better educated than the other women here. She likes to talk to you, doctor; you both speak the same language."

Virgilio dropped his gaze, and Horacio went on, after lighting the cigarette, which he had finished making.

"But that business last night, doctor, was a nasty affair. Do you know, sir, what Juca Badaró is going around saying?"

"I don't know, and, to tell you the truth, colonel, I'm not interested. I realize that the Badarós have no reason for liking me. I am your attorney, sir, and, what is more, attorney for the party as well. It is natural that they should speak ill of me."

Horacio put his foot on a chair; he was standing almost alongside Virgilio.

"It is your affair, of course, doctor. I don't like to meddle in the lives of others. Not even when the other person is a friend of mine, as you are."

"But what is it all about, anyway?" Virgilio wanted to know.

"Don't you realize, doctor, that unless you do something about this, no one will ever again—you will pardon me for saying so—take you seriously in these parts?"

"But why?"

"Juca Badaró is going around telling God and everybody that he snatched a woman out of your arms, that he insulted you, and that you, sir, did nothing about it. He is saying—you will pardon me for repeating it—that you are a coward, sir."

Virgilio turned pale, but controlled himself.

"Anyone who saw what happened," he said, "knows that is not so. I had already had my dance and was waiting for an encore. Even so, when he took Margot by the arm, I was about to interfere, but she asked me not to do so. And afterwards, when he made that insulting remark, it was Colonel Maneca who held me back."

Maneca Dantas now put in a word for the first time.

"It's plain enough, doctor. If I had let you raise your hand at that moment, we would all be attending your funeral; for Juca already had his hand on his revolver, and no one around here wants to see you killed, sir."

"Doctor," said Horacio. "I've been in this country ever since I

219

was a lad—that was a good many years ago—and I don't know anyone who's better acquainted with Ilhéos than I am. Our friend here is right: no one wants to see you killed, sir, above all myself, for I have need of your services. But neither do I want you to be disgraced around here, with the reputation of a coward. That is why I am talking to you like this."

He stopped as if he had just made a long speech. Lighting another match, he stood holding it in his hand as he looked straight at the attorney, as if waiting for him to speak.

"And what do you think I ought to do, sir?" Virgilio asked.

The match had burned his finger, and Horacio tossed it to the floor; his cigarette remained unlighted, a small object clinging to his big lip.

"I have a *cabra* here," he said, "a fellow you can trust. On Thursday Juca Badaró will be going up to the plantation, so I'm informed. For fifty milreis, sir, you can have the matter taken care of."

"How?" Virgilio did not quite understand.

"For fifty milreis," Maneca Dantas explained, "the man will do the job. On Thursday he will wait for Juca along the highway, and there's not a saint in the calendar will be able to save him."

"And," said Horacio, encouragingly, "there is not the slightest risk, for the Badarós will say that it was I who sent the fellow. If there are any legal proceedings, it will be against me. But don't let that worry you."

Virgilio rose from his chair.

"But, colonel, that's not courage, sending out a *jagunço* to kill a man in cold blood. That's not what I call courage. Now, if it were a matter of my meeting Juca in the street and punching him in the face, that would be something else. But sending out a *cabra* to shoot him—no, I certainly don't call that courage."

"Well, that's the way it is, doctor. And if you expect to make a career down here, you'd better let me call the man. Otherwise there is nothing to be done. You may be the best lawyer in the world, but no one would employ you."

"Not even the party," said Maneca Dantas.

Virgilio dropped back into his seat. He was thinking. This was something he had not looked for. He knew that Horacio was right. In this country, sending out to kill was an act of courage; it made a man respectable. He knew very well there was no plot here. If there should be any trouble with the law, the blame would be on Horacio. But still he could see no good reason for his having Juca Badaró assassinated.

"Let me tell you one thing, doctor, for I'm a friend of yours."

It was Horacio speaking. "In any case, I am going to have Juca Badaró put out of the way. I had already made up my mind to this. He has killed four of my men"—he corrected himself—"that is to say, his men did it; but down here it's the same as if he had done it himself. He set fire to Firmo's plantation and attacked Braz's home. And that's not all he's done. It's better to put him out of the way once and for all. Next week I'm going to begin felling the forest, and Juca Badaró is not going to be there to watch me."

He paused, once again struck a match, and puffed on his cigarette. He looked hard at Virgilio, and his voice was laden with meaning:

"I am merely trying to do you a favour, sir. All you have to do is to give the order to the man, and everybody will know, even though I take the blame, that it was you who sent him to dispose of Juca Badaró. After that no one will bother you, sir, nor any woman of yours. They will respect you."

Maneca Dantas slapped Virgilio on the shoulder; to him it was the simplest thing in the world. "It doesn't cost you anything to say four or five words." And Horacio concluded: "You know, doctor, I like an educated man, but in this country nobody can get along on education alone."

Virgilio lowered his head. The colonel was sending out to have Juca killed, but he wanted him to give the order to the *jagunço*; that way his name would be put on the roster of the brave in Ilhéos. He thought of Ester in the next room, crocheting, eating her heart out with jealousy. He thought of going away with her, of leaving this country for a civilized one—of going far away, away from these forests, these towns, this barbarous city, from this room, where these two colonels were advising him for his own good—*for his own good*—to send out and have a man killed. To flee with Ester, where the morning of every day would be different, the afternoons more beautiful, while at night the only laments would be the gentle sighs of love. In another, distant land—

Horacio's voice came to him across the room:

"Better make up your mind, doctor."

4

The long winter rains were heavy ones, with the water singing on the roof-tops and running down the window-panes. The wind from off the sea was shaking the trees in the garden as the leaves

221

and green fruit fell to the ground. Ester closed her eyes and had a vision of a floating leaf whirling madly in the air, with the raindrops falling on it and weighting it down until it sank to earth. It made her shudder and want to sleep, and she huddled with her lover, her thighs intertwined with his, her head on his broad bosom. Virgilio kissed her lovely hair and put his lips gently to her closed eyelids. She threw out a bare arm and encircled his waist. Sleep was coming, her eyes were growing heavier every moment, her body was exhausted from the violence of their recent embrace. Virgilio in a quick, nervous voice continued talking to her, for he wanted her to stay awake and keep him company. It was midnight and the rain had not stopped, but was coming down harder than ever, and with it came the sleep that relaxed Ester's body. He talked on, telling of things that had happened to him in his student days in Bahia. He even told of other women he had had in his life, to see if this would awaken her, cause her to fight against sleep. But Ester replied with monosyllables and ended by turning over on her stomach and burying her face in the pillows.

"Go on, dear, tell me—"

He saw that she was already asleep; and then it was that all the emptiness of his words came to him, all the things that he had been saying about his life as a student. Empty, wholly void of meaning and of interest. The raindrops were running down the window-pane—like tears, Virgilio thought. It must be good to be able to weep, to let suffering come out by way of the eyes and run down your face. That was the way it was with Ester. When she had learned of his dancing with Margot at the café, she had let the tears come, and after that it had been much easier to listen to and believe Virgilio's explanations. Many people were that way: they found consolation in tears. But Virgilio did not know how to weep. Not even when he had received the news of his father's sudden death in the backlands. And he had loved his father intensely; for he knew all that it had cost the old man to keep him in school; he knew of the pride his father had felt in him. But not even on that day had he wept. With a lump in his throat he had remained standing there in the street where an acquaintance had handed him his aunt's letter containing the news. A lump in his throat, but not a tear in those dry eyes, so dry they smarted. Not a tear.

Down the window-pane the tears of the rain were falling, one after another. Virgilio thought that the night was weeping for the dead of this land. There were so many of them, only a cloudburst would ever be able to atone for all the blood that had been shed! What was he doing here in this land; why had he come here? It was late now, there was Ester—the only thing was to go away with her. When he came, he had been filled with ambition, had had visions of rivers of money, a seat in the Chamber of Deputies, a political career, with all this fertile cacao region in the palm of his hand. At first that had been all that he thought about, and things had gone well; everything had turned out according to his wishes: he had made money, the colonels had confidence in him, he had won success as a lawyer, and things were going very well politically, also; the breach between the state government and Rio was widening, and for anyone who had eyes to see, it was a certainty that the former would not be able to maintain itself in power after the coming election, while it might even fall before then, seeing that there were those in Bahia who were talking of federal intervention in the state. The opposition leaders were in Rio de Janeiro at the moment, engaged in negotiations; they had been received by the President of the Republic, and the situation was becoming clearer every day. There was a very good chance that he would be the candidate for deputy next year, and should there be a change of régime, there was no doubt as to his election.

Then Ester had appeared upon the scene, and all this had ceased to have any importance for him. The only thing that mattered now was her body, her eyes, her voice, her desires, her love for him. After all, he could make a career in Rio just as well as here; as a matter of fact, that was what he had first thought of doing, upon taking his degree in law. If he could get a place in a law office with the right kind of clients, he would not fail to get ahead. The time that he had spent in Tabocas and Ilhéos would not by any means have been wasted. He had learned here in a year and eight months more than he had in five years at school. It was commonly said that an "Ilhéos lawyer" could practise law anywhere in the world, and it was the truth. Here all the subtleties of the profession were called for; a thorough knowledge of the law and of the methods of making a farce of it were necessary. Wherever he might go, he undoubtedly would have a splendid chance of success; for it was not for nothing that here in Ilhéos he was looked upon as one of the best attorneys at the local bar. Naturally, it would not be quite so easy there; he would not get ahead so quickly as he would here, where he already had made a name for himself and had entered upon a political career. Easy and quickly: those two words stuck in Virgilio's mind.

His rise here may have been a rapid one, but it had not been easy. Was it, by any chance, easy to have to send out and have men killed in order to be respected? In order to win the esteem of everyone and be able to hew out a political career? No, it was not easy. Not for him, at any rate, reared as he had been in another land, with other customs and other ways of looking at things. For the colonels down here, for the lawyers who had grown old in this country—for them it was easy—for Horacio, for the Badarós, for Maneca Dantas, for Dr. Genaro with all his pretensions to culture and his reputation for sobriety as a man who never visited a house of prostitution. They sent out to kill as they would to prune a grove, or as they might take out a birth certificate at the registry office. Yes, for them it was easy enough, and Virgilio had given some little thought to this strange fact. But now he found himself viewing differently these rude men of the plantations, these tricky lawyers of the city and the towns, who calmly sent their *cabras* out to wait for their enemies along the highway and fire upon them from behind a tree. His ambition now was, first of all, to go away with Ester; and second, to forget all about the terrible dramas that were a daily occurrence in this region. It had been necessary for him to be put in the position where he himself had to send out and have a man killed in order for him to be able to realize the horrible ugliness of it all and the manner in which this country weighed men down.

The workers in the groves had the cacao slime on their feet, and it became a thick rind that no water could wash away. And they all of them—workers, *jagunços*, colonels, lawyers, doctors, merchants, and exporters—they all had that slime clinging to their souls, inside them, deep in their hearts, and no amount of education, culture, or refinement of feeling could cleanse them of it. For cacao was money, cacao was power, cacao was the whole of life; it was not merely something planted in the black and sap-giving earth: it was inside themselves. Growing within them, it cast over every heart a malignant shade, slaying all good impulses. Virgilio did not hate Horacio, Maneca Dantas, much less the smiling Negro to whom he had given the order to ambush Juca Badaró that Thursday night, words that it had cost him so much to utter. No, if he hated anything, it was cacao itself. He felt himself dominated by it, and resented the fact that he had not had the strength of character to say no and let Horacio, alone, assume the responsibility for Juca's death.

The truth of the matter was he had not known to what an extent this land and its customs, everything that had to do with

224

cacao, had taken possession of him. Once in Tabocas he had slapped Margot, and it was then that he realized for the first time that there was another Virgilio whom he did not know, different from the one who had sat on the bench at school, gentle and lovable, ambitious but merry-hearted, sympathetic to the troubles of others, sensitive always to suffering. Today he was a rude fellow—in what way was he different from Horacio? He was, indeed, like him; his reactions were the same. When he had first known Ester, he had thought of saving her from a monster, an abject and sluggish being. But what difference was there, after all? They were both of them assassins; they were both of them men who sent out *capangas* to kill; they both lived off the golden fruit of the cacao tree.

At that moment, Virgilio reflected, Juca would have received the bullet and would be no more than another corpse along the highway. But he would not, like the others, be buried beside a tree, with only a rude cross to mark his resting-place. Juca was a wealthy planter; his body would be brought to Ilhéos and buried with great ceremony, and Lawyer Genaro would deliver an address at the cemetery comparing the deceased with historical figures of the past. Virgilio himself might even go to the funeral; for in this country it was nothing new for the assassin to follow his victim's casket to the grave—it was said that there were even those who, with mournful air and clad in ceremonial black, would help carry the coffin of the man they had killed. No, he would not go to Juca's funeral; for how would he ever be able to look Dona Olga in the face? Juca had not been a good husband, he had lived with other women, had gambled in the café; but all the same, Dona Olga would surely weep and suffer. How would he be able to look at her at such a moment as that? The only thing for him to do was to go far away, to travel, where he might forget all about Ilhéos, cacao, and deaths in the night; where he would no longer recall that night in Ester's house, the scene in the colonel's study when he had consented to their summoning the *cabra*. Why had he done so if it was not that he was irremediably bound to this land? As for his longing to take Ester away, what was that but a dream that was always receding into the future? Yes, he was bound to this land, hoping himself to become a cacao-planter, hoping in his heart of hearts that Horacio would be slain in one of the Sequeiro Grande fracases so that he might be able to marry Ester.

Only now did he admit to himself that this had been his desire all along, that he had been waiting day after day for the news of the colonel's death, for word that he had been brought down by one of the Badarós' bullets. Even as he laid his plans to procure employment in Rio and exerted himself to make more money so that they might be able to leave, meanwhile finding excuses for postponing his flight with Ester—all this while he had simply been waiting for what he looked upon as the inevitable to happen: for the Badarós to send out and have Horacio killed and thus put an end to the problem. This thought had occurred to him once before and he had endeavoured to put it out of his mind. If anything did happen and Horacio *was* killed, he told himself, he would advise Ester to come to terms with the Badarós, to agree to a division of the forest and the termination of the feud. But on this occasion he had deluded himself by the thought that he was regarding it merely as a likely event, telling himself that he could not fail in his duties as a family lawyer.

Now, in the bed here, as he watched the tears of the rain glide down the window-pane, he forced himself to admit the truth: that he was no longer free to leave this land, that he was definitely bound to it, bound to it by a corpse, by Juca Badaró, for whose murder he was responsible. And so there was nothing to do now but to go on waiting, day after day, until Horacio's turn should come and he too should be buried. Then he would have Ester; he would have the estate and the forest of Sequeiro Grande as well. He would be rich and respected, a political leader, a deputy, a senator, what would you? They would talk about him in the streets of Ilhéos, but they would greet him servilely and bow low to him. There was no other way out. There was no use thinking any longer of flight, of going away and beginning life anew; for wherever he went he would take with him the vision of Juca Badaró tumbling from his horse, a hand to his wound, a vision that Virgilio saw reflected in the dripping window-pane. He beheld it with dry, tearless eyes, and the thought came to him that his heart too was withered, overcast with the sombre cacao's shade.

There was no use thinking of flight. His feet were caught now in the slime of this earth, the soft cacao slime, a blood-slime as well. Never more would it be possible to dream of a different life. On this Thursday night, along the Ferradas highway, a man was bringing Juca Badaró down from his horse. Virgilio turned to embrace the woman beside him. Half asleep, Ester smiled.

"Not now, dear."

His anguish increasing, he threw on his clothes as quickly as possible. He must let the rain fall upon him, upon his burning head, he must bathe his hands, foul with blood, his hands and his blood-stained heart. He forgot to exercise his customary caution as he went out through the garden and onto the railway tracks. Removing his hat, he let the rain trickle down his face, as though these were the tears he himself was unable to shed.

5

There was, however, no foundation in fact for Virgilio's anguish, any more than there was for those high spirits which Dr. Jessé thought he could discern in Horacio's face when the colonel came to spend the night at the physician's home in Tabocas that Thursday. Ever since the start of the struggle for Sequeiro Grande, Horacio had left off travelling along the highways after dark, in spite of the guard that accompanied him. Since it was too late to set out for the plantation that afternoon, business having detained him in the town, he had put off his departure until the following morning, and meanwhile amused himself, toward the close of the day, by sitting in Dr. Jessé's consulting-room as the doctor interviewed his patients. Inasmuch as nearly all of them were acquaintances and political followers of his, he was not wasting his time. He had something to say to each of them and asked after their business, their private affairs, and their families. He could be amiable when he chose to be, and today he was in a particularly pleasant mood, and his feeling of goodwill increased as the day wore on.

From the window of the doctor's office he caught sight of Juca Badaró, booted and spurred, coming out of Azevedo's hardward shop and going down the street. There was a satisfied smile on Colonel Horacio's face as he surveyed his enemy walking along with a nervous gait. By this time the *cabra* whom he had sent out would be on his way to his hiding-place on the Ferradas road. It had cost Lawyer Virgilio something to make up his mind to that. Horacio liked the young attorney and was certain that he was doing him a real favour by thus giving him the credit, without any of the risks, for Juca Badaró's "liquidation." He turned from the window to speak to a woman who had come in, the wife of Silvio Mãosinha, who owned a little piece of land near Palestina and was one of Horacio's right-hand men in that region. Her husband was burning up with fever and she had brought him in from the grove that day and had come in search of Dr. Jessé. They were stopping in the

227

little house that they owned on the other side of the river. The woman was alarmed over Silvio's condition. It had been necessary to carry him in a hammock, she said, for he had not been able to mount.

Horacio accompanied Dr. Jessé to the patient's house and helped lift the sick man onto the bed so that the doctor could examine him. He asked the woman if she needed any money and proffered his assistance. Dr. Jessé knew that the colonel was friendly toward his political henchmen and his friends, but today it struck him that there was something exaggerated in his manner, for he would not even leave the room while the physician was making his examination, but insisted on helping the wife adjust the urinal, change Silvio's clothes, which were sticky with sweat, and administer the medicine that had been sent over from the pharmacy.

As Dr. Jessé was leaving, he took the colonel to one side.

"It's a hopeless case."

"You don't say—?"

"This fever takes them off. He won't live the day out. You had better come with me, sir, take a bath, and wash your hands with alcohol. It's nothing to fool with."

But Horacio only laughed. He remained at Silvio's house until dinner time, promising to come back later. It was not until just before he sat down at the table that he did wash his hands, laughing still at Dr. Jessé's fears. The fever, he remarked, would keep its distance from him. Dr. Jessé thereupon went into scientific explanations; for this unclassifiable fever was one of his major preoccupations. It killed in a few days' time and there was nothing that could be done for it. Nothing, however, could dampen Horacio's spirits tonight. He was feeling so good that he went back to Silvio's to play the nurse again, and he was the one who came running for Dr. Jessé as the patient lay dying, stopping on his way to notify the priest. By the time they arrived Silvio was already dead and his wife was weeping in a corner of the room. Horacio then remembered that by this time Juca Badaró also would be lying dead, stretched out along the highway, his eyes wide-staring and glassy like Silvio's. He informed the widow that he would be glad to pay the funeral expenses, and again assisted her in changing her husband's garments.

The truth was, nevertheless, that Horacio had no real cause for his high spirits nor Virgilio for his mood of depression; for the object of their thoughts, Juca Badaró, was at this moment riding toward his plantation, leaving behind him in the road the body of the man who had been sent to ambush him. Bent over a burro, which Viriato led by the rein, was Antonio Victor, who a second time had saved his boss's life and who had been wounded. It has happened quite by accident. Just as the man in hiding was getting his rifle ready, listening attentively to the approaching hoof-beats, his eyes fixed on the horseman up ahead, whom he recognized as Juca—just at that moment Antonio Victor had heard a slight rustling sound at the side of the road and, thinking it must be a cavy or an armadillo, he had ridden his burro over to the underbrush with the idea in mind of taking some game home as a little present for Don' Ana. Catching sight of the *cabra* with his upraised weapon, he had fired at once, but had missed his aim. The man had then whirled on him and fired, wounding Antonio Victor in the leg. If the latter did not receive the bullet in his chest, it was because he was in the act of dismounting. Hearing the shots, Juca and Viriato came running up and the *cabra* did not have time to flee. Before killing him, before they attended to Antonio Victor's wound, even, Juca had questioned the fellow.

"Tell us who sent you and I will let you go in peace."

"It was Lawyer Virgilio," said the man, "but Colonel Horacio—"

As the *cabra* walked away, Viriato raised his rifle, there was a flash in the night, and the man fell face downward. Juca, who was engaged in bandaging Antonio Victor's leg with a piece torn from his own silk shirt, upon hearing the shot rose to his feet.

"Didn't I say that he could go in peace?" he shouted angrily.

Viriato sought to excuse himself. "It's one the less, boss."

"I'm going to have to teach you to obey me. When I say a thing, I mean it. Juca Badaró doesn't go back on his word."

Viriato hung his head and made no reply. They then went over to the man, who was dead by now. Juca made a face.

"Come give me a hand," he said to Viriato. They placed Antonio Victor on the burro, Viriato took the reins, and they were on their way. By the time they reached the plantation, the kerosene lamps had been lighted, which showed that Sinhô was worried, for he had expected his brother much earlier than this. They all came out on the lawn, and a number of *jagunços* and workers came up to help get Antonio Victor off the burro. There was a babble of questions as the plantation folk crowded around in their anxiety to help the wounded man; and it was Sinhô Badaró himself who took the lad by the shoulders and helped carry him inside. They put him down on a bench and Don' Ana shouted for Raimunda to fetch the alcohol and cotton. At the sound of the mulatto girl's name, Antonio Victor turned his head; and only he and Don' Ana noticed that Raimunda's hands were trembling as she handed her mistress the bottle and the package of cotton. She remained close by to help Don' Ana treat the wound (the bullet had torn the flesh but had not reached the bone), and her rude, heavy hands now became tender and delicate ones, as soft as the hands of a woman should be; and to Antonio Victor they seemed gentler by far, softer and more tender, than Don' Ana's light and finely shaped ones.

6

On a bright, mild, sunny morning the mulatto girl, Raimunda, entered the workers' bunkhouse, bringing with her some bread and milk that Don' Ana had sent out to Antonio Victor. The place was empty, the workers having gone to the groves to gather cacao, and the wounded man was tossing fitfully in a feverish slumber. The girl paused beside his bunk and looked down upon him. His bandaged leg was sticking out from beneath an old counterpane and she had a glimpse of his enormous foot covered with dried cacao slime. This evening he would not be waiting at the river bank to help her lift the pail of water.

Suddenly Raimunda was afraid. Could it be that he was going to die? Sinhô Badaró had said that his wound was nothing at all, that in three or four days Antonio Victor would be up and around again, ready for another one. But even so she was afraid. Had balck Jeremias been alive still, she would have taken her courage in hand and would have made her way through the forest in search of a remedy from the witch-doctor. She had no confidence in this medicine from the pharmacy, which stood beside the bunk and which she had to give him now. She knew a prayer against fever and snake-bite that her mother had taught her in the kitchen of the Big House; and so, before giving Antonio Victor his medicine, she knelt on the floor and prayed:

"Cursed fever, I bury you three times in the bowels of the earth. The first in the name of the Father, the second in the name of the Son, and the third in the name of the Holy Ghost, with the grace of the Virgin Mary and all the saints. I conjure you, cursed

fever, and order you to return to the bowels of the earth, leaving my—"

According to old black Risoleta, upon reaching this point it was necessary to specify the relationship of the patient to the one who was praying—"my brother," "my husband," "my father," "my boss," and so on. Raimunda was undecided for a moment. Perhaps if it had not been so serious a matter, and if he had not been asleep, she would not have concluded the prayer:

"—leaving my man cured of all evils. Amen."

Antonio Victor awoke, and Raimunda's face grew hard again, her manner brusque. "It's time for your medicine." She raised his head with her big round arm and he swallowed the teaspoonful of liquid, then gazed at her with feverish eyes. She went over to what was called a hearth: three stones with a few spent coals and bits of half-burned wood and a kettle of water resting on the stones. Throwing out the water, Raimunda filled the kettle with milk from the bottle she had brought and lighted the fire. Antonio Victor followed her movements with his eyes. He did not know how to begin. The girl was squatting beside the hearth, waiting for the milk to boil.

"Raimunda," he called to her. She turned her head and looked at him. "Come here." She came over with ill grace, taking short, slow steps. "Sit down," he said. making room for her on the bunk.

"No," was her only reply.

Antonio Victor looked hard at her; then plucking up his courage, he asked: "Will you marry me?"

She appeared to be half vexed still; her face was expressionless and her hands played with the hem of her petticoat as she gazed down at the earthen floor. She did not answer, but ran over to the milk, which was beginning to boil.

"It almost boiled over."

Antonio Victor sank back, exhausted with the effort he had made. She was now heating water for coffee, serving him in a tin cup and moistening the bread to save him the trouble. Then she washed the cup and put out the fire.

"I'll be back at lunch time."

Antonio Victor said nothing, merely looked at her. Before leaving she paused beside his bunk again, her eyes once more on the floor and her hands busy with her petticoat, a look of vexation on her face and a trace of annoyance in her voice as well.

"If godfather will let me, I will."

With this she went out the door, and Antonio Victor felt his fever mounting.

7

Juca Badaró had just done arranging with Sinhô, down to the last detail, for the felling of the forest. They were to begin on Monday. The men for the job had already been picked: those who were to do the actual work of cutting down the trees and burning over the land, and those who were to stand guard over them with their rifles.

"It's understood, then: I'm starting Monday." Seated in his high-backed Austrian chair, Sinhô waited, for he knew that Juca had more to say. "He's a good *cabaclo*, that Antonio Victor."

"Yes, he's all right," Sinhô assented.

"He's funny, though," Juca went on with a laugh. "I went down to the bunkhouse to have a talk with him. This is the second time, you know, that he's got me out of a tight place. The first was that time in Tabocas, remember?"

"Yes, I remember it."

"And then again last night. So I went down there to find out if there was anything I could do for him. I told him I was thinking of giving him that piece of burnt-over land which was left from last year and which has not been planted yet. Down by the Border Line Plantation. It's good land and you could raise a fine grove there. But do you know what he said to me?"

"No. What?"

"He said," and Juca laughed again, "that there was only one thing he wanted, and that was for you to let him marry Raimunda. Well, there you are. Everyone has his—here I was, wanting to give the poor wretch a piece of land, and all he could think of was that horrible-looking hag. I promised him you would give your consent."

Sinhô had no objections. "He can marry her," he said, "and have the land besides. The next time I go in to Ilhéos, I will have Genaro enter title for him at the registry office. He's a good mulatto. And Raimunda, she's all right, too. I promised her father that I would take care of her when the time came for her to marry. I give my consent."

He was about to raise his voice and summon Raimunda and Don' Ana to tell them the news, when at a motion from Juca, he paused.

"I have another marriage offer to lay before you."

"Another one? Are you becoming the St. Anthony of the plantation hands?"

"This is not one of the hands."

"Who is it, then?"

Juca was trying to find a way of broaching the subject. "You know," he said, "Raimunda and Don' Ana are both the same age; they were both suckled at black Risoleta's breast; they grew up together; it would be nice if they could be married together."

"Don' Ana?" Sinhô Badaró narrowed his eyes and ran a hand down his beard.

"It's Captain João Magalhães. He spoke to me about it in Ilhéos. He seems to be a right kind of fellow."

Sinhô shut his eyes, then opened them.

"I saw how things were in that quarter," he said. "I could see how flustered Don' Ana was in the captain's presence—both here and at the procession."

"Well, what do you think about it?"

"No one really knows him," said Sinhô reflectively. "He says he's this, that, and the other thing. Lord knows what, down in Rio. But no one really knows anything about him. What do you know yourself?"

"I don't know anything more about him than you do; but I don't think it makes any difference. This is a new country, Sinhô; everything is new down here; you know that very well. Everybody starts from nothing, and it is by what he makes of himself afterwards that you judge a man. Who knows what he was before he came here? It's what lies ahead of him that counts. And the captain impresses me as being a man who's capable of taking care of himself; he has nerve."

"It may be."

"He went ahead and surveyed that land without any legal right to do so. I know he did that for the money and not out of friendship; but it's not for her money that he wants Don' Ana; he's in love with her. I know people as well as I know land. He'd marry her if she didn't have a penny and he had to start clean as a whistle. He has nerve, that's the main thing; it's better than loafing around and complaining all the time."

Sinhô was thinking it over, his eyes half-shut, his hands stroking his black beard.

"There's one thing I want to say to you," Juca went on. "You

233

have only one child, a daughter, and I have none, nor am I likely to have, for the doctor has told me that it is out of the question so far as Olga is concerned. One of these days they are going to bring me down with a bullet, you know that as well as I do. Some enemy of mine will get me—I'll never live to see the end of this business. And then, when you get to be an old man, who is the Badaró who is going to gather cacao and pick the mayor of Ilhéos? Who, I ask you?"

Sinhô did not reply.

"He's a man of our own sort," continued Juca. "What if he is nothing but a professional gambler, as they tell me? Isn't all this a gamble in the end? We need a man like that in the family, one who can take my place when they put me out of the way."

Striding across the room, he took up his riding-whip from a bench and began tapping his boots.

"You could marry her to a professional man, a doctor or a lawyer, but what would that get you? The fellow would merely live off the profits of cacao without ever planting a grove or felling a forest; he would simply run around spending it. But the captain's been around; what he wants now is to become a cacao-planter. That is why I think it is a good thing."

Raimunda came into the room to sweep it, but Sinhô made a gesture for her to leave.

"What I said to him was this: 'There's only one thing, captain. Whoever marries Don' Ana has to take her name. I know it's contrary to custom; it's the woman who takes the man's name. But in Don' Ana's case her husband has to become a Badaró.'"

"And what did he say to that?"

"He didn't like it at first. The Magalhães family, he said, was all this and all that; but when he saw there was no getting around it, he agreed."

Sinhô Badaró now called to the other room: "Don' Ana! Raimunda! Come here!"

The two of them came in. Don' Ana appeared to suspect what her father and her uncle had been talking about. Raimunda had a broom in her hand, for she thought that they were calling her to do the sweeping. It was to the mulatto girl that Sinhô spoke first:

"Antonio Victor wants to marry you. I've given my consent. I'm also giving you the land in back of the Border Line Grove as a dowry. Does that suit you?"

Raimunda did not know in which direction to look: "If godfather thinks it is all right—"

"Very well, then, get ready for the wedding. We don't want to lose any time. You may go."

Raimunda left, and Sinhô then called Don' Ana over to where he sat.

"I have a request for your hand, also, my daughter. Juca thinks it is all right, but I don't know what to say. It is that captain who was down here. How do you feel about it?"

Don' Ana was like Raimunda in Antonio Victor's presence, her eyes on the floor, her hands toying with her skirt; she was at a loss for words.

"It was Captain João Magalhães?"

"That's who it was. Do you like him?"

"Yes, Father, I do."

Sinhô Badaró slowly stroked his beard. "Get the Bible. We will see what it says."

Then it was that Don' Ana took her eyes from the floor, her hands from her skirt; her voice was strong and resolute:

"Whatever it says, Father, there's only one man in the world that I would marry, and that's the captain. Even without your blessing."

Saying this, she dropped at her father's feet and clasped his legs.

8

Dr. Jessé had to go away in the middle of the performance, leaving the amateurs of the Tabocas Group without a stage director or a prompter. This somewhat spoiled the show, as a number of the actors were not letter-perfect in their parts and had to rely on the prompter. It did not make a great deal of difference, however, for the townspeople had little time to spend in commenting on *Social Vampires*. The man who had come in search of Dr. Jessé had brought with him a piece of news that created a commotion: Horacio was ill, laid low with fever. And so it was that the doctor had to leave in the middle of things. Stowing the various remedies in his bag, he mounted his horse at once and was off, accompanied by the messenger. The news none the less flew from mouth to mouth down the aisles; and when at eleven o'clock the next morning Ester got off the train and, without stopping for lunch, mounted the horse waiting at the station and rode away surrounded by *cabras*, the whole of Tabocas by that time knew that Horacio had caught the fever while helping to care for Silvio, who had died three days before.

Silvio's widow had already begun a novena for Horacio, "such a good man," as she said. Indifferent to gossip, Virgilio had accompanied Ester as far as Tabocas, but he did not go to the plantation that day. He would come out if the colonel took a turn for the worse. He too now carried a revolver, ever since he had learned of Juca Badaró's escape from ambush. The town, meanwhile, lived in expectation of the next messenger who should come for medicine. Dr. Jessé's office was closed, and his wife was informing patients that the doctor would not be back until Colonel Horacio had "passed the crisis," a statement that was interpreted by the local residents to mean that Dr. Jessé would come back accompanied by Horacio's corpse, for none ever recovered from that fever. Innumerable cases of plantation hands, colonels, professional men, merchants, were cited to bear this out. And once again among the pious old ladies the story began circulating about the Devil in a bottle, who one day would come out to carry off Horacio's soul. It was said that Friar Bento was already on his way from Tabocas to the plantation to give the colonel extreme unction and to confess him and absolve him of his sins.

But Horacio did not die. A week later his fever began going down, until it had left him completely. It was in all likelihood his rugged frame rather than Dr. Jessé's medicines that had saved him, for he was a man without vices or physical weaknesses and with perfect organs. And no sooner had his fever begun subsiding than he ordered his men to start the felling of the forest of Sequeiro Grande. Virgilio was summoned out to the plantation, for the colonel wished to consult him regarding certain legal fine points. He had been out once before, but Horacio at that time was delirious and was raving of cacao, of forests being felled, groves planted, and crops harvested, as he shouted orders to his men. Ester, a thin little wraith of a figure, would not leave the sick man's bed, but exhibited a boundless devotion. When Virgilio had come the first time, she had merely asked him for news of her child in Ilhéos, and he had scarcely had an opportunity to see her alone. When he did see her and kiss her, it was but for a moment, as she was returning from the kitchen to the bedroom with a basin of hot water. They had exchanged but a few words, and Virgilio felt hurt, as if he had been betrayed. There was, further, a look of veiled uneasiness in his eyes, as if he felt that he was to blame for Horacio's illness and for his death, which he regarded as inevitable—as if the colonel had fallen ill in fulfilment of the young attorney's hidden wishes. He realized that Ester shared this feeling; but all the same, her attitude hurt him, as if she had been unfaithful to him.

When Horacio, out of danger now, summoned him for the consultation, Virgilio endeavoured to put on an aggrieved look with Ester, whose own face wore a tired and downcast expression. Clad in his nightgown, the colonel was lying between the white sheets, and his wife was seated on the bed, one of her husband's hands in hers. Never had Horacio felt so happy, now that Ester's devotion had been put to the test. His high spirits made him want to be active, and he began giving orders not only to the workmen, but also to Maneca Dantas and Braz, who had come to visit him that day. Virgilio, as he came into the room, bent down and embraced the colonel, gave Ester a cold hand-clasp, embraced Maneca Dantas also, and proffered his congratulations to Dr. Jessé "on the miracle he had performed." Horacio laughed at this.

"Next to God," he said, "the one that saved me, doctor, was this girl here," and he pointed to Ester. Then he apologized to Dr. Jessé: "Of course, my friend, you did all you could— medicines, treatment, what the devil. But if it hadn't been for her, who didn't sleep a wink all this time, I don't even know—"

Ester rose and left the room, and Virgilio, without noticing, took the place on the bed that she had left vacant. Beneath him he could feel the body-warmth of his beloved, and a sudden anger at Horacio came over him. Horacio had not died. For an instant Virgilio permitted his most deeply hidden thoughts to come into his heart. He had not died. Ah, if he could only send out and have him killed!

For some time he paid no attention to the conversation, being wholly absorbed in his thoughts. It was a question put to him by Maneca Dantas: "And what do *you* think about it, doctor?" that brought him back to his surroundings.

Afterwards he met Ester down near the troughs. She clung to him, sobbing. "You don't think I ought to have done that, do you? I couldn't do anything else."

He was deeply moved by this, and caressed her loved body underneath her clothing. He kissed her eyes, her face—then broke off suddenly. "Why, you've got fever!"

She assured him that it was not that; she was just tired. Kissing him again and again, she begged him to stay at the plantation that night; she would be able to visit his room as she came and went about the house, caring for the sick man. He

237

promised, touched by her entreaties and being anxious for her caresses. It was only when they saw a group of labourers coming down the road that he let her go.

At dinner, however, Ester was unable to eat or to remain seated at the table. Complaining of cold chills and seized by a fit of vomiting, she left the room. Virgilio turned very pale. "She's caught the fever!" he said to Dr. Jessé. The doctor rose and went in search of Ester, who was locked in the toilet. Virgilio also rose, paying little regard to the presence of Maneca Dantas and Braz. He stood at the doctor's side in the hallway until Ester opened the door, her eyes glowing strangely.

"Do you feel bad?" he asked, taking her by the arm. She gave him an affectionate smile and pressed his hand lightly.

"No, it's nothing. It's just that I can't stand on my feet. I'm going to lie down for a while. I'll be back."

Then, giving directions to Felicia, she went into the room where Virgilio had slept that night long ago, on his first visit to the plantation. He stood in the hall and watched her as she lay stretched out on the bed. Dr. Jessé came in after her and, begging Virgilio's pardon, closed the door behind him. From the front room Horacio called, to know what was going on. Virgilio now went into the colonel's bedroom.

"She's caught the fever," he announced in a shaken voice. He wanted to say something more and could not, but stood there staring at Horacio. The colonel's eyes opened wide, his mouth gaped; he too wanted to speak, but could not get the words out. He was like a man hurtling through the air with nothing to which to cling. Virgilio felt like embracing him, like mourning and weeping with him, the two of them together, two poor wretches.

9

It was the unanimous opinion in Ilhéos that the Badarós obviously had the advantage in the struggle for the possession of Sequeiro Grande. It was not merely what the pious old ladies said in the church sacristies; the knowing ones were saying it in the wine-shops as well, and even the lawyers at court; all were agreed that the Badaró brothers had practically won the victory, thanks in no small part to Horacio's illness. The court proceedings were at a standstill, having been brought to a stop by the opposing petitions of Lawyer Genaro, which the judge had granted. And Juca Badaró had already gone into the forest, was clearing that portion of it which bordered on the Sant' Ana Plantation, and had begun burning over the land.

It was true the shooting affrays still kept up, with Maneca Dantas, Jarde, Braz, Firmo, Zé da Ribeira, and the other small planters of the vicinity doing all in their power to impede the efforts of the Badarós' men. Maneca Dantas had laid an ambush for the workmen as they were going out to cut down the trees in one part of the forest, and this had led to a big gun-battle. And Braz with a few men had invaded the workers' camp on a night when Juca was not there. But in spite of all this the work went forward and the Badarós had won a foothold in the tract.

The attacks by Horacio's followers then flared with greater violence than ever. And so, while Juca was accompanying and guarding the workers, Teodoro das Baraúnas took the offensive. Appearing one night at José da Ribeira's plantation, he set fire to the latter's store of dried cacao, causing the loss of two hundred and fifty hundredweight which had already been sold. He also fired the manihot plantations, and Zé da Ribeira had great difficulty in putting out the blaze.

In Ilhéos people were saying that, after having set fire to Venancio's registry office, Teodoro das Baraúnas had become a pyromaniac. In the *Folha de Ilhéos* he was never otherwise referred to than as "the incendiary." Lawyer Ruy even wrote a famous article in which he compared Teodoro to Nero, fiddling while Rome burned, José da Ribeira and his workmen being compared to the "early Christians, victims of the criminal and bloodthirsty madness of this modern Nero, more monstrous even than the degenerate Roman Emperor." Of all the articles published during the Sequeiro Grand fracases, this was the one that achieved the widest renown, being reprinted by the opposition daily in Bahia under the heading: *"Crimes of the Government Party in Ilhéos."* Criminal proceedings were started against Teodoro.

But what definitely turned the tide of opinion in favour of the Badarós was the fact that Horacio, even after he had recovered, had not been able to begin felling the forest on the side that bordered his own plantation. This lack of energy on his part was attributed to Ester's illness; but be that as it might, the fact was that the workers and *jagunços* sent out by the colonel had returned once or twice without having been able to start the clearing and burning. This time it was Sinhô Badaró himself who for two rights in succession led the attacking party against Jarde's camp; and Horacio's men had ended by abandoning the undertaking. Braz alone, with a few of his followers, had been able to burn over a small plot, but it was as nothing compared to the Badaró clearings.

Even so, there were those who were betting on Horacio. They based their opinion chiefly on the colonel's larger fortune; for he was a man with much money in the bank and was capable of carrying on the struggle for a long time. Not only did the felling and planting eat up money, but above all there was the tremendous cost of maintaining an army of ruffians. In addition to all this, Sinhô Badaró was getting ready to marry off his daughter, and he wanted to do it in grand style. He had sent to Rio de Janeiro for a multitude of things and was completely remodeling his house in Ilhéos, adding to it a whole new wing in which the young married couple were to live. He was even giving the Big House at the plantation a coat of paint; and meanwhile, dressmakers and lace-makers were busily at work on the bride's wardrobe; for the marriage of a colonel's daughter was an event. The bride-to-be had to have enough linen to last her for many years, and it would afterwards serve for her children and grandchildren: counterpanes, sheets, coverlets, pillowcases, table napkins, all of them richly embroidered. Messengers were sent out into the backlands to buy up the finest of lace. All in all, what with paying the *jagunços* who were hired to kill, and paying the dressmakers, shoemakers, and others who clothed and shod the bride, money was freely spent. In Ilhéos there was almost as much talk of this marriage as there was of the Sequeiro Grande frays. João Magalhães had left the city and gone out to the plantation to aid Juca with the clearing; but from time to time he would come back to Ilhéos for his game at the café, to pick up a little money at poker. At the Big House he had no expenses and was able to economize.

However, various persons were aware that Sinhô Badaró had already spent practically all the income from this year's crop. Maximiliano told his intimate friends that Sinhô had even proposed selling, at a sufficiently low price, his next year's crop in advance, whereas Horacio had not as yet disposed of half the cacao he had gathered this year. Nevertheless, those who were putting their wagers on him were few in number. The majority were for the Badarós; they could see no possibility of the latter's losing; and for this reason they sent out to have new clothes made for Don' Ana's wedding. The pious old ladies and the married women would gather of an afternoon at Juca Badaró's house, where Olga would show them the expensive apparel that had just arrived from Rio: under-garments of embroidered cambric, nightgowns that were a dream, the most fashionable of corsets, and fine lacework from Ceará. Mouths would open wide with "Oh's" of admiration, for these were things Ilhéos had never seen before, denoting a luxury that bespoke the power of the Badaró family.

And as Sinhô, his melancholy face framed in his black beard, went down the narrow streets of the city, merchants would bow low to him in greeting and, pointing him out to travelling salesmen from Bahia or from Rio, would say:

"There goes the squire of this region, Sinhô Badaró!"

10

Ester died on a bright sunny morning, just as the bells in the city were pealing, summoning the inhabitants to a feast-day Mass. The ravages of the disease had destroyed practically all her beauty; her hair had fallen out, and at the end she was but a ghost of the woman she had once been, her eyes protruding from her emaciated face—for she was certain that she was going to die and she wanted so badly to live. At first she had been horribly delirious and, lying in pools of perspiration, had muttered disconnected words. Once she had clung to Horacio, screaming that a snake was encircling her neck and was about to strangle her. Maneca Dantas, who was spending a few days at the plantation, and who had grave suspicions regarding the relations between Ester and Virgilio, fairly trembled with fear that she would mention the lawyer's name in one of her delirious spells; but she appeared to see nothing but snakes in the forest pools, silent and treacherous, ready to leap on an innocent frog. And thus she would scream and suffer, tearing at the hearts of all those who stood by, as the mulatto girl Felicia silently wept.

When Dr. Jessé saw that the fever was not going down, he advised that Ester be taken in to Ilhéos. It was a mournful scene as the hammock, borne by workmen, left the plantation.

"It's like going to her funeral already, poor girl," Dr. Jessé remarked to Virgilio.

Horacio accompanied his wife, and the three of them went along in silence. Virgilio for his part had had nothing to say ever since she had been taken ill. All he had done had been to wander through the Big House, finding each day some fresh excuse for not returning to Tabocas. No one paid any attention to him, however, for all was confusion in the house, with *cabras* riding off for medicine, Negro women heating basins of water, and Horacio now giving orders to his men about entering the forest and now rushing back to the bed where Ester lay delirious.

As they went to lift her into the hammock, she had a moment of lucidity and took Horacio's hand, as if he had been the master of the world's destinies. "Don't let me die."

Despairingly Virgilio went out on the lawn. That look in her eyes was for him, a suppliant look, a mad desire to live. It lasted but a second, but in it he beheld their dream of another life in another land, the two of them free to love. He now felt no hatred for anyone—only for this land which had killed her, which had taken her away forever. But it was more than hatred; he was afraid. No one ever got free of this land; it took all those who sought to flee. It had bound Ester with the chains of death; it was binding him, too, would never let him go. He strolled out into the groves and walked up and down until they called to him that they were ready to leave. The hammock, covered by a sheet, went first and the men followed. It was a terribly long journey. When they came to a halt in Ferradas, they found that Ester's fever had increased. She was screaming now, screaming that she did not want to die.

They reached Tabocas early in the evening and Dr. Jessé's house was soon filled with visitors. Virgilio did not sleep the entire night, but lay tossing in the solitary bed that he had not occupied for so long a time. He remembered the nights with Ester, the endless caresses, their bodies quivering with love, nights of passion in the house in Ilhéos. The next day he saw her leave in a special coach, on an improvised bed, Horacio seated on one side of her and Dr. Jessé, half asleep, on the other side. The physician's face was tired and careworn and his eyes were deep-sunken in his fleshy face. Ester looked at Virgilio and he felt that it was a good-bye. The curious ones thonged the station. When the train had left, they fell back to let him pass, but their remarks followed him out into the street.

The following day he could stand it no longer and went in to Ilhéos. When he came back from Horacio's house, a visit that he prolonged as much as possible, there was nothing for him to do but drink in the wine-shops, for he was in no condition to go to court that day. Drowsy and irritable, he had the feeling of being alone, without a friend. He missed Maneca Dantas's company, for the colonel had conceived an attachment for the young lawyer. The latter would have liked to talk to someone, to unburden his soul, to tell everything—all that had happened and all that he had dreamed: the beautiful part, the life together in another land, the two of them with their love; and the wretched part as well, the longing for Horacio to die from a bullet fired by an enemy. He still thought at times of going away, but he knew it would never be, knew that he was bound to this land once and for all.

The only thing that could wrest him from his somnolent state was conversations having to do with the Sequeiro Grande affrays. They seemed somehow to bind him more to Ester, for it was owing to the forest of Sequeiro Grande that they had come to know and love each other. As for Horacio, however much his wife's illness may have grieved him, he never for a moment neglected his business, but had the other planters and the foremen come down to Ilhéos to talk things over with him. Maneca Dantas on one of these trips brought Dona Auricidia to help about the house and with the care of the child. Virgilio, meanwhile, would engage in long discussions with the colonels on the subject of politics, the method of conducting the court proceedings, and the articles in *A Folha de Ilhéos*. Horacio spoke of the attorney's candidacy for the post of deputy as now being an assured thing. In the course of Ester's illness Virgilio had come to conceive an esteem for her husband; he was conscious of a tie with the colonel and was grateful to discover that, however incapable of feeling and of suffering he might appear to be, Horacio *was* suffering none the less, and was doing all in his power to save Ester, by calling in physicians for consultations and through religious vows and Masses said in church.

Only once was Virgilio able to speak to Ester alone. She seemed to have been waiting only for this. It was the night before her death. Horacio had gone out and Dona Auricidia was dozing in the parlour when he slipped into the room to relieve Dr. Jessé, who was so tired he could hardly stand. Ester was sleeping, her face bathed with perspiration. Virgilio laid a hand on her head, then took out his handkerchief and wiped away the sweat. She stirred in bed, moaned, and finally awoke. When she recognized him and saw that they were alone, she raised a fleshless hand from beneath the sheet and, taking his own hand, laid it on her bosom. Then, with a great effort, she smiled and spoke to him:

"What a pity that I have to die—"

"You're not going to."

"—die, no." She smiled again, as sad a smile as ever was. "Let me see you."

Virgilio knelt beside the bed, his head upon hers as he kissed her face, her eyes, her fever-parched lips. He let the tears come, let them bathe her hands, the cold tears streaming down his cheeks. They did not say anything for a number of minutes—her feverish hand in his hair, his anguished mouth kissing that fever-disfigured face.

The sound of Dona Auricidia bestirring herself caused him to rise, but before he did so, she gave him a farewell kiss. He then went out where he could be alone and weep unseen. When Dona Auricidia came into the room, Ester appeared to be much better.

"It was the last rally before the end," Dona Auricidia remarked the next day, when Ester died. Only Virgilio knew that it was love's farewell.

Many people came to the funeral. There was a special train from Tabocas, bringing many from Ferradas also, including Maneca Dantas and the other planters whose groves bordered on Sequeiro Grande. There were friends from Banco da Victoria, and all Ilhéos turned out. In the black coffin the dead woman's face recovered some of its beauty, and Virgilio beheld her as she had been the evening before her death, smiling, happy at loving and being loved.

Ester's father wept, and Horacio, clad in black, received the condolences, while Dona Auricidia kept watch beside the body. The burial took place late in the afternoon, and twilight had already fallen before the service in the cemetery was over. Dr. Jessé said a few words at the grave and Canon Freitas blessed the remains, as the bystanders sought to discover traces of grief in Virgilio's pale face.

When the attorney invited Maneca Dantas to have dinner with him, the colonel declined; he had to keep Horacio company on this first night of mourning. Virgilio accordingly roamed the streets. Dropping in at a wine-shop, he was conscious of the curious stares of the others in the place, and so he went on down to the wharves, where he stood watching a boat unload its cargo. He also chatted for a while with a man in a sky-blue vest who had been drinking heavily. What he wanted was someone with whom he could have a long talk, someone on whose bosom he might weep out all the tears that were in his heart. He finally ended by going to Margot's house. She was sleeping and received him with much surprise. But when she saw how sad and wretched he was, her heart opened to him and she took him to

244

her breast with the maternal love with which she had taken him in that other night in Bahia, the night he had received the news of his father's death in the backlands.

11

The winter rains passed and the hot days of summer came. The trunks and boughs of the cacao trees were putting forth buds, the first signs of the new crop. Huge gangs of labourers, who had no groves to tend or cacao to dry, were now employed in felling the forest of Sequeiro Grande for the Badarós and for Horacio. For after Ester's death the latter had thrown himself into the struggle for the possession of the wood. He too had gone into the jungle, repelling the attacks of the Badarós' ruffians, opening clearings, and burning over enormous tracts. Progress was being made on each side of the forest, and it was indeed a race as to who would get there first. The gun-frays had subsided somewhat, but those who were in the know asserted that they would begin again the moment Horacio and the Badarós met on the banks of the river that cut the woods in two.

In Virgilio all this while Horacio had his most efficient collaborator. Not only were the court proceedings making headway, owing to the petitions with which the attorney daily bombarded the judge, but the brief he, as Zé da Ribeira's lawyer, had drawn up against Teodoro das Baraúnas was by way of being a legal masterpiece. Moreover, Virgilio had carefully studied the title to the forest that had been entered by Sinhô Badaró and had discovered in it great legal flaws. The survey, for example, was incomplete; it did not specify the true boundaries of the tract in question, but was very vague, wholly lacking in precision. Virgilio made a long exposition on the subject to the court, and this was added to the other documents in Horacio's suit.

Then the warm days ended and the long winter rains came back again, hardening the fruit of the cacao trees and illuminating with gold the shady groves. Once the slack months were over, the highways of Tabocas, Ferradas, Palestina, and Mutuns were filled with travelling salesmen, and the boats from Bahia as well, all bound for Ilhéos. Immigrants came also, whole swarms of them, travelling third-class in the overladen holds. Syrians came and at once made for the forest, their worldly possessions on their backs. Many of the burnt tree-trunks were

245

now putting forth fresh green shoots, and the clearings were bright with colour. New roads were already in existence, and with the winter rains flowers sprang up around the crosses that had been planted in the ground the winter before. This year alone the forest of Sequeiro Grande was diminished by almost half. It was now surrounded by clearings and burnt tracts and was, in brief, living its last winter. On rainy mornings workers would go by, scythes on their shoulders, singing their sad songs, which died away in the mysterious depths of the giant wood:

> *Cacao is a good crop,*
> *And there's a new crop coming....*

12

Don' Ana Badaró and João Magalhães were married at the beginning of winter. Juca and Olga stood up with the bridegroom, Lawyer Genaro and Dr. Pedro Matta's wife with the bride. Canon Freitas, who blessed the nuptials, at the same time joined in wedlock, "until death shall part," Antonio Victor and Raimunda. Antonia wore a pair of black boots that caused him a great deal of discomfort, and Raimunda's face held its usual cross-grained expression. Don' Ana had told the other couple that they need not do any work that day, but Raimunda had insisted on helping in the kitchen, and Antonio Victor had served the drinks to the guests, limping a little on account of his boots.

It was an epoch-marking occasion in Ilhéos. Don' Ana was very pretty in her white gown, with her bridal veil and orange blossoms and her big gold wedding ring, while João Magalhães, clad in a very fashionable frock-coat, drew admiring exclamations from the marriageable young ladies. Sinhô Badaró, looking a little sad, presided over the festivities, his gaze following his daughter as she went about seeing that the guests were served.

Those present then filed into the bridal chamber and past the big bed laden to overflowing with wedding gifts. There were tea-sets, silverware, articles of wearing-apparel, knick-knacks and ornaments, and last but not least a long-barreled Colt .38 revolver of plated steel and ivory, a masterpiece of the weapon-maker's art, the gift of Teodoro das Baraúnas to Captain João Magalhães. Teodoro drank champagne and cracked jokes with the captain about the stains on the bed-sheets, as the ecstatic guests went out into the ballroom, where a band in full uniform was playing waltzes, polkas, and an occasional maxixe.

When the time came for the newly wedded pair to retire, at early dawn, Juca Badaró took them to one side.

"How about starting a little one, eh?" he said with a laugh. "A legal Badaró."

The honeymoon, spent at the plantation, was rudely interrupted by the news of Juca's assassination in Ilhéos. After the wedding he too had come out to the plantation and then had gone into the forest with a gang of men. He had come back to the city for the week-end, being anxious to see Margot.

On Sunday he was having lunch with a physician who had just come to Ilhéos with a letter of introduction to Juca from a friend in Bahia. The physician was staying in a boarding-house kept by a Syrian in the centre of town. What once had been a parlour had been transformed into a restaurant, and Juca and the doctor were seated at the first table just inside the door, the former's back being turned to the street. The *cabra* stuck his revolver through the door and fired once, and Juca slumped down slowly over the table as the physician put out his arms to support him. Then suddenly he got to his feet, one hand grasping the side of the door while with the other he raised his revolver. The assassin had taken to his heels down the passageway, but the bullets from Juca's weapon reached him, three shots in all, and he dropped with a thud. Juca then sank down by the door and the revolver slipped from his hand and clattered over the stone pavement. It had all happened in a minute's time. The other guests now came running up to Juca, while passers-by in the street surrounded the fallen *cabra*.

Juca Badaró died three days later in the bosom of his family, having first stoically endured an operation as the physician endeavoured to extract the bullet. Resources for such an operation were wholly lacking in Ilhéos; there was not even any chloroform; yet Juca had smiled through it all as the doctor did his best for him.

"Save my brother's life," Sinhô Badaró said to the latter, "and you may ask of me what you will."

It was in vain, however; nor were any of the other medical men in Ilhéos, or Dr. Pedro, who came up from Tabocas, of any avail. Before dying, Juca called Sinhô over to him and asked him to give Margot a sum of money. Then he spoke with the captain and Don' Ana, although the room was by now full of people.

"Let's have a little one, eh? Don't forget! A Badaró." Then he took Don' Ana's hand and stroked it.

"Give him my name," he said.

Olga carried on scandalously, but Juca paid no attention to her and died peacefully enough. His only regret, expressed in his last words, was that he would not live to see the forest of Sequeiro Grande planted in cacao.

That night, in the house of mourning, Sinhô strode up and down the room. He was thinking of vengeance. He knew that it would mean nothing to shoot down Horacio's hired assassins; the other planters who were associated with him would feel as he did that the only thing to do was to have the colonel himself put out of the way. Only one life could pay for Juca's, and that was the life of Horacio da Silveira. He accordingly made up his mind that he would go through with it, come what might. He had a conversation on the subject with Teodoro and with the captain, at which Don' Ana was present. Lawyer Genaro and the deputy had felt that Horacio ought to be prosecuted; for Juca's assassin was one of his *jagunços*, who, as everybody knew, was employed on his plantation. But Sinhô violently waved this aside. This was no matter for a lawsuit. It would not be so easy to prove Horacio's guilt, now that the *cabra* who had committed the murder was dead; and besides, Sinhô Badaró would not feel avenged by seeing his enemy brought to trial as a criminal. Don' Ana was of the same opinion, and the captain agreed, although he was rather frightened by it all, not knowing how it was going to end. Teodoro das Baraúnas came over the next day to discuss their plans.

But killing Horacio was not so easy. He was well aware that both the country highways and the city streets were dangerous places for him, and he seldom left his own plantation. When he did come in to Ferradas or Tabocas, he was surrounded by a huge bodyguard, composed of men who were crack shots, and Braz almost always rode by his side. He did not return to Ilhéos for months, but instead Virgilio would come out to keep him in touch with things. For after a time Lawyer Genaro had succeeded in convincing Sinhô that he ought to institute legal proceedings against Horacio. Sinhô had agreed to this for reasons of his own. The police deputy at Ilhéos had thereupon begun an inquiry and had come to Tabocas to take the testimony of a number of witnesses, all of whom asserted that Juca's assassin was a worker on Horacio's plantation. And some fellow from the wharves with an imitation ring on his finger was quite emphatic in telling of a conversation he had had with the murderer on the eve of the crime, in a wine-shop kept by a certain Spaniard. The *cabra* had been very drunk, and the man with the imitation ring had led him on to talk. He had displayed a hundred-milreis note and had confided that he was "doing an important job for Colonel Horacio." The prosecutor accepted this evidence, Sinhô brought pressure to bear upon the judge, and the best that Virgilio had been able to do had been to prevent Horacio's being taken into custody. The judge on this point had excused himself to Sinhô by inquiring: "Who would dare go out to arrest Horacio on his own plantation? With all respect to the majesty of the law, it would be better if Horacio were arrested on the day of the trial." And Virgilio had promised that his client would put in an appearance.

Lawyer Genaro had great hopes of being able to get a jury that would bring in a verdict of guilty against the colonel. After all, the Badarós were political bigwigs, and it was by no means impossible that the jurors would decree the maximum penalty. Sinhô, on the other hand, had hopes of his own—of being able to do away with his enemy before the case came to trial; or as a last resort (as he told João Magalhães) he would take care of Horacio when the latter came to court. For this reason he let them go ahead.

Horacio himself, however, did not devote a moment's thought to the criminal proceedings. What he wanted, first of all, was news of how his own suit against Sinhô and Teodoro over the Sequeiro Grande property was coming along. As a result of all these legal bickerings the lawyers of the town grew rich, with their briefs, writs, petitions, and counter-petitions, as they diligently prepared their speeches to the jury.

Despite the difficulties in the way of Horacio's assassination, his life was twice seriously endangered. The first time was when one of Teodoro's men succeeded in getting as far as the guava tree beside the Big House. He waited there a number of hours until the colonel appeared on the veranda and, sitting down on a bench, began cutting up cane-stalks for a burro he had that was very tame. The bullet hit the animal, and Horacio dashed after the *cabra* who had fired the shot, but did not overtake him. The other time was when an old man attempted to kill him. This old fellow had previously appeared at the Badaró plantation, where he had made an offer to Sinhô to put Horacio out of the way. He wanted no pay for it; all he wanted was a weapon. He had an account to settle with the colonel, so he said. Sinhô had told them to give him a rifle, and the old man had tried to sneak up to the Big House one moonlit night. Someone afterward recalled that he was the father of Joaquim, who once had owned a grove that now was in the possession of Horacio.

As a result of these attempts Horacio strengthened his bodyguard and rarely went out of the house; but, for all that, his men went on clearing the forest of Sequeiro Grande. It would not be long before his workmen and those of the Badarós met up. The jungle was thinning out all the time, and the storehouses on either plantation were filled with cacao shrubs to be planted where the giant trees had stood. When Horacio's *cabras* and those of the Badarós did meet, there would certainly be a pitched battle and blood would flow in the highways.

13

But just as the men in the forest were hearing the sound of their adversaries' axes on the other side of the river, Ilhéos was awakened one morning by a sensational piece of news brought by the telegraph. The federal government had decreed intervention in the state of Bahia, army troops had occupied the city, the Governor had resigned, and the opposition leader, who had come back from Rio on a warship, had taken over as interventor. This meant that Horacio was now the government party and Sinhô Badaró was in the opposition. There was also a telegram from the new interventor, dismissing the prefect of Ilhéos and appointing Dr. Jessé to take his place. On the first boat coming down from Bahia a new judge and a new prosecutor arrived, bringing with them the the appointment of Braz as municipal police officer. The former judge was appointed to a small town in the backlands, but he refused to accept, preferring to retire. It was said that he was already a rich man and had no need of a magistracy in order to live. In honour of the occasion, *A Folha de Ilhéos* came out with a front page printed in two colours.

It was only then that Horacio appeared in Ilhéos, in response to a telegram from the interventor summoning him to Bahia for a conference. He was showered with congratulations from friends and political followers, and a large crowd followed him and Virgilio down to the wharf; for the attorney went with him.

"Doctor," said Horacio, when they were aboard ship, "you may consider yourself a federal deputy."

Sinhô Badaró also came in to Ilhéos. That night he had a conference with Lawyer Genaro, the former judge, and Captain João Magalhães. Meanwhile he ordered his men to continue felling the forest. The next day, when he went back to the Sant' Ana Plantation, he found Teodoro das Baraúnas waiting for him there.

14

Braz's telegram snatched Horacio away from his political talks with the interventor, from the arms of the women in the cafés of Bahia, and from *apéritifs* with politicians in the more fashionable bars; he caught the first boat back. The Badarós' men, it appeared, had fallen on his workmen while the latter were engaged in cutting timber and had wreaked a veritable carnage. What was more important, they had set fire to a large number of cacao groves. Throughout the whole of the struggle thus far the groves had been respected, as if by tacit agreement. Fire might devour registry offices, millet and manihot plantations, and warehouses full of dried cacao; men might be killed; but the cacao trees themselves were spared.

But Sinhô now knew that he had played his last card. The change in the political situation had robbed him of his best trumps. A proof of this was the disagreeable surprise that he met with when he went to sell his next season's crop in advance to Zude Brothers and Company. That firm was quite uninterested. They spoke of how tight money was, and finally proposed buying his cacao, but only with a guaranteed lien upon it. Sinhô was furious. What! Ask a mortgage on his, Sinhô Badarós', groves? He became so violently angry that Maximiliano feared a personal assault, but he nevertheless persisted in his refusal to buy the crop unless the guarantees he had asked for were given. "Those are orders," was all he would say. The result was that Sinhô had to dispose of his cacao to a Swiss export house at a wretched figure. And so it was, in view of all this, that he had been led to give Teodoro carte blanche to do what he liked so far as the forest was concerned. The firing of Firmo's and Jarde's groves had then followed, and even a few of Horacio's were burned. Carried by the wind, the conflagration lasted for days, as the snakes hissed and fled.

On the pier at Ilhéos the colonel's friends were waiting to grasp his hand and sympathize with him over the Badarós' barbarous conduct. Horacio, however, said nothing, but sought out Braz from among those present and went off with him for a long talk at police headquarters. He had promised the interventor that everything would be done legally; and if the *jagunços* were now given orders to assault the Badaró plantation and lay siege to the Big House, they found themselves in the newspaper columns transformed into "police troopers seeking to capture the incendiary, Teodoro das Baraúnas, who, as was well known, had taken refuge at the Sant' Ana Plantation."

This siege of the Badaró Big House marked the end of the struggle for the possession of the Sequeiro Grande tract. Teodoro had wanted to give himself up and thus deprive Horacio of his legal pretext. Sinhô, however, would not hear of this, but had him smuggled out and taken to Ilhéos, where friends put him aboard a ship bound for Rio de Janeiro. Later, word came back that he had taken up residence in Victoria do Espirito Santo, where he was attached to a commercial house. Horacio, it may be, had learned of Teodoro's flight; but if he knew of it, he said nothing, but continued to surround the Sant' Ana Big House just as though Teodoro was really in hiding there. The forest of Sequeiro Grande had been felled, and the burnt-over tracts in the wood were now indistinguishable from the burned groves, there being no longer any boundary lines between them. The jaguars and the monkeys had long since fled, and the ghosts as well; and the workers had come upon old Jeremias's bones, which they had buried, with a cross to mark the site.

Sinhô Badaró and his *cabras* held out for four days and four nights; and when at last he fell wounded and, on Don' Ana's orders, was taken to Ilhéos, Horacio was then able for the first time to come near the house. Sinhô had been taken away one morning in a hammock borne by his men, and that night Captain João Magalhães had Olga and Don' Ana mount and follow him. Raimunda went with them, the women being accompanied by five *jagunços*. They were to sleep that night at Teodoro's plantation and catch the train for Ilhéos the next morning.

João Magalhães, with the men that he had left him, now entrenched himself on the river bank. At his side was Antonio Victor, who now and then would raise his rifle and fire. The captain, with eyes accustomed to the lights of the city, was unable to distinguish anything on this night without a moon. At whom could the mulatto be firing, anyway? But the answering shot proved that Antonio Victor was right; his eyes, used to the darkness of the groves, could make out perfectly the figures of the men who were drawing near. They were being surrounded and there was nothing to do but retreat to the highway, the majority of them falling into the hands of Horacio's ruffians. Their number was being constantly diminished, until at last there were but four of them left. Antonio Victor then disappeared for a moment and came back with a burro ready saddled.

"You must mount and go, captain. There's nothing more to be done here."

It was the truth. Horacio's men, with Braz at the head of them, were now on the lawn of the Big House.

"And what about the rest of you?" said João Magalhães.

"We'll go along to guard you."

At the very moment they were leaving, Braz stepped onto the veranda of the seemingly deserted house. There was a dead silence that seemed to go with that moonless night. Horacio's men were gathered on the lawn, ready to go in. In obedience to an order, one of them struck a match to light a lantern. From inside the house came a shot, putting out the light but, by a miracle, not killing the man. The others now threw themselves down and began crawling along over the ground in an effort to enter the house in that manner. Again someone fired from within, aiming at Horacio in the midst of his *capangas*.

"There's still one left," said Braz to the colonel.

They entered the house, weapons in hand, eyes on the alert. They were filled with hatred now; they wanted to do to these last defenders even more than they had done to those who had fallen on the river bank and on the highway, whose eyes they had gouged out and whose lips, ears, and testicles they had cut off. They overran the house without finding anyone. The shots had ceased.

"They've run out of ammunition," Braz remarked.

He now took the lead, with a man on either side, and Horacio followed. The only place left was the attic. They clambered up the narrow stairs and Braz kicked the door in with his foot. Don' Ana Badaró fired and a *cabra* fell. And then, seeing that this was her last bullet, she tossed the revolver down beside Horacio.

"Now, then, have them kill me, assassin!" And she took a step forward.

Braz opened his mouth wide in astonishment. Had he not just seen her fleeing down the road with Olga and Raimunda, guarded by a handful of men? He had let them pass within bullet-range without firing on them. How the devil had she managed to get back? Don' Ana took another step forward, filling the attic doorway.

Horacio stepped aside. "You may go, my girl, I don't kill women."

Don' Ana went down the stair and crossed the parlour, glancing up at the chromo as she passed. A bullet had shattered the glass and had torn open the breast of the young shepherd lass who was dancing in the picture. Don' Ana went on out onto the lawn. The men were silent.

"Hell of a brave woman!" one of them muttered.

Don' Ana took one of the horses that were standing there saddled, and with a last look at the Big House she mounted, spurred the animal, and rode away into the night without a moon and without stars. Only then, after her figure had been lost to sight along the highway, did Horacio raise his arm and his voice at the same time, as he gave an order to his men to set fire to the Badaró homestead.

15

Lawyer Genaro, who was fond of aphorisms, was accustomed to remark years afterwards, when he had moved to Bahia in order to be able to give his children a better education: "All that tragedy was to end in a comedy." He was alluding to the Sequeiro Grande affrays and to Horacio's subsequent trial in Ilhéos.

Shortly before the trial started, the court had handed down an opinion in the suit brought by Horacio in defence of his rights to the Sequeiro Grande tract. This opinion recognized Colonel Horacio da Silveira and his associates as the rightful owners and directed the public prosecutor to proceed against Teodoro das Baraúnas for the burning of Venancio's registry office in Tabocas. Action was also to be taken against Sinhô Badaró and Captain João Magalhães for having registered an illegal title to the property. This latter case, however, was dropped, for the reason that Horacio, on Virgilio's advice, did not press the matter. Economically the Badaró family was in a very bad way; they owed money to the exporters, two of their crops had been sacrificed, and their holdings had by no means increased during this year of strife. On the contrary, not only had the Big House, the troughs and ovens been destroyed, but the young cacao shrubs in the warehouses had been burned and a large amount of damage had been done to a number of their groves. It would take many years for them to rebuild even a part of what had once been a great fortune. There were no adversaries for Horacio now.

As for the trial, it was no more than a justification of the colonel. He had surrendered the night before, and the best room in the municipal prefecture, which served also as court and prison, was transformed into a dormitory. Braz had stationed a number of police troopers as a guard, and he himself kept Horacio company. The room was filled with the colonel's friends, and the "prisoner" kept up a lively conversation, sent out for whisky, and in general held open house until morning.

The trial began at nine a.m. the next day and lasted until three a.m. the following morning. The Badarós had brought down from Bahia a lawyer with a great reputation, one Dr. Fausto Aguiar, who with Dr. Genaro was to serve as an assistant prosecutor. For everybody was aware that the new public prosecutor would make a very weak plea, seeing that he belonged to the same political party as Horacio.

Clad in his black robe, the judge came into the room accompanied by his clerks and bailiffs and took his seat in the high-backed chair above which there hung a crucified Christ shedding blood of a deep-red hue. Beside the judge sat the prosecutor, and chairs were placed for Dr. Genaro and Dr. Fausto, the assistant prosecutors. On the defense side were Virgilio and Lawyer Ruy. The judge uttered the regulation words and the trial was opened. The courtroom was packed and the crowd overflowed into the corridors outside. And a small lad, who years afterwards was to write the stories of this land, was then summoned by a bailiff to draw from an urn the names of the citizens who were to constitute the jury. He drew out a card, the judge read the name, a man rose, crossed the room, and took his seat on one of the chairs reserved for the seven jurors. Another card was drawn, and the judge read: "Manuel Dantas." Colonel Maneca Dantas had risen when Lawyer Genaro's voice rang out: "I refuse to accept him."

"Refused by the prosecution," announced the judge.

Maneca sat down, and the lad continued to draw the cards. From time to time a name would be objected to by the prosecution or the defence, until the jury was finally selected.

Meanwhile, the courtroom was buzzing:

"Unanimous for acquittal."

"I don't know—there are a couple of doubtful ones." And names were whispered.

"Maybe three," said someone else. "José Faria is no great friend of Horacio's, he isn't. He may vote against it."

"Lawyer Ruy was down at his house today. He'll vote for acquittal."

"They'll take an appeal."

"They won't have to; it will be unanimous!"

Bets were then laid as to the likelihood of an appeal. The state supreme court still represented the overthrown government, and if there was an appeal, Horacio might be found guilty, or at least a new trial would be ordered. The majority of those present, however, were confident that the jury would unanimously acquit the colonel, and in that case there would be no grounds for an appeal. The jurors were now sworn to "decide the case in accordance with the law and the evidence and their own consciences," and took their places in the box. The lad who had drawn the cards from the urn then left the judge's dais and took a seat behind the attorneys for the defence. From there he followed the entire proceedings, drinking it all in with eager ears and kindling eyes. Even at dawn the next morning, when some of those in the courtroom were dozing on the benches, this small boy was still nervously watching the show.

The whisperings suddenly ceased and a silence fell on the room, for the judge had just ordered the municipal police officer to bring in the defendant. Braz then went out and returned, accompanied by Colonel Horacio da Silveira with a trooper on either side. The colonel wore a black frock-coat, his hair was brushed back, and his face wore a serious, almost a penitent look. He stopped in front of the judge amid a heavy silence, as the onlookers leaned forward in their seats.

"Your name?"

"Horacio da Silveira, Colonel of the National Guard."

"Profession?"

"Farmer."

"Age?"

"Fifty-two years."

"Residence?"

"Holy Name Plantation in the municipality of Ilhéos."

"Have you heard the charge?"

The colonel's voice was clear and strong: "I have."

"Have you anything to say in your own defence?"

"My attorneys will speak for me."

256

"You have attorneys? Who are they?"

"Dr. Virgilio Cabral and Dr. Ruy Fonseca."

The judge motioned to the criminals' bench. "You may sit down."

But Horacio remained standing. Braz took the hint, removed the humiliating bench, and substituted a chair. Even then Horacio would not be seated. This created a sensation in the courtroom. Lawyer Ruy then requested of the judge that the accused might have the right to stand in place of being seated on that symbolic bench. This request was granted, and from all corners of the room the colonel's gigantic form could be seen, his arms folded over his bosom, his eyes fixed on the court. The young lad rose up to get a better view of him. He found him superb, an unforgettable figure.

The court clerk read the charge. The reading lasted three long hours as the depositions made by the various witnesses followed one after another. From time to time the attorneys would take notes on sheets of paper, and beside Lawyer Genaro was a stack of ponderous law-books. It was one o'clock in the afternoon when the clerk finished reading the charge, and the judge then recessed court for an hour, for lunch. The jurors, who were not permitted to talk to anyone, remained in the room and a lunch was sent in to them from the hotel, paid for by the prefecture. The only exception was in the case of Camilo Goes, who suffered from a stomach ailment and had to follow a special diet; his meal was brought to him from home.

The small lad watching the trial left the room holding his father's hand, but he was back in the doorway again as the bailiff was ringing his big bell to summon the clerks and attorneys. Once more Horacio came in and stood in front of the judge. The public prosecutor now took the floor, and as had been expected, his plea did not amount to much. He talked for half an hour, leaving innumerable loopholes for the defence. Nevertheless, in accordance with custom he ended by asking for the supreme penalty, which was thirty years in prison. He was followed by Lawyer Genaro, who spoke for two hours, mingling citations taken from law-books, some in French and some in Italian, with a detailed examination of the evidence, which, according to him, went to prove beyond a doubt that the assassin was a *cabra* in the employ of Horacio. He made much of the deposition of the man with the false ring, who had held a conversation with the slayer on the eve of the crime. He went into the history of the Sequeiro Grande affrays, and concluded by declaring that "if the defendant were not found guilty, justice in the Ilhéos region

257

would be no more than the most tragic of farces." Then, with a few Latin phrases, he sat down. The courtroom audience had understood little of this babel of tongues and citations, but their admiration for Lawyer Genaro was undiminished. It made no difference which side he was on; they esteemed him as a thing of worth that belonged to Ilhéos.

Dr. Fausto then followed, and curious necks were craned. His fame as a great orator had preceded him, for his defence pleas in Bahia were celebrated ones. If the truth were told, the Ilhéos residents would much rather have heard him on the side of the defence in this instance; but it was known that Sinhô Badaró had paid him fifteen *contos de reis* for his services. He did not speak long, for he was saving himself for the rebuttal, but the speech he made was a high-sounding one, and his voice was filled with emotion. He spoke of the wife left without a husband, the brother bereft of his brother, and went on to praise Juca Badaró as "the knight-errant of the land of cacao." His voice rose and fell, and was filled with hate as he came to speak of Horacio, " a *jagunço* who has become a leader of *jagunços*." On the other hand, it was in the gentlest of tones that he referred to Olga, "the poor, inconsolable widow." With a last appeal to the noble sentiments of justice on the part of the jurors he concluded; and court was then recessed for dinner.

That night there was a larger crowd than ever, and the lad had difficulty in holding his place. The clerks in the business houses had not been able to come in the morning or afternoon, and they now struggled for standing-room all the way to the prefecture stairs.

The first speaker at the evening session was Virgilio, who replied to Lawyer Genaro. He proceeded to demolish the evidence presented by the prosecution, showing the weakness of the entire case against Horacio; and he created a sensation when, in referring to the man with the false ring, whose deposition constituted the cornerstone of the state's evidence, he revealed that the fellow in question was a thief by the name of Fernando, who had arrived in Ilhéos a few years before and who had there become a vagabond with unknown means of livelihood. And "this witness so dear to the prosecution" was at that moment to be found lodged in a prison cell in Ilhéos, having been arrested on a charge of vagrancy and disorderly conduct. Of what value was the word of a man like that? A thief, a vagabond, a liar. Virgilio then read a deposition he had obtained from the Spanish proprietor of the wine-shop where the man with the false ring was alleged to have had his conversation with the assassin. The Spaniard declared that the witness in question had always had the reputation of being a liar, that he liked to tell stories and make up things, and that he, the Spaniard, suspected that it was the man with the ring who on two occasions had been responsible for the disappearance of money from the cash-drawer of the shop. Of what legal value, then, were any statements which such a witness might make? Was any credence to be given to what a fellow of that type had to say? At this point the speaker glanced first at the judge, then at the jury, and after that let his eyes roam over the courtroom. He went on to give his own version of the Sequeiro Grande affrays. He recalled the other suit, for the possession of the land, which had been lost by the Badarós. He also recalled the setting fire to Venancio's registry office. And after talking for two hours, he closed with a plea that justice be done his client.

It was Lawyer Ruy who replied to Dr. Fausto. His powerful voice, a little shaky with drink, now resounded through the courtroom. He trembled, he wept, he grew emotional, he hurled accusations, he defended his client, as his auditors alternately wept and laughed; but he was particularly violent toward Dr. Fausto, who "had dared to spew cowardly words upon the stainless character of the Bayard of Ilhéos, Colonel Horacio da Silveira." With the exception of the lawyers and the young lad, no one knew who Bayard was, but they all thought it was a very nice comparison.

Still standing erect, his arms folded over his bosom, Horacio all this while showed no trace of weariness. Occasionally he would smile at Lawyer Ruy's more savage and venomous ironies directed at Dr. Fausto.

Then came the summation speeches, and they all took the floor again, to repeat what they had said before. The only thing new was a deposition that Lawyer Genaro had obtained to offset that of the Spaniard, the wine-shop proprietor whose testimony Virgilio had introduced. This fresh bit of evidence came from an acquaintance of the man with the false ring, another frequenter of the Spaniard's place—the man in the sky-blue vest. This latter asserted that the man with the ring "was a good fellow, even though he might not appear to be." His stories might be made up, but many of the things he told had actually happened. And Lawyer Genaro then went on to declaim against "the wretched local police, who had thrown an innocent man into jail simply to keep him from testifying at the trial."

Dr. Fausto then rose for his big speech. He tried hard to make his voice tremble more than Lawyer Ruy's, and a few of those in the courtroom wept again. In short, he did his very best. Virgilio spoke again for ten minutes, dealing only with the question of the man with the ring.

The closing address was made by Lawyer Ruy, who compared Justice to the figure of Christ above the judge's head. He ended with a resounding sentence which he had been preparing for the past couple of days:

"In acquitting Colonel Horacio da Silveira, gentlemen of the jury, you will prove to all the civilized world, whose eyes at this moment are turned upon this courtroom, that there is in Ilhéos not only cacao, money, and fertile land; you will prove that in Ilhéos there is Justice, mother of all the virtues a people may possess."

In spite of the exaggeration in this statement—the eyes of the world turned upon that Ilhéos courtroom—or possibly for that reason, it drew a burst of applause from the spectators, and the judge had to have his bailiff ring for order.

The jury then retired to consider its verdict of guilt or innocence. Horacio also retired and stood in the corridor talking to his lawyers. Fifteen minutes later the jurors filed back, and Braz returned with the colonel. The latter had just had the word from Virgilio: "Unanimous!"

The judge read the verdict unanimously acquitting Colonel Horacio da Silveira. With this, some began leaving the courtroom, while others came up to embrace Horacio and his attorneys. Braz issued the order freeing the colonel from custody, and the erstwhile defendant departed with his friends, who accompanied him to his home.

The father of the young lad, seeing that his son was very tired, lifted him to his shoulder. The boy's eyes were still following Horacio as the colonel left the court.

"What did you like best about it?" his father asked.

The lad smiled a little, then confessed: "What I liked best, yes, the very best of all, was that man with the false ring who knew stories."

Lawyer Ruy in passing overheard this and stroked the lad's blond head, then dashed down the stairs to overtake Horacio, who was just going out the main entrance of the prefecture into the bright morning that was rising out of the sea, above the city of Ilhéos.

VI
PROGRESS

1

Some months afterwards, early one afternoon, Colonel Horacio da Silveira unexpectedly dismounted from his horse in front of Maneca Dantas's house. Dona Auricidia appeared, dragging her mountainous flesh, and extremely solicitous, wishing to know if the colonel had had lunch. He informed her that he had eaten. His face had a tightly compressed look, his eyes were small, and his mouth was drawn out of shape in a hard line. One of the workmen was sent to call Maneca, who was out in the groves, and Dona Auricidia meanwhile strove to entertain the guest. She did almost all the talking. Horacio barely replying with a "Yes" or a "No" when she paused for breath. She was relating anecdotes about her children, praising the intelligence of the oldest boy, who was named Ruy. Maneca finally came in, embraced the colonel, and they began conversing. Whereupon Dona Auricidia retired to see about "a little bite of something to eat."

Horacio then rose and stood gazing out the window at the cacao groves. Maneca waited for him to say something. The minutes went by in silence, with Horacio still staring out at the highway that ran near the Big House. Suddenly he turned.

"I was going through some of the things in the house in Ilhéos," he said, "some things of Ester's."

261

Maneca Dantas felt his heart beating more quickly. Horacio stood gazing at him with his swarthy, all but expressionless eyes, but there was a hard look about his mouth.

"I came upon some letters." And he added in a dull voice: "She was Virgilio's mistress."

Saying this, he turned once more to stare out the window. Maneca Dantas now rose and laid a hand on his friend's shoulder.

"I've known it for some time," he said, "but I didn't like to meddle. And the poor girl paid for it, dying the way she did."

Horacio left the window and, seating himself on a stool, gazed down at the floor. He appeared to be remembering things that had happened long ago, good times, happy memories.

"It's a pity. At first I thought she didn't care for me. All she did was go off in the corner and cry. She said she was afraid of snakes. Even in bed she used to huddle up when I touched her. It made me angry, but I didn't say anything, for it was my fault, marrying a young and educated girl like her."

He shook his head and looked at Maneca Dantas. The latter listened in silence, his face resting in his hands; he did not make a gesture.

"Then suddenly she changed, she became affectionate, and I came to believe that she was fond of me. Before that, when I went into the forest or when I got into shooting scrapes, it had been only for money—partly for the little fellow. But after that everything I did was for her, for I was certain that she cared for me.

"You cannot imagine, my friend," and he pointed a finger at Maneca, "how I felt when she died. I went on giving orders to my men, but all the while I was thinking of killing myself. And if I didn't put a bullet through my brain, it was on account of the little fellow, her son and mine. It was true, she hadn't loved me then, when he was born, but all that was past; she was kind and loving now. Otherwise I *would* have killed myself."

He laughed, a terrifying laugh.

"And to think that all that was for another, for that little shyster. If she was kind and loving, it was for his sake. I had the left-overs."

Dona Auricidia now came in and summoned them to the dining-room. The table was laden with sweets, cheeses, and fruits. As they ate, the mistress of the house kept up an incessant chatter; bragging about her oldest boy, she compelled the child to answer historical questions, to read from a book so that his godfather could hear him, and to recite a few stanzas of poetry.

After they went back to the parlour Horacio had no more to say, but seated himself in a chair and listened to the conversation without paying attention. Maneca Dantas tried to fill up the gaps by talking about the crops, the price of cacao, and the saplings that had been set out on the Sequeiro Grande tract. Dona Auricidia was so sorry that their good friend could not stay for dinner, for she had had them kill some young roosters to make a brown sauce that was "something special."

"I am sorry, my dear lady, but I can't."

And so the afternoon went by, with Horacio chewing on the end of an unlighted cigarette blackened with saliva. Maneca did the talking. He realized that what he had to say was of no interest, but he could think of nothing else; his mind was a blank. All he knew was that Horacio did not want to be alone. On another day, now distant, it had been Virgilio who had wanted company. Maneca paused as he thought of this.

Twilight was falling and the workers were coming back from the groves. Horacio rose and once more gazed out on the highway, now veiled with the melancholy of dusk. Then he went into the other part of the house to take leave of Dona Auricidia, and gave his godson a small coin. Maneca accompanied him outside to where his horse was waiting. As he placed his foot in the stirrup, Horacio turned and said:

"I'm going to have him put out of the way."

2

Maneca Dantas felt like tearing his hair. "That headstrong little lawyer!" He had already exhausted all his arguments in an effort to convince him that he should not go to Ferradas that night, and here Virgilio was, bent upon going in spite of everything. He was more stubborn than a mule, which is the most stubborn animal there is. And yet everybody in Ilhéos was agreed that Lawyer Virgilio was an intelligent man.

Maneca could not have told you why he had taken such a liking to the young attorney. Even after he was certain that Virgilio was engaged in planting horns on Horacio's brow, even then he had not ceased to hold him in high regard, despite the fact that Maneca all but idolized the colonel, to whom he owed the greater portion of his worldly possessions. It was Horacio who had lent him a hand when he was in a bad way and had helped him come up in the world. Yet even after he had discovered that Virgilio was sleeping with Ester, Maneca Dantas had not found it in his heart to be angry with the lawyer. When Ester had died, his sorrow had been mixed with a certain feeling of relief. It was sad, no doubt of that; but it would have been worse, far worse, if Horacio had discovered everything and she had died a still more tragic death. What kind of death that might have been he could not have told you; but while he was endowed with no great powers of imagination, he could picture horrible things—such, for example, as Ester shut up in a room with snakes, like that story he had read in a newspaper once upon a time.

Accordingly, when the fever had carried her off, Maneca had felt badly about it, but at the same time he had breathed a sigh of relief: the problem was solved. And now why did Horacio, after all these months, have to discover those love-letters, which, understandably enough, made him want to kill Virgilio? The thing he could not understand was why those who played the dangerous game of deceiving husbands should permit themselves the luxury of writing letters of that sort. It was an utterly stupid thing to do. He himself, once in a while, had had a mistress—not a married woman, to be sure, but some pretty little prostitute who had caught his fancy and for whom he had set up housekeeping. He would go to her place, sleep there, eat and drink—but write a letter? Never. Now and then he would receive a note from one of them, but these were almost always more or less urgent requests for money. Requests for money, mingled with kisses and terms of endearment. But Colonel Maneca Dantas always tore these letters up before Dona Auricidia's keen scent should have detected the unpleasant odour of cheap perfume of which they always reeked. Requests for money, that was all.

Maneca was thinking of these letters while Virgilio was out in the dining-room preparing the drinks. Had he destroyed them all? The truth of the matter was, there was one letter that he had not destroyed and that he still carried to this day hidden away among the papers in his bill-fold. This was a daily risk that he ran—just imagine if Dona Auricidia should come upon it! She would certainly bring the roof down. Although he was alone in the room, Maneca glanced about him to make sure no one was looking, then opened his wallet and, from among the bills of sale for cacao, took out a letter written in a scrawling hand with numerous blots and mistakes in spelling. It was from Doralice, a little girl whom he had had in Bahia once when he had spent two months in the capital having his eyes treated. He had met her in a café and they had lived together during those months; and of all the women he had known, she was the only one who had ever written him a letter without once asking for money. For this reason he had kept her note; and despite the fact that Doralice was by now a dim memory, far in the past, it was a pleasing memory just the same. Hearing Virgilio's steps, he replaced the letter in his purse as the lawyer came in with a bottle and glasses on a tray.

Maneca drank his rum and then fell back once more on the story, which represented for him the furthest stretch of his imagination, to the effect that he "had heard a rumour that Sinhô Badaró was going to lay an ambush for Virgilio that night, along the road to Ferradas, to avenge himself for Juca's death." Virgilio laughed.

"But, Maneca," he said, "that's idiotic, absolutely idiotic. The Ferradas highway is in Colonel Horacio's territory. If there's one safe road, it is that one. And I'm not going to leave my client cooling his heels. What's more, he's an elector of mine."

What appeared to amuse him was the idea of an ambush by the Badarós under such conditions as that: "On the road to Ferradas, under Horacio's very nose?"

Maneca rose from his chair.

"And so, my dear sir, you're determined to go in spite of everything?"

"Yes, I'm going, that's certain."

"And supposing," said Maneca, "that it was our friend himself who wanted—"

"Colonel Horacio?"

"He knows everything." Maneca glanced away; he could not look the lawyer in the face.

"Knows what?"

"That business of you and his wife. That crazy habit of writing love letters—He was rummaging through her things—" Again he averted his gaze, lowered his head as if he were to blame for everything; he could not meet Virgilio's eyes.

Virgilio, however, was not in the least embarrassed. He had Maneca Dantas sit down beside him and tell him everything. Letters? Yes, he had written letters; he had had letters from her, too; it was their way of keeping close to each other, those days when they could not be together with their love. He went to tell the whole story: how happy they had been; their plans for flight; their nights of love. His words were passionate ones as he recalled her death. He had understood and sympathized with Horacio's despair the day she had died, and for that reason he had not gone away but had remained to keep the colonel company.

"It was a way of being near to Ester. Do you understand that?"

Maneca was not sure that he did; but that was the way it was with these lovers. Virgilio went on talking, without a pause. Why had he not gone away? Why had he wanted to stay with Horacio and go on helping him with his business? Because everything there reminded him of Ester, whom death had taken from him forever. With others it was the cacao that snared them, the ambition to make money. He too was trapped by cacao, but not for the money that was in it. It was the memory of her that held him, her body there in the cemetery, her presence, which was everywhere, in the house at Ilhéos, in Dr. Jessé's home, down there at Tabocas, at the plantation, and in the person of Horacio—above all, in Horacio. Virgilio had no ambitions; he spent money like a fool, all that he earned; he had no desire to buy a cacao grove; all that he wanted was to remain close to her—and she was in those towns and plantations. Each time that a frog cried out in a snake's mouth, he held her in his arms afresh, as that first time in the plantation Big House.

"Do you understand, Maneca?"

He gave a melancholy laugh. No, Maneca could not understand him, he was sure of that. Only when one had had a mad love, once in one's life, only then would he be able to understand. At this point Maneca could think of nothing better than to show Virgilio the letter from Doralice. It was the one way of expressing the bond between them.

Virgilio took the letter and read it, as Maneca's eyes grew dim.

My dear Maneca I hope these poorly written lines will find you enjoying the best of health. Maneca you are a very bad boy not to write to your Doralice who you have forgot but who is waiting for you. Maneca I write to ask when you are coming so that I can wate for you on the keys. Maneca every night when I go to slepe I dream of you. Of the walks we used to take you and me and Editi and Danda singing that song called I Gave My Heart. Maneca when you come to Ilhéos I don't want you to go down to the strete where the hores are bekause I don't want you to get sick. When you come here I want us to have a good time. My handsome little sonny boy when are we going to be together again???!!! I think of you all the time. Maneca write to me even if its only a few lines. Excuse the mistakes in this letter Maneca with many kisses from your black girl DORALICE. *Thats all. Notise the adress 98 2nd of July Strete. Goodby from your* FORGOTTEN *Doralice.*

"Was she pretty?" Virgilio asked when he had .finished reading the letter.

"She was a little doll." Maneca's voice was tremulous. They could find nothing more to say to each other, as Virgilio watched his friend put the letter back among the papers in his bill-fold. So even an Ilhéos colonel had a love-story to tell. Virgilio served another drink of rum.

Maneca Dantas then stubbornly came back to the subject they had been discussing.

"I like you, doctor," he said, "and I am asking you not to go. Take a boat, go to Bahia. You are young and intelligent; you can make a career for yourself anywhere."

But Virgilio refused. He would not give up the idea of going to Ferradas that night. Death meant nothing to him; the terrible thing was to go on living without Ester. Did the colonel understand that? What was life to him, anyway? He felt unclean, up to his neck in that filthy cacao slime. So long as Ester was alive there had been the hope of going away with her. But now nothing mattered.

It was then that Maneca Dantas made his supreme offer, all that he had to give.

"If it's a question of a woman, doctor," he said, "I can give you Doralice's new address if you like. She's a beauty, and you'll forget."

Virgilio thanked him: "You're a good friend, Maneca Dantas. The curious thing is how you people can do such things and still be so good." Then he concluded abruptly: "I'm going to Ferradas tonight. And if there's time, I'll die as the law here commands, the law of cacao—by taking someone with me. Isn't that the way?"

And so it was that Maneca Dantas that night saw the young attorney ride off alone, in the direction of Ferradas, smiling sadly.

"And he's so young, poor fellow," said Maneca to himself.

Along the highway Virgilio heard a voice singing a song that had to do with the affrays of Sequeiro Grande:

I am going to tell you a tale
Will make your blood run cold.

A tale to make your blood run cold, a tale of this land, a tale of love. A frog screams in the mouth of a snake. Virgilio had dreamed a dream once, a romantic dream: he had appeared at night, mounted on a black horse, on the veranda of the Big House; in the heavens an enormous yellow moon, above the cacao trees and above the forest. Ester had been waiting for him, timid and afraid. He had calmed her fears, however, had clasped her around the waist and lifted her to the crupper of his horse; and then, on his night-black steed, they had set out through the cacao groves and down the highways; through the towns and the cities and over the sea, among the freighters and the ocean liners, they had gone galloping to other, far-distant lands. The snake hisses, the frog screams. But Ester, her arms about him, is safe. A tale to make your blood run cold. They will go to the end of the world, their feet free of the cacao slime that holds them there. That steed has wings, and they go far from the snakes, far from the assassinated frogs, far, very far, from the groves of cacao, the dead men along the highway, the crosses lit up by candles on nights of longing. The black steed soars through the air, over the groves, over the forests, over the burnings and the clearings. Ester goes with Virgilio and they will moan with love this moon-drenched night. Through the air they go at an unbridled gallop. The moon envelops the night, and from afar there comes a song. A man is singing:

And now I have truly told you a tale
To make your blood run cold.

It is like a wedding march. None would ever have thought that the last verse of the song was to be written this very night, along the road to Ferradas. What does it matter—what does death matter—a bullet in the chest, a cross by the roadside, a candle lighted by Maneca Dantas—so long as Ester goes with him on that galloping black steed, to other lands than this, the land of cacao? The song accompanies him like a wedding march. A tale to make your blood run cold.

268

3

The city of Ilhéos awoke in a state of feverish excitement. Its streets were carpeted with flowers, flags hung from the house windows, and bells were pealing merrily on this festive morning. A huge crowd was on its way down to the waterfront and filled the pier to overflowing. The pupils from the schools marched in a body: the young women from Our Lady of Victory Seminary, which was the nuns' school (the building had recently been completed, on top of the hill overlooking the city); the boys and girls from the private institutions; and finally the children of the poor from the public school. They all were in holiday garb, and the nuns' charges each wore a blue ribbon symbolizing the religious confraternity to which she belonged. There was a band as well, in showy red and black uniforms, playing a lively air on this day of stir and bustle. Braz was in command of the police troopers, who carried rifles on their shoulders, and on the crowded pier were all the most important citizens of the town, clad in the black Prince Alberts they donned on state occasions. Dr. Jessé, the present prefect of Ilhéos, was sweating in a stiff collar and was doing his best to remember the words of the speech he was shortly to deliver, which he had spent two whole days in embellishing. Sinhô Badaró was there also, with his daughter and son-in-law. The colonel still limped a little in his right leg, where he had been wounded at the time of the assault on the Big House. Here at the waterfront today members of the government party and members of the opposition mingled together, along with priests and nuns. Even Friar Bento had come down from Ferradas and stood conversing with some of the sisters in that foreign-sounding voice of his. Business houses were closed for the day, for everybody had gone to meet the boat.

The wine-shop kept by the Spaniard, which was near the wharves, was filled with customers. The man with the false ring, who had generously forgiven the Spaniard for having turned him in to the police, was talking to the man in the sky-blue vest.

"And now," he was saying, "it's a Bishop—what's a Bishop that they have to make so much fuss over him? Why, I once knew an Archbishop, down south. And do you know what he looked like? Like a broiled lobster, that's what!"

The man in the sky-blue vest did not argue the matter. It might be the truth, who could say? In any event, the first Bishop of Ilhéos was arriving this morning; for a recent papal decree had elevated the city from a parish to a diocese, and a canon from Parahyba had been consecrated Bishop. According to the newspapers of Bahia, he was a man of great virtues and great learning; but for the residents of Ilhéos he was *their* Bishop, a symbol of the importance their city had achieved, a sign of progress. Despite the lack of religious sentiment that, if one was to believe Canon Freitas, was so characteristic of this region, the town was proud of the honour the Church had conferred upon it and was prepared to give the first incumbent a right royal welcome.

People now came running down the beach: the boat had been sighted, out near the Rapa rock. Men and women, meanwhile, were still hurrying down the street on their way to the pier. The pious old ladies wore black shawls over their heads and were so nervous that for once they had lost their tongues. The young girls and their swains took advantage of the occasion to do a bit of ogling, and even the prostitutes had put in an appearance. The last, however, gazed on from a distance, having formed a convivial group in back of the booths where fish were sold. There were numerous priests in the throng also, and the inhabitants could not help wondering where they had all come from. They were from the towns of the interior, the vicars of Itapira and Barra do Rio de Contas having made a long and tiresome journey to pay their respects to the new Bishop.

The big carpet from the grand staircase of the prefecture had been laid upon the pier, and over this the Bishop was to pass.

The boat, decked out with flags, was now crossing the bar, and its whistle could be heard from a distance. Rockets went up in the air from the island of Pontal, and the police troopers discharged their rifles in a mock salute. The priests, the prefect, the colonels, and the nuns, the wealthy merchants as well, all crowded forward, and as the ship drew up to the pier, the sky above the city was filled with exploding rockets and the bells pealed, as the Bishop, a short, fat little man, descended the gangplank and Dr. Jessé began his address of welcome.

The crowd accompanied the prelate to the home of Canon Freitas, where breakfast was served for the select few, and that afternoon there was a solemn benediction in the Cathedral of St. George. Maneca Dantas had brought his children along, and his son Ruy declaimed a few verses by way of welcome to the "spiritual father." The Bishop praised the precocious lad's

270

intelligence. Sinhô Badaró likewise paid a visit to ask a blessing for his grandchild that was about to be born.

That night there were more fireworks, while at the prefecture a state banquet was held, the tribute of the city of Ilhéos to its first Bishop. The new prosecutor spoke in the name of the people, and the guest of honour said a few words in reply, expressive of his happiness at finding himself among the *grapiúnas.* Following the banquet the Bishop withdrew, for he was tired; but the festivities kept up until a late hour, and it was two o'clock in the morning when Lawyer Ruy, thoroughly drunk, staggered out into the street. Finding no one with whom to talk, he went down to the waterfront and there, happening to run into the man with the false ring, he proceeded, for want of any other listener, to expound to him his view of things.

"In this land, my son, a cacao grove can even produce a Bishop. It produces railroads, assassins, ousters, town houses, cafés, schools, theatres—even a Bishop. Yes, this country doesn't only yield cacao, it yields everything."

All of which was not quite in keeping with an article that Lawyer Ruy had published that day in *A Folha de Ilhéos.* For the first and only time that paper and *O Comercio* found themselves in full agreement. Both praised the city and the municipality for the progress they had achieved; both stressed the importance of the Bishop's coming; and both prophesied a brilliant future for the town.

"Its elevation to a diocese," wrote Manuel de Oliveira, "is no more than a recognition of the dizzying progress which Ilhéos has made, a progress that is due to the efforts of those great men who sacrificed everything for their country's good."

"Ilhéos, cradle of so many sons of toil," wrote Lawyer Ruy, "of so many men of character and intelligence who have blazed the path for civilization in the black and barbarous land of cacao...."

In the meantime, still trying to steady himself on his feet, Lawyer Ruy was bellowing to the man with the false ring:

"Cacao, my son, is everything. It even yields a Bishop at the foot of the tree—even a Bishop."

To the man with the false ring nothing in the world was impossible.

"It may be," he said, "who knows?"

4

Following the election that elevated Dr. Jessé Freitas to the
Federal Chamber as a government party deputy ("What's that
jackass going to do there?" Lawyer Ruy had inquired of his
acquaintances), and which at the same time transformed the
interventor into the constitutional Governor of the state of
Bahia, a decree was issued creating the municipality of Itabuna,
which was thereby dismembered from Ilhéos. The seat of the
new municipality was to be the former borough of Tabocas, now
the city of Itabuna. A bridge, in the interim, had been
constructed joining the two portions of the town on either side of
the river.

Horacio, who had picked Maneca Dantas to succeed Dr.
Jessé as prefect of Ilhéos, now chose for the corresponding post
in Itabuna that same hardware dealer, Azevedo, who had been
the Badarós' devoted follower and who had gone bankrupt on
their account. For Azevedo could not stand being the under-dog
in politics and had come to an agreement with Horacio. His
electors had voted for Dr. Jessé for deputy and so, in exchange,
he was given the new prefecture.

It was the day for the new municipal government to take
over, and a triumphal arch of flowering cacao boughs had been
erected in Church Square. Within record time they had thrown
up a modern building to house the prefect, and a special train
from Ilhéos now brought Horacio, the Bishop, Maneca Dantas,
the judge, the prosecutor, planters and merchants, married
women and young ladies. At the station the residents of Itabuna
crowded forward to grasp Horacio's hand.

The inaugural ceremony was an impressive one. Azevedo,
having taken the oath of office, delivered a speech in which he
further swore undying loyalty to the Governor of the state and to
Colonel Horacio da Silveira, "that benefactor of the cacao
region." Horacio looked on, his eyes very small, as someone at
his side, alluding to Azevedo's turncoat propensities, remarked:
"Anyone who didn't know you, colonel, would say that you'd
bought an old nag."

"He'll go all right, with a tight rein," was Horacio's reply.

In the afternoon there was a fair with an auction of gifts in the
public square, and that evening a grand ball was staged in the
main room of the prefecture. The Bishop did not deem it fitting
to be present in the ballroom, but he was ensconced in another

room, where a buffet supper was being served, consisting of sweets of various kinds, under the auspices of the Pereira sisters—"real artists," according to Maneca Dantas, who was a connoisseur in such matters. There were all kinds of drinks as well, everything from champagne to rum.

Round the Bishop a circle had been formed—Horacio, Maneca, Azevedo, the judge, Braz, and various others—and the finest of fine goblets were now filled with the finest of wine. Someone proposed a toast to the Bishop; and then the prosecutor of Ilhéos suggested that, by way of showing their gratitude to the colonel, they drink a toast to Horacio. In the course of his remarks he took occasion, innocently enough, to express a regret that "in this hour of the city's great triumph Colonel Horacio da Silveira could not have at his side his devoted wife of ever living memory, Dona Ester, that self-sacrificing martyr to a true wife's love for her husband—or that other townsman of theirs, whose memory likewise was with them always and who had contributed so much to the progress of the new municipality of Itabuna—Dr. Virgilio Cabral, who had died at the hands of his cowardly political enemies." But those days, the speaker went on to assert, while still quite recent, were a thing of the past now; they belonged to a time when civilization had not yet reached this region, a time when Itabuna was still Tabocas.

"Today," he concluded, "all this is no more than a painful memory."

The prosecutor then raised his glass in a toast, Horacio clinked glasses with him, and together they drank to the memory of Ester and Virgilio. As the rims of their goblets met, little clear-ringing sounds were heard.

"Baccarat crystal," Horacio observed to the Bishop, who was seated at his side.

And he gave a calm and satisfied laugh.

5

It ordinarily takes five years for cacao trees to bear their first fruit, but those that were planted on the Sequeiro Grande tract began budding at the end of the third year and were yielding fruit the year following. Even those agricultural experts who had studied in the schools, even the old planters who knew cacao as no one else did, were astonished at the size of the nuts that these groves so precociously produced. Those nuts were enormous ones, and the trees were laden with them to their topmost boughs. Nothing of the kind had ever been seen before; for this was the best land in the world for the planting of cacao, a land fertilized with human blood.

Glossary of Brazilian Terms

Boi tátá (bôh-e tah'tah'). Mythical fire-breathing ox.

Caapora (kah-poh'rah). A goblin.

Caboclo (kah-boh'kloo). A Brazilian Indian (literally, "copper-coloured").

Cabra (kah'brah). Term applied to the offspring of a mulatto and a Negro; comes to mean, in general, a backwoods assassin. Cf. *capanga, jagunço*.

Capanga (kah-pahn'gah). Hired assassin; backwoods Negro. Cf. *cabra, jagunço*.

Carioca (kah-ree-oh'kah). Resident of Rio de Janeiro.

Cigarro (see-gahr'roo). A cigarette made with millet straw, with the aid of a penknife; or, simply, cigarette.

Conquistador (kohn-kees'tah-dohr). Literally, a "conqueror"; one who opens up a new country.

Conto (kohn'too). Brazilian coin worth 1,000,000 reis (*q.v.*), or, at the time of this story, a little more than $500 (about $546).

Fazenda (fah-zen'dah). A plantation; in this book, a cacao plantation.

Fazendeiro (fah-zen-day-ee'roo). A plantation-owner, a planter.

Grapiúna (grah-pee-oo'nah). Resident of the Ilhéos cacao region.

Jagunço (zhah-goon'soo). This term was originally applied to ruffians at a fair; from this it derived the meaning of backcountry ruffian, which is the sense that it has in this book (cf. *cabra, capanga*); is sometimes used as practically synonymous with *sertanejo,* or inhabitant of the backlands.

Milrei (meel'ray-ee). Brazilian coin worth 1,000 reis, or about 54 cents in United States currency.

Mingau (meen'gow). A dish (paste) made of manihot flour, sugar, and eggs.

Rei (ray'ee). Brazilian monetary unit, worth one twentieth of a cent.

Tirana (tee-rah'nah). A melancholy love-song, slow in movement, on the theme of love's "tyranny."